Alexandra Raife has lived abroad in many countries and worked at a variety of jobs, including a six-year commission in the RAF and many years co-running a Highland hotel. She lives in Perthshire. She is the author of six previous novels, *Drumveyn*, *The Larach*, *Grianan*, *Belonging*, *Sun On Snow* and *The Wedding Gift*, all of which have been richly praised.

Praise for Alexandra Raife

'A welcome new storyteller'   Rosamunde Pilcher

'An absorbing story with a perfectly painted background'
                                                                    Financial Times

'A love story with an unconventional twist and a very readable novel'   *The Times*

'A compelling read'   *Woman's Weekly*

'The power of a natural-born storyteller'   *The Lady*

'Warm, friendly, involving . . . lovely'   Reay Tannahill

'*Drumveyn* had me hooked from the first page'
                                                                    Barbara Erskine

MOVING ON

Alexandra Raife

CORONET BOOKS
Hodder & Stoughton

First published in Great Britain in 2001 by Hodder & Stoughton
First published in paperback in 2000 by Hodder & Stoughton
A division of Hodder Headline

A Coronet Paperback

10 9 8 7 6 5 4 3 2 1

A CIP Catalogue record for this title is available from the British Library

ISBN 0 340 79290 6

Typeset by Palimpsest Book Production Limited,
Polmont, Stirlingshire

Printed and bound in Great Britain by
Mackays of Chatham, plc

Hodder & Stoughton
A division of Hodder Headline
338 Euston Road
London NW1 3BH

For Sheila

It was nearly dark before they lowered the heavy, already stiffening body into the grave. The gusty wind and fitful rain of a cold September day had died away but there was a rawness in the air that warned of winter, and matched the bleak hopelessness in Catriona's heart to see this friend of so many years laid in the earth.

She stood for a moment to look down on him, but the memories and the thoughts she wished to accord him in farewell seemed to float and jumble, elusive and refusing to take coherent shape. Only the practical would emerge in words.

'Have we put him deep enough?'

'Oh, aye, he'll rest easy there, never fear.'

Watty's voice was full of the comfort he could only express in such prosaic reassurance, but she heard in it his own sadness for Braan, and his anxiety for herself. Yet Watty's life at Glen Righ was ending too, on this dank evening with the last watery gleams reaching from below the sullen cloud banks in the west to give them enough light to fill the grave they had dug together for the old dog.

How many years was it since Watty had 'started at the big house' as a lad? His role had been no more defined than that, had never needed to be. He had simply been a pair of extra hands for the seasonal jobs of lambing, gathering, clipping, the hay, the harvest, beating, ghillieing, tattie picking. He had dug over the garden in the days when it was still productive; he had driven the tractor, run up and down the glen in an old canvas-topped Land Rover fetching and carrying from Luig or Fort William, till the elderly chauffeur had been pensioned off and he had gravitated to what interested him most, looking after the estate vehicles, and making a comfortable niche for himself as general handyman about the house.

How old was he now, Catriona wondered, knowing she was keeping her mind away from the reality of the wet clods of earth thumping down on Braan. In his forties, perhaps even fifty? She had wanted to find him a new job, for Watty had been the mainstay of her existence at Glen Righ House since he had taken over the care of her grandfather, frail and 'a wee bit wandery' as the glen phrase had it. Fergus had died three years ago, and since then Watty's care had been transferred to the decaying house, and, though neither of them could have said exactly in what terms, to Catriona herself. But Watty had been visibly alarmed at the idea of working somewhere else, to a set timetable, among strangers.

'Ach, there'll be this and that,' he said vaguely, when she tried to discuss it. 'I'll pick up a few hours here and there.'

That was how it would work out, she knew, just as he had been able to acquire an ancient caravan which was slowly disintegrating on a derelict piece of ground behind the Old Mill in Luig, the small fishing town beyond the high barrier of the Luig Moor to the south.

'Rest easy, lad, rest easy,' Watty was saying quietly now, in his own farewell to Braan, the big gentle retriever. 'I'll keep an eye on him, you know that,' he added to Catriona in awkward reassurance, wanting to put out a hand to her in comfort. That was unthinkable, of course, but it hurt him to see her, so vulnerable yet so resolutely self-contained. The lassie had had more than enough to thole in her life, that was certain, and there was worse to come, with Glen Righ gone, where her family had lived time out of mind. She looked so alone without Braan at her heels. Watty's eyes were wet as he scrupulously patted smooth the slight mound they had made. There would be no marker; sentimentality of that sort was entirely alien to Catriona.

They walked together up the moss-grown path which climbed beside the half acre of long-neglected lawn, and up the steps to the terrace.

'Here, I'll get these.' Watty added the spade to the shovel and mattock he was carrying, and paused to face Catriona in the dying light. The tools in his hands would be left behind with everything else, a week from now no longer Finlay possessions. There was nothing to say. After all the years, the sharing and trust and ease between them, there were no words, just a stiff nod on either side, mouths tight.

Then Watty was gone, his unhurried tread fading across the weed-choked flagstones, drowned almost at once by the rushing noise of the burn, high after the rain, pouring itself down the gorge below the end of the terrace, the ever-present background sound of Glen Righ. The gorge where her brother had died. Catriona shivered. It was no moment for such memories.

She turned to the house, its great bulk climbing high and black against the grey cloud-shredded sky. No light was on. From a long habit of spartan living Catriona never put lights on till she needed them.

Suddenly she knew she could not sleep there. The house where she was born. The house where, once the brief unhappy experiment of sending her away to school had been given up in her early teens, she had spent nearly every night of her life. The house which she had been dreading leaving for the terrifying challenge she had set herself. Now she could hardly bear to go in. For sixteen years, apart from those brief wretched periods of exile, Braan had been with her, going everywhere with her, sleeping in her room at night. What would her cold, gaunt room be like, the two old-fashioned leather suitcases which were all she would carry away with her ready packed, without that living breathing presence?

Now tears threatened. She dared not let them come.

She would never, never cope with all that lay ahead if she gave in to them so soon.

She went in, running up the wide steps, flicking down as she passed the pear-drop brass switch which dimly lit the high, dusty hall, its chilly expanses strewn with objects more usually found in outhouses than indoors, and going quickly on up the dark carved stair. The house felt inimical, as though it had already passed into the hands of strangers. She wished for a moment she had asked Watty to come in with her, then realised how odd that would have seemed.

In her room, comfortless, stark, unchanged since childhood, she hurriedly gathered up the few things she had left out for the night, and slammed down the lids of the cases, clicking shut their dusty locks with four sounds of cold finality. Without a glance around she picked them up and by taking small steps managed to carry them both at once, her face set grimly. She did not think she could deal with a second journey to this room.

She pulled the heavy front door shut behind her; it had stood open as it always did for most of the summer. There was no key. She didn't remember ever having seen one. Perhaps the door should be locked now. The house was being handed over, in this moment, to its new owners, who for some reason inexplicable to Catriona had bought it with everything it contained. She didn't think there could be much of value in the dilapidated, uncared-for, disregarded Finlay possessions. But such issues had been the business of those larger powers whom she was accustomed to having in charge of her life – the factor, the estate office, the bank, and now the new player on the scene, Glen Righ Enterprises, a Japanese-based company which had bought the house and all that was left of the estate for an ambitious sail-shoot-stay scheme which had been the subject of much sardonic glen humour.

Well, if the door should be locked then no doubt Mrs Macgillivray would lock it. She and dour Macgillivray, the gamekeeper, had been kept on as part of the contents, and more local wit, of an even more pleasurable nature, had been expended on wishing yon Japs joy of them.

Struggling now, but for some reason she didn't examine determined not to put down either suitcase, Catriona went along the terrace to where the Fiat was parked ready for an early start in the morning. It was tuned and serviced, tank full, oil and tyre pressures checked. Watty had even cleaned it, which had amused her, but had also brought a lump to her throat, for she understood the mute message of these untoward attentions. She put the cases in the back with relief, then, habit trapping her with treacherous ease, turned to call to Braan, 'In the back,' a time-honoured command which meant nothing more than Get in, since he always sat where he preferred, beside her in the front.

Raw facts swept coldly over her – the bundle in the hairy blanket with its familiar smell which she found wholesome and agreeable; the big drops spattering off the leaves onto the newly turned bare earth.

Go, go. Don't think. With shaking hands she started

the car and, without turning her head to the dark bulk of the house, bumped down the drive and out onto the glen road. Farewells had been said to the Macgillivrays, the only people left on the place. Somewhere down the winding miles ahead Watty would be rattling in his old jeep. The thought consoled her, as though he hadn't quite gone yet.

She clung to specks of contact as she drove down the familiar road: a lighted window on the steep hillside, the pale pattern of new fence stobs as she left Glen Righ ground behind her, a weathered nameboard at the entrance to a track, a house sign, all things she would normally not register at all. Now, her throat tight, she rehearsed to herself the names, pictured the faces, turned over memories, tenuous and haphazard, fleeing away as the little car hummed on.

Coming down the last mile before Inverbuie village she remembered with a stab of guilt that she had promised to drop off the layered roots of japonica Watty had potted up and set aside for her. He had left them by the front door so that she couldn't miss them, but going out in the dark of course she had. And because she had intended to leave them as she passed she hadn't said goodbye to Helen.

What would become of them? Would Mrs Macgillivray appropriate them? She had a reputation for having a heavy hand with growing things. 'I wouldn't like to be a flower in her garden,' Catriona had heard it expressed.

She knew these thoughts were a defence against the reality of driving past Tigh Bhan without a word. It was a house with many precious associations and leaving it behind hurt almost as much as saying goodbye to Braan. But it was too late to call now, and indeed she didn't think she had the courage.

It had been so good to find that when Lilias Markie died, that friend whose affection and support had been a mainstay for Catriona for almost as long as she could remember, the house had been bought by someone who in many ways could take her place. It had meant that the huge gap Catriona had dreaded had largely been filled, and Helen Rathbone's unfailing welcome, her quiet humour, her love of books and her readiness to be part of the new scene in which she found herself, had much softened the blow of Lilias's death.

And now not to say goodbye. But Helen, of all people, would understand what had impelled Catriona to go tonight, go without knowing where she would sleep, or if she would stop at all, launching herself blindly into the unknown world everyone else seemed to deal with so easily, starting out upon this challenge she had set herself, the importance of which she had been unable to explain to anyone.

She had steeled herself to face all the things she most feared, in an environment quite alien to her. Since her grandfather died she had been helped and protected by her friends, given jobs which made little demand on her, her shyness and self-doubts understood and allowed for. She was twenty-four years old, without qualifications or training of any kind, and with no experience of life outside her sheltered circle, and this remote glen where she had been known all her life and where she was accepted for what she was.

She went through the tiny village at the head of Loch Buie without looking at anything. Scarcely a movement on the street, the carpark half empty, a big white and orange coach outside the hotel. The season winding down. Dark coming early.

Unseen, without so much as an arm lifted in farewell as the well-known little car scudded on, Catriona, momentarily blinded by tears, took the empty road which looped up onto the moor, and slipped away across its dark emptiness towards her new life.

Chapter One

Helen Rathbone sat at the kitchen table at Tigh Bhan, her elbows propped upon it, fingertips to her temples, thumbs to her jaw. Her hands were not so much propping her head in despair as blinkering her from everything around her, the big, well-equipped, sunny room with its long window which looked across the garden and a single field to the gleaming length of Loch Buie between its high hills, where the heather was now the colour of rust and the bracken flaunted great patches of yellow. Helen loved both kitchen and view; the latter perhaps had been the clinching factor in the decision to buy the house — to be able to stand at the sink, if one was obliged to stand at a sink, with such beauty before one's eyes . . .

But had it been her decision? Had anything, ever, since she married Walter, been done because she had chosen or wanted it? And had she truly seen her role as tied perpetually to the kitchen sink? It was these questions and where they led her which had held her here for the past hour, shutting out anything that might distract or divert her.

The morning had begun much as usual, except that the moment she woke she had remembered that this was the day Catriona was leaving, and had got up at once, moving quietly so as not to disturb Walter who detested any change to their fixed routine, so that she would be down however early Catriona called to say goodbye, as she had promised she would do. But Catriona hadn't come, and Helen, realising how hard it must be for her to leave Glen Righ now that the moment had come, and picturing with affectionate amusement the trouble she was probably having with unaccustomed packing, had kept an increasingly uneasy eye on the clock. It would be unfortunate if Catriona came during breakfast; that above all Walter hated to have interrupted.

When Postie told her Catriona had already left – 'No, no, you'll not be seeing that one the day, she was away down the glen last night' – she had felt an instant's hurt blankness which it had taken a moment to deal with sensibly.

Perhaps Catriona had decided to spend her last night with friends in Luig, so that she could make an early start this morning. It must have been too late to call as she passed. But might she have left the plants she had said she would bring? Something ought to be done with them if she had. But Helen knew as she hurried to the back door to look that that wasn't the real reason for her sudden purposefulness. She needed some token that Catriona had not departed without a word. The step was empty of everything but the boot-scraper. Even then Helen had not given up, going through the house to the front door, and opening with care, so that he wouldn't hear her, the new bolts and locks Walter had insisted upon. Nothing.

She had felt rebuffed, though knowing it was absurd. There would be a perfectly reasonable explanation. But, as the morning wound along its undeviating route, she had been forced to acknowledge just how much she was going to miss Catriona, and also what her degree of disappointment that there had been no proper goodbye revealed about her own life.

Catriona, in spite of her shyness and almost crippling lack of self-confidence about anything outside her own known world of the glen, had nevertheless been Helen's most important link with this new life at Tigh Bhan. Not that Catriona had appeared there nearly often enough; she would always be too unsure about the value of her own company for that. Helen had only been once to Glen Righ House. It rarely occurred to Catriona to ask anyone there, and when Helen had finally been invited into the comfortless caverns of its rooms, where furnishings not only unaltered for a century, but by the look of them untouched as well, mouldered quietly with a certain grandeur of unimpaired assurance, she thought she saw why.

She had come to understand that for Catriona to have made the effort to call at Tigh Bhan soon after the Rathbones had arrived in Inverbuie had been something rather out of the way, and she knew now that she owed it to the long-standing friendship there had been between the two houses, which Catriona had felt it her duty to preserve. On that first visit she had been as tongue-tied and farouche as a child, and indeed she had looked like one, with her undeveloped figure and untidy clothes, her small never-quite-clean-looking hands and thin neck. Helen had since discovered that Catriona was in her mid-twenties, but still quite often saw her as that shy child.

The link had really been Lilias Markie, the previous occupant of the house. She had been much loved and respected locally and, more than a year after her death, shopkeepers in Luig over the headland to the south, or in Fort William, over twenty miles away, or tradesmen doing the jobs Walter had insisted upon in a house Helen had thought more or less perfect, made friendly references to her. As Helen had learned more about Catriona's strange existence, alone in the crumbling castle-like Glen Righ House, living a hand-to-mouth existence helping friends who owned a hotel on Loch Luig, or on a farm which had by now swallowed up much of the land her family had once owned, or in the health food shop down by Luig harbour, she had guessed, and hoped, that in some measure she had replaced Lilias in Catriona's life. In a small way, she would always amend, for it was clear to her that the benefits she received were far greater. Because of the friendship with Catriona had come a swifter acceptance than she and Walter could ever have achieved on their own merits, an unknown retired couple, still with English accents unaltered by the years in Edinburgh.

Attractive West Coast villages like Inverbuie were surfeited with affluent and elderly incomers who had not paid their dues, social or financial, into the community during their working lives, but wished to enjoy the pleasures of retirement there. The fact that their spending power helped to keep such tiny places alive did not always seem to Helen adequate justification for the invasion.

But apart from the warmer welcome the Rathbones had received as a result of being befriended by Catriona there had also been, for Helen, the pleasure of being with someone young. How deeply she had missed the school, the years and years of children. Walter, on the other hand, had never given the slightest sign of missing them at all. Had he actually disliked them? It was just one more of the large, inexorable questions of this morning, which were beginning to boil and surge in a manner at once alarming and exciting, as she sat still, head in hands, at the empty table in the tidy kitchen.

The school. The children. She had learned to use the terms, but in her mind had always thought of their charges as 'the boys'. Walter had continued to say it, resenting the infiltration of girls which changing times had thrust upon them. It was perhaps as well, Helen had allowed herself to think even at the time, that he had by then withdrawn almost completely from active involvement, reserving to himself the most rewarding group of high flyers, and with them teaching only Latin and mathematics, and Greek to a few bright stars.

Helen looked back, with a detachment which rather impressed her, over the years to the beginning. She knew she must do this. She had to be sure. And honest.

She had met Walter just when she was beginning to be ashamed of having fallen into that most unenterprising of traps, going back to her own old school to teach after taking her degree at London, and her Certificate of Education at Nottingham. How she had loathed that post-graduate year and those surroundings. How appealing Shrewsbury had looked by contrast in the Easter sunshine, how familiar its hilly streets and splendid black-and-white Tudor buildings. She had run into friends, they had descended in a cheerful crowd on the Copper Kettle where tables had been pulled together for them in the inner room, and they had eaten the famous cream cakes and drunk the coffee which at that time even small provincial tea-shops were getting more ambitious about.

Had her future been decided by cream cakes? Helen half smiled and half winced at the thought. The truth was that at this stage she could hardly remember anything more significant swaying her to take the junior English post at St Chad's. She had enjoyed her years at school there. Did anyone ever admit that nowadays – or anyone above prep school age, at any rate? She liked the town; she liked her parents, and she had liked living with them in the comfortable old house with lawns sloping to the river in the pretty village of Withedine a few miles away.

It had all been too easy, too obvious. For the first term she had been blissfully happy, finding her feet in the job, enjoying the joke of being a member of staff where four years ago she had been Head Girl. Not a brilliant one, and only chosen, she knew, because she had stayed on to take an extra A level after doing university entrance exams in third year sixth.

Then after Christmas the depressing truth had suddenly struck her. She had progressed nowhere. The lively student years, the vac jobs on the Continent, the friendships, the choices and opportunities, had all been thrown away. She had a 'good' job, it was true, an enviable first job. She had, all in all, an enviable existence. But here she was, shivering on the same draughty stairs, trying to warm her hands on the same luke-warm radiators, on duty in the same dark cloakroom and in the hideous new dining-room which had been built on what, when she first arrived at the school fourteen years ago, had been the top tennis court. Some things had changed, it was true. At prayers she no longer faced the platform but, one of the row of mistresses under the jut of the upper gallery, looked past the navy and white rows to the rib-stalls opposite, or let her eyes range up to the long windows above, trying to remember what she had decided to do in first period with the Lower Third.

How archaic the language sounded now. But she still could not use easily those then frowned-upon words, classroom, teacher . . .

Walter had been staying with friends at Cressage.

There had been a tennis party. God, I feel old, she thought, mocking herself. Spongy grass and hairless balls, tennis shoes stiff with fresh whitening which had dried in the sun on the kitchen yard wall all morning, cakestand on the tea table, embroidered napkins smaller than handkerchieves. And what adjectives, after all the years of marriage, could she find to describe that not particularly striking, not particularly personable young man, who had engaged most of her attention that afternoon? Well, not so young; ten years older than she was, and that had mattered at twenty-two, and made it flattering when he singled her out. Medium height, medium build. Straight brownish hair falling diagonally across a high forehead. A curly Petersen pipe which, inexplicably now, had seemed attractive then. She loathed the fact that Walter had taken to smoking again in retirement; the smell permeated the house and seemed especially distasteful in this environment.

They had been polite to each other, she supposed, her mind returning to their developing acquaintance, both brought up to respect other people's ways and views, accustomed to restraint, capable of self-discipline. And neither, though the thought would scarcely have been put into words, even privately, believing that in the shuffling of the courtship deck they merited any spectacular hand being dealt to them. He would do. She would do. Was that how other marriages came about?

Helen shivered in spite of the enervating level of heating Walter liked. But the main lure, surely, had been his dream, and the way he had changed when he talked of it, seized by an unexpected ardour which had made him suddenly much more likeable. Starting a prep school in the house in the western suburbs of Edinburgh which his aunt had left him. What had seemed so dazzlingly original about that? But the enticement had been there, to break out of the mould into which she had so unthinkingly cast herself, to start out on a new enterprise for which, she had felt in her soul, she was well equipped.

What had they done in time spent together during the months of their engagement? She couldn't remember. When she tried memory simply clicked up again the images of that first tennis party, or others very like it. There must have been, certainly had been, family dinner parties round the table which now stood in the dining-room next door. What could she remember of them? Nothing in particular. Good food, good manners, a mild formality. Her father, the local GP, had probably been absent for half of them.

Her parents had approved of Walter; there was nothing of which to disapprove. Everyone had been pleased at the engagement, even Walter's cantankerous widowed mother who lived near Whitby. He had always been terrified of betraying the slightest breath of a northern accent, Helen remembered, and she also remembered, as though it concerned two barely known people belonging to another time, noticing the occasional stressed 'con' prefix or strong final 't'. She had made no comment.

Then had come the busy satisfying years. Satisfying? She checked there, decided it was a question for another day, and shivered again. What would other days bring?

The busy years then. The comfortable, well furnished, but not entirely suitable house to adapt to their purpose. The combined roles of wife – she had not expected Walter to insist on that as her priority, but she had not contested it – matron, active teaching partner, and housekeeper both for the school and their own flat, two very different levels of activity. The busy years and the best.

The best? Before Reggie was born? Well, she had set herself to ask these questions. And the answer was yes, harsh though that was. In fact it was with the arrival of her son that her life had turned into the solely domestic channel from which she had never fought free, and which itself had narrowed and narrowed, as the school expanded and flourished, into housekeeping and nothing more.

And had narrowed again, ominously and unendurably, here. When they had first moved to Tigh Bhan she had discovered with relief that they had inherited, as well as Catriona's diffident friendship, regular domestic help. It had come in the form of a brawny, hatchet-jawed and opinionated village woman called Barbara Bailey. She had always cleaned at Tigh Bhan, and as far as she was concerned she always would. The rate she demanded was startlingly low, and Helen had suggested something a little more realistic.

'I'll just be on Tuesdays and Thursdays,' Barbara had warned, disconcerted, searching instinctively for something else on which to take a stand.

'That would suit me very well,' Helen had agreed, and so it had been settled.

Barbara Bailey had been a crasher. Helen had her own categories after the long years of suffering domestic help, though 'help' was often a misnomer. Barbara had also clung resolutely to familiar terminology. Asked to clean those areas of the study which were not on the proscribed list before Walter finished breakfast, she would say crushingly, 'That'll be the sewing-room you're meaning.' Required to sweep the back doorstep she would remark when she came back, 'I wasnae sure what you were meaning, so I just did the step at the garden door to make sure.' Every time she went out to the dustbin she moved it six feet to where it had formerly stood, and she always took the hoover out of the cupboard in the kitchen passage and put it back in the cupboard under the stairs. Helen didn't specially mind. Arbitrating on such subjects had been necessary when several people used the equipment and time was at a premium. Now she was done with battles. She was nearly fifty-nine. Retirement age was close. Who cared, truly, where the hoover lived?

Walter, however, couldn't bear Barbara. He saw nothing funny in her vehement support of a previous dispensation. At Tigh Bhan he found himself too tediously close to domestic activities, missing the cushioning of Netherdean where his study had been a sanctum never invaded, where scarcely a sound or indeed a demand of any kind ever reached him.

He sacked Barbara. Tigh Bhan was not a small house,

Walter's standards had not dropped an inch since the staff had numbered eight, and he continued to demand the sort of meals he had always been accustomed to. As a consequence Helen had found herself if anything busier than ever before, certainly occupied with even more mundane chores than, barring emergencies, she had had to face for a long time.

There had also been the question of entertaining. Helen had been long resigned to the social obligations which had gone with the territory of school. There unrolled in her memory now an endless procession of the stuffiest of duty dinner parties, drinks parties, Sunday lunches, buffets at every traditional school function in the calendar. She had not foreseen that in 'retirement' Walter would want to cling to the same style, which she had seen as something they could at last blissfully escape from. Somehow, even here in Inverbuie, he had collected around him a stifling group consisting of the local minister and his counterpart in Luig, a retired archaeologist, a retired professor, and an inexpressibly dull Air Commodore who Helen was convinced could neither read nor write, and who seemed to be included on the grounds of rank alone. For this rarefied clique, plus their wives, with none of whom had she been able to make the slightest contact, she found herself obliged all too frequently to shop, clean and polish, prepare canapés and rub up glasses and silver, cook large elaborate dinners and clear up afterwards. Attempts to find help for a few hours drew a blank; word had gone out, though now she thought ruefully, with a renewed pang for her departure, she should have taken the problem to Catriona.

And so her thoughts circled back. It would make such a difference not having Catriona in the glen. Helen hated to think of it. The possibility of making ordinary, warm friendships through her had barely begun to be fulfilled. The insights into local ways and humour, the contact with day-to-day events, the fascinating glimpses of the past, the usefulness of being able to tap into Catriona's intricate knowledge of where to walk, where to obtain things, who lived where, who was related to whom, as well as the pleasure of her company, would all be lost.

After Postie had gone Helen had, as always, ground some beans, made coffee, set a tray with a starched tray-cloth, bone-china cup and saucer, and plate with four fingers of homemade shortbread, the cream jug and two bowls of soft sugar, light and dark (Walter liked to be given the choice), which had to be freshly filled every time or the sugar set like rock. She had placed the mail in the space she had left for it, graded in order of size, and added the bubbling percolator. Then she had carried the tray to the pleasant south-facing French-windowed little room which Walter had appropriated to himself without discussion, and had tapped lightly as Walter required. It seemed that knocking did not disturb the vital train of thought, but opening the door did.

He had not acknowledged her appearance, beyond hastily and protectively moving some papers as though she would be incapable of comprehending their importance.

She was used to this, and saw no sense in minding it. As she turned away, leaving intact his mental link with the author of a paper putting forward the clearly untenable theory that Caelius exceeded Cicero in epigrammatic power, she had heard him take a first greedy gulp of coffee, had, indeed, tensed herself for the sound.

Today, however, he had spoken.

'Not up to your best standard, perhaps.'

It was said semi-jokingly, suavely, but with an undercurrent of pettish spite; a tone she had heard him employ a hundred times. But not to her. To some clumsy housemaid perhaps, or condemning the offerings of an inadequate cook, or flensing a brash or underconfident new master, but not, till now, to her.

She had turned, her heart quickening a little in shock, and had seen that he was not even aware of what he had done. His hand was out for the first piece of shortbread, his head was down, his lips pursed as his fountain pen flowed smoothly in some vitriolic phrase which evidently pleased him.

She had said nothing, feeling the tide of anger rise hotly in her cheeks, but he had not noticed that she had halted. She had turned away and left the room and come to sit here at the kitchen table.

But she could sit here no longer. She had to cook lunch, which must on no account be late. She took fish from the fridge ('refrigerator, please. You know better than that,' came Walter's pained voice), removed the clingfilm, split the fillets in two, rolled them neatly up, secured them with cocktail sticks. These were once living creatures that swam in the sea. Now they are white, slippery, semi-translucent pieces of edible substance, which I do not cook flat but make into little rolls because that egocentric, lazy, spoiled man on the other side of the house makes a boring fuss if I don't. I have allowed him, in all fairness, to behave like this. And today, for his lunch, I shall roll up the whiting, make an egg sauce, boil and cream potatoes, cook green beans, heat up the lentil soup and be prepared for him to complain because we had it yesterday as well. I shall serve him with coffee mousse and sponge fingers, but not with coffee because it spoils his nap. I shall do all this, today, once more.

She did it, and called Walter at one, and Walter came in with his scholarly abstracted air and talked to her because he was temporarily detached from his pen and wished to go on polishing his wit about the pusillanimity of soul of a man who could stigmatise Cicero as verbose. He ate without noticing what he was putting in his mouth, except to object about the soup, and as he dropped his napkin, which he never bothered to put back in his napkin ring, Helen said, 'Walter, could you pay attention for a moment, please. I have decided to leave you.'

Chapter Two

It was hot in the train. At first that had been welcome; Helen didn't feel as though she had been properly warm for weeks. But before long it had become oppressive and devitalising. As she approached the end of her journey April sunshine poured down on the unassuming landscape of north Shropshire, where the rich green of spring was an actual shock after the cold Edinburgh winter, the grey vistas of stone.

The network of small roads, the neat towns and villages she looked out on, were at once deeply familiar as the landscape of childhood always is, yet oddly alien after the years away. Her eye was unaccustomed to the red brick of cottages and farmhouses, the flash of black-and-white. Also there was a prosperous air which was new, huge barns everywhere, wide gateways hung with metal gates to accommodate today's monster machines, bigger fields, bare farmyards where she remembered a friendly scene of hens and bantams pecking about, ducks on duckponds, cats sunning themselves in warm corners out of reach of the dogs, horses looking over half doors, the mixen in the middle of the yard. Mixen. Was that Shropshire for midden? She had never thought about it, it was just the word that was used. But that was fifty years ago. Half a century of change. And for nearly half that time, since her father died and her mother had found she couldn't endure living in the well-loved house without him, Helen had not returned.

Was that Wem already? The train was flashing down the line where, when she used to go to visit friends, the little local train had puffed peacefully from tiny station to tiny station, each bright with flowers for the Best Kept Station competition. And earlier, in the war, coming this way occasionally with her mother, tired shoppers who had queued for hours had been crammed into the couple of carriages, squeezed close on the seats with their knees sideways to make room for those standing. She, like the other children, would be taken onto the lap of some friendly stranger if her mother couldn't find a seat. Sometimes they rode in the guard's van, and that would be packed too.

The last station seemed to have vanished altogether and before she expected it they were running into the outskirts of Shrewsbury, now stretching greedily out into the farmland. They passed a grid of empty pens covering a wide area she had known as fields, and she remembered being told some time ago that the cattle market had moved from its old site at Smithfield. She had liked, on market days, hearing through the form room windows the cattle being driven along Town Walls, country thoughts intruding in town, home thoughts agreeably breaking in on school.

Don't look back, Helen reminded herself, don't compare. It wouldn't help her to adjust, and it would be maddening for Reggie and the family. The flow of memories, inescapable as they were, must be kept to herself. Hopefully they would have less power to hurt than the visions of gleaming Loch Buie and the hills of Glen Righ and the Luig peninsula, which had caught at her so often and with such an acute sense of loss in the lonely weeks in the city, while the painful unravelling was being completed.

She had had to go. How many times a day did she assure herself of that? She had had to leave Walter before she was drowned, stifled, obliterated by his monumental selfishness. With a wry grimace she recognised that this time she was also rehearsing her defence against Reggie's criticism – or Nadia's, for her daughter-in-law had already made her feelings abundantly clear. Women of Helen's age, their tenor had been, did not divorce their husbands. Apart from any moral considerations there had been the crushing rider that there was no sense in doing so. What sort of life could a woman approaching sixty expect to make on her own? What was the *point*? Helen smiled briefly, hearing Nadia's baffled and exasperated voice, then the smile faded as she realised that all too soon she would hear it in reality, hammering insistently at these same questions. Nadia never saw any reason for holding her tongue.

The town was rushing towards them. Not much was recognisable, but Helen supposed that no matter what other changes had been made the Victorian splendours of the railway station would still survive beside the warm sandstone walls of the castle.

Nadia was alone on the platform. Helen had not expected to see Reggie but as it was the Easter holidays she had thought Phoebe and Sebastian might be there. Was that because I am longing to see my grandchildren, she asked herself, or because their presence would have been a useful buffer? All she knew for certain, as the train slid to a halt, was that she did not, did *not* want to be where she was.

Nadia had spotted her and pulled open the carriage door exclaiming, '*There* you are!' in a tone which implied that Helen was either late or had been deliberately attempting to hide. Helen, smiling warmly, wished for a moment that she had.

'Nadia, how good of you to come to meet me.'

Nadia bumped a kiss onto Helen's cheek and before it could be returned began to grapple energetically with the luggage. That was only, Helen knew, because her daughter-in-law regarded kissing as an obligatory social rite, and performed it on that basis, wasting as little time on it as possible.

'Here, I'll take those. You shouldn't be carrying them.' At your age. Already the words hung in the air. 'I've still got one or two things to do in town, but they won't take long. You wouldn't believe the rush I've had getting here, but the holidays are always ghastly, aren't they? And on the way home we must collect Sebastian, he's at a chum's this afternoon, don't let me forget. He and Phoebe are dying to see you, of course, only they do so hate being dragged into town on a day like this, and honestly, who can blame them? It's boiling today, like summer already. Got your ticket? Well done. I managed to squeeze the car in not too far away, which is an absolute miracle. The town's a complete nightmare already, even though Easter's barely over. You pop yourself in, I'll see to this lot.'

Heat hung stiflingly below the high walls, bounced back from cars and buildings. Helen wished she had put on a thinner blouse under the lambswool sweater which had seemed very light in Edinburgh's morning chill, with the early haar still clinging along the firth. Yes, thank you, Nadia, I had a good journey.

'How is Reggie?' she asked, as Nadia manoeuvred the long vehicle out with firm competence.

'Oh, frightfully busy, poor old lad. Terrific competition these days from the EC countries. God knows why we ever let them in.'

An interesting view, Helen thought, in a conscious effort to cheer herself up as they joined the unbroken line of vehicles grinding up Castle Street. She hadn't seen the town since that last sad visit to pack the things her mother had wanted to take to the house she was to share with her sister in York, and to arrange about letting Roden House.

ALEXANDRA RAIFE

There had been little time to look about her then, and she found she was still unconsciously expecting to see the familiar outlines of her youth, jarred by the disappearance of dignified old buildings, disliking the tourist-crowded pavements.

That's ridiculous and pointless, she told herself sharply. Don't do it, don't even think that way. But she knew the flurry of nostalgia was part of a deeper dread of the unknown future, and doubt about the wisdom of what she was doing. Not what she had done. Never for one second had she doubted the rightness and good sense of that. The only wonder was that she had waited so long to do it. But to come here, to allow herself to be persuaded that her 'place' now was with her son and his family, in the surroundings where she had grown up – had that been wise? Had she once again taken the easiest, the most obvious route? For nothing there either would be as it had been, and she had never till now had the courage to face it.

In the early years of their marriage Walter had resisted coming back, saying, in what he meant to be taken as a humorous tone, that during his engagement he had had his fill of rural somnolence and barren exchanges with sons of the soil. When Reggie, knowing he would inherit Roden House, had come to live here and had met and married Nadia, the second ten-year lease on the house was still running and they had rented a bungalow in the village, soon too small for them as first Phoebe and then Sebastian arrived. The obvious arrangement for family visits had always been for them to come to Netherdean, though since Walter detested Nadia that had hardly been ideal either. But the children liked the intriguing playground of an empty school and its grounds, and could conveniently be left while their parents went touring further north.

'These wretched tourists, just look at them,' Nadia was complaining. 'I don't mind them going to see Rowley's House and Fish Street and all that boring old stuff, but I do wish they could be kept off the streets so that we could get on with our lives. Oh look, not an inch to park in, wouldn't you know it? I shall have to go right round again. But Phoebe will be so upset if I don't collect her new Frizzle and Fry video. Don't you know them? Well, I suppose you wouldn't. I can see we're going to have to educate you. There are these two hysterical characters and they – oh, yes, thank you, I can get in there, if you don't take all day about it. Go on, masses of room!' Nadia stuck her head out of the window to call commandingly to the driver about to pull out.

Helen didn't think he appreciated the assistance.

'Shan't be a tick, but I really can't go home without it. It's been in for two days, and Phoebe's been awfully good about it, poor sweet. You know what girls that age are like when they're mad keen on something. Or no, actually, I don't suppose you do.'

I think perhaps I might, actually, Helen said temperately to herself. After the first shy and uncertain half dozen, just Phoebe's age, there had been so many more, in the end nearly equalling the boys, and so fascinatingly different to look after.

'Never having had a daughter, I mean,' Nadia added helpfully, fishing for her handbag among the mounds of shopping on the back seat. 'Now, you'll be all right, won't you?'

What if I had said, No, I'm afraid to be left sitting alone in your car on a spring afternoon in an English country town? Would Nadia still have cloven a way across the pavement as though her errand was self-evidently more important than the amblings of the holiday-makers? Yes, she would, confident and unheeding, in her navy blue skirt and navy-striped shirt with the collar standing up, her crisp red, white and navy scarf. She too had been at St Chad's. Did she feel safe in navy blue? Did it hint at the hankering never to have left school which Helen had always suspected in her, the longing to be Games Captain still, her large firm breasts and sturdy thighs barely contained by the gym-tunic across whose yoke a long row of badges was sewn, all for physical prowess.

I'm tired, Helen thought, shutting her eyes against the glare from the long bonnet, and trying to shut her ears against the roar of the traffic struggling up the steep street. I am tired and lonely and afraid.

The web of ring-road and roundabouts which now seemed to encircle the town, once contained in the great defensive horseshoe loop of the Severn, was so confusing that Helen completely lost her bearings for a time, more than half her attention in any case absorbed by Nadia's driving. I do not think you can discourage other vehicle-owners from ever using the road again, however combatively you deal with them, she longed to suggest, and realised bleakly that there might be much silent dialogue in a similar vein in the days to come.

Then, without warning, more than four decades fell abruptly away. Time rolled back, to drowsy afternoons of summer terms, bouncing slowly homewards with the orange and brown plush of the seat of the 4.10 bus warm through blue check gingham, panama hat with its school band (or later the sixth form boater which she had rather liked) on the seat beside her, as it was not supposed to be. The quiet road they had turned into, twisting among small hills crested with woods and dotted with farms, was startlingly the same as it had always been. She had walked, cycled, ridden, driven and been driven along here a thousand times. As the road wound and dipped towards the river valley and the village she felt unbearably stirred, at once enchanted and apprehensive and, oddly, fiercely protective of the scene, as though Nadia was an intruder in it. A vision of the house rose vividly before her, the house as it always looked whenever she thought of it, its small time-worn bricks rich and mellow in the afternoon sunshine, its three rows of windows, the lower ones half smothered by wistaria, overlooking the river, down the slope made into a lawn again after the vegetable growing of the war years. She felt her throat constrict, her eyes smart.

The intense, unlooked-for moment of recognition and homecoming was wiped out as they turned the last corner and the village came into sight. It straggled now far along the river, a desirable 'rural' environment within easy reach of the town, its old cottages tarted up, new housing estates on three sides, more building work in progress. And there, spreading like a stain across the meadows of the slope opposite, hideous in the primary colours of machinery, with stark sheds, concrete paths and roadways, neat breeze-block offices, sprawled Reggie's kingdom.

My son is responsible for that, Helen thought, shaken to her soul at the hideous sight.

'Not bad, is it?' Nadia asked with pride. 'We'll show you round properly tomorrow. Best thing that could ever have happened to the village, keeps the school going and the village shop and all that sort of thing. Reggie hadn't a clue when he started, but Dad got him going on the right lines, and no one could deny he's made a go of it since.'

'He certainly has,' Helen agreed. Her voice sounded dangerously faint to her own ears, and she rallied to try again. 'It does look most success—'

'Goodness, there's Deirdre Bracegirdle. Whatever's she doing calling at the vicarage? She's not religious. Oh and look, I knew it, he promised me faithfully they'd only play in the garden. And that's Kurt's bike he's pinched, it's far too big for him . . .'

Nadia's voice as she pulled up had taken on a note

of besotted indulgence which made Helen carefully wipe all expression from her face.

Sebastian was riding a bicycle round and round the oak tree in the centre of the village green (both of which Helen was glad to see had survived) and its angry owner was trying to stop him every time he came round.

'Darling, look who's here! Come and say hello,' Nadia shouted.

Sebastian looked across at the car, wobbled, scowled and rode faster.

'His balance is usually jolly good,' his mother said defensively. 'He is only six. I took him by surprise calling like that.'

Of the various points at issue, this was not the one to which Helen would have given priority. She waited in silence. The pub, she saw, had been extended and was now pink, and a couple of cottages had been removed to give it a carpark. The shop had become a plate-glass-fronted minimarket. What had formerly been where that modern garage was? She couldn't remember. Did it matter?

'Sebastian, let Kurt have his bike and come and say hello to Grannie,' Nadia shouted again, with no inhibitions about disturbing anyone.

Sebastian stood on his pedals and spurted away across the green, followed by a protesting Kurt.

'Oh, don't worry, he'll come home when he's ready,' Nadia said, as though it was Helen who had been doing the shouting, but her well-fleshed cheeks were an unbecoming scarlet and her mouth was tight with annoyance as she started up the car.

Helen was not offended by Sebastian's rudeness. She had not expected much spontaneous delight from either grandchild at the sight of her. Of all the children she had known, these two she had always found it especially difficult to relate to, and she did not think them entirely to blame.

The thoughts were a smokescreen, and she knew it, for the car was now following the curve of road down towards the River Roden. The moment was close, and she wasn't ready.

When Reggie had inherited from her mother, at Helen's own request, the house that had been in the family for four generations and was to have come to her, he and Nadia had knocked it down.

Chapter Three

Although Helen had known this had been done, and although she had received many enthusiastic descriptions of the new house from Nadia, loaded with invidious and tactless comparisons with the old one, and had even seen bits of it as a background to endless photographs of the children, nothing had prepared her for the physical shock, this stunned, sick, hollow feeling. The mellow beauty of two hundred and fifty years, the great trees, the semi-wild garden with its winding paths and hidden corners, the orchard, the outbuildings of that same weathered brick grouped round the cobbled yard with the handsome iron pump in the middle, had all been erased. The brain had long ago accepted the fact, but the eye had to see for itself before the pain of loss struck home.

'Now, isn't that better?' Nadia cried complacently, swinging into a drive of dark tarmac. 'I don't know how anyone could have put up with that beetly old place, it gave me the creeps. You should have seen the state it was in, the floors all sunk and uneven, woodworm in the beams, and still those awful old flagstones in the kitchen, absolute dirt traps. But you'll be warm and cosy in this one, don't worry . . .'

Ignoring the hard lump in her throat Helen made herself look properly at the house as, dragged down by reluctance, she got out of the car. It was two-storied, with a hexagonal conservatory joined to it at the hip. It boasted a multiplicity of architectural detail: a fanlight, a colonnade, a balcony, and much herringbone brickwork in a curious shade of mauve-red. Even so early in the year strident colour was added by massed plants in troughs of imitation carved stone. A lawn at the left was gaudy with swing, trampoline, climbing frame, slide and portable sandpit. Everywhere were straight lines and hard edges. Graded terraces made giant steps of what had once been the easy slope of the lawn. Where it had ended at the river's edge in a grassy bank there was now a wall of pierced concrete. That somehow seemed worst of all, a deliberate shutting out of everything natural, gentle, peaceful.

'Frightfully dangerous for the children, open to the river the way it was before,' Nadia said, seeing where Helen was looking. 'I flatly refused to move in till that wall was put up. I wouldn't have had a moment's peace without it.'

I was a child here, and I survived. So did my mother, her father . . .

'Now come along, let's find Phoebe. I expect she didn't hear the car. And Reggie said he'd try to be home early for once, though to be honest I shan't hold my breath.'

Disorientated, numb, Helen had to make a conscious effort to set her limbs in motion. 'I'll bring something in with me,' she said, feeling scarcely able to remember normal behaviour.

'No, no, don't bother about that.' Nadia sounded impatient and must have realised it, for she added in a tone at once bracing and patronising, 'Can't have you struggling in with all my awful shopping, can we?'

Virtually the entire ground floor of the new house seemed to be one room, made even bigger by the conservatory beyond, the doors to which were open. Acres of pale blue carpet were dotted by grossly stuffed sofas and chairs covered in glazed chintz in a Florentine design of pale blue and pink. Each was mated with a glass-topped table in a frame stained a purplish 'mahogany'. The biggest television Helen had ever seen was pumping out Children's BBC at maximum volume. No one was watching it. There was no sign anywhere of any furniture from the original house, and Helen was thankful that she had been able to preserve the few pieces her mother had taken with her when she moved. She put the thought aside. Accept what's here, concentrate on the present. The present seemed more than anything to consist of an ambient temperature which was making her face flush and her skin prickle under her too-heavy clothes.

'Phoebe, Phoebe, where are you? Grannie's here,' Nadia was calling.

I think we've played this scene before, Helen thought,
with the flatness of exhaustion.

'Did you bring my video?' a high voice called from
upstairs, over the blare of a second television.

'Yes, darling, I did. And I'll give it to you when you
come down.' Nadia flashed Helen a look of triumph at
this brilliant piece of child management.

Phoebe appeared on the stairs, sliding her expensive
trainers off the edge of each step and letting herself drop
with a thump onto the next, her narrow face at once
resentful and duplicitous.

'Hello, Phoebe.'

'I didn't hear the car,' Phoebe said to her mother,
using a defensive baby voice that sought her support.

Helen wondered if lying was her habitual approach to
Nadia. She regarded her grand-daughter with a wish to be
impartial, but knew it was going to be difficult. Phoebe
had her mother's flat yellow hair and pale blue eyes, but
not her high colouring or sturdy build. She was as weedy
as Reggie had been at that age, but a hundred times more
confident, and her eyes held a contempt of which he had
never been capable.

'Hello, Grannie.' Phoebe came down the last few
steps and twisted her cheek upwards to be kissed, closing
her eyes.

Helen pressed her lips against the pale skin and was
conscious of a strong wish that it had been her hand.
Appalled, for never in all the years of children had such
an impulse seized her, she put her arms round Phoebe

and hugged her. This was her son's child; and they were to live together.

'Ow,' said Phoebe. 'You bumped me with your bag.'

'Come and show Grannie the lovely little new home we've made for her,' Nadia suggested, more cajoling than brisk, Helen's experienced ear noted. 'Phoebe was such a help to me, getting it all ready for you,' she added to Helen, who saw by Phoebe's cold stare that she had been no such thing and didn't care who knew it.

'Where's my Frizzle and Fry?' Phoebe demanded.

'In the car, darling, of course. I shoved it into one of the Marks and Spencer bags – the one on top!' Nadia raised her voice to add as Phoebe scudded off. 'Otherwise she'd go through the lot like a hunt terrier after a fox,' she explained in what sounded like admiration, but which Helen chose to believe was apology for yelling so loudly.

Phoebe dashed in again clutching the video and disappeared upstairs. Helen thought she could have brought in the bag she had found it in. Nadia, clearly, had expected nothing of the sort.

'Now, come and see your new domain.' Nadia switched back to bright hostess mode. 'Then I can bring in your things and get you nicely settled in.'

Helen found herself longing with the passion of weariness for the refuge of the grannie flat she had heard so much about. To shut the door on her own self-contained accommodation seemed at this moment the most desirable thing in the world. Nadia had warned her

— Reggie never wrote — that it wasn't huge, and she could see from the size and layout of the house that it couldn't be, but to be peaceful and alone was all she needed.

Nadia led her through a dazzling kitchen, open to the living area but stepped back from it, and into a brief corridor with two doors. 'Bathroom,' she said, tapping with her knuckles on the first, 'and *here* you are,' throwing open the second, 'your own special quarters. As I said in my letters, you can be completely shut away here and no one will disturb you. What do you think? Aren't you thrilled?'

She so evidently was that none of Helen's startled protests could be voiced. The 'grannie flat' of the letters, where she was to be 'absolutely independent, free to come and go as you choose', was this? This square bedroom with its square window looking out onto the children's play area, with its single armchair, one of the glass-topped tables beside it, a television taking up a third of the dressing table and a small desk huddled in a corner.

'Even though the cupboard doors slide you probably won't be able to get into the end bit behind the desk very easily, but you can always put things you don't wear often there. Anyway, I don't suppose you need many clothes now, do you? Reggie wasn't sure but I told him you couldn't do without a desk, didn't he remember what you were like, you and Grandpa, forever scribbling away at something or other? Oh, heavens, sorry, I suppose I shouldn't have said that, but you know what I mean. Anyway, we gave you your own television, so you'll be able to watch all your favourite programmes in peace. The children each have one, naturally, but they prefer the one in the lounge because it's bigger, and anyway, it's quite nice to watch together as a family thing, isn't it? In my opinion they can spend too much time in their rooms, with all these video games and so on. Now I'll just lug in your stuff and then we can—'

With a look at her watch Nadia was hurrying off, her voice trailing away as her mind totted up the things she still had to pack into her day. The door from the corridor to the kitchen whined as it closed.

Very still, though with an inner trembling beginning to take hold, Helen stood where she had come to a halt, just inside the door. This barren cube was to be her home. The visions of a pleasant little sitting-room, with her books around her and the few possessions she had sent on, and which she had thought might already have arrived; of a separate bedroom, no matter how small; of her own tiny kitchen which would give the independence Nadia had been so adamant she should have, fled in the face of this bald reality.

'Goodness, what have you got in these, Edinburgh rock?' Nadia cried gaily, dumping the cases on the floor and laughing at her own wit. 'Everything all right for you?' She didn't pause for a reply, sure everything she had arranged must be perfect. 'We planned this flatlet originally as a guest suite. Of course we had to take the double bed out and put a single one in for you, because we thought you'd like more space, and what a sweat that was, let me tell you! No, no, only joking. Oh, and I forgot to say, the bathroom's more or less yours. I'll try to make the children go up to their own loo during the day now that you're here. Right, must dash now. Supper sixish, if that's OK with you. Bit early tonight, I've got choir practice. A bit of a bore on your first evening, but there it is. I'll give you a shout when Reggie pitches up.'

Helen stood, her heart beating so hard, yet so strangely slowly, that she could hardly take a proper breath. To the right of her window, through which the sun poured without interruption – there used to be elm trees by the bridge, she thought, but confusedly, as though for the moment she could recall nothing clearly – Sebastian appeared, still cycling. He dismounted by the swing, let the bicycle fall with a crash onto its concrete base, and disappeared round the front of the house.

He's stolen it, Helen thought detachedly, and without surprise. She knew she wasn't going to be able to contain the tide of tears rising up in her. She needed somewhere to bury her face, some place of comfort to absorb them. There were no clothes in the wardrobe, familiar and hers; the blue quilted counterpane with its rectangle of piping and box-pleated valance made the bed as impersonal as any in a hotel room. Moving almost without being aware of it, she went to the window and leaned her forehead against the shiny blue folds of the glazed cotton curtain. Did everything have to gleam and shine; did everything have to be in straight lines? Then choking, dismaying tears overtook her, and she clung there, all her normal calm and quiet humour shattered, doing her best to muffle the racking sobs.

When finally she steadied her breathing and straightened up, she saw that the pristine curtain not only had a dark damp patch on its flattened folds but that there were two little starbursts of creases where her hands had clung. She wondered, without caring, how long they would take to vanish. Then, with a deliberate resolve to face what had happened to this loved place, she lifted her chin and looked out past the gaudy expensive toys which had been lavished on her grandchildren. Behind what she supposed would be called privacy fencing, though it was mostly hidden itself by slow-growing conifers of different colours, she could see the maroon pantile roof of the bungalow built where the old grass court had been. How passionate they had all been about tennis when she was in her teens; how many long afternoons and evenings had been passed there, and on friends' courts, playing on till it was impossible to see the ball. And how as they mowed and rolled and marked out the lines with the little tray of whitening on its wobbly wheels, they had longed for a hard court. And equally, hunting for balls in the rhododendrons and the long grass, how they had longed for new netting. But in the post-war years few people had the money for such luxuries. Certainly not her father, the local GP worn out by the demands of a rural practice previously covered by three doctors.

Now there was the ridge of a plastic greenhouse, a

rotary washing line, the tips of flimsy trees with crepe paper blossoms in pastel shades.

She must wash her face, brush her hair. She must concentrate with all her determination on what was there, on what existed, not what had been. With a slight effort she lifted one of the cases across the wooden arms of the 'easy' chair. The months in the Edinburgh flat, recovering, adjusting, marking time, had made her much less fit than when she had had the garden at Tigh Bhan to look after, the hills of Glen Righ to explore.

Don't think of that, she pleaded with herself in anguish, tears threatening again at the image of the big comfortable house, the loch before it, the burn pouring down its rough gorge from the moor behind it. She found the presents she had brought, a fresh blouse, her washing things and make-up. Glen Righ and its beauty were as inaccessible now as the picture she had had of the comfortable flat where she was to build her new life, the life which would carry her beyond the barrier of 'retirement', and into old age.

She thought she heard a car arrive, but no one called her. Going through the kitchen, which still had its arid high-gloss look as though no preparations of any kind were in hand for 'supper', she heard voices raised in argument.

'Of course we'll have to take it back.'

'He should take it back himself.'

'He's far too tired to cycle all that way again.'

'Nadia, it's less than a mile.'

'But then he'd have to walk home afterwards. No, it's out of the question, he's far too small to be expected to do that, poor little soul. I've got choir practice, so you'll have to go, and that's that. Now for heaven's sake let's have — Oh, there you are at last,' Nadia cried, dutiful whipped-up welcome barely cloaking the irritation in her voice as she saw Helen.

Reggie greeted his mother with the awkwardness he had always exhibited with her since his resentful teens, and which she hoped would at last disappear now that they were, at his and Nadia's insistence, to live under the same roof.

But there was something else too, Helen sensed as she stepped back from his flabby hug and looked up into his bony weak-jawed face. His eyes were blinking in the familiar way behind his thick lenses, not meeting hers. He was uncomfortable about something. He felt guilty, she was suddenly certain, because he knew the provision that had been made for her was less than adequate. Good. That gave her the first faint hope for the future she had felt since she stepped off the train.

Chapter Four

Almost due north of the changed and swollen village of Withedine and more than three hundred miles away, Catriona, fitting her key with reluctance into the door of a dour, shabby house in a Dundee suburb, was shivering in an evening colder by several degrees. The wind off the Tay scoured up the steep street, where the once comfortable Edwardian villas were now chopped and jigsawed into a warren of flats and bedsits, largely occupied by the student population; of which she was one.

The door fell to behind her with its dead thud. Once, in the dark sunless days of last term, when the raw east coast cold seemed to have penetrated her bones and the muffling haar never seemed to lift from the river and the dilapidated graceless city, she had counted up, in a sort of desperate test of her capacity to see this through, the number of times she would hear that prisoner's sound. The answer had been too appalling to contemplate. Now she closed her ears to it, crossing to the darkly varnished stairs, hefting with both hands her leather suitcase, an antique piece of luggage nearly as heavy as the belongings stuffed into it. Like the rest of her possessions, Catriona never looked at it; never saw it as eccentric or dated or different from the things other people owned. As she had done all her life, while the big house of Glen Righ sank year by year into decrepitude and decay, she had simply used what was available, without complaint and without much noticing.

When she had embarked on her course at the Taybridge College of Business Studies, in those autumn days so tense with fear, and so baffling with the thousand unfamiliar things she had to grapple with that they had become an indistinguishable blur in her mind, her fellow students had seen her as a freak, a one-off, something else. At first they eyed her in hostile silence, unable to add up the weird clothes, whose subfusc dinginess bore no relation to any current fashion of student scruffiness, her delicate build, gentle manner and cultured voice, and her capacity to absorb and retain information, which they soon saw far exceeded their own. They took her accent and natural courtesy to be patronising and imitated her behind her back. Then, as familiarity with each other and their new environment grew, they became more confident and began to tease her with a snide mockery which made them feel they were in control. Like their earlier silence, Catriona appeared not to notice the jibes and unkindness, and they were forced to accept that she was genuinely oblivious to them.

Having worked through their own insecurities, most of the group, fundamentally good-natured, began to accept this oddity among them for what she was. Catriona continued to appear punctually each day and apply herself single-mindedly to whatever was being taught; she promptly fulfilled every assignment and when her fellow students, beginning to feel protective about her, told her no one had to work that hard, she looked at them with the polite incomprehension of someone being addressed in a foreign tongue.

Eventually, getting over their ingrained antipathy to something they didn't understand, and seeing Catriona floundering in a world not only unfamiliar but daunting, three or four of the girls decided kindly to 'drag her into the real world'. Although Catriona was older than they were by six or seven years, they never saw her as a 'mature student', one or two of whom were also taking the information technology course. Physically she was less developed than any of them, and in her dull black needlecord skirt and sagging sweaters in oatmeal or lovat green, her Harris tweed coat and damp-stained zipped suede boots, looked like some anxious child in a wartime film, about to be bundled onto a train with a label round her neck to escape the bombs. Also, making even more of a nonsense of the age gap, her mentors came to accept her innocence, naivety and her amazing ignorance of the basic mechanics of what they regarded as normal life.

Once she had mastered such mysteries as the soap dispenser in the loos and the self-service system in the cafeteria and could get herself across roads, her struggles with all of which in the first days of term had made her fellow students demand blankly, 'Is she real or what?' they felt she should learn there was more to life than vanishing with a shy smile every afternoon, never to be seen again till she slipped into her seat the next morning.

They started by insisting she join them for lunch in the clattering, resounding restaurant, shouting questions at her over the racket, reduced to puzzled 'Yeah?'s at her half-heard, only half-believable replies.

'So where's this place, then?' they would ask, and 'On the West Coast,' Catriona would reply containedly, though seared by a vision of the beauty and peace she was denying herself in this painful attempt to catch up, get into step with the world.

But she knew she had been right to uproot herself. The life she had led in Glen Righ had been so sheltered, so untouched by reality, as to be quite abnormal. She had been eight when her parents were killed in an aircraft accident, but even before that she and her brother had been left for most of the time at Glen Righ with their grandfather. Then her brother had died too, falling into the rocky gorge at the end of the terrace, and she had been alone with her grandfather, whose mind had been unhinged by the triple tragedy. She had been briefly sent away to school, where she had been utterly miserable, but Fergus's condition had deteriorated in her absence, and the experiment had been abandoned. So for years she had been accustomed to the spartan, threadbare rigours of the big house, too large to heat properly, even if she and Fergus had thought such a luxury necessary, with Watty Duff to do the odd jobs and, latterly, to look after Fergus as he sank more and more swiftly into frailty and confusion. The estate had limped along, managed as it had always been by a factor who rarely came to the glen. Mismanaged, or unmanaged, Catriona had discovered when two years after Fergus's death selling up had become the only course open to her.

It had been a turning point for her, not merely in the physical upheaval of losing the only home she had ever known, but by bringing her up against a decision she had been turning over in her mind for some time. After Fergus's death, living alone at Glen Righ, she had been rescued from her isolation and, she could see now, a dangerous slide into apathy and reclusiveness, by the concern of a small group of friends. One was her nearest neighbour, Clare Macrae, who lived at Rhumore, a farm once owned by the Finlays and now in its turn owning large tracts of Glen Righ Estate. Then the Urquharts, who a few years ago had turned their family home of Ardlonach on the Luig peninsula into a hotel, had offered her a job and she had helped there for a couple of seasons, filling in the winter months by looking after the meal and health-food shop on Luig harbour belonging to yet another member of their circle who was about to get married. These jobs had been fun, and Catriona knew how much she owed to them, but an awareness had grown in her that all along she had been looked after and shielded by other people. Her way had been made easy, her gaucheness and inexperience understood and allowed for. Nothing had been asked of her that she would find too difficult, and she had slipped into these jobs without a qualification in the world.

So, consulting no one, she had set herself this challenge, to remove herself from the beloved and well-known landscape of the glen, beyond the protective reach of her friends, and meet head on other people's reality. Working in the office at Ardlonach she had learned the rudiments of using a computer, and because she had no other ideas about what she would like to do, or could do, she had settled on the IT course and found a place at Taybridge. But nothing had prepared her for the arid seediness, the crudeness, the raw cold of this place. She knew her own terrors and self-doubt coloured her view, and that her memories of the first two terms had to be exaggerated and distorted. There must have been bright days, mild days, pleasant days. But in memory they remained harried, oppressed and grim, and always there seemed to have been this mean wind off the river eating into her bones.

Disconcerted more by the bad manners than the animosity she had encountered, for since she came from a world where she never met the latter she had hardly recognised it for what it was, she had done her best to integrate, to drink down without shirking the whole dose. She had been persuaded to go to student clubs but, deafened, bored and confounded, had decided after one or two experiments that this arcane form of entertainment was not for her. She had established workable day-to-day relationships with a handful of people on her course, all female, for being unversed in the signals she was so oblivious to male interest that she killed off at birth what little there was of it.

For the rest she had settled into a semi-solitary existence which was just endurable, though a world away from her life in the glen, where she knew and was known by everyone, and accepted for what she was. Letters were her comfort and reassurance and, surprisingly, it was Una Urquhart who proved the best correspondent. Catriona would not have expected it, partly because Una was naturally reticent, always ready to let her more forceful and articulate cousin Rebecca hold the floor, but also because she was usually, from Easter to October at least, run off her feet in the hotel kitchen. It was Una's marvellous food which had made Ardlonach the success it had become, and she still did most of the cooking herself. But during the quiet winter months, when Catriona had most needed support, Una, recently divorced and in her own way almost as solitary as Catriona, had written often, providing the day-to-day gossip and news of friends which Catriona yearned for. Clare wrote less often, busy with the farm and her two small children, and Trudy Colquhoun, whose shop Catriona had looked after last winter, wrote with astonishment that she was already pregnant. Since her husband was a doctor her friends thought the astonishment overdone, but Fitz declared himself as surprised as anyone.

All these jokes and scraps of information Catriona

fed upon as avidly as a prisoner of war, and only two pieces of news distressed her. One was that Watty Duff had failed to hold on to any of the jobs he had tried since leaving Glen Righ, and had slipped into a hand-to-mouth existence of drinking his dole money as soon as he got it and scrounging odd jobs to get by on for the rest of the week.

And in the New Year Helen Rathbone had written to say that she was leaving Tigh Bhan. This came as a deep shock to Catriona, who had valued more than she realised the continuity and security of her link with the house. It had forced her to realise that Lilias Markie had represented a mother figure for her, and to acknowledge for the first time how easy it had been to let Helen fulfil the same role when she came to Tigh Bhan. Only at this distance of time could Catriona see how amazing the arrival of someone like her had been. Even during that nervous first call, which it had taken Catriona so long to bring herself to make, there had been instant ease and communication. Shared pleasure in books, an appetite which never lessened for Catriona, had been at the core of the friendship, for apart from Lilias only Clare had previously provided that, and her present active life left her little room to indulge it now.

It had been even more startling to hear that Helen was divorcing her husband. Not that Catriona didn't think it an excellent idea — she applauded it from her heart. She had disliked intensely the mixture of patronising jocularity and thinly veiled irritation at the intrusion with which Walter Rathbone had greeted her, and had always been relieved when he took himself off, muttering importantly about his 'work', to stink out what had been Lilias's pretty little sewing-room with his foul pipe. Even so, divorce was surprising. It seemed so odd at their age. Walter was seventy at least, and though Helen, trim and active, with only two rather stylish badger streaks of white in her brown hair framing a thin intelligent face, was obviously much younger than her husband, even she must be well into her fifties.

How sad that they had stayed at Tigh Bhan for so short a time. It had been a relief to have what Catriona vaguely thought of as nice people there – some dreadful incomers were infiltrating the glens these days – and as the friendship with Helen developed she had hoped it would extend to include the rest of her small circle. But though Clare too had called at Tigh Bhan, and Helen had met Trudy in the meal shop, which she still looked after part-time, things had not progressed much from there. Walter had been the problem, preferring to move in a very different group, chiefly composed of members of his own generation, and openly dismissive of everyday glen activities. Whatever Helen had felt about it, the Rathbones had, until the time of Catriona's departure, remained aloof. And now they were gone, the friendly white house by the hump-backed bridge was on the market again, and Catriona felt a sense of emptiness whenever she thought of it.

*   *   *

She let herself into her own corner of the student warren, dropping her bag with relief, not looking about her. The furnishing of the room was fifties drab — brownish roses on a dingy cream wallpaper, wooden-armed sofa and chairs scantily stretch-covered in a wincing mixture of greens. There was a huge rattling bay window and a chimney which quietly howled in most weathers, the most homelike aspect of these depressing quarters for Catriona. Long inured to discomfort, it never crossed her mind to introduce any improvements. This was simply a place where she could do any work which didn't need a computer, where she could huddle up in a bed far more comfortable than her worn-out childhood one at Glen Righ, and where she could read and read. Her other solace and refuge, or more accurately her other hungry need, was to walk. She had sold the car as soon as she arrived. She didn't need it here and didn't want the expense of running it, but the lack of wheels made her feel cut off from the surrounding countryside, dull though she thought it. However, she was only fifteen minutes away from open ground, and she would go up the dull streets at a rapid pace, always feeling faintly separate and threatened, heading for the tree-clad spaces of Balgay Park and the barer heights of the extinct volcano of the Law Hill. Although there was always a sense of curtailment, for at home she had been able to range for miles without crossing a road or seeing a soul, the views over the Tay and out to sea offered reminders of the long sea-lochs she missed so much, and the exercise always made her feel better. The downside was that walking made her long for Braan's company, and deepened the ache of nostalgia for all she had left behind, reminding her that 'home' existed no longer.

But two terms, the worst, were over, and the last one was beginning. That was what she must cling to. She had not gone back to the West Coast in the intervals between, not sure she would have the courage to leave again. In spite of invitations to stay at Rhumore or Ardlonach at Christmas she had held to her decision, knowing better than anyone the temptation she would face.

Also she had needed to earn some money. She had found work in a Perthshire hotel, a friendly place which had offered her a job again at Easter, from which she had just returned. Though there had been little free time at such peak periods it had been good to be in the hills again, and she had found friends among the young and lively staff.

Now one more term, spring must surely be close at last, summer waiting like a hazy golden dream beyond. Now she could begin to think what she would do once it came. She had hardly dared let herself wonder about it, not sure she would ever get this far, but now she knew she would pass, and probably pass well, for nothing on the course had seriously tested her. And in personal terms, which she knew was where the real test had lain, she had survived.

Chapter Five

Buffeted by sound and hubbub, light and heat, with a need whose almost physical urgency she would hardly have imagined herself capable of, to fight clear of complications and confusion, of unfinished conversations and half-grasped changes of plan and counter-plan, Helen stepped out into the early dusk. She drew a breath of pleasure and relief to find the air deliciously cool after the hot day and the overpowering warmth of the house, which sailed above her lit from stem to stern, casting into black shadow the unfamiliar steps of the new terraces. She felt her way down, trying to refuse the rush of memory — sweet scents of dew on mown grass, of long-gone lilacs, of the wash of apple blossom from the orchard where now two more bungalows squatted, each with outside lights deepening the dusk still further.

She came to the concrete balustrade and checked. She had known it was there, had seen there was no gate in it, did not even know if there was any space left beyond where it was possible to walk, yet irresistibly she had been drawn down to the river; needed, before anything else, to make her private contact with it. She put her feet in the decorative holes and leaned over the cold concrete, so grittily angular, so much less comfortable than stone. The base of the wall fell sheer to the water. No path led now to the wooden bridge over the stream which fed down through the orchard; there was no way to reach the fields. Probably they had been built over too. But the air was fresh with river smells, light danced gold through the gaps in the wall on the smooth black ripples, and swallows wove their swift patterns low over the water as they always had.

It could work. It must work. She had seen so little of Reggie since he had left school. Did he still carry with him his sense of injustice about Netherdean and being the headmaster's son? But he had been the one to suggest that she came. She had not expected it, and surely it must be a good basis for getting to know him better? And though she had not perhaps fully allowed for the impact of Nadia, self-assured and untrammelled in her native environment, Helen had known roughly what to expect there. The hardest thing to adapt to, apart from the shock of her tiny room, would be the way Nadia dealt with the children. Supper – Helen heard herself putting the word into inverted commas – had been a marathon of whining, argument and upheaval.

Helen had offered to help get it ready.

'Nothing to do,' Nadia had said breezily, slapping dishes into two microwaves and setting timers. 'Saves all the quarrelling,' she had explained, seeing Helen's face. 'Now, plonk yourself down anywhere you like, no ceremony here. This is the breakfast nook, but when we're in a hurry – Phoebe, Sebastian, come on, buck up, I'm not telling you again.'

'We're just watching *Home and Away*,' had floated down angrily from above.

'Don't be silly, you can watch it down here.'

'Shall I lay the table?' Helen had asked.

'Oh, no one goes in for all that rigmarole any more, do they?'

Helen had felt a bleak certainty that she would hear this crushing tone a good deal in the days to come.

'Simple, you see.' Nadia had jangled onto the shiny table a metal stand hung with blue-handled cutlery. Helen thought she might soon become tired of blue. Reggie had wandered through from what Nadia called the lounge, saying, 'Sorry, didn't offer you a sherry. But Nadia never does, do you, old girl?'

Have I brought my only son into the world to use the expression 'a sherry'? Helen had wondered, attempting to mask her sense of being lost and alien with amusement, though the latter had not survived the arrival of the children, after a lot more shouting up and down stairs. They had taken one look at their plates and chorused, in agreement for once, 'Oh, no, yuk, not *lasagne*! Yuk, horrible stuff.'

The phone had rung and Nadia, busy with high-pitched greetings, had broken off to snap, 'Shut up, you two, you like lasagne. But if you're not going to eat it just get out whatever you like. Yes, my two horrors. Oh, in great form, thanks. Tuesday would be fine – no, hang on, haven't I got badminton that afternoon? I swapped with Nancibel, she has some ghastly old—' Nadia had here broken off to turn her back on Helen, highlighting a remark which otherwise would have passed unnoticed. 'I'll come back to you on that, if that's all right with you. And how's – yes, Phoebe, of course you can have chips, just get on with it, you know where they are – look, usual chaos here, and I'm off to choir practice in ten minutes and haven't even had the chance to get my nosebag on yet, so why don't we talk about it after the Pony Club committee meeting? Yes, you idiot, tomorrow. Half-two. God, you're hopeless . . .'

Throughout the gabble and shrieks of this conversation, the children had scrabbled in the freezer, fought over things they both wanted, slammed their choices into a microwave oven each, and left strewn behind them ripped-open bags and packets. Reggie had focused on his lasagne, making a little uncontroversial conversation about the hot weather with his mother.

The whole uncomfortable meal had been the same. The children had squabbled, left three-quarters of their food, got up to help themselves to ice cream, crisps and Coke. The phone had rung. The television had poured forth sound. Helen had thought Nadia might want it off so that she could hear, but all she had said after the fourth phone call was, 'Bother, now I've missed that entire episode. What happened, Phoebe?'

'Don't know,' Phoebe had said, shrugging. 'Can Nikki come tomorrow?'

'Oh, darling, perhaps not tomorrow.' The warning face Nadia pulled in Helen's direction had been embarrassingly obvious.

'Oh, Mummy, you promised! You said once Easter was over. You said she could come all day. You are mean, you never let her come here, I have to go to her house all the time. It isn't fair, you *said* she could come—'

This had been poured out in a querulous monotone of considerable anger, and Nadia had given in at once. 'Well, if she doesn't come till after my meeting, and if you stay up in your room or play outside, only remember you mustn't make too much noise . . .' Again the grimace, the meaning tilt of the head.

The fragmented scene played itself over again in Helen's tired brain. It was all quite normal, she assured herself. No one nowadays expected formal meals with tablecloths and polished silver, with children being told to take their elbows off the table and sit up and not speak with their mouths full. Indeed, Nadia had said as she rammed in the aerial of her mobile for the last time and ran her bag to earth, 'Nice for you to be in a family, isn't it? It must have been jolly boring for you in that flat all alone,' and had whirled complacently away.

She meant to be kind. The picture she had drawn of Helen's quarters here, the picture which had made the plan seem feasible, had not been intended to mislead. To Nadia the words 'completely independent' probably meant shutting a bedroom door. 'Your own separate entrance.' The little corridor? It was Helen's imagination which had run away with her, and after all what more did she need? What would she have done in a sitting-room except read, watch television, or write letters, all of which she could do in the room she had been given. Despair filled her at the thought. Was that truly all she did; was that all her life had dwindled down to?

But no, there could be much more. Here she wouldn't feel trapped as she had in the city flat. Here there was the garden, however altered, beyond it the village where she had been brought up and where there were certain to be even now familiar names and faces. Beyond that lay a countryside she looked forward to exploring again. And here, to get to know properly at last, was her own family.

Where else had there been for her to go, in all honesty? Apart from the precious remnants of her furniture in store in Edinburgh, furniture that had come from this house, there was no link now with any other place. She had swiftly discovered, after Walter's retirement, how evanescent the links with school had been. She had seen for herself through the years how unsatisfactory return visits from ex-staff and ex-pupils alike could be. Because Netherdean had been Walter's, hers and Walter's, she had been betrayed into believing that for them the links would be stronger, but the truth was that everyone had been too busy to make them very welcome. And a blunter truth hit her for the first time: Walter had been deeply unpopular. No matter whether she herself had been liked or not, when she went back with him they were seen as an indivisible unit, not merely unwelcome but positively resented.

Reaching this comfortless dead-end in her thoughts, Helen turned from the cold barrier, rubbing her arms. This was a dead-end too, shutting her in not only from the river but from access to the wider landscape. But did she want to explore it? There were several lights across the river where once there had been a single farm. She must go in. Reggie had gone to return Kurt's bicycle, and when Helen had said she would look after the children, he had looked delighted, as though unused to such freedom.

'Oh, well I wouldn't mind a natter with Kurt's father. Haven't seen much of him lately. But the kids don't need much looking after. I mean, they do pretty much what they like.'

He had looked suddenly uneasy, imagining how Phoebe might receive her grandmother's old-fashioned ideas about things like bed-time.

'It's all right,' Helen had said, understanding him perfectly. 'I'll just be here if they need anything.'

It would have been good to have had the chance to talk to him alone, she thought, going with a reluctance she was ashamed of up the ruled concrete steps. But she still hadn't unpacked. That would occupy what remained of the evening.

* * *

Nadia was oddly resistant to the idea of Helen walking to the shop.

'I never go into the tacky little place, the prices are outrageous. Just tell me what you want and I'll get it in town. Lord knows I have to go in often enough.'

'Thank you, Nadia, but I'd enjoy the walk.'

'It's far too hot for walking. We don't want you collapsing on us, do we? That would never do, when you've only just arrived. Now, where's my blue folder?' Helen's silly idea was evidently considered squashed. 'Phoebe, have you seen my blue folder?'

Phoebe, watching cartoons, neither moved nor spoke.

'Nevertheless, there are one or two things I need,' Helen said quietly. It seemed important to insist on her right to come and go as she wished.

'Oh, well . . .' Nadia wasn't pleased, pushing her lips out in a very grumpy expression, but her attention had now moved to the hunt for the folder. 'Come on, you two, if you're coming.' She had not said where they were going, and had not offered to take Helen.

Helen walked down the drive, edged with its neat kerbstones, its weed-free rose beds, and remembered the lane that used to lead from the yard, the hump of grass and wild flowers in the middle, the wild roses against the high wall, whose small, crumbling, hand-made red bricks contained colours from yellow through orange to purple. Reaching the road she glanced left; across the bridge houses now clustered where open fields had been. She turned right and walked up into the village.

The volume of traffic surprised her. This was a quiet village no longer. The other thing that struck her was the difference in the gardens. Where there used to be hedges and wooden fences, brick paths and borders full of cottage flowers, damson and plum trees, box and elder, now there were open areas with plenty of parking space, garden centre plants, shaven grass.

In Scotland the lawns would barely have received their first cut. Abruptly Helen was gripped by home-sickness for Scottish voices, Scottish friendliness, for space and coolness, wind and stone.

The feeling was accentuated in the shop, which was indeed tacky. It used to have, tiny as it was, a small hardware section, and Helen had hoped to buy a kettle. She had woken at three, stifled with heat even though she had turned her radiator off, and had been unable to get to sleep again, appalled at what she had done to her life, feeling trapped in the barren room, in the hideous modern house. At last she had gone through to the kitchen, wincing at the squeal of the passage door, and made tea. But it would make such a difference to be able to do that in her own room. Not that Nadia was likely to approve.

Helen rather enjoyed the thought as she searched the shop; not so much as an electric plug. She had also thought she might find someone here who would know some of the old village names. One glance at the yawning lump of a girl in a grubby pink and white tabard over T-shirt and jeans told her the idea was fatuous. Though it was even more fatuous to feel rebuffed.

She walked round the green feeling oddly self-conscious, as though half-expecting to be recognised, yet at the same time aware of being uncomfortably alien, searching for the solid bones of the place under the cosmetic surgery of the present. Here unchanged was a row of black and white cottages, their thatched roofs differently pitched, their small windows uneven, their steps at different heights. The cricket field boasted a bigger pavilion, the wooden hall where gallons of rabbit stew had been dished out to unenthusiastic evacuees, and where countless items of worthless rubbish had changed hands at sales of work, had been rebuilt. She still had the copy of *The Key Above the Door* she had bought there for twopence, opening up to her the world of a new author.

But as she roamed, adding up, this was here, this is new, she felt more and more remote from her surroundings. What was she looking for; what did she hope to feel? The recognition of some unaltered detail brought an instant of satisfaction, then meant — what? There was no one there to share the moment, and its pleasure could not be held onto. Nor could it be recaptured. In the moment of being identified objects stepped from past to present, were what they were, without significance.

Wandering aimlessly, edgy and frustrated, as though somewhere lay some reality she was missing, Helen found herself at the church, and paused in the cool shade of the lych-gate, sniffing the earthy smell of the path that never saw the sun, mingled with the harsh scent of yew. After a while she went along the mown paths and stood before her father's grave. Younger than she was now. Had he worked himself to death, she wondered, with a fresh adult perception. Her mother wasn't here, but all her family were, for none survived. But both those loved ghosts remained as inaccessible here as they had been last night in the new house that would have so deeply dismayed them. Wandering on, other names brought back memories, and she decided with new resolution that without delay she would do as she had planned, and go in search of friends from school, friends from the years before she had met Walter.

Walter. Above her head the clock in its square tower resonantly struck noon and she remembered the bells bursting out in exuberance for her wedding, the flowers, the sun, the wind tugging at her insecure veil, the smiling faces along the path. Walter had been there too; she found it hard to include him in the picture.

She sat on a lichened tomb like an ottoman, its lettering long smoothed away, and in the drowsy midday heat let her thoughts rove back. During the weeks in Edinburgh her mind had been numb, not ready to grapple with anything beyond the step-by-step undoing of the nuts and bolts of marriage. For the mechanics of the process, as with everything else that concerned Walter and herself, had been her responsibility. Which was one of the reasons she had quite simply, in the kitchen of Tigh Bhan, come to the end of the road.

How many women, she wondered, admiring the colours of a Red Admiral against weathered stone, women intelligent and competent as she knew herself, relatively speaking, to be, would be ready today to put their partner's career so unquestioningly before their own? Well, a good many, probably, just as it was less than honest to pretend that in 'her era' such a sacrifice was inevitable. It hadn't been. More usual, certainly, but there had been a choice. She had allowed her brain, her skills, her life to be made subordinate to Walter's. Why? Because she had wanted to please? Just as she had tried to compensate Reggie for what he later referred to as his unnatural childhood. Would he still call it that? Would he be prepared to talk about it at all?

Walter has been pushed aside again, I see, she mocked herself lazily, leaning back on her hands so that the crusted lichen pitted her palms, closing her eyes against the sun's dazzle. When she had said she was leaving him he had been incredulous in a dismissive, impatient way that had strengthened her purpose as nothing else could have done. Ridiculous woman, take an aspirin, do the ironing, nip a few leaves off the geraniums and you'll feel better. Only don't forget to bring my tea and scones at four-thirty sharp.

When she had convinced him that she meant what she said he had been panicky and aggrieved. 'But what about me? What do you expect me to do?'

The unexpected part — and perched upon the tomb of some doughty Shropshire knight, in the secluded peace of the churchyard, Helen made herself face the unpalatable truth at last – had been that Walter had so swiftly designed for himself an alternative which was patently going to suit him better than marriage to her. A friend of his, or more accurately a correspondent with whom he disagreed in every particular, recently widowed and now living in his Edinburgh club, which was also Walter's, had written describing life there in enviable terms – efficient service which demanded no recognition other than financial, peace to work, a choice of roasts every day, excellent port and no emotional demands. Walter couldn't wait, and on the understanding that Helen should see to all chores like selling the house, packing his belongings, arranging the move and, since she was the one defaulting on the marriage, organising their separation on terms advantageous to him, declared himself ready to go at once.

Now, all these arrangements complete, for the first time Helen was able to laugh about it. Walter hadn't missed a step, and at the same time he had wrung from her the last drops of guilt, for in contrast to the eagerness with which he had hurried off to his new utopia, Helen felt she was abandoning responsibilities. Also, long as it had taken her to reach this point, she had no vision of what she could be or do, alone.

She had loved Inverbuie, but had felt distanced from it by Walter's selective involvement. He had always had the idea of retiring to the West Coast, but once there it had been obvious that he could have lived anywhere so long as his creature comforts were in place. Once Tigh

Bhan was sold Edinburgh had seemed the natural focus, but the miserable weeks there had sharply pointed up the fact that friendships had centred round the school, and that within that context Helen had been half of a couple.

The concept of living exclusively for herself had been strange, and when Reggie, so unexpectedly uncritical of her decision to leave his father, had asked her to come here it had seemed the obvious decision. Though she and Reggie had grown so far apart, and Nadia was as different from her in temperament and outlook as a daughter-in-law could well be, it was time to get to know them better, and the children too. She would get used to the house, rediscover a countryside once loved, find old friends and make new ones.

With fresh determination she went out through the black shadow of the gate. There used to be a short-cut to the bridge from here, a path which ran down the churchyard wall and through a favourite haunt, where the grassy mound of the old castle was still surrounded by its moat, and where ancient oaks and walnuts overhung the river. The path was there, and the iron kissing gate. Most of the trees had gone, there were seats bolted to concrete bases, the grass was bare, trodden, silted with litter. An iron railing with incurved spikes along the top barred the way along the river bank.

Ashamed to find herself unreasonably rattled at this minor setback, her new resolution so swiftly dampened,

Helen turned back up the ravaged slope and, more tired than she had any right to be, took the longer route home through the indifferent village.

Chapter Six

The house was locked. Helen, hot and thirsty, was annoyed with herself for not having thought of this. Then Nadia's car – Helen was blind to makes – turned in, and they were plunged into the chaos Helen was beginning to think Nadia preferred. In spite of yesterday's shopping she had more today, dumping it down at random, ignoring her mobile which pealed among the carrier bags, and apparently regarding Helen getting herself shut out as one more thing done to plague her.

'I must find you a key. Only then I'll have to show you all the business with the alarms, and I'm not sure you'll – yes, sweetie, I did get a chocolate fudge cake, but you're not to start on it now. Phoebe, quick, grab that bag, the one that's slipping. What a slowcoach! Oh, well, nothing that mattered. Sebbie, do shut up, I don't *know* what's for lunch, I haven't even thought about it. All right, anything you like, go and look. So what did you do this morning, Helen? It must be nice to be a lady of leisure — bother that phone. Find it for me, Seb.'

But Sebastian had gone and Phoebe, with a triumphant look at Helen which suggested that her grandmother wouldn't approve of whatever she had persuaded her mother to buy her, was sidling towards the stairs.

Nadia found her mobile. 'No, I don't mind a bit, bring them round any time that suits you. Don't be silly, of course I mean it. Do you want me to feed the troops? No? Sure? Fine, then, see you whenever . . .'

She slammed the phone down muttering, 'That's all I need,' then raised the voice that had rallied teams on many a playing field. 'Sebastian, Kurt and Denzil are coming over so don't disappear.'

Good Shropshire names, Helen thought, clutching at anything to keep depression at bay.

'Oh, no, not *them*,' came an angry protest from the lounge. 'I'm fed up with them.'

'Can I help you to put the shopping away?' Helen asked. Find out where things go; settle in.

'Oh, no, please don't bother. I'll be quicker doing it on my own, actually.'

'Can I do something about lunch then?'

'No, honestly, don't worry. I've got a couple of calls to make then I'll stick a pizza into the mike and fling some salad into a bowl. Not that the children will look at salad, but one must be seen to try. You take the paper and sit outside in the sun or something. Damn, now someone's

ringing me. I shall never get hold of Deirdre at this rate.
Yes? Hello?'

Helen felt the words, 'Now look what you've done,'
had a place there. It doesn't matter, she reminded herself.
The years of reducing muddle and creating order are over.
Now it's time to sit in the sun with the paper, out of
the way.

A car pulled in beside Nadia's. 'Mum, it's Aunt
Wendy,' Sebastian shouted. 'She's brought the dogs ...'

Nadia's brothers both farmed, and their wives, who
had been at St Chad's with her, came of farming families.
How had Reggie found his way into this group, Helen
marvelled, as the bedlam of lunch, with extra confusion
added by three gluttonous cocker spaniels, clashed round
her. Perhaps it was a refuge from the intellectual demands
his father had made upon him, the pressure to be something he was not. And I was too busy to see it, or to protect
him. This was what he chose instead: undemanding gossip
and cheerful turmoil; inclusion in a large busy circle whose
members were happy with who they were and what they
did; Nadia in command, unchallenged. Helen remembered
Walter's disbelief when he had first met her, and the acid
sarcasm with which he invariably referred to her. Nadia
had been gloriously unaware of it, clinging to the 'what
an old pet' line she had originally chosen, though taking
unconscious revenge by treating him as a generation older
than her own father.

All that was required of Reggie now was to provide
financially which, to his mother's surprise, he more than

adequately did, having made excellent use of the opening offered him by his father-in-law.

Helen would have preferred to be shown round the works by Reggie, for she would have been interested to see him in control in his own kingdom, but he appeared not to mind Nadia, a complacent guide, leading the way along the shadeless concrete paths, light bouncing back from monster machines. Some of her facts and figures might not bear examination, Helen suspected, seeing Reggie push up his spectacles more than once in a familiar gesture of uneasiness, but he didn't correct her. Inaccuracies notwithstanding, there was a prosperous air about the place, which Reggie now owned outright, and Helen received the impression that there was little fear of orders falling off or the gates closing.

She tried hard in the days that followed to convince herself that she was settling in. She bought her kettle, and though Nadia was annoyed, feeling that Helen had somehow escaped her control, and protested more than once, 'We do want you to be part of the family, you know,' she let it go at that. Helen established the habit of having coffee and fruit in her room for breakfast, and tea alone whenever it seemed appropriate. The bathroom which, as she had feared, was not regarded by anyone as hers, remained a minor source of irritation. The children saw no point in going upstairs when a loo was handy nearby and always took their friends there. Visitors said airily, 'I'll just pop in here, shall I?', but since there was no other downstairs cloakroom Helen could hardly find this unreasonable.

There were more rewarding things on which to concentrate, the most important of which was finding a workable contact with Sebastian. This was mainly achieved by letting him beat her at computer games. He invariably behaved badly when Nadia was around, but Helen found him ready to be friendly when she wasn't, and she thought this promised well. It was much harder to find any common ground with Phoebe, and in spite of all the years spent with children Helen found herself baffled by an egotism and hostility which she had never encountered in any other eight-year-old.

She was also baffled in her hopes of being useful.

'I have a girl,' Nadia said dismissively. 'Pretty incompetent, I have to say, but why worry, they never last five minutes.'

Helen, suppressing a smile, could imagine it.

If not the house then the garden? The grounds at Netherdean, where they weren't built over by science rooms and gym, had over time been reduced to lawns and shrubs, but at Tigh Bhan Helen had enjoyed keeping in order the garden which Lilias Markie, knowledgeable and zealous, had made when she was younger.

This suggestion too was summarily dealt with.

'Someone comes over from the works,' Nadia said, and it was true that the garden, regularly mown, raked and weeded, didn't seem to have a blade of grass out of place. How could a piece of lush and leafy Shropshire look so barren, Helen would wonder sadly.

But leafy Shropshire still existed, and as she walked further afield, mainly to fill unaccustomed tracts of empty time, she found many unspoiled corners which she remembered, and discovering them gave her much private pleasure. For comfort and mental contact she always had reading, though her deepest sense of deprivation came from being cut off from her books, the bulk of which were in store in Edinburgh. Still, she reminded herself, it was fortunate she had sent on only a few here, because she barely had space even for those. The only bookcase in the house held a row of videos.

She had long ago discovered that Nadia was allergic to the printed page.

'Goodness, I don't have time for *reading*,' she would cry, making the very idea sound disreputable. Helen could still see Walter's shudder. 'All right for some,' she said now when she came across Helen, who had joined the library without delay, immersed and content.

It came as a shock, however, to find that Reggie never read. Books, Helen had believed, were part of the heritage she and Walter had given him, and his rejection of them was an indication, more disturbing even than his reluctance to talk to her, of how deep his aggrievement had been. She had hoped, when she made up her mind to come here, that in time they would be able to draw this old resentment into the light and put it behind them, but Reggie had long ago learned not to expose himself in words. Having refined a system of living where no intellectual activity disturbed him, and he could bumble along without falling too far short of expectations, he had no wish to be made to examine or justify it.

As she absorbed the changes which had overtaken the village, Helen gradually found more sources of warmth and comfort were to hand. Going to church, more because that had been part of life here than from any deep personal conviction, she was startled at how overwhelmingly the past wrapped her round, and how close her younger self seemed. Emerging into the sunshine it was difficult to remember for a moment who she now was, but the conventional greeting from the vicar, the smiles and nods from members of the congregation, gave her a first hope that new friendships could be formed.

Although, as she went down the road to Roden House, as busy as on any weekday, she couldn't help regretting the closing of the Moat, she was able by now to ask herself more realistically what she had expected to find here. She had vaguely supposed the village would still be inhabited by the families who had lived there for generations, but what had she seen them as doing? Shoeing horses, ditching, road-mending, laying hedges, scissor-grinding, rabbit-catching, thatching? Well, someone must still thatch, she pleaded in self-defence, beginning to smile. But where, today, would those people be employed? If not on the farms then perhaps in Reggie's factory?

When she checked she could find only two names she recognised on the roll. She hesitated about going in search of them, but when she did call, rather self-consciously, first at an ex-Council house down by the disused mill, then at a bungalow nearly overrun by a garden which looked as though everything in it would win a prize at the West Midland Show (if it was still called that) she was reassured by her welcome. It was offered, she knew, more on behalf of her father than herself, but that didn't matter. The small burst of reminiscence, the recalling of names and events, cheered her. She knew, as she walked away, that these were not contacts that held the promise of anything more than being remembered as the doctor's daughter, now back to live with her son, but they made her feel less alien, and she valued that.

There remained her own friends, with whom correspondence had lapsed over the years as their lives diverged. The first she phoned was, amazingly, still at the old address, and it was fun to hear the incredulous 'Helen Woodward? I don't *believe* it!' After the rush of words to sketch in their present situations, and the insistence that she must visit without delay, Helen, reviewing the route, regretted having been persuaded to sell her car.

Why had she agreed to that? Long habit of giving in to Walter, she supposed. His selfishness so far exceeded her own that it had been the only way to peaceful coexistence. Nadia had been airily certain that it was simple to get everywhere by bus. When, Helen wondered, studying timetables, had Nadia last used one? It was the grannie flat all over again, and though Reggie had the temerity to suggest that Nadia could run Helen wherever she wanted to go, how could Nadia find time, with tennis and badminton, sitting on every village committee, the choir, propping up the Conservatives and endlessly ferrying the children? She kept in touch too, not only with family and relatives scattered about the county, but, as far as Helen could see, with most of her year at school as well.

She no doubt regarded her mother-in-law as a duty to be shouldered with the rest, and Helen could imagine her comments. 'Just have to get on with it, I suppose. Someone has to do it.' Perhaps even, 'Could be worse'? But as long as Nadia could get on with her own life, and Helen didn't interfere with the children and kept to the role assigned to her, 'putting her feet up and not worrying about a thing,' Nadia hardly noticed her in the scrimmage.

It was in a mood of determined optimism that Helen set out on the expedition which held out the strongest promise of renewed friendship. For most of her school years her closest ally had been Janet Madeley, who lived in a neat stone farmhouse tucked away under the Long Mountain where Helen had often stayed. Their shared passion had been riding and together they had explored miles of the beautiful, sleepy Welsh Border country. Now, exactly as in those faraway days, Helen took one bus into Shrewsbury and waited hours for the next.

When she was a child the time had dragged horribly, but now there was much she wanted to see. Walking up the hill from the bus station, as she had done so many times, she felt happier than she had for days. She stood and looked at the school from across the road, surprised by the vividness of the memories, but also by a reluctance to go closer. What was that about? She had enjoyed school. Standing there, a trim middle-aged figure in her blue Chambray dress, a life-time away from the schoolgirl who had hurried in through the high gates opposite, she realised that still, after all this time, there was a residue of guilt about having come back to teach, knowing in her heart that it was the easy option.

Had marrying Walter been a decision made in the same way? Had she loved him? Had she known what love was? Getting married had simply been the next thing one did, just as having Reggie was the next after that. Bringing a human being into the world without any compelling desire to do so; surely that was unforgivable?

Her face a little bleak, she crossed the road to the Quarry, following the winding path down to the early summer brilliance of the Dingle, exactly as it had always been which, public park though it was, pleased her. As she went back into the town, threading well-known alleys and tiny streets, finding long-forgotten corners with names like Shoplatch, Dogpole and Wyle Cop, discovering with amusement that the shoe shop at the top of Mardol still sold Clarks sandals and brown lace-up shoes, she forgot the crowded pavements and ambling throngs.

She felt happier than she had for some time as she stepped off the second bus and headed down the narrow road, its grassy banks overhung with hawthorns. In less than a mile there in front of her was the farmhouse, dwarfed by more buildings than she remembered. Behind them rose the steep green field where the stream came down. The Hangings; the name came readily back. Hanging valley, she supposed. She had never thought about it before. Here was the gate into the garden, the short-cut to the house. Here they had gone in, hats off, brown leather satchels on their backs, brown polished shoes on their feet.

No one had bothered to change much here, she saw with pleasure, except that the once velvet lawn looked as though it was now cut not quite often enough with a Flymo, rather than being faithfully mown and rolled as before. Here, familiar to her hand, was the gate leading to the yard and the back door. No one had ever used the front door. And here was the bench, or one very like it, where she and Janet had been made to sit after hunting days, to brush and scratch with their fingernails every speck of dried mud from their jackets.

Then the past fled in the immediacy of the present. Round the corner of a new building came a figure at once instantly recognisable and utterly changed, a stout woman in grubby jodhpurs and green quilted waistcoat, grey hair pulled back into a band, halter in hand. The image fragmented as she came forward grinning broadly, and Helen found in the changed face the good-natured schoolgirl she had liked so much.

'Helen? It is you! Hey, isn't this great? Who'd have thought you'd ever come back?'

They embraced willingly but awkwardly, the gesture new between them. But, at their age, one did such things.

In the welter of exclamations and questions, with too much to register, too much to establish, the fact that Helen had come on the bus seemed to make most impact.

'On the *bus?*' Janet exclaimed. 'But why on earth? It must have taken forever. Don't you have a car? I could have fetched you, it's no distance, or surely your son or somebody could have run you over?'

In the dimensions of today, of adulthood, of car-owning, of course it was no distance. Feeling foolish, Helen realised she had seen the journey as the gently paced one of her youth, full of nostalgia and promise.

'It was rather fun,' she said. 'It brought back lots of memories.'

'Well, rather you than me, but if that's what you wanted ... I'll take you home, though. Don't be daft, of course I will. Now, what will you have? Coffee? Something cold? I can't believe you've walked down from the bus stop. Dotty.'

At least frankness of speech between them hadn't disappeared, and as they adjusted to their nearly-sixty-year-old selves, Helen found herself relaxing. She had loved this place, counting the days to her visits here, and had been miserable when she left it. But, as at Roden House, the pace had quickened, friendly shadows had been chased away by a new light.

On the bus, Helen had lectured herself on the futility of expecting things to remain static, but she couldn't stop herself saying almost in dismay, 'I see you've done quite a lot to the kitchen.'

'Yes, taken Dad's old office into it,' Janet said, clicking the kettle on and turning to survey the big bright room with satisfaction. 'What do you think?'

It could be anywhere, Helen thought. She had wanted to see again the low-ceilinged, dark-beamed kitchen with its big range, and the long table where meals which in the post-war years had seemed sumptuous had been served, with 'the men' sitting spaced below the family and served on different plates. She had never considered the ethics of that; it was how things were.

She smiled, said how modern and efficient it all looked, and accepted her coffee gratefully.

Catch up on the years, shrug over husbands, both ex, take the taste of that away with a little bragging about children, run down names from school, feel a brief interest in the lives of those people Janet was still in touch with – it was all agreeable and effortless, and they gossiped an hour away before going out to look round the farm. Most of the land had been sold, and Janet's brother was farming the land his wife's family owned over the border in the Berwyns. Janet and her two daughters were deeply and successfully involved in the world of show-jumping.

'Such a shame you won't meet them. They're off at Fontainebleau which is why the yard's so quiet. But come on and I'll let you see everything else.'

With happy pride she showed Helen new stables, tackroom and feed stores, jazzy jumps of terrifying scale, the swimming bath (for the horses, of course), and the ultimate glory of the indoor school. A couple of girl grooms chatted for a while, and various horses figured too, but not as individuals, Helen felt, slightly jarred by Janet's new unsentimental approach.

Through it all, in the blinding sunshine which seemed to have prevailed ever since she came south, Helen sought in her mind cool buildings with dipping roofs, the untidy stackyard with the barrel of treacle which they used to suck up messily with straws pulled from the stack, the shady place in the stream where they watered the ponies, the warm mealy scents of the granary on summer afternoons, and the dense soft coats of Welsh hill ponies who barely came in all winter.

It was pointless to cling to such images, she knew, and she must learn not to do it, but as Janet swept her home, sticking to the main road the bus had come by, where Helen had hoped for a glimpse of remembered byways, she knew that too little remained, in themselves and in the routes their lives had taken, to draw either of them to re-establish any close friendship.

Accepting this, she felt reluctant to seek out other former friends just yet, and she knew it also made her feel less hopeful, for a few days after this visit, of ever being able to communicate with Reggie. Love him as she might as her son, shouldn't she face the fact that the chance of finding any adult contact with him had passed her by?

So it was a great and very pleasant surprise when Reggie diffidently suggested she might like to go with him one day when he had a business appointment, and Nadia was taking the children to visit cousins at Yockleton.

'It's at Hawkcliff, and I know that used to be a favourite place of yours. I shall be tied up for the meeting, and for lunch as well, I'm afraid, but I wondered if you'd like a wander round as it's such a nice day.'

Hawkcliff, a hotel a few miles away where her father had often taken her mother and herself for Sunday lunch, was indeed a favourite place. It was surrounded by a large park with delightful outcroppings of sandstone cliffs adorned with crumbling follies, hidden valleys and stretches of woodland. Bracing herself for every kind of despoliation, Helen was thrilled to find it virtually unchanged, and she spent a couple of magical hours rediscovering its delights.

Though the time spent with Reggie was no more than the drive there and back, plus having an excellent tea in the conservatory she remembered so well, there was no constraint between them, and Helen realised it was the first time they had truly been on their own. She was careful not to touch on any personal topic, and Reggie, after a successful meeting, was still very much in his professional mode in which, Helen had noted before, he could be unexpectedly impressive.

She knew such occasions would be rare, and there was no evading the fact that Nadia's presence and Nadia's overwhelming personality would always interpose a barrier between her and Reggie, her and the children, but Helen nevertheless treasured the memory of this day, heartened by the undemanding but positive contact achieved. The secret, she knew, would be not to hope for more.

Chapter Seven

Catriona sat tense and shaken by delight as the train pulled away from Bridge of Orchy and up by the Water of Tulla to cross the Rannoch Moor. Not that she knew or cared about these names. Until she went to Dundee she had barely been further than Glen Righ or the Luig peninsula. She only knew that this journey seemed twice as long coming this way as it had when she had driven to college last autumn, but one of her fellow students had offered her a lift to Glasgow so that she could get onto the West Coast line, and it had seemed the best way home. Now, names or not, she was in her own country. The great hills swam up on either side, spectacular after the months on the Tay estuary, and the Rannoch Moor, that place of changing moods and a dozen different faces, lay sombre under a sky of wind-scattered cloud pierced by shafts of pale light.

Catriona didn't care what the weather was like. She had done it, done what she had set out to do, and she was home, her relief and happiness barely containable. Reserved as she was, and accustomed to solitude, she felt an urgent need to share this delight, and she crushed her hands together, pressing her elbows into her sides, simmering with the pleasure of knowing she would soon be with people who would understand exactly what she felt. If she had ever experienced sex, she might have longed for a glorious bout of love-making as the perfect release for these feelings, but she hadn't and didn't. She merely sat through these last miles, these most splendid of miles, while the train left behind on the bleak moor tiny dots of stations which didn't even have villages around them, and took the long curve into Glen Spean and down again to Fort William.

Trudy was waiting on the platform as she had promised she would be, a Trudy hugely, splendidly pregnant, her usual capacious, floaty and what Clare called earth-mother clothes perfect for her present shape. She beamed at the sight of Catriona, and clutched her close against the solid curve of the baby, and Catriona, who wasn't good at hugging, accepted the embrace laughing but feeling closer to crying.

'God, it's good to see you! It's been far too long. Why didn't you come back for Christmas and Easter, you silly goose?' Trudy demanded, shaking her head and looking ready to shake Catriona.

Catriona didn't answer, her face bright with pleasure; for none of that mattered now.

'Oh, well,' said Trudy, 'at least we've got you back now. Where's the rest of your luggage?'

'What luggage?'

'This is it?'

One leather case stamped with Fergus's initials squatted on the platform.

'This? After almost a year away?'

Catriona shrugged. 'I didn't need the other one. Most of my stuff was worn out anyway,' she added vaguely, as though she couldn't think how it had happened. 'Some books are coming in the post though,' she added, sure that would please.

Trudy laughed. 'Oh, Catriona, I cannot tell you how we've missed you,' she exclaimed, seizing her arm and giving it a little shake, as though still needing to express some of the anxiety they had felt to imagine Catriona, alone, without their support, tackling her personal challenge in an environment so different from any she had previously known. 'Still, you're here now, so come on.'

She stooped for the case and Catriona dived to prevent her. 'I'm sure you shouldn't carry things.'

'That? Pooh, that's nothing to me. I'm indecently fit. Fitz says it's alarming, and he can't imagine what I'm about to produce.'

'A winged horse, a phoenix, a unicorn,' chanted Catriona, high on being home, high on the brisk tug of the wind, the soft, salt-laden wind of the West, high on hearing again the scrabbling cries of the gulls, sniffing the smells of the summer town, catching her first glimpse of the jabble of small waves on the loch, driving grey and fast towards the narrows.

Trudy laughed. 'Do they have black unicorns?' Her husband came originally from Jamaica and she was looking forward with interest to finding out what colour her baby was to be.

Catriona laughed too, laughed as she rarely did, freely and happily, carried away by the sheer pleasure of being here, of not being alone. Soon she would be swept over the moor and along the lochside to Luig, and she would sleep tonight in the little flat overlooking the harbour, above the shop Trudy used to run and still owned.

'Are you sure you really need me to help and aren't doing this as a favour?' she asked as Trudy shook clear of the tourist traffic clogging the town and headed west.

'For pity's sake, Catriona, how many more times?'

In letters and in the single phone call when Trudy had finally managed to make contact with Catriona in her lodgings, she had given the same assurance over and over again. 'Look at me. Do you honestly think I could lurch around the shop in this state? I'd knock over piles of baskets and sweep away packets of herbs every time I turned round. And can you see me grovelling under the counter and nipping up stepladders? I told you, my wretched assistant, who was a pain in the neck anyway, did a bunk, no notice, no explanation. I've been scraping round for help from anyone and everyone. Sadie's been marvellous, but she can't do full-time. Clare did a few hours, bless her, but she had to bring both the children with her, and Isla's been having trouble with her ears and howled most of the time, which wasn't very soothing for the customers – or particularly good for trade. God, I suppose I'm in for all that soon.'

With a fleeting, almost secret smile she laid a hand on her stomach, which even in the big car and with the seat fully back almost touched the steering wheel, and Catriona, bravely for her, shyly touched it too for a second.

Trudy put her strong hand over the small tentative one, holding it there, and flashed a smile, this time wide and warm, at her passenger. 'Honestly,' she said seriously, 'I can't think of anyone I'd rather have to be there just now. I don't want to have to worry about the shop for the next few weeks. You've done it all before, you can run the place standing on your head. The only thing I'm concerned about is that I'm grabbing you up when you may want to be off on more worthwhile pursuits, qualified and trained and all as you are nowadays.'

A look of intense satisfaction flitted across Catriona's small face. Though Trudy had ended up on a teasing note, seriousness being generally alien to her, her words gave Catriona a glow that was new, and good. She had, for the first time in her life, gone out there and competed on a level field. And she had achieved. She had been top of her course, though that particular detail she had told no one, because it was important to no one but her.

'To be honest,' she said, 'I don't know what I'll do yet. I know I should have been trying harder to find a proper job, but it was so tempting to come back and have the summer here.'

A wistful note in her voice as she looked away across

the thin grass and stony outcrops of the moor, patterned by swift changes of shadow and sunlight, told Trudy how much determination it had required for Catriona to see her exile through. She respected her for it, and had no wish to dissuade her from whatever course she saw as right, but she thought Catriona had put herself through enough for the moment, and as tactfully as she could attempted to say so.

'There are "proper" jobs to be had here,' she suggested carefully. 'Not many, it's true, but it may not be necessary to go away from us all again — or away from this.'

On cue, they had breasted the ridge, and before them stretched away, to the furthest grey merging of sea and sky, the hills and glens, promontories and islands, pale beaches of sea-lochs and fast-running currents of the sound, which were Catriona's home. Trudy didn't pull up; a coach and a couple of cars were parked on the open space of turf at the top, and people were taking photographs in spite of the indifferent light. Nor did she say more, for Catriona's reaction of joy and thankfulness was almost tangible in the confined space, and Trudy felt unexpectedly moved by it.

'I just don't want to rely on you all for ever,' Catriona said after a while, sounding touchingly like the awkward immature girl Trudy had first known, who at nineteen had seemed barely out of childhood. 'It would be so easy to come back and be looked after by everybody again. I ought to stand on my own feet.'

'So that's why you turned down poor old Una when

she begged you to help in the hotel again?' Trudy teased. Una and Rebecca Urquhart, who together ran Ardlonach, had perfectly understood Catriona's refusal, however, and while it was frustrating to be denied an experienced and urgently needed pair of hands on idealistic grounds, they respected her determination to be independent.

'Of course I'll help out if she's stuck,' Catriona was saying anxiously. 'I could do evenings after the shop closes, or Sundays, which are always hectic in the summer. Until she finds real staff, I mean.'

'It's OK, don't panic.' Trudy swung round a caravan in a place where no caravan expected to be overtaken and received an indignant blast from a horn. 'And don't you panic, either,' she addressed her rear-view mirror. 'They're managing at the moment. One of the staff had a friend staying and she's agreed to work for a couple of weeks. They'll find someone, they always do.'

Catriona leaned back in her seat. Trudy's easy manner, the blissful sense of being back in a place where she was accepted for what she was, the very sound of familiar names, reminders of familiar hotel problems, combined to give her a marvellous sense of peace. She hardly recognised it for what it was. She had never as an adult been away and come home before.

When Trudy took the left fork for Luig, and the right curved away towards Inverbuie, Catriona barely noticed. She had made herself face the fact of leaving Glen Righ with an almost violent resolution last autumn, and her thoughts had rarely turned since to the old house. That was part of the past. What she had longed for was the beloved group of friends and the equally beloved high, wide, dramatic landscape, and those, she was learning with delight, would never go away.

A squally shower hit them as they ran along beside Loch Luig, purple and flattened under the beating rain. The lochside caravan park looked run down and squalid in the downpour. In Luig people were sheltering in doorways and sitting in cars or buses, as huge drops bounced off deserted pavements. Catriona didn't care. Crossing the cobbles in front of the shop at the panting hobble which was all Trudy could rise to, and diving into its herb-and-spice-scented sanctuary, they gasped and giggled like children, wiping the rain from their faces, and the two or three customers already there laughed with them.

'I'm converted to the no-luggage system,' Trudy admitted. 'Hi, Sadie, how's it going? Wow, who'd have thought one could get so wet so quickly? And now we've got to go out again to dash up the stairs.'

'Well, Catriona, it's grand to see you back. You've been sorely missed,' the calm, slow-moving woman in charge of the shop came to welcome them in her soft Highland voice. 'And don't you be dashing anywhere, Trudy Colquhoun, especially up that rickety old stair, when it's running with water too. The doctor'd be having something to say to me if I let you. Just wait now till it stops, like a sensible body.'

'It's stopping, look.' Catriona was at the door leading to the small white-washed back yard with its hanging baskets draggled by the fierce shower. Through the gap in the far wall, where steps led down to the harbour, lurid yellow light was spreading over the water. She had a sudden wild feeling that it was all too much to take in, that she wouldn't be able to hold on to it.

The flat above the shop was one long coom-ceilinged room, with a bathroom in the L-shaped extension over the old wash-house which Trudy had turned into a workroom. Dormer windows looked over the harbour to the bracken-clad hills across the loch. A small kitchen was fitted into one corner, a careless collection of basic furniture was scattered through the room. Trudy was an indifferent housekeeper and had more than enough to do keeping her square granite house above the town even halfway to Fitz's standards. But Catriona had slept here many times before and loved this room. She could not have asked for anything more perfect to return to on this day of joyful liberation.

The huge family lunch, argumentative and noisy, with astonishing quantities of hot food being disposed of, course after course of solid country cooking produced by Nadia's scurrying, worrying, down-trodden wisp of a mother, had been an endurance test even more taxing than the duty lunches of the Netherdean years.

Then, when with weary relief Helen had at last heard Nadia, at the top of her powerful voice, begin rounding up the children, she had realised with dismay that three of the cousins were coming back to Roden House for the night, one of them a truculent tearaway she had already twice crossed swords with, once for trampling on her handbag and then kicking it out of his way, and soon afterwards for pinching the baby to make it yell. Whose baby? She didn't know and didn't care.

Packed into the back of the car with the hot restless children, who kicked her ankles and sprayed bits of chocolate onto her light skirt, she counted away the miles and the minutes till she could be quiet and alone in her own room, though not sure she could settle to reading. After such an afternoon even *Songs of Praise* might be a panacea, with its ever-rewarding sight of crammed rows of washed, brushed and tidy people belting out the well-known hymns with exaggerated lip movements, light winking on ranked rows of spectacles.

The children came to play, shout and in the end fight, outside her window, till Phoebe, furious after being pushed off the climbing frame which she had in any case outgrown, ran in with hysterical complaints to her mother. When Helen went to see if any damage had been done, and if she could help, Nadia snapped, 'I should think you might have kept an eye on them in the first place,' ostentatiously soothing Phoebe, who had failed to produce any blood or even a scratch to substantiate her story.

Helen felt a rage boil up in her that she feared might burst out in a storm of tears. She could never in her life remember feeling such shaking frustrated anger. She turned and, just as she was, went out of the kitchen door, taking the only exit route, the drive.

Over the bridge was the one small field Reggie had kept to preserve something of the former view, then came a small estate of what she supposed might be called middle-management houses, spruce and indistinguishable from each other, all with more than one car outside. Beyond them a lane still led off to a farm on the right.

Here Helen used to come, one of a little gaggle of children each carrying a quart or pint pail, for the evening chore of fetching the milk. Helen had minded the fact that she carried a big blue and white jug. The more daring of the boys used to swing their tin pails in a circle over their heads without spilling a drop, and she had longed to do the same. Though she had been down here several times since she had come back, this evening, emotions churned up, her feeling of being alien and alone too raw to crush down with self-discipline and good sense, the images which swarmed back were unbearably piercing.

Dusky air sliced by bats, rooks noisily gathering in the elms, whiffs of wood-smoke and dank undergrowth; the lamplit shippen with its long row of black and white backsides, the rhythmic hiss of milk into pails, the over-sweet scent of cud from the cows' breath steaming up with the stronger smells of hay and dung; the dairy by contrast bitingly cold, milk rippling blue-white down the ridges of the cooler, the row of measures from a half-gill upwards neatly on their hooks, the stark smell of wet stone, and the children pressing themselves against the wall in an obedient queue, for the farmer was an ox of a man with a broad leather belt who roared at them if they got in his way.

Ghosts. Time past. Where cowsheds and calf pen and tractor sheds had clustered round the great pile of the midden the neat terraces of sheltered housing surrounded a tiled space with seats and a couple of weeping birches in round plots. The farmhouse was a guest house.

These were facts. This was how it was. There must, Helen knew, be many corners of this lovely county which still held their unspoiled rural peace. Withedine was just too near the town and had suffered accordingly. Or gained? She knew her view of it would not be shared by everyone.

That was the problem. Where were the like minds, how could she find them? What options were open to her? She could not, she admitted at last, live in the room she had been given. Buy a cottage in the village then? Or in another, quieter village? She could get a car, be independent but still near the family. And alone. Yes, that was the core of it all. At Roden House, in Withedine or ten miles away she would not be close to her son, his wife or children. How awful it must be for them to have her in the house. She realised she had been refusing to acknowledge this, dreading the bleak questions it would force upon her. She walked for a long way, and though she grew calmer she found no solutions.

But waking with a jerk after a few hours of broken sleep the plan was there, waiting for her, rounded and complete, breathtaking in its rightness and simplicity.

Chapter Eight

Sebastian delivered the large white envelope to her room, post-marked Fort William, her name and address neatly word-processed in its shiny window, a reference number below. He also brought her *Times*, and stapled to it her second month's newsagent's bill (which Nadia had not included in the household account). Sebastian had been eating peanut butter by the spoonful when sent on this errand and all three items bore traces of it.

Helen didn't care. With pulse quickening and hands unsteady she turned to the desk for her paperknife, then with an exclamation of impatience with herself, ran her finger along the flap, tearing it raggedly open. And there it was.

The envelope contained three folders but afterwards she could never recall what had been in the other two. For in spite of many long walks, and many wakeful hours spent dutifully 'thinking things through', her mind, crazily, delightedly and irresponsibly, was made up in that moment.

*   *   *

Catriona had left the glazed door and both dormer windows open, and she woke to the cry of gulls and the pungent reek of sea air and harbour water, oil and diesel, tar and seaweed. Since it was midsummer a slant of early sunlight reached the corner of the room and, in a juxtaposition of associations that for a moment unsettled her, she was reminded of the sliver of morning light which had reached her room in the gaunt house in Dundee. But she need never think of that dark place again; it was over. She was not much given to tears, never having had on hand the comfort of having someone to dry them which encourages the habit. Now her relief to wake and find herself here was so intense that with a dry little sob she turned her face into the pillow. It was the sounds and scents of home which flowed into this casual room she liked so much.

For the time being the questions of what she would do, where she would live, could be put on hold. Until Trudy had permanent full-time help in the shop she would have a roof, an income that exceeded her needs, and for emergencies she had safe the pitiful capital which was her inheritance from her once-wealthy, land-owning, spendthrift family. Waiting for her were the small circle of close friends and the wider network of people who had known her since she was born, people who with a friendly word would absorb her once more into the pattern of their lives, not needing to know where she had been or what she had been doing, or why.

She washed so sketchily that the water didn't have time to run hot. Such details had no importance for Catriona. Pulling on a grey sweatshirt, a pair of narrow-hipped, washed-out grey jeans from Oxfam, and canvas rope-soled shoes with the toes just about through, she ran down the outside stair and crossed to the gap in the harbour wall. A shiver of cold air met her off the water. The morning was crisp-edged but had none of the dour bite of the eastern seaboard. Watching a couple of fishing boats putting out, the chug of their engines coming quiet and even across the water, a sound of the utmost nostalgia, looking at the rows of sailing dinghies and small yachts dipping at their moorings alongside the marina, and past them to the island in the mouth of the loch, the sense of homecoming was so acute it almost hurt.

She mustn't let herself feel too settled here, she reminded herself sternly. Soon, if she were to survive independently as she was determined to do, there would have to be another journey to a strange place. But for now, for this intoxicating moment, she was here and, since Sadie had insisted on looking after the shop, the day lay empty before her.

She would wander, till the sleeping town awoke, round the harbour, then go, as invited, up the steep winding streets to have breakfast with Trudy and Fitz. After that, as soon as possible, she must find Watty and set him about the business of finding a car for her. Then she would head up onto the moor, scarcely able to wait to disappear again into the space and solitude of this longed-for landscape. Later she would go down the three miles of gently falling headland to Ardlonach, to see Una and Rebecca and Dan, and whoever else she knew who was still involved in the hotel.

In the late morning sunshine of a day which had turned out better than its early promise, Catriona perched on a boulder high on the spine of the Luig Moor. Larks climbed above her till they were dots so tiny it was impossible to believe the lavishness of song pouring into the blue heights could come from them. The curlew's call, rippling across slopes patterned with bog-myrtle and blaeberry, where bell heather was already bright though bracken fronds were still pale and curled at the tip, brought a lump to her throat.

How good it had been to see Fitz again, his big smile flashing, a happy man with his busy practice, his elegant well-proportioned house, his child due soon and slapdash Trudy to hold at bay too much order, too much precision. Catriona tipped her head back to watch a buzzard circle with a leisurely indolence which belied its predatory intent. She would be here when Trudy's baby came; that was so good.

Ferreting out Watty hadn't been so satisfactory. He was still in his seedy caravan behind the Old Mill, which was now being converted into rather horrid flats. Trudy and her first husband had once owned it, she with her meal shop, he with his pottery. At that time the ground above the burn had been grassy and open. Now it looked like a piece of wasteground, scattered with rubble and building material, ground up by machines. Here the old caravan squatted, tiny, devoid of comfort, insulation or modern fittings, and when Watty opened the sticking door there had seeped out past him a disagreeable whiff of damp, mildew, rotting hardboard, whisky fumes and God knows what from old Dunlopillo.

All that had been forgotten, though, in Watty's welcome. His round red face had creased up in emotion, and from his eyes had squeezed an unmistakable dampness. Words had come jumbling out as he saw the present, of which he was suddenly ashamed, in relation to the very different ways of the past.

'My, Catriona, is that you? I canna' hardly believe my eyes! Well but, that's just – I'd no word of you coming, not a word. I've no' been seeing all that much of folk lately, to tell you the truth. Wait now, till I put a few things past, and then you can come in. You'll have a cuppie wi' me, surely? It'll no' take more than a minute to bring the kettle to the boil. You'll not be in all that of a hurry?'

Catriona had noted that he hadn't shaved for days, and that he still wore, jacket pockets bulging, trousers bagging round his ankles and in shreds at his heels, one of the cut-down tweed suits that had once belonged to her grandfather. Fergus wouldn't have worried at its condition; his tailor would have wept.

Long-instilled good manners and the local tradition of

hospitality had made Watty ask her in, but she had seen in his eyes his embarrassment at what she would find.

'Come down to the café with me,' she had suggested. 'It seems hours since I had breakfast at the Colquhouns and I hardly ate anything anyway, we were all talking so hard.'

By the way Watty's face had brightened, and the alacrity with which he had reached for his cap and pulled the door to behind him, she had guessed that the prospect of a fry-up pleased him even more than her arrival.

Watty, as she had been warned, appeared to have been largely adrift since Glen Righ was sold.

'Och, I get by,' he had said airily. 'I do this and that, ye ken what it's like.'

When pressed, he had raked up a few details. He had driven the hill buggy during the stalking for Donald Macrae, Clare's husband, on Rhumore, a farm which now included a large part of both grouse moor and deer forest once owned by the Finlays. He had been handyman at the caravan park but had been paid off before the end of the season because they hadn't been doing well. He had had a fencing job for a couple of weeks.

'By rights I'd have been at the tattie picking after that, but it's all squads these days, squads for the beating, squads for the clipping. There's no' the jobs to be had, and that's the truth of it.'

Catriona didn't believe him, Watty had had too many years, ever since leaving school, secure and indolent at Glen Righ, taking its perks for granted. This protected

existence had not equipped him for coping alone. Part
of his redundancy money had bought the caravan, but he
would have been hard put to it to say where the rest had
gone. Without the estate to subsidise it he had found it
impossible to run his old jeep, so had been restricted in
the seasonal jobs he could pick up, though he had worked
through the lambing on Luig estate, which owned most
of the headland on which Catriona now sat. Since then
he had done little, existing on state handouts and sliding
rapidly down a spiral of laziness and indifference.

'Right, Watty, to business,' she had said briskly, as he
finished tucking away a mound of bacon, eggs, sausage,
black pudding, fried bread and tinned tomatoes, sluiced
down with mugs of sweet milky tea. 'I need a cheap little
runabout which will do umpteen miles to the gallon and
get through at least one MOT. Any ideas?'

A light had come into Watty's eyes which had not been
there for many months. 'Wheels, is it?' He had tapped the
side of his nose. 'Just you leave it to me.' Cars, his chief
interest in the world, his one-time kingdom . . .

What he had not understood, as he gestured Catriona
to the door ahead of him with the natural courtliness of
his kind, was that his satisfaction had more to do with
looking after her again than with finding a car. He was
needed once more, by a Finlay, in the way he had been
used to, and which he had missed without ever realising
what had made the last nine months so long and empty.

'And don't forget you're quite capable of cooking a
meal for yourself, Watty,' Catriona had reminded him as

they parted. 'You know what I'm talking about.' To her, shy and reticent as she basically might be, a blunt authority over Watty was entirely natural, just as it was natural to him to be on the receiving end of it.

'Aye, well, you're right enough at that,' he had agreed, grinning. He had been neglecting himself, and it was time to take a pull. Full of new purpose, pausing only to pick up his essential daily forty and his *Record*, Watty had hurried off.

In one of the many wrinkles on the southern face of the moor below the Luig–Inverbuie road, where a seepage spring gathered into a trickle and began to cut its way through the peaty ground, swiftly turning into a small burn, Jake Macleod sat below a bank shaded by thin birches and hazels. He was, from habit and training, not too absorbed in what he was watching to miss a peripheral movement on the open ground to his right, and equally from habit he eased himself further into the leaf-pattern of the shadows and was still. Whoever was coming off the moor – a teenage lad, Jake thought, by the height and light build – he was fit and active and knew the ground, moving with a balance and speed which told of long familiarity. And he was heading for this burn.

The boy was very close before Jake decided he was a girl. Nothing in the slight silhouette had told him so, except the clumpy dark hair. Would she go straight past without noticing him; would she squawk if she did spot him, squatting half naked under the bushes?

Catriona saw him, quelled a jolt of surprise, for the high sunny moor had seemed all her own, then checked, glancing down to where he had been looking.

'Have I disturbed something you were watching?' she asked, speaking quietly and turning to him with a grimace of apology for her clumsy intrusion.

Jake decided he liked this leaping of preliminaries as much as her calm acceptance of his presence. With a quick shake of his head – he wasn't much given to smiling – he made a quiet movement with his hand, and following it the girl, with a small indrawn breath of delight, picked out the tiny pair of dappled fawns, hardly discernible against their perfect camouflage to any but a practised eye. They lay motionless, one on each side of a flattened circle of grass, the bracken curling over them adding its dapple to their own neat lines of white spots.

'Where's the doe?' Catriona asked in a low voice, folding herself in a fluid movement to sit on her heels and beginning to search the available cover nearby.

Jake grinned, with a pleasure rarely seen on his thin saturnine features. This girl, whose face he somehow felt he knew, got straight to the salient facts in a way he liked. Had these been red deer calves the hind would have left them tucked up on their own for the day, relying on that camouflage for their safety. This pair, as was to be expected at this relatively lower height, were roe and not so likely to be left alone for long periods.

'She's gone downwind, not far away, in that first bit of dead ground. If we go down the burn keeping out of sight she'll circle back.'

'Let's go then, she'll be worried,' Catriona said, and after one more look at the pretty creatures, two days old at most, she straightened up and began to thread her way down the sheep-path beside the miniature falls of the burn. Jake, amused, reached for his shirt and followed her. A couple of hundred feet down a sheltered bowl opened out, its floor carpeted with wild flowers, its air faintly scented by the wind-crippled larches which sheltered it.

'She won't worry about us here,' Jake said, slowing as he reached the sunny hollow, and hoping the girl would stop too. He wanted at least to discover who she was. She had amused him by her directness, her economy with words, and, in a way he was not accustomed to encountering, by her unawareness of him other than as a source of information about the deer. In fact she had shown no reaction of any kind, coming across an unknown, half-clad male on a deserted hillside. Jake wore combat boots with no socks and a Black Watch kilt which had belonged to an uncle, his Macleod one having finally fallen to bits. He was not the sort of man to go to the trouble of having a new kilt made when a perfectly good one, which happened to fit him, was up at the big house doing nothing.

Suddenly, though he wasn't sure the sums computed, memory clicked up the name he had been looking for.

'You're a Finlay of Glen Righ,' he said. 'Yes?' He had

known Alastair best, the heir who had been killed in the light aircraft disaster. He had been a few years older than Jake, and had married a stunningly beautiful girl who was rarely seen in the glen. He had had a son and a daughter, Jake remembered, though tragically the boy had been killed too, drowning in the gorge beside the house. Old Fergus had bravely gone in after him but had been unable to save him. But the sister would be older than this, surely, well out of her teens by now. Yet the look was there, in the dark eyes and fine-boned build.

'Catriona Finlay of nowhere,' Catriona was saying, with a shrug and a smile. 'Glen Righ's been sold.'

'Ah yes.' Jake recalled now hearing that it had been taken over by some consortium who wanted to develop it as an upmarket sporting hotel. 'I haven't been here much in recent years. I'm sorry, that must have been hard for you.'

'Bearable.' She used the word not dismissively, but as though she had chosen it as honestly as she could.

Jake, who normally had little patience with social trivia, was interested enough to ask, 'Who bought the place exactly? What's happening to it?'

Catriona flashed a brief smile at him from under the thick fringe which looked as though she hacked it off herself. 'A Japanese group bought it. They have plans for sail-stay-shoot-stalk holidays – very expensive ones, of course.'

'They'll have their work cut out,' he commented, and Catriona laughed outright, a thing she rarely did.

'I didn't mean the house,' Jake said hastily, though he was grinning too. He had gathered it had sunk into a level of decay eccentric even for this part of the world. She must have had a bizarre life up there, alone with the old man, who had by all accounts been seriously out of touch with reality towards the end. 'I was thinking of the sail-stay part. Coming into Righ Bay? Tricky at the best of times. The logistics sound daunting.'

'Oh, the state of the house too,' Catriona assured him candidly. 'The whole thing. And yes, relying on guests arriving by water they'll find themselves producing dinner at some very odd hours. It's bad enough in an ordinary hotel where they come by road and think by the time they reach Glasgow that they've practically arrived. I helped the Urquharts at Ardlonach one summer, so I know about that.'

It was a long speech for Catriona but, though she knew she was absurdly ready to find home in everything today, it was a joy after the months of non-communication to be with people who spoke her own language again. And somehow, coming upon Jake while he was watching the roe twins, sharing the pleasure of it with him, there had been no time for shyness or self-consciousness.

'Who runs the hotel at Ardlonach?' Jake had known the Urquharts well in his youth but he had a lot of catching up to do.

'You know the family? Then you'll remember all the cousins? Tony inherited the house and left the Navy to turn it into a hotel, with a sort of survival school attached, leadership training for business executives and all that sort of thing. But he didn't really like it and gave it up after a while. His ex-wife, Una, runs it now, and Tony's cousin Rebecca helps her.'

'Ah, Rebecca.' A feisty lady. Jake had had a brief fling with her some years ago, always drawn to sophisticated and competent women with minds of their own. 'I must go down and reacquaint myself.'

'You're one of the Macleods, aren't you?' Catriona too had been trying to chase down elusive memories. 'I'm sorry, but I don't remember which. There were always so many of you.'

The big house of Luig, so much more worldly and cosmopolitan than Glen Righ, had been a terrifying place which Catriona as a child had dreaded visiting, in the faraway days when Fergus had still taken part in the social life of the glen.

'I'm Jake. Connor owns Luig now. My father was his father's cousin. I can never remember what that makes me, but anyway, I was mostly brought up there, and it's still home base.'

He had the Macleod looks, lean and predatory, and the Macleod arrogance, Catriona thought, though quite objectively, but not the flamboyant Macleod colouring. His hair was as dark as hers, the grey which peppered it still almost imperceptible. It was also quite long and she couldn't imagine him knowing or caring what the current fashion was.

'You seem at home on this bit of ground,' Jake remarked. 'This is quite a way from Glen Righ.'

'I sometimes rode this far, and sometimes when I was at Ardlonach I used to come up here.'

'Where are you living now?'

Catriona looked at him frowning, as though for the first time conscious of the strangeness of talking to him like this. Then she said in her light courteous voice, 'I must go now. Goodbye,' and, without any sign of being aware that her reaction was odd, went quickly away over the rich June grass, dropping without a glance behind her down the steep bank where the burn tippled over into a frothing pool.

Well! Jake said to himself, with a small grunt of amusement. He wasn't used to being disconcerted. What an odd little thing. Did she take after her grandfather? But he had enjoyed talking to her. Content, he stretched out on his back on the carpet of grass thick with heartsease and tormentil, eyebright and bedstraw, unbuckled the straps of his kilt and spread it wide on either side. The sun glinted on the inverted V of black hair which ran down from his navel and widened over his flat brown belly. Jake slept.

Chapter Nine

Unlike Catriona, who thought the only way to buy a car was to set Watty Duff to work, expecting him to do the legwork, checking, dealing and even, when she had paid up, to deliver the vehicle to her door in a roadworthy condition, Helen believed that you must go to a main dealer at a reputable garage. She had not known till now, however, that you could complete the entire transaction over the phone. But she had bought a house that way; why not a car? Heady with rebellion – for by this time Nadia had become recklessly outspoken in her protests – and with a sense of achievement which was new and bracing, she had laid her plans, and was now being carried by taxi from Perth railway station to Marlee Motors at the north end of the city, a welter of supermarkets and garages and seedy bed and breakfast places with traffic pouring endlessly by. It was a less attractive aspect than she remembered from the days when she and Walter used to stay at the George. Walter had always preferred the hotels his parents had liked; and Walter had driven staid solid motor cars (never dropping the word 'motor'). But this was not a day to think of Walter. In fact no day was going to be a day for thinking of Walter ever again, if she could manage it.

She was welcomed by a friendly young salesman, who didn't appear to mind showing her every switch and dial, and who offered to go for a turn round the block with her before she drove away. Though grateful that everything was being made so easy Helen felt she could manage without that. She had done a lot of driving over the years. The car had always been Walter's, but it had been she who had done the never-ending chores of shopping at the cash-and-carry, ferrying children to doctor's, dentist's or optician's, meeting parents at the airport or station. Once they had moved to Tigh Bhan it had been she who went back and forth to Fort William for all the household needs, trying but usually failing to fulfil Walter's precise demands.

The blue VW Polo, smart and gleaming, was the first car she had ever owned herself, and even as she angled back towards town to pick up the road west she began to appreciate its nippy responsiveness. But today she was in a mood to find everything marvellous, and she knew it. Scottish voices, easy Scottish friendliness, how she had missed them. And now, almost before she had time to take in that it was really happening, she was heading deep into Scottish hills, past Loch Earn, through Glen Ogle and Glen Dochart, and after a brief stop for food taking the swings of the road up from Tyndrum with a sensation of exuberance and liberation she could never remember feeling even a shadow of before.

She was so happy that she felt almost guilty about rejecting Shropshire, once so well-loved. Had she given it a fair chance? But she could go back, she would go back, for she had no intention of cutting herself off from the family. But she would go back on her own terms, for visits, not thrust haplessly into the close quarters which had been so claustrophobic for them all. Had she truly done her best over Reggie? She had tried, many times, during the busy weeks while the house purchase was going through and she was sorting out her finances, arranging to have her furniture taken out of store, buying the car, organising electricity and telephone and somewhere to stay while she moved in, to talk to Reggie, not just about these practical matters, but about their feelings for each other. He had never been able to voice his feelings, however, and his concern had been displayed by little more than the number of times he cleaned his spectacles and the difficulty he found in concentrating on this month's *Engineering*.

Nadia, on the other hand, had protested, argued and poured out warnings, producing one horror story after another about house-buying disasters run into by her friends.

'What a great many incompetent people you must know,' Helen had eventually been moved to comment, and Nadia had flounced off indignantly.

Phoebe had given the most away, watching the preparations for her grandmother's departure with unconcealed satisfaction. 'Mummy says we'll be able to have guests to stay again.' 'Will we be able to make a noise when we play outside now?' 'The downstairs bathroom's really best for us when we've been outside. We make the stairs so dirty trekking up and down.' 'How do kettles make white marks on furniture, Grannie . . . ?'

Nadia had made several pointed remarks about her hospitality not being found adequate, but had been patently relieved to abandon the experiment.

'Only it's ridiculous to go so far away,' she would complain. 'I can see that it didn't really suit you to live with us, though I have to say we did our best to make you comfy, but I'm sure Reggie could find you some nice little cottage nearby.' Then, finding Helen unresponsive, 'Well, you might think of us, having to come all that way to see you if anything goes wrong, I mean if you're ill or something.' Which soon degenerated into the frankly unkind, 'At your age, no one could call it a sensible idea.'

She worried away about having an independent valuation done on the house. 'You'll find the place a ruin if you don't,' she warned, not very logically but clearly hoping this would be the case.

Helen serenely kept to herself the fact that she had had a search done, sure Nadia would not care for some of the details it had revealed.

Now, coming into Glencoe village, with the tumbled

splendour of the hills of Ardgour against a sunset sky before her, the realities she had so blithely ignored began to stir a faint trepidation. If those warnings of damp and 'giving' floors were serious, and if the phrase 'some replacement of windows would be advisable' meant the whole lot would have to be renewed, then funds might be stretched. She had not insisted on an equal division of resources when the divorce went through, knowing that it was more important to Walter than to her to cling to certain luxuries. Indeed he saw them as his due. Most of her capital had gone on Hilltop House and the car, but though such concerns seemed more real now that she was actually on her way to the unknown, unseen house, she still couldn't bring herself to worry much. It was a first intoxicating glimpse of being truly, at last, answerable to no one but herself. She smiled, her spirits lifting another notch, remembering Nadia's hints that she was squandering Reggie's heritage. Reggie hadn't done badly from her so far, and had done unexpectedly well for himself. He needed nothing. He could have whatever was left over.

It had been a long day, and in spite of her happiness, and the deepening conviction that she had done the right thing, which she had feared might waver when the moment of departure came, it had contained a lot of mixed emotions. She could not escape the sense of having failed, in spite of her best intentions, with the family, the only people close to her in the world. She felt guilty for not having tried harder, for staying so short a time, for not making more effort to adapt, and for being in general an inadequate mother.

She decided, driving at last along Loch Luig, tired now but filled with tingling excitement to be here again, almost unable to take in the scale and beauty of her surroundings or believe that she would actually be living here from now on, that it would be sensible to find the place where she was booked in, have a long soothing bath and go straight to bed.

Once in her pleasant room in the Harbour Brae Guest-house, however, she knew that late as it was it would be impossible to wind down sufficiently to sleep. It was still light, much lighter than it would be in the south at this time, and almost without conscious decision she found herself slipping downstairs again, and going out to the car.

She drove down into the town, where the shops she had often used ringed the big carpark above the harbour, and with excitement gripping her took the road which for almost a year had led home, across the Luig Moor and down again to Inverbuie and Tigh Bhan. It was a steep pull, and she remembered how laboriously lorries and coaches had ground up here, but she had never specially noticed the lane which turned off to the right above the last houses. She swung into it, her heart thumping. Above it the moor began; below, a dry-stane dyke almost invisible under wild roses and hawthorns enclosed the huge garden of the last house on the hill road. Two hundred yards or so along the lane the dyke turned into the rear wall of a house, with a small gate in between. The back door of the house, and further along the door to a single-storey extension, opened onto a turning place which had been carved out of the rising bank sheltering the house to the north.

The last of a watery sunset was far round to the north-west by now, sending lances of yellow light across the moor from a citrus-green sky, catching the side of the house even at this late hour. Up here, it was as if the town did not exist.

Helen got out of the car clumsily, shaken by a mixture of relief and delight to be here, and apprehension at what she would find, though, since she had no key, whatever dire secrets the house held would remain hidden tonight. Taking a deep unsteady breath of the cool air of dusk, laden with garden scents and the faintest tang of salt water, she crossed to the green-painted gate, covered with rusting rabbit netting which curled up uselessly at the bottom, and for the first time went down the path which led past a glazed verandah to the front of the house, and looked out over harbour, loch and guardian island, to the hills of the headland beyond, their crests still outlined by golden light. Her view. Impossible to believe that yet.

Thrilled, eager, but tense with uncertainty as the doubting voices came back, Helen went down the first set of steps of a steeply terraced garden and turned to look at the house.

In the deepening gloaming the white harling looked almost luminous. The verandah ran as far as the central front door. Apart from that the house was a simple two windows up and two down, and to the right, stepped back from it, was the second cottage, which she knew had formerly been used for holiday letting, and which had been one of the chief reasons for her instant decision to buy. The grannie flat in reverse, she thought, trying to lighten her tension.

She knew this picture by heart, for this was what had stared up at her as she drew the folders from that large white envelope in her bedroom at Roden House. But the reality, as she stood here in the cool dusk, feeling swept away by the sense of height and space this marvellous position gave, was so infinitely more satisfying.

The heavy dew of an untended lawn was soaking her shoes, but she barely noticed. Last night, after a final family supper when Nadia's theme had been, 'Now, it's not too late to change your mind. We can always sell the place again, even if it means losing on it,' she had been finishing her packing, hot, harried and anxious, in that soulless little box of a room. Now she was here.

And Nadia, alas, would shortly be here too, to check the place out.

'We shall have to re-arrange our holidays, of course,' she had said, crossly flipping over the pages of the scrawled calendar in the kitchen. 'It looks as though you'll have to wait to go to Aunt Wendy's till the end of August this year, my pets. Yes, I know I promised, but I didn't know Grannie would be buying a new house, did I? And that will mean missing the Edgethorne Show. What a shame! Mummy will just have to make it up to you. But we can't have Grannie struggling to move into a new house all on her own, can we? She won't know a soul up there . . .'

Somehow I don't feel I won't know a soul, Helen thought. It had been impossible to say so to Nadia, when trying to reassure her that she wouldn't need help. She pushed the memory away, turning to go down the next set of steps, the plants which had spread unchecked across them brushing cold and wet against her ankles. She didn't care, feeling released and heedless. Catriona, whom she had known best, had left the area, certainly. Helen had hardly heard from her since she left for Dundee without saying goodbye, her departure triggering the decision, contemplated for so many months, to separate from Walter. When Helen had left Inverbuie for Edinburgh she had written giving Catriona her new address, but when she had moved to Withedine she had not, thinking the link between them by that stage too tenuous, and also feeling she should cut the ties with Scotland for good if she was to make a successful new life in Shropshire.

The occasional contacts with Catriona's friends during the time at Tigh Bhan had never developed into more than acquaintance, for Walter had always said damningly that he couldn't work up much interest in hotel-keepers and farmers. Yet, though there was no single person she would get in touch with or go to see now she was back, there was a reassuring certainty of being in a friendly place. There would be faces she would know in the shops and about the town; people who would remember her. The voices would be voices she wanted to hear, the pace and ways would be the pace and ways she felt at home with and had missed. If she could survive alone contentedly anywhere in the world, it would be here.

'But what on earth will you *do* with yourself?' she heard Nadia's exasperated cry.

Oddly, the question didn't worry her. At Roden House the days had seemed endless, and she had worked at filling them with little routines to break up the arid stretches of time. She had found herself watching the clock, looking forward to the day being over, to closing her door at last and going to bed with a book. That was no way to live. Here, though she would be living alone, she somehow had no fear of the days being empty.

There would be more than enough to do reducing this garden to order for a start. With the shoulder of the moor cutting off the last of the light from the west as she went further down the slope, it seemed abruptly darker, but she could still see the rampant growth everywhere, the crammed borders and the shaggy shapes of unpruned bushes. But what entranced her, and what the photograph of the house had not hinted at, was this succession of levels which drew her on to one unexpected corner after another, fragrant, silent and mysterious. There had been no mention, either, of the burn which tumbled down inside the eastern wall, beyond which rose the dark shapes of trees. This magical garden was a world on its own and she went on almost in a dream, unable to believe it could possibly be hers.

Perhaps the kind half-dark of the summer night was

concealing all kinds of dereliction, and the house still waited with whatever problems it had in store, but she could hardly wait to come back. At the earliest possible moment tomorrow she would collect the key, and equip herself to do as much cleaning as she could before the furniture — and her books, her books! — arrived.

But for now she had done what she had come to do; she had put a finger on the quiet pulse of this place, and had felt welcome.

Chapter Ten

'Catriona, have you heard who's moved into Hilltop?' Una Urquhart sounded delighted to be imparting news bound to give pleasure. 'Those friends of yours who bought Tigh Bhan after Lilias died.'

'Oh, you've heard? I came specially to tell you. Helen Rathbone, yes. She hasn't moved in yet, though, that's tomorrow. I can still hardly believe it. Watty's just told me – he had to come down to tighten my clutch or something.'

Watty had run to earth a van of a certain age but, he swore, of unblemished history, and was now enjoying tinkering with it whenever Catriona would let him. She hadn't regretted her decision to buy it. One of her main reasons had been exactly this – to be able to slip along to Ardlonach whenever she could, the friendly comfortable hotel west of Luig in its sheltered bay looking out to the island, which Una still owned.

'Trust Watty to have his ear to the ground,' Una commented, smiling at Catriona's excitement.

'Yes, usually lying on it, plastered,' Rebecca put in. She, more caustic of tongue and more crisp and vivid in appearance than gentle dreamy Una, was the driving force behind Ardlonach. She had arrived two years ago, having abandoned her high-powered career in the financial world in order to make a major decision about her own life, just when her cousin Tony had walked out on Una. She had stayed to help her open for the summer, and had never gone away. She now lived with Dan McNee, who ran the survival school part of the business, in a cottage a little way down the loch.

They were in the small office she and Una used as a sitting-room, and she was busy at the computer entering the day's arrivals and putting through dinner charges, but she too was glad to see Catriona, younger than the rest of the group by ten years or more and very much protected by them, looking and sounding so thrilled.

Una, too thin these days and looking tired already though the season was barely into its stride, was still in the whites in which she had cooked dinner, and after drinking her coffee was planning a retreat to bath and bed. Rebecca, whose resilient energy rarely failed her, was rattling through the evening office work before going to socialise with the guests. Dan would already be in the bar and still, for Rebecca, time away from him was holding time.

'How nice it will be for you to have Helen back,

Catriona,' Una was saying warmly. 'You got on so well with her when she was at Tigh Bhan.' She knew how hard Catriona found it to make new friends.

'It sometimes seemed almost as though Lilias hadn't gone,' Catriona said, not looking at either of them as she spoke, shy of expressing this thought.

'I know,' Una said gently. She understood better than anyone the emptiness of Catriona's life, and her need for the security of affection and permanence. 'But didn't you know Mrs Rathbone was coming back to live?'

'We lost touch. Well, I stopped writing. I thought when she'd gone from Tigh Bhan it would be a bit boring for her to keep up the contact.'

'Is she buying or leasing Hilltop?' asked Rebecca, who liked facts. 'And is she back on her own? Wasn't there a pompous old bore of a husband? Damn, I'd forgotten that extra bed in Room 7, haven't put in children's rates. Damn, damn, damn . . .'

'They were getting divorced,' Catriona said, then glanced at Una. It was over a year since Una's divorce had been finalised, and though she had never expressed the slightest doubt that it had been the right thing to do, there was still a sadness about her, a look of having been wounded which her friends minded on her behalf. 'I thought Helen was going to live in Edinburgh. That's where she went after leaving Inverbuie. Anyway, I'll go and see if I can help tomorrow, after I finish in the shop. It will be lovely to see her again. I'll rope in Watty too. Hilltop's been empty for quite a while. I don't know what state the house will be in but the garden's a jungle.'

'How do you know that?' Una asked with interest. Catriona had been back such a short time, and though she was only working part-time Una found her capacity for being absorbed into the landscape, while apparently never going anywhere or doing anything, amazing.

'Oh, you know, going up onto the moor,' Catriona said evasively. She had used the Hilltop garden as a convenient short-cut. Accustomed in the glen to owning virtually all the land within walking distance — and whatever bits of the estate had become Rhumore over the years she had still felt belonged to the Finlays by natural laws, a view Donald Macrae wouldn't have dreamed of contesting — she had already covered most of the ground around Luig.

'You and your faithful Watty,' Rebecca teased. 'You actually think he's some use, don't you?'

'Not a huge amount,' Catriona conceded, with a glimmer of a smile. 'Which is why I was wondering — you couldn't possibly spare Bern for a couple of hours tomorrow, could you?'

'Oh, Catriona, I would have, gladly,' Una exclaimed, 'but he's done something to his back and can't do any heavy work for a week or two.'

'Very conveniently,' Rebecca added tartly. 'Just as things are beginning to hot up in the hotel, and everything in the garden is ramping to the skies.'

'Oh, Rebecca, you know he's more concerned about

that than anyone.' Una leapt to his defence. 'You can't believe he's malingering.'

'No, hasn't the brains to think of it.' But Rebecca was grinning at the screen. It did Una good to be wound up occasionally; she could get too serious.

'But it's a bore for you about the garden,' Catriona sympathised, knowing it was the chief love of Una's life, though she was usually too busy to get into it much. 'How about Watty coming to give a hand?'

'Don't tell me you're actually licking him into shape?' Rebecca demanded. 'He was quite happy drinking his dole money and sitting on the harbour wall with his cronies smoking himself to death. Do you think he'll appreciate having to work for his pleasures?'

'Yes,' said Catriona simply, and Una laughed.

'I think you're right,' she said, giving Catriona's arm a little pat as she got up to go. 'And if Watty wants to put in a few hours a week while Bern's laid up I shall be very glad to see him.'

'So long as he isn't let loose on the bar,' Rebecca ruled, turning over the last dinner chit and closing down the computer.

'Can't Bern do the bar either? Perhaps I could help on the odd evening,' Catriona suggested.

The cousins stared at her in amazement.

'You?' said Rebecca.

Catriona coloured. When she had helped in the hotel before she had been adamant that the bar was beyond her. Now, after her year away, she had, without being aware of it, left behind her fears of tackling such a job, of being watched, keeping people waiting, being inept in what she saw as an area where everyone else was at ease.

'It's probably a silly idea,' she said quickly. 'I just thought if you were really busy ...'

'It's very good of you,' Una assured her warmly. 'We're getting by at present, but if we have any gaps in the roster we'll certainly ask, and thank you.'

'You're getting braver,' commented the more out-spoken Rebecca. 'Good for you.'

'I'll probably be useless,' Catriona warned, but she said it without anxiety. Many of the terrors which had ridden her seemed to have evaporated, not while she was in Dundee, but since she had come back, in the simplicity and security of this well-known place, her private testing time behind her.

'You'll be fine,' Una said, an affectionate look in the dark eyes that could look so sad and withdrawn. 'Now I really am off, if you don't mind. I feel exhausted for some reason, though no one could say we had a huge number of dinners tonight. I don't know how I'm going to cope with August at this rate. Oh, and by the way,' she added, turning at the door, 'Mrs Rathbone isn't the only person who's turned up in Luig again. Ask Rebecca, she'll tell you all about it.'

She was gone, and Catriona turned to find Rebecca putting her desk into the meticulous order she preferred with an unusually self-conscious expression on her face.

'So who else has come back?' she asked.

'No one. Una's just being silly.'

'But who did she mean?' Catriona thought it no bad thing to see the self-possessed and often far too sweeping Rebecca discomfited by Una for once.

'You know anyway,' Rebecca remembered, recovering her poise. 'He said he'd run into you. Jake Macleod.'

'Oh, yes, I met him up on the moor. We were watching some baby roe. He said he was coming to see you soon. Do you know him well?' From anyone but Catriona the question might have been pointed, scenting gossip. From her it was innocent and direct.

Rebecca couldn't quite control a grimace of wry humour. 'For a brief period, a long time ago. He looked in to see how life had treated me and, knowing him, to check out my present status. Dan wasn't too impressed.'

'I'd have thought they might get on rather well together,' Catriona remarked. 'Both outdoor types, I mean. And Jake seemed very easy to get on with.'

Rebecca blinked at her, but at the same time couldn't suppress a grin. Dan, ex-RAF Regiment sergeant and a tough, resourceful, truculent individual, was the first man Rebecca had had any real relationship with who refused to be swamped by her vigorous assertiveness. He was also deeply possessive. Jake, though his official military career had been no more than a brief commission in the Scots Guards, had earned his living after that in some very unforgiving parts of the world, at some periods certainly bearing arms, though no one ever knew exactly what he did. At first glance perhaps the two men did have much in common, but Jake had come here checking out Dan's woman. And lively and enjoyable though their brief affair had been, Rebecca had never heard anyone describe him as easy to get on with, and would have thought gauche and under-confident Catriona the last person to find him so.

'Let's just say they didn't hit it off,' she temporised, hiding her smile.

'What a shame,' Catriona said nicely. Meeting Jake as she had, on the hill, in her own environment, she had felt instantly at ease with him and found him friendly and kind, adjectives not often applied to him. 'Is Jake living at Luig now?'

'He was at the big house, but Connor and Michaela are coming up early this year, and the whole crowd will be up in August and you know what that's like, so he's moving into the old bothy.'

'The bothy where they used to do the shooting lunches? What a marvellous place to live!'

Rebecca raised an eyebrow. 'Marvellous? It's four stone walls. Most people couldn't begin to imagine living in a place like that.'

'It's got water, it's even got a loo out at the back. And think of its position, away up there, the views, the silence. Imagine waking there early in the morning, and just stepping out of the door and onto the hill . . .' Catriona's voice betrayed her wistfulness, and Rebecca looked at her more attentively.

'How much longer do you have in Trudy's flat?'

'Oh, a couple of weeks still.' Catriona spoke more

briskly, realising she had given herself away. 'Trudy said I could stay with her if I haven't found anything else by then, but I can easily rent somewhere.'

Rebecca, who was kinder than she pretended to be, refrained from reminding her how high rates were in the summer. She guessed Catriona still felt she had some sort of duty to go out into the world and get a 'normal' job, and knew until she found it she could make no plans about where to live. She also understood how Catriona in her soul longed to stay, near her friends, piecing together any patchwork of jobs which would support her.

'Apparently Jake's going to be here for a while this time,' she remarked casually. Once he and Dan got over locking horns it would be fun to have him around. She had no interest in him now other than as a friend, a member of the established circle whose families had lived here for generations. She had no interest in any man but Dan, with whom she was happier and more satisfied than she had ever imagined it was possible to be. 'His uncle, or perhaps great-uncle, I can never work out the intricacies of the Macleod clan, has left him the little bookshop at the top of Harbour Brae.'

'The antiquarian bookshop? Oh, no, has darling Percy died? How sad, I hadn't heard. But he must have been ninety at least. I used to take him books sometimes from the library at home and I'm sure he always paid me far too much.'

He probably did, Rebecca guessed. Neighbours and acquaintances had watched with sorrow the decline of the Finlay fortunes, and had been concerned about the strange life Catriona had led, growing up there with only her mentally unstable grandfather for company.

'I think he was more interested in collecting than in making money,' she said. 'It seems he had contacts world-wide in his field. His correspondence was huge, Jake was telling us, and some very weird people indeed turned up at his funeral.'

'I wish I'd been there,' Catriona mourned. 'But what will Jake do with the shop, do you think? Will he sell it?'

It hurt her to imagine it, just as it had hurt her to carry each separate volume to Percy Macleod when times were hard. She still could hardly bear to realise that the entire library at Glen Righ had gone, included in the sale of the house. With scrupulous fairness she had decided very few books in the house could be judged hers. The couple of boxfuls she had kept were stored with Trudy but she still felt, particularly when for some reason she couldn't sleep, the chill space where these familiar and comforting companions should have been.

'He might not sell,' Rebecca was saying. 'There's a bit more to Jake than that unprepossessing exterior suggests. He's a cagey devil, and the years can scarcely be said to have mellowed him, but he does have a brain, and wider interests than he always lets people know about. I can't see him tying himself down to looking after the business himself, though. He must be one of the most restless people in the world – and he might not find enough beautiful, rich and powerful women in Luig to keep him happy for long.'

As they all had the habit of doing with Catriona, forgetting she was in her mid-twenties and had by now had a taste of what was known as the real world, she suppressed the term 'ball-breakers'.

Hilltop House seemed a very different place in the morning light. Last night it had hung, ghostly and gleaming, full of promise, high above its shadowy scented garden. Today it seemed altogether a more down-to-earth place, not even very like the photograph which had drawn Helen to it in the first instance. That had made it look wider, more elegant, certainly in better repair.

With a slight sinking feeling, where she had expected to feel only the joy of ownership, she pushed open the door from the lane and went tentatively into a minute dark lobby. She had wanted to be alone, had battled for that very thing, longing for this moment with the keenest anticipation, but now, disconcertingly, she wanted someone else to be there. She supposed you couldn't be one of a couple for thirty-five years and not find it daunting to embark on so major an adventure completely alone.

The door to the right led into a depressing loo, brown stains spreading down its bowl. The door on the other side led into a narrow kitchen, fitted adequately but unimaginatively in mock-pine. She hardly looked at it; if it worked it would have to do. She must have been mad to buy the place without coming to look at it. It would only have taken a couple of days to come up from Withedine and go back. But if she hadn't liked it? She knew that was why she hadn't come. She had wanted to like it, had been utterly resolved on liking it. The illogical sequence of these thoughts struck her, and she laughed in the strange heavy silence which empty houses hold. Turning back to the lobby she went through the door leading to the hall and the front of the house.

Ahead of her was a glazed door, the verandah beyond that, then light and space, loch, hills and sky. Trembling, Helen stood still, relief filling her. This was why she had come.

The verandah was the salient feature of the house, all of whose rooms faced out over that glorious view to the south. It had been added, Helen guessed, by someone with a taste for amateur building, and was a stout, no-nonsense structure intended to withstand the winds which no doubt would come raging in over the moor. Its chief beauty was that it continued, though narrow as the ground fell steeply away, round the western gable end. How lovely it was going to be to sit and watch the sun set over the far sound and its scatter of islands.

Her heart beating with a stifling excitement, as though she was beginning to believe this could be all right after all, Helen went up the steep stairs and turned first into the westward room. Here she found a small window had been knocked through the thick end wall, to one side to accommodate the chimney, low to allow for the slope of the roof, and not made to open on this storm-ridden side of the house. Glancing over her shoulder as she knelt to peer through it, Helen saw how she could place one of the low guest-room divans she had kept so that she could lie and look out of that deep-set window as the light faded on summer nights.

The house was shabby, that was undeniable; it not only needed thorough cleaning but much re-decorating. And when, after a brief tussle, she got the front door open and stepped out and looked down into the garden she saw with dismay that last night's impression of richness and abundant flowering translated into a reality of wild neglect. There was no doubt about the lush growth, but most of it seemed to be in the form of sagging bushes, mad tangles of collapsing climbers in the grip of ivy or convolvulus, rank grass thick with weeds, and borders invaded by couch grass and ground elder.

She would scarcely know where to begin on such a wilderness, yet, exploring it with trepidation, she soon forgot her dismay, entranced by its variety and unexpectedness. Now she had descended three lots of steps and passing between rough pillars of granite found herself in what had once been an extensive fruit garden. Many of the bushes, overgrown as they were, would soon bear fruit, and looked as though care and attention might reclaim them.

But what struck Helen most was the still, sheltered air of the place, as though there was no road busy with tourist traffic a couple of hundred yards away, no tight-crammed town below. A dry-stane dyke bounded her property, and stepping up on a solid boulder at its base she looked over. A narrow path dipped away out of sight between gardens. A path into the town? Helen looked along the wall and saw a wooden gate half-smothered by honeysuckle. Examining it she found it fastened with wire too tough to unwind. Struggling out from the strangling stems, wet with dew, dizzy with the overpowering scent, she decided getting it open would be one of her earliest jobs.

As she climbed up the levels again, this time by grass-choked steps beside the burn, she knew she could delay no longer looking at the smaller cottage. It had been described as self-contained and suitable for holiday letting. Helen knew she had been reluctant to go in because, fatally, she would find herself looking at it through Nadia's eyes. She should be capable of making her own judgements, and in time she would, but for now Nadia's voice was still in her ears, Nadia's negative and irrational views all too recently frustrating, and Helen felt nervousness return as she opened the faded green-painted door.

It led straight into a sitting-room, meagrely furnished, two bedrooms opening off it. A door at the back led to bathroom and kitchen, the latter with a 'dining area' which consisted of two bench seats and a table the size of a suitcase. All walls were smothered in heavily patterned wallpaper, woodwork was dark green. The whole cottage gave off a smell of damp and forsakenness which even the shabbiness of Hilltop had not exuded.

The rumour of confrontations to come stirred in the fusty air, and Helen shivered. She reminded herself that it was not necessary for Nadia to approve – Reggie was a cypher in such matters – but the habit of years was too strong, the habit of pleasing. And this, patently, would not please. Nadia and Reggie would be here in a matter of weeks; there was so much to do.

Distractedly, Helen hurried back to the main house. She must scrub and clean before the furniture arrived. She shouldn't have been wandering in the garden, wasting time. She should have been heating water, measuring spaces, planning where things would go. Her delight in the house had fled; it had become a monumental task she wasn't sure she could handle. All morning as she cleaned she found more things to worry about – spongy sills, floorboards sagging in corners, a network of mildewy cracks in the bathroom basin, signs of damp by the chimneys in both bedrooms, dry now but doubtless ready to return when winter came. And all the time, worse by far, Little Hilltop waited, and the garden, larger every time she thought about it, spread in a chaos it would take her years to reduce. Whatever had she done? Helen scrubbed feverishly on.

'Hi! Helen, where are you? Can we come up?'

Startled, disorientated, she sat back on her heels. Who knew her name? That sounded like a voice from another time. Pushing her hair off her hot forehead with her wrist, getting a whiff of rubber glove and dirty water as she did so, she felt a dazed incredulous hopefulness flood through her.

Chapter Eleven

'But how on earth did you—?'

'You didn't think you could turn up in Luig to live and keep it a secret?'

'But to find me on the very first day! I'm just so thrilled—'

'You remember Watty?'

'Yes, of course. How are you, Watty?'

Watty rolled his cap up into a spill.

'We've come to help. What can we do?'

'But are you — where are you living? I thought you were in Dundee.'

'Done that. All over. I'm helping Trudy in the shop at present, part-time. Someone else is looking after it this afternoon. I just hoped we'd get here before your furniture van arrived.'

'It's due at any moment. Oh, Catriona, it's so good to see you, such a marvellous surprise. Not for the help, though that will be most welcome, of course. But to find you here ...' I had felt so alone, and so unfitted after all to deal with it. Now that sense of aloneness had vanished at a stroke, never to return. 'But you can't plunge straight into work. Let's have coffee first.'

'Bother, we should have brought something with us. We never thought of that, did we, Watty?'

Helen gave her a quick hug of delighted affection which had to be expressed somehow. No, nothing so domestic would have occurred to Catriona, let alone Watty. But she had come as a matter of course to help, and though she was so slight and looked fragile Helen remembered how surprisingly tough she was, and knew her assistance would be nearly as valuable as the squat and powerful Watty's.

'Of course you didn't need to bring anything,' she said. 'I had a flask filled in case the electricity wasn't on, but it's all been faithfully done as arranged, and I bought a few other things on my way up.'

With Catriona and Watty there, with the simple actions of boiling the kettle, setting out mugs and breaking open supplies, with the moving-day scene of biscuits from the packet, milk from the carton, and the single teaspoon going wet into the sugar and leaving damp marks on the worktop, the dull kitchen became hers.

'You've got masses of cupboards in here, haven't you,' Catriona commented, looking round with approval.

'And there's the plumbing in ready for your washing machine,' said Watty, prowling. 'That's handy, mind. And you'll never want for water here. That burn starts away up on the moor.'

'And the bank above not only shelters you from the north but also means your catchment tank's high, so the pressure will be good,' Catriona added.

How did they know these things, Helen wondered, amused, feeling tensions ironed away. Because they were natives; they absorbed such details by osmosis.

The furniture was in, and the last boxes of books were being stacked in the sitting-room, when a big car pulled into the lane.

'Have I timed it right? I saw the van coming through the town, and since I'm not much use to anyone at present I thought I'd give you time to get the hard work done.' Swaying ponderously, her big smile flashing in her brown face, Trudy came across the gravel to the door, a covered tray in her hands. 'Welcome back,' she said to Helen.

'How truly kind of you to come.' Helen knew Trudy only slightly, having met her occasionally in the meal shop, but she used to hear a lot about her from Catriona and, liking her easy manner and ready friendliness, had always hoped to get to know her better. She had also warmed to Trudy's husband the doctor, meeting him professionally when she had sliced open her eyebrow slipping off the kitchen steps and Walter had ruled that she needed stitches, but had not driven her to Luig to have them put in. Fitz's comments on his absence had done her almost more good than his sewing skills.

'But of course you mustn't think of doing anything,'

she added to Trudy, with a mock-alarmed glance at her splendidly gravid bulk.

'Specially as I'm two days overdue,' Trudy agreed cheerfully, and laughed at the expression of the passing removal man who had overheard her. 'So here's my contribution,' she went on, whipping aside her cloth to reveal two golden quiches and a tub of salad. 'There's another basket in the car, Watty.'

Apart from plates and forks it contained a couple of bottles of Sauvignon and several glasses.

'I take it you won't be complaining that I'm blocking you in for a minute or two?' she remarked to the men, whose interest had switched from her girth to the provisions.

'Aye well, we're no' in all that of a hurry,' they agreed, grinning.

'Trudy, are you expecting a party?' Catriona demanded.

'Flitting is a party, isn't it?' Trudy said, handing one of the bottles to the nearest male to be dealt with. 'Here you go. Rebecca said she'd come along if she could, just to say hello because they're pretty busy with Bern laid up, and Fitz has a call somewhere up here this afternoon and might be able to look in.'

'You're all so kind,' Helen said helplessly, feeling an unexpected prickling behind her eyes.

'Marginally warmer outside, don't you think?' Trudy appeared to have taken charge.

So, for the first time, they spilled out of the verandah door, and spread wherever it suited them on the doorstep, the flagstones around it, and the first flight of steps down to the unkempt lawn, and Rebecca, bringing Una with her, and also bearing wine, came round the end of the house to find them there. Fitz didn't make it, and the removal men soon left, pretending sanctimoniously that they couldn't drink on the job but actually wishing, like Watty, that someone had had the sense to put in a few bottles of beer.

Rebecca and then Trudy had to reverse onto the busy hill road to let them out. 'Though believe me, backing is my least efficient thing in present circumstances,' Trudy warned. 'It all has to be done by mirrors.'

When Watty offered to shift the Chrysler for her, however, she lumbered to her feet in a hurry. 'I'm the one that has to live with Fitz afterwards,' she reminded him. 'You can leap about and see us out if you want to be useful.'

'Am I disturbing any neighbours?' Helen enquired of Catriona while this was going on, not having had time yet to work out who might be affected.

'Everyone understands about flitting day,' Catriona assured her. 'Anyway, there's no one near enough to mind.'

It was easy to forget that any houses lay below at all. Nothing could be built above because of the steepness of the bank, and the lane only went as far as Little Hilltop and the deep declivity of the burn. All considerations, Helen reflected, conscious of having been a great deal luckier than she deserved, which sensible people took into account when buying houses.

'Right, Helen, what can we do to help?' asked brisk Rebecca when she and Trudy came back.

How strange the pleasure of hearing my name so simply used; what a feeling of acceptance it gives. Catriona regards herself as my friend; these are friends of hers, ergo ...

'It's very good of you, and I'm grateful a thousand times, but if you don't mind I'd quite like to do nothing for a while. We got on so well earlier,' with a nod of gratitude to Watty and Catriona, 'I think we should just enjoy the party. And I've hardly had time to take in this fantastic setting yet. I was quite mad, you know, and bought the place sight unseen.'

'That was very adventurous,' Una commented, opening her eyes. 'I don't think I'd ever be brave enough to do something like that.'

How nice that she sees it as courage. Nadia saw it as being disgracefully irresponsible.

'And are you pleased with your purchase?' Trudy wanted to know.

'I can't tell you how pleased.' Helen heard her voice sounding suddenly shaky, and knew she could never explain how by simply being here they had banished to oblivion the nervous doubts of the morning.

'But isn't there quite a lot to do if you want to sleep here tonight?' Rebecca persisted. 'Can't we unpack a few boxes, put up some curtains, or at least make up a bed for you before we go?'

'No, truly, thank you for the offer, but I won't do

much more today. And I'm not sleeping here. I'm at the Harbour Brae Guest-house for another night.'

'But Mrs Cowie doesn't do dinner, does she? Just high tea at six or some ungodly hour.'

'I could just be in time for that, I suppose,' Helen said, glancing at her watch, but not in the least wanting to break up the gathering.

'Ah, but did you put your name down?' Trudy asked solemnly. 'If you didn't put your name down this morning you won't have been Counted In. You have to know how these things work. Two chops each and none over. No, what would be much nicer would be if you came to dinner with us. Catriona's coming, and Fitz is obviously not going to show up now, and I know he'll want to say hello. So won't you come? Please do.'

'But you won't want to worry about guests—'

'In my condition? Oh, Fitz cooks and does all that stuff,' Trudy said, and the others laughed.

'And tomorrow come and have dinner with us,' Una suggested. 'Then you won't have to think about cooking for another night. The only problem is, we have to wait till the end of dinner when everyone's gone in. Will that be a bore for you?'

After the child-orientated régime of Roden House it sounded like heaven to Helen.

'I'm afraid we'll have to go now,' Una said regretfully, 'but we'll look forward to seeing you then.'

Helen, who had imagined she was desperate for solitude, found herself warmed to the core by this assumption that she was now part of their circle, and saw, with shame, that what she had sought so eagerly was not solitude at all, but freedom from Walter and, in her turn, Nadia. The regiment of family. It was something she must think about more honestly later.

The last guests drifted towards the dining-room and Catriona, pink and flushed with her efforts, came out from behind the bar to collect glasses, tidy cushions and set stools straight. She had done it. With a few minutes of whirling help from Rebecca when things had got out of hand — it was that wretched table who'd gone in for dinner so early that they were out again and asking for Gaelic coffee before most people had even ordered — she had coped with the pre-dinner rush without disaster. It would never seem an ordeal again, and even tonight had only been an ordeal in the sense that she didn't know measures or prices or where anything was. There had been none of that terrified sense of her own inadequacy which used to cripple her. And now there was this pleasant quiet time, with the action in the kitchen and dining-room. She only had to deal with the phone and be here in case anyone turned up. The early diners had apparently already gone to bed. Most non-residents would head for the Coach-house, the popular lower bar with its separate entrance, and once dinner was over one of the staff would take over here and Catriona would be free. Helen was already in the dining-room with Rebecca, where Una would join them as soon as she could for the single course which was all she ever wanted.

Catriona had had staff supper earlier, but didn't feel excluded. She was used to hotel life. How good it felt, she thought, relaxing in one of the cushioned window seats of her tidy bar, to have Helen back. Why did it matter so much? Her acquaintance with Helen had not been long, six or seven months at most, and it had been restricted by Walter Rathbone's all-too-evident irritation with her presence. Also, though this didn't strike Catriona even now, she had only once invited Helen to Glen Righ, so ingrained had been the conviction that its rigours were unsustainable for the casual visitor.

Initially she had called at Tigh Bhan because she wanted to welcome the newcomers for Lilias's sake. Then, Helen had been so oddly like Lilias, with the same perceptiveness, the same alert brain – though with a less tart vein of humour, it had to be said – that sometimes Catriona had almost forgotten the house had changed hands at all. What Catriona was circling round, though she shied away from the words, was that Helen had continued to provide the warm, supportive mother figure which Catriona had never had in reality.

To have Helen living in Luig – that lent, whether justifiably or rationally or not, a sense of stability which even the friendships Catriona had found in the last few years did not give. And to know that she needed the kind of help which it was within Catriona's scope to give was especially good.

When Catriona's relief arrived, bringing coffee for her, Catriona thanked her with a shy smile and slipped away, down to the big bar in the ex-coach-house below, its doors wide to a pleasant evening. Several people were still sitting outside though others had been driven in by the midges.

Dan McNee was behind the bar, and his habitually reserved face with its cold pale eyes looked less dour at the sight of Catriona, of whom he was very fond.

'Come down to see where the real work goes on?' he greeted her. 'Do you feel you've earned a drink?'

She smiled at him. 'I certainly do. No crises – or none that anyone mentioned anyway. But I'll stick to coffee, thanks.'

'Not even a glass of—' Dan broke off, forgetting what he had begun to say, as three newcomers appeared in the doorway. Catriona turned to look.

A tall and striking couple were coming in, both with red-gold curling hair, long faces and high foreheads, long legs and straight backs, and an unmistakable air of upper-class assurance. With them, swarthier than ever by contrast, but with a natural arrogance that exceeded even theirs, came Jake, his eyes sweeping the room with the thoroughness of a man accustomed to absorbing every detail of his surroundings.

'That bastard,' Catriona heard Dan say, not under his breath, as she exclaimed, 'It's the Macleods.'

Jake was in his kilt and a sagging black sweater with no shirt under it. Connor Macleod and his sister Michaela were dressed in urban casual style, everything about them saying glamour, quality and luxe. With their elegance and confidence, they were the sort of people who made Catriona fold in on herself like a threatened sea-anemone, feeling pale, plain, dumb and harried.

'It's Catriona Finlay, isn't it?' Michaela was asking, kindly, but in an accent which made Dan scowl. 'How lovely to see you again. Jake said you were living in Luig now. You remember Conn?'

Connor's eyes were hazel-to-yellow, and they too were smiling and friendly as he took Catriona's offered hand. She had rejected neighbourly advances during the years when poor old Fergus was failing, but perhaps now that she was on her own they could do more for her.

'Of course Catriona remembers me,' he said. 'Are you on your own? Won't you come and join us? Inside, don't you think? The last of the sun's gone by now.' He wasn't asking; he had decided.

Jake, his narrow dark face unsmiling, nodded at Catriona. He had been coming off the hill, crossing the road to go down to the loch, when his cousins had passed, and he had only agreed to come for a drink with them because he had thought there might be the chance to have a quick business chat with Connor. Uncle Percy had been the last of his generation and his death had brought several trusts and legal arrangements to an end, which affected them all. Once the annual August house-party was in full swing Connor would be impossible to pin down.

Now Jake was annoyed with himself for coming. He was going to be dragged into social time-wasting of the sort he most disliked. Also he wasn't pleased to see the Finlay girl here. He wouldn't have thought she was the type to spend her evenings perched on a bar stool, though he realised, seeing her in this setting and in the clothes she had worn for doing the bar, that she was older than he had supposed.

'You must come and see us up at Luig,' Connor was saying to Catriona, having swept aside her protests that she didn't want a drink and ordered wine for her. 'Yes, you must, no excuses. Tell her, Michaela.'

'Do come,' Michaela said more persuasively. 'There's no one there but family at present. We should enjoy the chance to get to know you better. I'll get in touch with you and we'll arrange something.'

Catriona, though shrivelling at the idea, knew this was the sort of thing she mustn't duck. She must go on facing up to challenges. It was no use thinking that by surviving the year in Dundee, now a blur of dark, cold and loneliness, she had conquered her fears for good. But it was bad enough now, at this moment, having to hold her own in a conversation with these formidable Macleods, and she was thankful when Rebecca and Una appeared with Helen.

Jake hunched lower over his whisky as they came over; this was getting out of hand, and even Rebecca's appearance didn't make up for it. He'd go after this drink.

Dan swore because he had offered to fill in this evening, in spite of a long day on the hill with his survivors, and it was obvious that Rebecca was going to be stuck with that lot all night.

But Jake didn't go, and Dan presently forgot his rancour, for a surprisingly pleasant evening evolved from these unpromising beginnings. Michaela Macleod was not only socially accomplished but genuinely kind, and soon found common ground with Una, not by nature a ready talker. Connor, unaware that Helen saw straight through him, was punctiliously attentive to the older woman, the newcomer and stranger, while Jake was unexpectedly charmed to find Catriona regarding him as a refuge from Connor's teasing.

Jake was not used to being seen in this light by a female, and had to accept that to Catriona he belonged to an older generation. Their meeting on the moor had been nothing more to her than a straightforward encounter, sharing the pleasure of an appealing sight, a beautiful morning and being back on home ground. Amused, Jake decided this was even quite good for him for a change.

The element that prevented him from doing what he usually did, simply walking off when he had had enough, was the surprising satisfaction he found in talking to Helen. He liked the thin keen face, the two sweeps of white hair back from her temples, he liked her laughter and quick intelligence and humour. He was also impressed, spending most of the evening talking to her, with her range of knowledge and interests. A definite asset in their circle, he decided. He scarcely noticed when Dan was free to come and join them, and he decided as he went, long after midnight, up the dusky hill to his new quarters in the bothy, that he was glad after all that he had run into Conn and Michaela.

For Helen, undressing in her still rather basic bedroom at Hilltop where little had been unpacked, the evening had been even more enjoyable – and astonishing and disturbing. She had found in Jake an element of potent physical attraction which she could never recall encountering before, and the discovery had severely rocked her. To put her reaction into some rational context, and thus if she could reduce its power, she tried to work out when last a man had made such an immediate, unequivocal impact upon her.

Certainly it had had no part in her relationship with Walter, even at the very beginning. But in those days, when she had first met him, had people thought in that way? A young man was rated good-looking because of his face, his manners, the way he dressed. You didn't think of his body. At least she hadn't, and she didn't think her friends had. They hadn't 'fancied' someone, and as far as she could remember there had been no equivalent word. Oh, there must have been. She must just have been excessively innocent. Well-brought-up; a key phrase of her time.

Since then there had been flurries of feeling along the way, the occasional junior master who had been flatteringly attentive. Sitting very still before her mirror, she allowed her mind to turn to something she generally refused it. There had been an entire term once when she had been conscious of the presence, the steps, the voice of someone, when her days, enriched, had revolved round the pattern of his days, when her pulses had been quickened by chance meetings, when she had swung helplessly between hope and despair. It had been, as she had known with shame at the time, based chiefly on her need to break free of the trap of her unsatisfactory existence, which at times had seemed to stretch before her in an unendurable sameness and pointlessness. But there had been real feeling too, and glimpses of a whole world of sensation and fulfilment which had made the final decision agonising. But there had only been one decision possible.

Had there, she thought sharply now. Why had that seemed so clear to them? Because of Walter, of course, but also because of their relevant positions. Yes, that had really seemed to matter. Labels; convention; behaving well. But the episode had left her feeling more defiant than ashamed, still inwardly protesting that there had to be something more to life.

This evening, watching Jake's sinewy brown hands, his lean brown face with the dark eyes that missed nothing, listening to his quiet cultured voice talking directly to her beneath the general conversation, she had felt a sense of recognition, of deep secret satisfaction, as though he was someone she had known somewhere, sometime, and had been sure she would meet again. And her body had felt alive, aware, eager, in a way she had imagined it would never feel again.

But this was madness. Jake was a stranger, a man met in a bar, and he must be twelve, fifteen years younger than she was. How surprised — or outraged and disgusted — he would be at her thoughts. Blushing and angry with herself, Helen hurried into bed. At least, thank God, not he, not anyone, would ever know about them.

Chapter Twelve

Registering the twinge between her shoulder blades as she picked up the tray, Helen knew she had probably done too much today. But the house was most satisfyingly taking shape. She went round the angle of the verandah to the table and chair she had set against the western gable. It was too cool to sit outside this evening, but from here, just as she had foreseen, every last second of light and sunset could be enjoyed.

She was still wearing the old shirt of Walter's and the fawn cords, the knees now damp and dirty, which she had put on when she got up. She would take pleasure in binning both as soon as all the grubby work was done; they were too dull for her present mood. It was such a luxury not to change though. She wondered, momentarily arrested by the thought, how many evenings there had been in her adult life when she had not. And it was luxury to eat salad and new potatoes and nothing else, and to contemplate afterwards a long relaxing bath and going to bed while it was still light.

Why did she have this almost reckless sense of freedom here? She had lived alone for weeks in Edinburgh after she and Walter had separated. But then, the shell of settled habit too rawly torn away, she had gone on blindly, numbly, following the same patterns as before, as though still subject to rules which other people laid down. Because she had been in Edinburgh, where not far away in his club overlooking George Street Walter was busily setting up once more a system of living which precisely suited him, had she felt still subservient to him? And at Withedine her chief aim had been to fit in with the ways of someone else's house. Why had it taken this long for independence to stir?

This morning she had woken to it, without question. She smiled, remembering. It had been nearly nine, and that in itself had been extraordinary. One of the miseries of Roden House had been waking hideously early, wincing at the hours that must be got through before the day could begin, yet dreading the first sounds of the house coming to life. Today she had stayed where she was without the least sense of urgency, not disturbed by the fact that her clothes were tossed on the floor, or that she had spent the previous evening in a bar with several people she hardly knew, drinking a lot of wine. She had only been gratified to find it had had no effect on her, other than to make her sleep so well.

She had reviewed the evening with lazy pleasure. How agreeably it had flowed by, how good everyone had been to her. Delicious dinner first, with Una and Rebecca, then easy inclusion in the larger group. Why were they welcoming her so readily? They were all younger than she was, Jake, probably in his mid-forties, the oldest of them. Helen knew she was asking the question out of a sort of self-protectiveness, hurrying to say she was old before anyone else did. At the same time she knew she would be the only person to whom the fact would occur. Never, anywhere, in any gathering, had she been accepted more straightforwardly for what she was. And Lilias Markie, whom they often referred to as one of them, close and much loved, had been in her eighties. To be honest, there were more years between the Macleods and Catriona than there were between the Macleods and herself.

After Dan had closed the bar, which had meant turfing everyone else out and locking the outside door, and he and Rebecca had joined them, Helen had been interested to observe the change in Rebecca when Dan was there. She was focused on him, not in any demanding or explicit way, but with a look of peace and completeness, and Helen could rarely recall so strong a sense of any couple being a unit. Without Rebecca, though, she thought Dan might be a chancy customer. There had been a crackle of latent antagonism between him and Jake which neither had made much effort to conceal.

And so to Jake, the thought of whom had been there since the moment of waking, had hovered behind all these lesser thoughts. She had luxuriated in lying there, lapped in indolence, the silence of the house around her, the day formless and full of promise, with no demands from anyone to cut across it. And at another deeper level there had been an awareness of the beauty which lay beyond the walls, hers too. She had forgotten how the continual sense of it formed a satisfying background to living here, a source of delight to be tapped a hundred times a day.

And still, she had seen, she was interposing layers of thought between her and the question that mattered most. She had made herself face it, pulling herself up in the bed, rejecting sloth and evasion, at the same time amused that she had to make this physical statement to bring herself to the point.

Why had Jake attracted her so strongly, in almost violent contradiction to her nature and habit? Because of his arresting good looks? No, she didn't think so, for his face held elements of hardness, of deliberate reserve, of impatient contempt for fools, which she had not entirely liked. His voice, yes. His brain, yes. His lean, hard, tanned body, yes.

Helen had laughed aloud in the silence to be able to acknowledge this so bluntly. What was happening to her? But even so she knew she had scarcely touched on the answer. The truth was that Jake projected a personality of compelling power and individuality. He could be fitted into no framework, placed in no conventional category.

And though she had estimated his age at perhaps forty-five he could believably be ten years on either side of that. He was one of those people for whom age is irrelevant, because he would not conform to the ageing pattern of his contemporaries. Did that mean that he was incapable of growing up? And did that in turn explain why he was unmarried (Helen realised with a small jar that she had assumed this) and living alone in some bothy up on the moor, rootless and apparently without possessions? And what was this mysterious job of his? Michaela had made some teasing reference to it and been rewarded with a black scowl. It took him away for most of the time, that much had been clear, and seemed to have led him over the years into many different corners of the world, but more than that she had not learned.

And probably wouldn't learn, she had told herself. He would be off once more and that would be that.

But for now, what fun it had been, what simple ordinary fun, to sit at a bar table with a lot of lively and attractive people, with the flow of talk surging around her, drink wine and fancy a bloke.

A noise below had startled her, and suddenly she had remembered the piece of laconic planning preferred in this part of the world.

'You must have masses to do still,' Catriona had said as she had left last night after driving Helen's car home for her. 'I'm doing the shop tomorrow but I'll get Watty to look in and give you a hand.' No wasting words over times, hourly rates, or what sort of help Watty would be prepared to give.

How beautifully simple, Helen had thought in her wine-happy haze and, though the emptiness of the day had been cut into, she had still thought it so as she sprang out of bed and reached for her dressing-gown.

What had Watty done all day, exactly? He'd made tea to start with. He'd made tea quite often. But he'd been so good-natured and patient, moving from job to job without question, peaceful, unhurried, ready to stop and blether whenever she came near him, but nevertheless getting through a lot of jobs she would have struggled with alone.

He'd freed windows and put up curtain rails, found battens to put under leaning furniture on uneven floors, unstuck the cast-iron canopy of the sitting-room fireplace which had been jammed in and looked as though it was rusted there for ever. And he had stopped the leak in the downstairs loo, which Helen had thought she would have to get a plumber in to do.

'Dirt in the valve,' he had said confidently, and though she had had misgivings when he began to dismantle the ballcock it had only taken him minutes to fix it. 'You'd no' want your water running away like that,' he had told her reprovingly. She had been more worried about the peaty stains in the loo bowl, but had got the message that the resources of the burn were not limitless.

He had measured the cracked window-panes and gone down to the town for new glass, at the same time fetching 'the messages' and adding a few items of his own while he was about it, such as putty, fire cement, a pair of 'nippers', and six cans of beer.

'Ye canna be doing without nippers,' he had announced

so firmly that although Helen thought since she had till
now she probably could in future, she had not had the
courage to argue with him.

He hadn't bought the paint stripper which had been
on the list. Helen had intended – I still do intend, Watty
– to clean old varnish and paint dribbles off the floors, and
wax them. Watty was prepared to resist this idea with all
the determination of the deeply lazy.

'But you'll be getting proper carpets at the end o' the
day,' he had objected. 'These ones' – her treasured Persian
rugs – 'will be just for now, will they no'? They'll never
reach, wait while I show you . . .'

It was clear Helen would be stripping the floors
herself. Though every room had had fitted carpets, as
was manifest by the hundreds of yawning staples around
the skirting boards which made cleaning such a nightmare,
the little house, a century and a half old at least, cried out
in Helen's view for rugs, and she was delighted at the
prospect of having her own in use again. And to have her
furniture about her and her pictures up, each an old and
loved friend. They brought back thoughts of home and
her parents with a more vivid nostalgia than all the weeks
in Withedine had done.

How patient Watty had been about letting her try
things in different places. But Watty didn't care how often
he shifted everything. It was all one to him what he did
while he was there. To be employed again, with money in
his pocket, was good but, though he would have been hard
put to it to find the words, what was better was to have

a share in other people's lives again, to be needed. And to have Catriona there. That, for Watty, put the world to rights.

There had been something about his pace which had been very soothing, Helen decided, leaning her head against the white-washed wall behind her. It had induced a wonderful feeling of time stretching limitlessly away. 'I have the rest of my life to do this,' she had found herself saying, not with great originality perhaps, but with great contentment.

Then she had remembered that she had no such thing. For soon Nadia and Reggie and the children would descend upon her, and not only did she have to have Little Hilltop ready for them, but her own house in order too.

Panic had swept her, as the familiar need to meet other people's requirements rushed back, and with it the inability to see the house as she had so happily seen it till now. Suddenly, unbearably, it looked gloomy, shabby and unwelcoming, its paintwork scarred, its floors uneven and possibly unsafe, its lighting minimal, its stairs steep and narrow. It had no central heating, no double glazing, and there was hardly a socket in the place for the battery of appliances Nadia would consider essential.

Then rare anger had overtaken Helen. She would be sixty next birthday. She had worked, effectively and competently, all her life. She had looked after a large complex of buildings and grounds; she had managed staff and cared for the wellbeing of hundreds of children; she had entertained, far from brilliantly she knew, but adequately, a multitude of guests from cardinals to — she struggled for an alliterative comparison. To crap artists. She giggled, seeing Walter's face.

So how could she be pitched into this sort of alarm by fearing the criticism, which hadn't even been voiced yet, of those closest to her? What was wrong with her; what lay beneath this desire to placate? Hadn't coming here, buying this house against all advice, freed her from that?

Well, she would free herself. This was her chosen place, her chosen life. She would do all she could in the time available to make the little house next door ready for the family, but essentially it would be as she wanted it to be.

A clear sea-green band of light lay along the western sky. Against it the islands stood out starkly, their pattern already beginning to print itself on her eye. Would she have, as she so much hoped, quiet years here in which to put down roots at last?

The phone rang faintly from the hall. Hurrying round three sides of a square to get to it Helen decided this was an arrangement which could be improved upon. Was Reggie getting in touch at last? He and Nadia had been out when she had phoned last night before going to Ardlonach. Perhaps he had tried later — if Phoebe had bothered to pass on her message.

It wasn't Reggie.

'Helen, so exciting — Trudy's gone off to hospital. She'd been saying all afternoon there were sort of pains starting but she was sure they weren't real ones, but when

Fitz came in he told her she was a lunatic and whizzed her off to Fort William at once. He promised to phone as soon as there's news, but I just thought you'd like to know what was happening.'

Catriona's excitement as she poured this out came vibrantly across, and Helen found herself beaming.

'Of course I do! How thrilling, and how good of you to phone. Will you let me know as soon as you hear?'

'The very minute. I'm going to phone Una now, and then Clare. Oh, and by the way, Watty asked me to say he won't manage tomorrow. He's going to Rhumore to help with the hay. They're late this year and Donald's anxious to get it in because the four-day forecast looks bad. Watty will look by in a day or two, if that's all right?'

'That's fine.' Helen had not been aware that any arrangement had been made for tomorrow.

'I'll tell him when I see him, then. Oh, Helen, it is good to have you here again.'

Helen knew that nothing but deep excitement would have made Catriona say such a thing, but she felt very happy as she went up the now carpeted stairs for the umpteenth time that day, and turned on the big brass taps of the high-sided, claw-footed bath.

Catriona phoned before eight next morning.

'Is this too early? Do you mind?'

Helen, already awake and reading, could hear the

thrill in her voice and liked the courtesy which made her remember to ask.

'Of course it's not too early. What's the news? How's Trudy?'

'It's all over. A little boy. Well, a huge boy, Fitz says. Born just after midnight, and everything went well. He weighed — oh, heavens, is it pounds or ounces, what an idiot I am, I can't even think about working it out, lots anyway. But Fitz says Trudy was marvellous. I knew she would be.'

'Catriona, that's wonderful news! I'm so pleased. When can you go and see them both?'

'That's partly why I'm phoning. I wanted to tell you the news of course but, misery and disaster, I've lent Watty the van to go to Rhumore—'

'Don't be silly, I'll take you in. Of course I will, I'd be delighted. Maybe I'll get a peep at the baby.'

'Oh, Helen, thanks. You don't mind? Sadie's offered to do the morning so that I can go, which is really good of her. But it would be such fun to go and see the baby together, wouldn't it?'

Helen thought so, taking the Fort William road a couple of hours later. What could be nicer than sharing this event, spinning away with Catriona on a summer morning, going to see a new baby on the very day that he was born? Much more important than the cottage cleaning which had looked so urgent yesterday.

'What are you going to call him?' she asked a smiling but tired-looking Trudy, whose usually shining mane of brown hair was lank round her shoulders and who had dark circles under her eyes. But she had had a few hours' sleep, and looked blissfully happy.

'Finbarr,' she said composedly.

'Finbarr?'

'Don't squeak like that, Catriona, you'll affect my milk.'

'Oh, please, spare me the mysteries of motherhood. But honestly, Finbarr?'

Trudy giggled. 'Fitz sees no reason to abandon an excellent tradition. If Fitzroy Colquhoun sounds extreme, then why not carry on in the same vein?'

'Helen, talk sense to her.'

'It is a human child,' Helen said, smiling down at the black crinkly hair and crumpled milk-coffee skin against her arm. ('Just exactly the colour I'd hoped for,' Trudy had declared joyfully.) 'It will have a life to lead.'

'Oh well, Finn will be all right. Anyway, you try and deter Fitz when he's in pursuit of a joke.'

It was all so good, Helen decided as they headed for home. The very downing of tools, leaving a hundred jobs waiting, had been an exhilarating freedom. And in Fort William she hadn't even tried to reduce her boring shopping list, instead taking Catriona to celebrate with coffee and cream cakes.

'Jake made a proposition to me last night,' Catriona said as they climbed towards the moor.

Helen was glad Catriona wasn't the kind of passenger to register the sudden change in speed as her foot came off the accelerator. The name itself was enough to jolt her; what Catriona had so casually said was even more startling. Not that, in her case, any innuendo need be suspected.

'And what was that?' Helen managed to enquire, hearing to her disgust that her voice sounded elderly, repressive even.

Catriona turned to her with shy eagerness. 'It sounds possible, I think. But I don't know whether I'm really qualified for that sort of job. It would be a big responsibility. I've been trying to think about it sensibly, but I'm still not sure ...'

'I think I need a few more clues,' Helen suggested, while her mind ran round the possibilities of jobs connected with Jake and remained baffled. And – oh, *what*? – was there a flicker of pique there? What's happened to you, woman?

'It's Percy Macleod's shop, the bookshop,' Catriona explained. 'Well, it's Jake's now. He wondered if I could look after it for him, not that it's open for very long hours, but he'd like everything catalogued as soon as possible. It seems to be in fearful chaos, it always was, I suppose, but apparently there's masses of correspondence piling up from all these weird people Percy used to find books for. Even to do holding letters, explaining why there's a delay, would help, Jake said. I wonder if I'd be any use at that?'

'Of course you would. How can you even ask? You'd be the ideal person to help.' Helen's enthusiasm was whole-hearted. Few people of her acquaintance shared

Catriona's genuine love of books, or the catholic tastes she had acquired by browsing all her life in the library of Glen Righ House.

'Do you think so?' Catriona's doubts of her own capacity were never far away.

'I'm sure. I know you're helping Trudy for the time being, but doesn't she have someone coming on a permanent basis soon?'

Catriona hesitated, looking away across the ridges of bright bracken and the darker patches where the heather would not be out for another month. 'I thought I ought not to keep on being given jobs by my friends,' she brought out at last.

How readily she has accepted that Jake is a friend. The taken-for-granted links of the years.

'So you want Jake to advertise for an assistant so that you can write and apply, enclosing your CV?'

Catriona laughed. 'When you put it like that I can see it's ridiculous. But I do have this feeling that I ought to stand on my own feet.'

'And where else in Luig is Jake going to find a suitable person to help him?' Helen asked. Then wondered whether, ideal as Catriona might be for the job, Jake would make the ideal employer.

Catriona giggled. 'He's put a notice in the shop window. Rather a cross notice. It says, "Assistant required," blah, blah, usual stuff, and then, "Please do not apply unless you have some degree of literacy." The local unemployed think it means a university qualification in some posh subject, Fitz reports, and naturally nobody's applied.'

'Then you will?'

Catriona's smile deepened.

Chapter Thirteen

Catriona was becoming dazzled by her own courage. She had agreed to help Jake in the bookshop, though making the arrangement, to his amusement, as tentative and indefinite as it could well be, and at present fitting it in with her hours at the meal shop, where Trudy still needed her. She was lending a hand at Ardlonach as required, and she was a godmother.

At first she had been more amazed and apprehensive than pleased when Fitz and Trudy asked her.

'Goodness, I couldn't do that, I'd be hopeless. I mean, what about Rebecca, or Clare? Wouldn't either of them be better?'

Clare Macrae was Trudy's closest friend and her own age, and had two children of her own. Rebecca, too, had a daughter, though the child was not Dan's and lived with her adopted family in the Borders. In Catriona's eyes these two were competent, mature people, far better fitted to care for Finbarr's moral welfare than she.

'Not Una?' Trudy had teased, but Fitz, scooping Catriona against him for a second with a long arm, had said in his deep firm voice, 'We want you.'

And now something else was happening in Catriona's life, something she scarcely dared examine in case she was imagining it, something that till now she had thought only happened to other people. Connor Macleod seemed to be chatting her up. It wasn't even a phrase she much liked, but anything else sounded too serious, made too much of an assumption.

She had gone, trembling with nerves, to lunch at Luig House. Parking the van on the smoothly raked gravel sweep on the east side of the house, she wasn't daunted by its size. She had lived all her life in a house even more imposing in its way, and at least twice as old, though Glen Righ had never had the cared-for air of this early nineteenth-century building, with its gleaming rows of windows, its roses and clematis trained up honey-coloured walls. Catriona dimly recalled coming here as a child. Two impressions had survived; the first of a blaze of light and delicate colours, the second of being teased by her brother when they got home for not having uttered a word the whole time they were there. As she stepped into the hall she had a momentary conviction that both memories were about to repeat themselves.

Luig was basically an English country house transplanted to overlook a Scottish sea-loch, and its interior reflected the Italianate tastes the Macleod of the period had acquired during an embassy to Naples. To Catriona it all looked immensely splendid but somehow unreal, as she followed the housekeeper through a long room with pale blue walls and decorated ceiling, some of the original white and gold chairs upholstered in painted silk still in their places.

But what really terrified her was not the setting but the people. She had literally had nightmares about coming to this lunch party, and all morning had swung between determination to phone and say she wasn't coming, and the even grimmer determination not to dodge any steps required of her in 'real life'. She could not have said what she meant by the term. She only knew that other people, all other people it seemed, did things and knew things which seemed to her to belong in a foreign country, and she must cross its boundary.

She would have been surprised to learn how carefully Michaela had planned this first visit on her behalf. Lunch not dinner; Gillian, her gentle-voiced blind cousin, the pianist, least threatening of people, present with her companion; her elder sister Mariotta and her Italian husband, both decided and voluble talkers, banished for the day; and only one other couple invited, people who had known Fergus Finlay for years and would be sympathetic to this shy oddity his grand-daughter.

Catriona was led out of French windows onto a sheltered lawn so luxuriously furnished that she felt for a moment it could have been a terrace on the Riviera. It was flanked by yew hedges clipped as rigidly as walls, and down a widening vista of smoothly mown grass statues gleamed white against semi-circles of flowering bushes backed by majestic Wellingtonias. For a dislocated moment even a distant blue glimpse of the sound seemed exotic and foreign. Catriona thought the statues a bit much.

Languid forms rose to greet her from deeply cushioned white wicker loungers. Although everyone was casually dressed, the women all bore the accoutrements of expensive sunglasses, gold jewellery, elegant sandals and painted toenails, creating a general effect of nerve-racking sophistication.

Catriona had given herself a stern lecture before setting out about it not mattering what she looked like; about never having cared what she looked like; and, less reassuringly, about being unable to do much about it now even if she wanted to. Nevertheless, in a cotton skirt from Oxfam and a pink blouse handed down by Clare, it had been impossible not to feel horribly dowdy in such carelessly glamorous company.

Connor appeared in the middle of the greetings bearing a misted silver bowl of fruit punch, its alcoholic content, with Catriona in mind, at roughly half the level he would normally have mixed in. He was wearing brief denim shorts and a rugby shirt which Catriona, failing to recognise its famous colours, was glad to see was washed out and faded. Though his tan had a reddish tinge to it he looked vibrant and handsome with the sun gleaming on his red-gold hair.

Connor was in a restless frame of mind at present, unexpectedly confronted with an ill-timed gap between liaisons. The girlfriend due to join him at Luig for the traditional house-party for the Twelfth had, without warning, announced her engagement to a member of the outer fringe of their circle so insignificant as never to have been rated competition by Connor, let alone a threat. As the person Connor had his sights on for his next affair was being unusually tedious about keeping promises to sail with her family in August and stalk with her husband in September, he could see himself spending most of the summer alone, by which he meant without a sexual partner. He was sufficiently interested in the projected relationship not to want to commit himself elsewhere in the meantime, and it had occurred to him it might be fun to encourage Catriona out of her farouche shyness. Though she was undeveloped and ungroomed to the point of unattractiveness, her innocence had its own appeal, and there was something titillating in the thought of helping her to shed her diffidence. Vague clichés about emerging from shells and breaking out of chrysalises suggested themselves. Catriona was twenty-five, as he and Michaela had worked out with some disbelief when planning this lunch. More than time she left behind that awkward reserve of hers.

To Catriona it was a huge relief to find that in spite of the unnerving setting all that happened to her was that she was put into a long comfortable chair with her feet up, given a tall glass of what she thought might be Pimms, offered delicious food, and gently drawn into undemanding conversation by a group of people as well-disposed and easy to be with as her own friends. Nothing was expected of her. The sun poured down and the dreamlike sensation of being somewhere in the south of France persisted.

The van drove itself home.

Helen was amused at Catriona's euphoria after the success of this sally into the great world, but from her account of the small party guessed it had been a sort of dummy run organised by Michaela out of kindness. She also suspected it was unlikely to be repeated on such an undemanding level, and couldn't imagine Catriona having much to contribute to the scene at Luig House.

Helen had gathered from Rebecca and Una that Luig was far from the average tweed-and-dogs-and-faded-chintz Scottish country house, lived in all the year round as a family home. It much more met the original meaning of the term, country house as opposed to town house, the place where one stayed for the shooting and stalking but which would be unthinkable at any other season. The guests who came and went in August and September belonged to a set whose natural base was the capital cities of the world, people at the centre of events, whether in politics, power or the arts. The Macleods themselves, even as children, had never regarded Luig as home.

The Macleods other than Jake. Everyone agreed on his love for the place, and it appeared he had been largely brought up there. Helen saw him as quite separate from the others and in spite of her efforts to put him out of her mind he continued to intrigue her. As far as she could see, for he was extremely elusive and disappeared for days at a time doing she knew not what, his present life was lived outside any conventional patterns, relying on minimal human contact.

The only things certain about him at the moment were that he had begun the job of sifting through the rare and valuable nesting litter with which his kinsman Percy had surrounded himself, and that he had taken on Catriona to help him whenever she was free.

Helen had not been sure how that would work out but Catriona, surprisingly, saw nothing alarming in Jake. His way of life seemed natural and even enviable to her, and because he now owned the bookshop she seemed to see him as a slightly less ancient version of Percy. As far as viewing him as a male, she was no more aware of him than she was of Watty, and indeed by now had eyes for no one but Connor.

Her interest there, however, had she known it, was almost equally asexual. She was flattered by his teasing attention and swept away by his looks. She went through the rituals of being seized by breathless pleasure to catch a glimpse of him in the town, of glueing herself to the phone in case he called, of thinking about him at the back of her mind during every waking moment, all the manifestations of infatuation which she had never got out of her system in her teens, but she was still physically unstirred.

Connor, discovering her innocence to be even more

profound than he had supposed, was wary about venturing onto that dangerous ground, with its snares of emotional dependency. In fact, her sexual unawareness quickly bored him, though he was still prepared to give her his attention when not otherwise engaged, and also, his interest having been briefly aroused, felt a certain lazy possessiveness about her. For the rest, she had a quick brain and a good sense of humour and her company, in limited doses, was reasonably rewarding.

Catriona would not have presumed to expect him to spend much time with her, only grateful for what meetings there were. Otherwise she was happily occupied, pursuing her various jobs, spending every moment she could with Finbarr whom she adored and with whom she was becoming daily more confident, and making sure Helen had all the help she needed at Hilltop.

Helen felt she was beginning to settle in. She now said 'Hilltop' with the stress on the second syllable in the Scottish manner, and found herself referring to the smaller house as Wee Hilltop, though she had not got as far as the local pronunciation of Hilltap. She had also begun to distinguish between Luig meaning the town and Luig meaning the estate, something which had confused her at first.

These were tiny signals, she knew, of her deeper sense of integrating, becoming accepted and involved in a way she had never imagined happening so swiftly. It could have been like this, she knew, when they had lived at Tigh Bhan.

These friends had been waiting in the wings, kept there by Walter's thirst for some level of self-gratification in every social exchange.

How completely he had vanished from her life. She could laugh now at the fact that, though she had been the one seeking a divorce, Walter, after his initial angry panic, had agreed without serious protest. As soon as he was sure his life would not suffer any intolerable disruption, he had embraced the idea with unflattering alacrity. Had that startled sense of rejection, of not being needed, been at the root of her inertia in the weeks before going to Shropshire? She imagined so. No wonder she couldn't remember much about them.

The thought of Shropshire brought her sharply back to the one thing she was dreading. No matter how contented she was in her new surroundings, how satisfied she felt with the way her beloved furniture looked so much at home in the simple rooms of Hilltop, or how every exploration of the garden revealed new delights or inspired new plans, like a dark shadow spoiling her pleasure was the prospect of the arrival of Reggie and Nadia with the children.

This is my son I'm talking about, she would remind herself, these are my grandchildren, and she would be horrified by this trepidation catching her unawares yet again. Reggie is coming to make sure I'm all right here. He is being caring and conscientious. He and Nadia want to look after me. But the feeling that Hilltop was about to be inspected and found wanting, and that she herself, by her indifference to its shortcomings, would equally be found wanting, could not be shaken off.

She dealt with it as best she could by abandoning tempting jobs on the main house and concentrating all her efforts on preparing the smaller one, deciding there was time to decorate it before the family arrived, in the hope that lighter walls and fresh paintwork would make other defects less obvious.

'Should I look in *Yellow Pages* for a decorator?' she asked Catriona.

'In *Yellow Pages*?' Catriona sounded as though the idea was wildly indecent. 'You mustn't do that!'

'No? Then what should I do?' Helen didn't imagine Catriona was in touch with the world of painters and decorators. 'Could Watty do it?'

'Goodness no, don't let him loose on it. Well, he might do some of the preparation. We can all help with that. Leave the rest to me.'

'Time's a problem, though. The family will be here in less than three weeks. I really don't mind paying the normal rates.'

But that, it seemed, was not how it was done. Not so much as a point of cost but as a point of honour. And so Helen, who disliked painting and thought she had done enough of it in the thrifty Netherdean years, found herself in honour bound joining the motley squad who came and went during the next couple of weeks, transforming Little Hilltop.

It included Watty and a very seedy mate, who dropped

a cigarette butt into a pile of stripped wallpaper and nearly burned the place down on his first morning; Sadie's husband who was receiving disability benefits for back problems, and discreetly withdrew before Helen, discovering this, could take issue on the matter; Dan McNee who put in four silent and intensive hours of work which covered more ground than Watty and his sidekick together had done in a day; and two friendly hunks of New Zealanders whose girlfriends were working at Ardlonach and who were 'blowing through' on their way round Scotland. They brought a radio and were messy workers, but they were cheerful and willing, and by this time Helen was going with the flow anyway, seeing how dull it would have been to have held aloof from the activity.

Catriona painted for ten minutes and had the dripping brush and run-streaked can removed from her hands, and herself removed to the garden to be cleaned up by a gently chiding New Zealander. Rebecca looked in occasionally, always on the run, and even quiet Una appeared once or twice, though her efforts were only marginally more acceptable than Catriona's. Trudy came every day with Finbarr.

'I'm making the most of taking him everywhere while he's a parcel,' she explained, wielding a useful brush for an hour or two while Finbarr slept in his carrycot in the long grass outside and then was passed round like a toy at coffee break.

Inevitably the job took them up to the last possible

minute on the last evening. Setbacks had included a rotting doorframe which had had to be renewed, crumbling plaster, damp patches on the kitchen walls which required treatment before paint could be applied, and window sills which needed more Polyfilla than paint, and which, had there been more time, should have been replaced. Helen had come to the conclusion that had she called in a professional tradesman the job would never have been finished on time.

As it was the whole working team was there, plus Fitz and Rebecca, laying carpets, reassembling bunk beds, fixing towel rails, putting up mirrors, changing plugs on lamps, and carrying back in the characterless furniture considered by the previous owners suitable for holiday letting. It looked less attractive than ever in its new setting, against pale emulsioned walls and white woodwork, and Helen knew she had made the wrong decision in keeping it. Then she realised she was seeing it through Nadia's eyes, and reminded herself of more sensible reasoning — the house wouldn't be used for more than a few weeks of each year and the family would be in and out of her own house anyway. What was here was perfectly adequate.

But a general dread of tomorrow crept up on her and she was thankful that the planning for the evening had been taken over by Dan. He was a valuable person to have around, Helen had discovered, quietly competent but with a driving energy which got things done at impressive speed. Also, once you got past the chilly exterior, he had more warmth and humour than she had given him credit for.

Tonight he had brought with him not only beer, lager and wine but, as Una's contribution since somebody had to hold the fort at Ardlonach, sausage rolls, smoked-fish patties and some very original pizzas.

It would have been churlish to let worries about the next day spoil the evening. The house was ready, and a lively party was getting under way in which Helen felt surprisingly at home. Also she relished the enjoyable irony of the contrast with tomorrow, and the self she would be then. Grannie. Grannie who had gone off the rails and must be reproved and dragged back onto them.

Well for now Grannie would have another glass of Sauvignon and enjoy herself. Fleetingly, looking round the relaxed noisy group, she wondered if Jake could have enjoyed this. She supposed he would have despised it.

Chapter Fourteen

Reggie and Nadia arrived without the children.

'Oh, poor Sebbie, the Edgethorne Show is the absolute highlight of his year, poor little chap, you wouldn't want him to miss that,' Nadia cried, as though Helen had unreasonably wished to inflict this deprivation on him. 'And these long car journeys are such a drag for them, aren't they? If you *will* insist on living at the other end of the country ...'

Jolly laugh accompanying the gibe. All too familiar exasperation filled Helen, at once, already, as she had promised herself so firmly it would not. As the business of exchanging welcoming hugs (Nadia gripped her like a wrestler, mercifully briefly; Reggie's thin arms in a short-sleeved shirt felt like spaghetti not cooked enough to stick), moving towards the house, getting jammed in the lobby, uncorking themselves into the hall and finally reaching the verandah was achieved, to a disjointed tangle of questions about the children and the journey, thoughts at a quite different level went through Helen's brain.

Had it never been intended to bring the children? But of course it had; there had been the ominous not-quite-warnings, 'I just hope there'll be plenty for them to do up there, you know how bored they get when the weather's bad,' and, 'They simply don't believe me when I tell them you haven't got a computer.' Had that been an indirect order to buy one? So when had it been decided that the children wouldn't come? And why, above all, had she not been told? Helen thought of the struggle Watty and Dan had had with the bunk beds, which had been found to be unsafe and which had had to be strengthened. And for which she had bought new mattresses, fetched from Fort William by Rebecca in the Ardlonach minibus.

No, stop, these are details, trivialities, they don't matter. There would be other visits. But Helen was honest enough to know what lay below her annoyance. When she had seen only Reggie and Nadia in the car she had been overwhelmingly relieved. Now that was a reaction she ought to be worrying about.

'What an impossible place to find,' Nadia was saying, still in the rallying tone which she believed excused her complaints. 'We tried steep hill after steep hill, all just as you described, didn't we, Reggie?'

There is only one road signposted Inverbuie; only one road called Luig Hill.

Reggie, who had learned long ago that it was simplest to accept the party line, because if he didn't thickets of irrational argument awaited him, summoned his protective wooden look and said, 'I'll go and fetch a few things in, shall I?'

'But you'll be next door,' Helen reminded him. Or had that fact been ignored like her directions about finding the house? 'Shall we have tea first?'

'Gracious, it's cold up here, isn't it?' Nadia remarked, pulling her cardigan more tightly about her and glancing disparagingly round the sparsely furnished verandah. 'Reggie and I love Scotland, as you know, but you must admit the temperature's about ten degrees lower than at home. And you could hardly have chosen a more exposed spot to live, could you?'

'Would you prefer tea by the fire?'

Helen knew she had played the view over loch and hills as her trump card, had awaited with confidence the moment when her guests would come through the hall door and exclaim with pleasure at what lay before them. She saw now that she had anticipated the moment as providing some sort of vindication of what she had done. So she felt vindication was needed; had she been hoping, against all experience and reason, for approbation?

'What a poky little room,' Nadia cried as they went into the sitting-room. Not for the first time Helen wondered why her daughter-in-law supposed the rules of ordinary politeness did not apply to her. How offended Nadia would have been by any criticism of her own house half as damning.

'Goodness, I actually think it's colder in here than

outside. Wouldn't you say, Reggie?' Nadia's tone was less jocular as she shivered ostentatiously, and her mouth was beginning to turn down in an unattractive way.

'I should have lit the fire earlier. I'm sorry.'

Helen knelt to put a match to it, annoyed with herself. She had become so used to using the verandah that she hadn't bothered with the fire for several days. That was where she had imagined they would sit, ignoring the fact that it wasn't a particularly bright or warm day. Now, perhaps because the paper had had the chance to get damp, the fire behaved more grudgingly than it ever had before, producing nothing more than a tiny plume of greenish-grey smoke at one side.

'I expect the chimney's badly designed,' Nadia said. 'These old places are always hopeless. Isn't there an electric fire we can put on? Reggie, go and look, there's sure to be something.'

'This won't take a moment,' Helen said, holding up a sheet of newspaper to improve the draught and wishing she could cross her fingers at the same time.

'Reggie, for heaven's sake do something. I'm frozen,' Nadia hissed in what she imagined to be a whisper.

'There's an electric fire in my bedroom, upstairs on the left,' Helen said, giving in. Reggie was clearly going to do as he was told anyway.

He disappeared, looking relieved.

'Shall I do something about tea?' Nadia asked. 'I'm starving after that awful drive. And of course, we are here to make your life easier, aren't we?'

Reminding herself of this obviously made her feel better, and Helen bent her head over the newspaper to hide her smile. Nadia was so outrageous that the only thing to do was laugh. A tiny, tiny stir behind the paper, too tenuous to be called a crackle, cheered her even more. Reggie could be heard blundering about in the room above, the room on the right. No wonder they had had trouble finding the house. He used to be quite bright, his mother thought detachedly. I'm sure I wasn't deluding myself in thinking so. But nowadays he seems to have perfected the technique of shutting down his brain as he leaves the office. Well, he's spent a few years with Nadia. Presumably he'd go mad if he didn't.

Smiling more broadly, she pulled away the browning paper before the first flames caught it.

Reggie appeared with a convector heater whose feet he banged against the door jamb. He pushed the door shut behind him with a thump of his bony backside, causing an acrid mushroom of smoke to billow into Helen's face.

Tea was over, and Helen was pleased that at least the results of her morning's baking (which after very few hours' sleep she would have been pleased on this particular morning not to have had to do) had been found satisfactory. The luggage had been carried into Little Hilltop, and though Nadia had fallen silent as she had looked around her, her lip thrust out, she had said nothing, and Helen had left them to it, in her relief to be alone running like a mad thing across the rough grass back to her own front door.

One thing she had decided. Since Phoebe and Sebastian weren't here there need be no nonsense about early supper. She dialled the Ardlonach number, noting with passing interest that it gave her pleasure just to do so. She had been persuaded to spend more than one evening there while the work was being done on Little Hilltop and supposed, to her amusement, that it had become something which had never featured in her life before, or which she had felt the lack of – her local. It was an even greater pleasure now to hear Rebecca's crisp voice, warming at once to friendliness.

'Of course we can manage a table. Would eight-thirty suit you? Right, we'll see you then, and we look forward to meeting your son and daughter-in-law.'

That's what you think. Helen felt almost light-headed, rescued from an evening of three-handed fencing.

A tall shadow passed the window, bowed down with care.

'Look, Mother, I'm really sorry, but Nadia absolutely refuses to stay in that house ...'

The one thing Helen clung to during the ensuing period of turmoil and held-in tempers, as she fulfilled the demands of hospitality and did her best to find some solution acceptable to Nadia, was that they should have dinner at Ardlonach. In any case, by the time her spare bedroom had been rearranged to Nadia's grudging satisfaction it was far too late to think of cooking. But principally she needed some sane company to steady her and keep events at Hilltop in perspective.

Nadia had refused to stay in Little Hilltop on the grounds that it was damp, it was cold (though in there at least heaters had been on all day) and she had seen a beetle in the kitchen.

'A beetle? An ordinary black beetle?' Helen had asked Reggie blankly.

'Well, you know, she thinks perhaps the house wasn't left very clean. By the last people, she meant, of course. It hasn't been lived in for a while, has it?'

'Not very clean.' Helen had spoken calmly, in her mind's eye seeing the willing workers, half of them unpaid, who had gutted and scrubbed and scraped and painted and polished.

'I mean, I'm sure it is. Of course it is,' Reggie had said hastily, uneasy at that toneless response. 'Only she did see this beetle,' he had added, remembering Nadia's fury.

'She's a farmer's daughter,' Helen reminded him, her eyebrows raised. 'Has she never seen anything more alarming in her life than a beetle?'

'Oh, well, you know what I mean. She's terribly keen on hygiene and all that sort of thing. Likes everything to be spotless.'

'So what do you suggest?'

'Well,' Reggie had had the grace to go a little pink, 'as the children aren't with us I think she'd rather be here in the main house, not the annexe you know. You do have a spare room here, don't you?'

'In my freezing cold house? You know I do, since you went in there looking for a heater earlier. You also know that it's stuffed with boxes that haven't been unpacked yet.'

'Yes, well, I could shift those out, I suppose.'

'And put them—?'

'I expect we could make room somewhere.'

'And then you'll shift another bed in?'

'She won't stay where she is.'

They had looked at each other, weighing the patent unreasonableness of Nadia's behaviour against such considerations as a bearable night for Reggie, a bearable visit for all of them, and the long-term importance of maintaining some level of workable accord.

'Then we'd better get to work,' Helen had said after a moment, adding, 'My poor Reggie,' in a tone which held more irony than sympathy.

Dinner at Ardlonach was a revealing experience. Nadia was on her best behaviour, as she always was when she knew she had gone too far and been lucky to get away with it. Listening to her outbursts of jollity Helen decided objectively that she was more entertaining when she was being unpleasant. At least then what she said stimulated some response.

Rebecca came to join them in the bar, greeting Reggie and Nadia as friends. Helen watched with sardonic enjoyment as her vivid face glazed over at Nadia's detailed account of why the children hadn't come, and was not surprised, whatever the message brought by one of the staff had been, that it required Rebecca's immediate attention.

Dan, coming in to serve for half an hour while dinner was at its height, trained a searching look on Helen as Nadia joked about her escape from the horrors of Little Hilltop, and clearly hoped for an invitation to enter the fray on Helen's behalf.

Una came to the table to say hello just as they were finishing dinner and found little to say. They were about to have coffee and Helen suggested she join them, but she murmured a polite half-heard excuse and slipped away.

Helen led the way down to the Coach-house after dinner in the hope of some company, any company, to dilute Nadia – Reggie she could cope with – and firmly ignoring a flurry of protests.

'But isn't this a public bar?' Nadia demanded too loudly. 'What's wrong with the one upstairs?'

No one uses it after dinner, except boring old residents having a nightcap. But Helen didn't say that. Nadia would doubtless put her in the nightcap category. The two New Zealanders who last night had sat on the floor of Little Hilltop in their ragged paint-streaked jeans, among the lager cans and paper plates, and sung some rather arresting songs in what was to be Nadia's sitting-room, raised their glasses in salute.

If I had been on my own I would have gone across to them, Helen thought. I could have gone quite naturally to speak to them and, I think, been accepted. Ah, a small doubt there. So the woman-about-to-be-sixty has reappeared, has she? She had been absent lately. Nadia, it seemed, had brought her back into existence. But the truth was clear. Helen would have felt more at ease with those two casual laid-back young men than she did with her own daughter-in-law, or her own son. At the very least they would have made her laugh.

Fitz and Trudy appeared soon afterwards, Fitz swinging the carrycot containing a sleeping Finbarr as easily as if it had been a handbag. They too came to say hello, but after a concentrated burst of Nadia decided they ought to take Finn up to Una's room. They didn't come back.

Back at Hilltop, waiting by the dead fire for the bathroom to be free, Helen decided that the whole evening had passed for her at one remove from reality. The friends, the laughter, the flowing talk she had enjoyed so much on other occasions had been beyond her reach. Not that the friendship had been illusory; on the contrary, everyone had been more than ready to extend it to the newcomers, but after each attempt the same conclusion had been reached – the mix simply wouldn't work.

Helen looked restlessly at her watch. How could anyone in the world take so long to have a bath at this time of night? This was exactly the opposite of what she had planned and intended. She had wanted her house to herself, had believed that living in two separate units would suit them all. How transparent Nadia had been in her rejection of the plan, seeing being put into Little Hilltop as being fobbed off with second-best. The 'annexe'.

Helen smiled. Rebecca would have picked up on her use of the word at once, her blue eyes snapping with ironic amusement; Fitz too would have seen through the dramas about the beetles and the damp.

I missed you all tonight, Helen told them ruefully. It was going to be a long two weeks.

But perhaps it was thinking of the quick perceptions of Rebecca and Fitz which made her wake up belatedly to the obvious. Why was she passively waiting while Reggie had his bath – there had been no question as to who would get the one before dinner when Nadia discovered that the immersion only heated enough water for one at a time – when there was a fully equipped bathroom next door where the water had been hot since afternoon? Idiot.

In slippers and robe she went down the steps from the verandah. Cool fragrant air flowed round her. The lights of the town below meant friendly people, the great black humped ridges of the hills across the loch shut out a less congenial world. With an enjoyable feeling of mild rebellion, she went on, down the the successive levels, brushing through the heavy dew and hearing her slippers squelch, taking them off when they became too coldly soggy, liking the icy feel of the wet grass because soon her feet would be stepping into hot water. She opened her robe and let the air, cool as a knife blade, slide over her skin. Then she took off the dressing-gown altogether, and without haste wandered back up through the garden.

Letting her shivering body sink with an exclamation of bliss that was near torture into the steaming pine-scented water it occurred to her, with a sweet simplicity, that if she felt too crowded and hassled in her own house there was no reason why she shouldn't move in here. What an excellent solution, she thought, charmed, and the prospect combined with the caress of the water to soothe away the evening's sensation of working perpetually against the grain. But she was honest enough to know that the new resolve to follow her instincts, and not be boxed in perpetually by other people's whims and demands, more probably had its roots in the final event of a long, jangled, exasperating evening.

For as they had turned out of the Ardlonach drive onto the road below the moor she had seen a dark shape ahead which she recognised. Jake, kilt swinging, was crossing towards the loch. Just a glimpse, caught in the headlights' beam, not even registered by Reggie or Nadia, who were disagreeing about what had been in the seafood cocktail.

'It can't have had shrimps in it. Shrimps make me ill at once, so I'd certainly have known by now.'

Another world, barely guessed at yet, had seemed to Helen to be represented by that figure swiftly swallowed up by the shadows. Her own personal, private world, where she was a woman of fierce feelings, capable of new experiences, ready for unguessed-at adventures. While at the same time, tucked away in the back seat, forgotten in the argument about the shrimps from which Reggie was now trying to extricate himself, she was tedious old mother-in-law, a duty to be dealt with, irritatingly disrupting the activities of real life, like going to the Edgethorne Show.

Chapter Fifteen

'Now we really should get down to business,' Nadia said, pushing back the dishes of a substantial breakfast to clear a space on the table and making a face at Reggie. He got up obediently and went out, and could be heard going up to their room.

'Business?' said Helen. What was going on? And though her voice was calm she was aware of a sudden unaccountable bumpiness in the beat of her heart.

'Well you know, we shouldn't waste time,' Nadia said in a brisk tone, though a small frown — of impatience, uncertainty? — appeared between her eyes, which were too small for the slabby planes of her face.

Is she talking about making plans for what we'll do during their visit? Helen wondered as Reggie reappeared carrying a fat document file, but instinct told her this was too simple an answer, seized upon to stave off — what? She didn't know.

'Now we appreciate that you like living in Scotland

and everything,' Nadia began, taking the folder from Reggie's unresisting hands and flipping it open in a down-to-brass-tacks manner. 'And we can quite see that because you've lived here most of your life you might think it a good plan to retire here. People do get these ideas – Reggie, I had all these in order, what on earth have you done with them? I do *wish* you'd leave things alone – and we can see now it wouldn't have worked having you with us at Roden House. It was too restricting for the children for one thing, and after all it is their home. Still, we did our best, didn't we? So anyway, we thought the best thing would be – now, where's the one I liked? Honestly, this is so annoying when I'd most particularly – the best thing, would be to let you carry on with buying this place since you seemed so set on it, and then when you'd had time to realise – ah, this is the one! *Now,*' triumphantly, 'what do you think of that?'

I hope she runs her committees more efficiently, Helen thought, hoping the sarcasm would help her to subdue her breathing, her speeding heart and the temper which she normally had well under control. She sat very still, her eyes on the stapled pages Nadia was pushing towards her. Below the heading of the top one was a photograph of a two-tone bungalow with a picture window, three dwarf evergreens and a yellow lawn.

'What is this?' Helen thought the strangled effect which holding onto calm had on her voice would have alerted anyone.

Nadia, however, continued to sift busily through the

contents of the file. 'Now, don't worry, if that one doesn't grab you, there are lots of others to choose from. We all have our own taste – be jolly dull if we didn't. But you didn't give yourself time to think when you went mad over this house, so we've worked quite hard, haven't we, Reggie, to find some super alternatives. We started in the village, naturally, but then we thought you might be happy being a bit further away, because you're an independent old thing when it comes down to it, aren't you?' Nadia might not survive this conversation, Helen thought clinically. 'So we looked in town as well, convenient for shopping and so on. Of course you hadn't told us you'd bought a car.' Nadia's tone implied that this moving of the goalposts had been distinctly underhand.

'Nadia, please stop there,' Helen said sharply, then paused, putting her fingertips to her forehead for a moment while she made herself winnow out the unimportant elements of Nadia's speech. The barbs could be ignored; she didn't think Nadia would have imagined for a second that they could hurt. It was essential to stick to the one vital fact. 'I have a house, which suits me in every way, and I intend to live in it.'

'But you must see that's impossible,' Nadia retorted, still rearranging schedules, and speaking in a semi-abstracted tone which showed she had no idea the discussion was over. 'We knew when you refused to come and look this place over before you bought that it would be a disaster, and you see how right we were.'

In spite of her resolve not to be drawn into useless

skirmishing, Helen could not prevent herself from repeating, 'Disaster?' Out of the corner of her eye she saw Reggie shift in his chair.

'Well, I mean,' Nadia glanced round her with a shrug, as though the problems were so self-evident that it was hardly worth enumerating them. 'You haven't got a room that's a decent size, and everywhere's so cold and uncomfortable and dark. I can hardly see what I'm reading at this very minute.'

It was true that the roof of the verandah did make the room on this side of the hall darker. That was why Helen had chosen it as the dining-room. She had not used it till now, and agreed that the single overhead light did little to brighten it on this grey morning.

'And that dreadful little kitchen,' Nadia continued fretfully. Preparing breakfast had not gone smoothly, partly because Helen had forgotten the enormous amount Nadia liked to eat when on holiday. 'There wouldn't be room to put in a proper one even if you wanted to, unless you built out, and that would take up your parking area. Then there's no central heating, no hot water supply, and not a single window that fits. The draughts are appalling – and I suppose up here they call this summer!' Nadia wound up with a laugh, deciding it was time for a joke. Jokes always helped. Helen was looking a bit boot-faced. Nadia hoped she wasn't going to be awkward.

Helen was not in fact capable of speaking for a moment. She knew if she released the anger swelling chokingly inside her it would wash them away on a great tide from which there would be no struggling back.

'And then it really is madly inconvenient for us,' Nadia pointed out, forced to play her ace, and giving Reggie such a ferocious look that he was galvanised into putting in weakly, 'Yes, it is a pretty long journey, you know, Mother.'

Nadia gave a click of exasperation at his apologetic tone. His mother turned on him a level look which made him blush.

'If you'd just look through these,' Nadia coaxed, returning to the safe realms of the material, 'I'm sure there'd be something that would suit you. Some cosy little house with no stairs, no fires, a modern kitchen, a shower for when you find it difficult to get in and out of the bath, because that day will come sooner than you think, and a tiny wee garden that would take no looking after at all. Not like that enormous jungle you've got here. I was looking at it out of our window this morning. I'd had no idea it was such a ridiculous size. You'd need someone with a rotovator to turn the whole thing over, but even then I suppose most of it's too steep. Anyway, we don't have to worry about that, because the whole idea isn't going to work.'

I won't say, 'Not work?' Helen decided. I can't keep on repeating what she says. And suddenly, blessedly, humour returned. Nadia's obliviousness to anyone else's point of view, her sweeping assumptions, her impertinent strictures on Helen's choices, Helen's life, which she didn't even appear to realise could offend, could only be funny.

'How kind of you to bring these,' Helen said briskly, sweeping together the fulsome blurbs without a glance. 'I shan't waste any time looking at them as I happen to be completely satisfied with the house I have. I intend to live here for the foreseeable future, and I'm sorry if that will be a nuisance for you. Now, let's clear breakfast away, and then I suggest that we walk down into the town so that you can see my new surroundings, and afterwards we'll find somewhere nice for lunch.'

'But that's not—' Nadia began angrily.

Helen cut across her. 'Reggie.'

She had not used that tone to him for a long time.

'*Reggie!*' Nadia's voice held a familiar warning but was also strangely uncertain.

Reggie, caught between a rock and a hard place, writhed as though in actual pain. But he couldn't fail to see, in all honesty, where logic lay. 'It is her life, you know,' he muttered to Nadia.

Are those the manners I taught him, Helen wondered with distaste. But he had said enough. 'Good, that's settled then. Now Nadia, if you'll take these? I'll bring the coffee pot. Reggie, perhaps you could fetch a tray? Between the sink and the washing machine.' She had no faith in his capacity to find one for himself.

Helen sat in the garden while battle was joined above. After a moment or two she moved down a couple of sets of steps to be out of earshot. It was chilly and she sat with her jacket wrapped tightly round her, but knew that was as much for comfort as for warmth. Riffles of anger spread through her, each in turn smoothed out with an effort and set aside. This would not be the end of the matter, she knew, and it would be up to her to avert open warfare. But the monstrous effrontery of getting those house details, without consultation or any apparent consideration for her wishes, was going to make her angry for some time to come, and there was no avoiding that. However, the anger must be contained, put on hold. Humour, she knew, was the key to achieving that, and she mustn't forget it.

In fact a moment of amusement helped her now, as an image came of herself flitting about the garden, naked in the summer night. How Nadia would have squawked at the sight, would squawk at the mere idea. A good thing, though, Helen thought prosaically, that her figure was still skinny. Hurrying about the sprawl of Netherdean had kept her trim without ever having to think about it. She had put on weight briefly at Tigh Bhan, with the combination of a drop in activity and eating her share of those ridiculous meals Walter had demanded. There had been little to burn them off, though walking and gardening had helped. In the Edinburgh flat, though she had been less active than ever in her life, she had barely eaten. Once at Roden House long walks in search of the remnants of remembered places had used up some of the empty hours.

Why am I going over all this, she wondered, but knew it was to keep other thoughts at bay. Once Nadia had worked off her temper on poor old Reggie there was a day to get through, and several days after that. On what terms; in what mood? It was not a pleasant prospect.

Nadia being Nadia, the topic of moving back to Shropshire was not relinquished, as Helen had foreseen, and she found herself defusing argument after argument in the days that followed. Reggie was no help. He had shot his bolt, it had landed with appalling success, and he had paid the price. He wouldn't do that again in a hurry.

Some sort of programme was patched together to fill the days. Rather usefully, though Helen could not have imagined being thrilled about it in other circumstances, friends of Nadia's brothers who had been touring further north were in Fort William for two nights, so large portions of time could be consumed in looking after them, visiting the site of the Glencoe massacre, shopping in Oban and looking at Dunstaffnage Castle, though on a squally grey day the latter far from came up to expectations.

'I like visiting these places when the family are living there,' Nadia said discontentedly, her cheeks an unbecoming purple, her thin hair whipped into string. 'You know, when you feel really close to their lives and can see little things like the dogs' graves and school photos and the children's toys lying about – and you can say to yourself, "Gosh, I wouldn't have chosen those curtains!" Do you know what I mean?'

Both wives eagerly assented. Helen never got as far as

their names. Had they too been picked by Nadia for her team in the distant days of school?

After this, history and culture were out, and the lengthy drives Nadia liked (good time-fillers) took them to smokehouses or distilleries or virtually any shop that said Highland over the door. Stocks began to build of tablet, whisky-flavoured marmalade, shortbread, Stag's Breath liqueur, tins of soup with tartan on the labels, sloe gin made in a castle, haggis, venison pâté and heather ale.

Helen took them to Trudy's meal shop, thinking that if Nadia wanted smoked fish she might as well get it there, and as Sadie had just arrived to take over she invited Catriona to join them for lunch. It was not a success. Nadia refused to go to the small restaurant on the other side of the harbour which Catriona suggested, and insisted on going to a hotel where the Scotch broth was like lukewarm dishwater and Reggie's smoked salmon had ice particles on it. Catriona had little to say, and afterwards Nadia dismissed her with, 'Well, I'm not quite sure why *she* was there. Jolly hard work, wasn't she?'

Apart from her strange compulsion for stocking up on food and drink, Nadia seemed to think it her duty to fit out every member of the family, down to the smallest cousin, with Shetland sweaters, Fair Isle mittens, and Tam o' Shanters. Helen thought every woollen shop (Nadia believed the ones that called themselves mills were cheaper) looked exactly like the last, and in fact most belonged to the same chain, but Nadia hunted inexhaustibly for bargains while Reggie drifted along without argument in the sort of mental twilight zone he had created for himself. Deprived of his working-day function, he exhibited all the capacity for torpor and suspension of the vital faculties of a hibernating animal, Helen decided, wondering with guilty dismay if she liked him at all.

Perhaps it didn't matter. Perhaps there was no 'ought to' in such things. And her mind would turn, as it often did, to Jake, with his strong individuality, his independence and freedom of choice. Though she had met him so briefly the impact of his personality had been huge. It seemed she was not alone in feeling this, for she had observed that his name often came up in conversation among his friends, as though they too found him and his life intriguing. Or was she just hyper-alert to picking up the references?

She knew she would never aspire to his level of solitariness herself, and indeed this period of being cut off from them was making her realise how important the new friendships had become, even in so short a time. But personal freedom, options, those perhaps she was learning something about. Not before time, she would remind herself tartly. But the anticipation of being free to return to her new life could not be dampened.

Nadia did in the end abandon her efforts to induce Helen to return south, though she didn't do it gracefully, merely shifting her attack to a new quarter.

'There's so much to be done to the house, if you're really set on staying, that I suppose we'll have to try and get up again sometime in the autumn to help you with it. Goodness knows how we'll fit it in. You'll have to move out temporarily, as there'll be such a lot of major construction work, but you'll be perfectly comfortable in the other house while it's being done.'

Helen, who had resisted as impolitic the tempting idea of retreating to Little Hilltop for the duration of their visit, longed to ask how Nadia could think of condemning her to its discomforts, but instead enquired meekly, 'What major work is that?'

Reggie's newspaper twitched and though it stayed in place he drew his outstretched legs under him as though preparing for flight.

'All the central heating and wiring and the new bathroom and kitchen and everything.' Nadia took it so much for granted that these improvements were needed that she didn't look up from what she was doing – removing the price tags from cashmere sweaters for the children which she could have bought more cheaply in Shrewsbury. 'I do hate these little plastic things, don't you? You always need a pair of scissors in the end.'

'Ah. The central heating and everything.'

'We should probably start getting estimates right away. For their kitchen, Rogie and Wendy got a marvellous German firm in, not cheap but well worth it in the end. I wonder if they'd come this far? It really does make life difficult living—'

'I don't want central heating, and I intend to leave the kitchen as it is,' Helen said.

'No central heating?' Nadia raised her head to look

at her open-mouthed. 'But what about the winter? I mean, it's just about bearable now, though I haven't really had a decent night's sleep since we came because no matter how high you have the heater the draughts cut back the temperature at once, but it will get jolly cold here in the winter. This isn't Edinburgh, remember.'

Much you know about it, Helen thought, remembering the penetrating east coast winds. 'Nadia, how about leaving decisions about my house to me?'

The words were spoken with such deceptive quietness that for a second Nadia didn't realise how brusque they had been. When it dawned on her that she was being ticked off her solid face took on a wounded, crumpled look, and she cried, stung, 'Oh, I say, that's a bit much! When we're only trying to help – when we're doing our very best – when we've come all this way—'

Helen thought she might storm out, but alas, she didn't, settling instead for offended incoherence.

'Oh, dear.' It was the merest resigned breath as Helen accepted the only alternative and went quietly out of the room herself. She made tea, but didn't return with it to steady the afflicted. Instead she sat peacefully sipping it in the kitchen, deciding that Reggie probably wasn't having the best holiday of his life.

At least it was to be a curtailed one. With no meddling to occupy her, with the car already full of shopping, with no compliance or gratitude from Helen to appease her, Nadia soon found that the children, whom she phoned twice a day, were frantic for her to go home.

'After all, poor preciouses, it is unfair to be away in the summer holidays. And Phoebe keeps saying she feels sick. I'm sure Wendy's giving her all the wrong things to eat, though I did explain everything several times before I left and made out the most comprehensive lists . . .'

Would they ever come here again, Helen wondered, as the car rolled away along the lane. She had made it clear that Little Hilltop was available whenever they wanted to use it. That was the deal, and she had not wavered from it. Did she want them to come? Yes, in spite of everything, she did, she was glad to find. Or, more accurately, she did not want the link severed. But she would meet them on her terms, hoping that over the years, with the children especially, some understanding or acceptance could be established.

For now, for the immediate present, she was conscious only of excitement to have her new life, barely explored, barely begun, handed back to her days before she had hoped for that pleasure.

Chapter Sixteen

There was a sense of rediscovery in wandering in the silence through her small kingdom which was almost more enjoyable than first making its acquaintance had been. Then there had been so much underlying worry; had she done something irresponsible; had she wilfully squandered her capital; would the roof be unsound, the fabric riddled with woodworm, were there problems with the drains? Now those anxieties had gone. No major deficiencies or insoluble difficulties had surfaced – whatever Nadia might think! Helen laughed as she crossed the grass to Little Hilltop. (Must mow this as soon as it's dry enough.)

Truly, was this house so bad? She paused in the doorway, which led straight into the sitting-room, and tried to make an objective assessment. Simple, yes, basic even, and not warm it was true, with its thick stone walls and single deep-set window and its air which still, in spite of all that had been done in here, had an unlived-in feeling. But it was fresh and neat, with bright curtains, and clean, if worn, loose covers on the sofa and chairs. Helen felt sad to think of the hard and generous work which had gone into its preparation. What a waste of effort, all in the end to do no more than provide a second bathroom for Reggie or herself. She was here now to turn off the water heater. Then she supposed she must shut the door, and wait and see if the family would ever decide to use the little house. Nadia had more or less ruled out the possibility by her objections, but then, Helen reminded herself, Nadia would be capable of any volte-face that suited her.

Now to work on her own house – and on the garden, which had been ramping and blooming and spreading so exuberantly during these rainy days that it did indeed look like a jungle. Watty hadn't appeared for days. Had he thought he wouldn't be wanted when she had guests, or had he, in the local manner, picked up vibes?

Then a chill thought struck Helen, making her pause on the weedy path. What if Nadia's bossy manner and boring monologues about the children, Reggie's well-meaning but indisputable dullness, had ruined the incipient friendships she had begun to enjoy so much? What if she had been seen in a new light by appearing with her family, who had so signally failed to strike the right note with anyone? What if, more dismaying and for a moment seeming even more likely, she had imagined that easy rapport, and there had never been real friendship in the first place? Of course there hadn't. Everyone had been kind, that was all. They were young enough to be her children. They had been looking after her, as they used to look after Lilias Markie.

Helen blushed as she stood there, remembering how confident she had been that the two young New Zealanders in the Coach-house bar wouldn't have minded her joining them. If she had done so they would surely have groaned to have their evening wrecked, pulling themselves together perhaps to be polite, but privately wishing she'd take herself off somewhere else.

How embarrassing, but how infinitely worse to think of, as inevitably she immediately did, the way she had been so compellingly attracted to Jake. Cheeks burning, shaking her head to ward off these thoughts Helen hurried towards the house. There were a hundred jobs to be done, beds to strip, washing to get going, unpacking still waiting. As she had before, she tried to quell her discomfiture by reminding herself that no one would ever guess the absurdity of her reaction over Jake. It was small comfort.

She worked hard, but the pleasure of at last having no dreaded barrier ahead was marred by new doubts. She cleaned and tidied all morning, never looking out of a window, trying to think of nothing but the job in hand. The phone didn't ring, no one came. She felt very much alone and then was angry with herself — wasn't that what she had wanted?

Then, disturbingly, she saw that in a wider context. Alone at retiring age, her useful life over, trying to push her way into a community where she had no ties, had made no input over the years ... Nadia was right – who would want her?

She had lunch, then, as a solace that had never failed her yet, decided to unpack the last boxes of books, now stacked along the wall of the dining-room. She was soon absorbed, the life-long magic working its charm. Among the leather-bound Collins Pocket Classics she came across her copy of Mrs Henry Wood's *Lord Oakburn's Daughters*. She sat back on her heels. She had promised to lend it to Catriona when she came across it. And surely among this lot would be – yes, here it was, *The Conscript of Waterloo*, Erckmann-Chatrian. Helen smiled. Who but Catriona would read him now, but she had said she minded parting with him when the Glen Righ library was sold, and Helen had made a mental note to put it aside for her when it came to light.

On an impulse she got to her feet, went through to the kitchen to find a bag, folded the slim books into it and pushed it into her jacket pocket. Without bothering to lock the house she went out of the front door and down through the garden. Ever since moving in she had been meaning to investigate the way out into the path below, but every trip into the town had involved shopping for things too heavy or cumbersome to carry back up the steep hill. Now, her spirits rising in the far from summery air, for the weather had performed poorly for the whole of Nadia and Reggie's visit, she pushed nettles and long grass flat with the side of her foot and, arms held high, avoided the rain-laden trailers of honeysuckle and the branches of seedling elders to reach the dyke. She wouldn't waste time today struggling with the wire that secured the gate. The latter didn't look too robust but the dyke did. She found toeholds and climbed up with ease then, making sure no stems would catch her feet, vaulted down, landing with perhaps a slightly heavier thump than in former times. Her shoes were soaked, her trousers dark with moisture, and it occurred to her that a passer-by might have viewed her arrival in the lane with surprise, but she felt purposefulness buoy her up again.

The path led down between neatly pointed stone walls. Perhaps it was private, perhaps she would wind up in somebody's garden and have to retrace her steps and go via Luig Hill after all, but a cheerful instinct told her she would have to do nothing of the sort.

And so it turned out. The path, crossing a road here, zig-zagging round gardens there, changing in character as it went lower, took her all the way to the harbour, something which, on that day and in that mood, seemed satisfactory out of all proportion. But again, who cared what pleased her or what didn't? She was accountable to no one.

Catriona was not in Trudy's shop, and nor was Sadie. A new face was behind the counter, and Helen had a strange disjointed feeling of having been out of touch with everything for much longer than she had. Of course that wasn't true. In fact Reggie and Nadia had originally planned to stay for three more days, but all the same Helen found herself groping for a moment to work out when this job was meant to end for Catriona. And if this was the new permanent person then she would have moved into the flat above. So where was Catriona living?

Helen introduced herself and was received with reserve. Trudy's new assistant, a serious and solidly built girl (Helen thought she could just be called a girl), gave the impression that she would prefer people to come in to buy her wares rather than on social quests. She revealed, after a second's hesitation, that her name was Glynis, and Helen found herself thinking that a friendly Scot might have been a better choice, then reproved herself for making such a judgement. Trudy had said she was looking for experience, reliability and maturity; Glynis would probably turn out to be ideal.

She was not effusive, however. Catriona might be at the bookshop, she didn't really know. 'I don't think it opens proper hours though, not like a real shop.'

'And do you happen to know where Catriona is living?'

'Sorry, haven't a clue. It was Sadie who showed me the ropes,' Glynis explained, not quite shrugging.

'I expect I'll find her. Thank you for your help. And I hope you'll be happy in Luig.'

'It's been a bit slow so far,' Glynis said dubiously. 'Maybe it will pick up a bit when the shooting and all that starts.'

This was a business rather than a social assessment, Helen concluded.

'Yes, Trudy generally does well with the big houses and hotels,' she agreed, doing her best, but noting that she felt defensive. Whether on behalf of Trudy, Luig or the Scottish way of life she couldn't have said.

Not tremendously impressed, she went out onto the cobbled space in front of the shop. The row of cottages of which it was part stood on the approach to the quay, and flittering sunshine breaking through the clouds lured her out along it. The wind was brisker as she left the protection of the buildings and she stood for a few moments with her eyes closed, letting it cream over her face, smelling of salt and boats and fish, threaded with the cries of the gulls above engine noises, the clunk of a mallet, the rhythmic sound of someone sawing. When she opened her eyes again the day was brighter and she stood, happiness filling her, looking across the choppy water of the little harbour to the hills beyond, where the bracken was now a darker green and the heather was just coming into bloom. It was the view from her own windows, altered only by looking at it from sea-level, yet she felt as though she had been cut off from it for far too long, incapable of seeing, smelling, feeling. She knew this was exaggerated, but she also knew it was true.

Feeling refreshed, elated, ready for anything, she turned back towards the town.

Catriona was absorbed at the computer, oblivious of her surroundings, the gloom, the dust of years, the tottering piles of books stacked haphazardly around her in the tiny back room. Books climbed up the walls and up the grimy window, obliterating most of the light, which was further reduced by a dark green blind stuck crookedly halfway down the top sash. Outside, across a narrow vennel, a high wall of damp-streaked granite completed the job.

An old-fashioned angle-poise lamp, ungainly as a praying mantis, craned from the top of the rolltop desk where the computer squatted awkwardly. Its brown twisted flex coiled across the floor to a single socket glutted with adaptors and plugs. There was a low clay sink against the back wall and on the dank wooden draining board stood a dust-furred kettle and a carton of yesterday's milk.

Catriona was deeply happy. Jake would be back in a couple of days, as nearly as anyone could ever guess his movements, and she thought he would be pleased with her progress. She had barely left the computer since Glynis's early arrival had freed her from the less enthralling job of selling herbs and oatmeal, leatherwork and frozen mackerel. It had been a surprise when Jake had decided to go for the computer. She would have thought it the antithesis of his ideals, which seemed to be based on living in as fundamental manner as could be achieved.

Apart from the contact in the shop she had met him several times on the hill, for like her he went out whenever he felt like it, at any hour of the twenty-four, and she had been impressed not only by his minute familiarity with the landscape, but by his skills in adapting its resources to his needs. He possessed a wealth of knowledge about plants and their uses, and a range of information about all aspects of the area, which there had barely been time for more than tantalising glimpses of so far. At first, coming across him on the moor, Catriona had wondered if he minded her presence, or felt it to be an intrusion, but on each occasion he had talked to her easily, never appearing to be in any hurry, and more than once he had taken her with him to locate some special plant, describing to her in fascinating detail its properties or application for healing or survival. He was as interesting as Percy had been, and she couldn't see why he was generally considered brusque and short-tempered. A coarse bugger, in local terminology. As far as she could see, he just didn't like frittering his time away in pointless chat, and she could understand that.

She was improving on the social front herself though, she thought with a complacency unusual for her. Looking back on her time in Dundee she could see that the only test she had satisfactorily passed had been the course itself. For the rest she had hidden away, sitting out the lonely months, and that could hardly be called much of an achievement, though it had seemed so at the time.

But now ... A smile hovered for a moment, curling a mouth which was mostly anxiously set. Her fingers flickered over the keyboard, accurately transferring to disk the minutely detailed information Percy had built up on thousands of reference cards in his scholarly writing, but her mind was elsewhere; was at Luig House.

She was beginning, tentatively, to enjoy her visits there, free of the admixture of alarm which had made the early ones such an undertaking. No one was hostile, no one expected anything of her. The talk always raced along, in the way she was accustomed to with her own friends – in fact the two circles overlapped – and if she had nothing to contribute no one minded or appeared to notice. And Connor was such fun. Her fingers paused. He made her feel – how could she put into words how he made her feel? Grown-up. Feminine. Alive.

She smiled again, flipping over the card for *Joseph Crawhall's Shooting Notebooks*, then realised she had entered its details twice without noticing. Deleting rapidly, she mocked herself for being so pleased, at twenty-five, to feel grown-up. That was pathetic. Then her mind turned to the second word; feminine. The sight of Connor coming into a room, the doubt and expectancy as she wondered if he would come to talk to her, the profoundly disturbing pleasure when he did, all these were feelings she had assumed other people experienced but had accepted were not for her. She was different. She had always known that, and with her new perspective she could see how far from normal that isolated existence at Glen Righ with her grandfather had been. But her response to Connor had made her realise, with a vast relief, that after all she could be like other people. She had no views as to where these feelings might carry her, had no specific longings, in physical or any other terms. It was enough for now that, two or three times a week at least, she could be sure of seeing—

The raucous jangling of the bell as the shop door opened made her jump so violently that a great space

appeared on the screen. A customer. They were so infre-
quent – the musty contents of the window, the damp-
spotted sporting prints, the leather-bound tomes, the dead
flies, did not appeal to the average strolling tourist – that
she felt wildly disorientated for a moment, struggling to
organise her thoughts, her face, her smile.

But it was Helen standing inside the door, Helen without the overpowering daughter-in-law who never stopped
talking and who had made everyone feel so protective on
Helen's behalf; Helen without her gangling, ineffectual
son, who by contrast never had anything to say for himself
at all; Helen on her own again, her thin intelligent face
keen and happy, her deep-set eyes smiling.

'How lovely to see you!' Catriona exclaimed, with no
idea of how radiantly her own face had lit up.

'I went to the meal shop—'

'Glynis was free a week earlier than she'd expected and
so she – but never mind that, what about you? Where are
– your—?' She couldn't even remember their names, so
thoroughly had they been dismissed.

'They had to go back a few days early,' Helen said
composedly, and Catriona laughed at her tone, stepping
forward to give her a quick clumsy hug.

It was a gesture absolutely foreign to her, and Helen,
responding, thought a little blankly, Um, what does that
say about my precious son and his wife?

'But where are you living? The rather repressive Glynis
said you were working here full-time, but she didn't know
where you were staying.'

'She's a bit heavy, isn't she? I'm not sure Trudy had bargained for that. But yes, darling Jake has given me a proper job, and guess what, come and look, something I never expected and I'm so excited about it ...'

She actually took hold of Helen's sleeve, and Helen decided that whatever she was about to be shown must be thrilling indeed to prompt this contact. But she knew the thought was cloaking a sharp reaction to that 'darling Jake'. Only Catriona, with her strange unawareness, her view of him as some sort of junior Percy, could use the term so carelessly.

'Look! Isn't it marvellous?'

Helen had never thought computers rated much wild enthusiasm, though she had determinedly beaten down Walter's resistance to having one in the Netherdean office and had found it a huge boon.

'Jake wants the whole inventory put onto disk. It will make such a difference. And he's letting me do it, he's trusting me.'

'And you're coping?' Small need to ask; Catriona's happy face and the slim index finger, grubby from her excursions among the books, which she laid lightly on a key without depressing it in a gesture of love, answered that question. But the other had not been dealt with.

'Are you staying with Trudy?'

'With Trudy?' Catriona looked puzzled for a second, as though turning her mind with an effort to practical matters. 'Oh, no, not with Trudy, though she did suggest it. There was no need, Jake said I could stay here.'

'Here?' Their surroundings were unprepossessing to a degree, and Helen suspected that whatever domestic accommodation was available would be just as uninviting. 'Is there a flat above, like at the meal shop?'

'Oh, no, I mean here.' Catriona nodded to a dark green bundle in a corner and returned her attention to the screen. 'It's brilliant being given the chance to put in a whole program like this myself—'

'You're sleeping in this office?'

'It's going to take time of course, but I can start as early as I like in the morning and go on as late as I like at night. I think Jake's going to be pleased at how far I've got. What did you—?' Some quality in Helen's tone dragged Catriona out of her concentration on the computer. 'Oh, yes, Dan lent me the sleeping bag and stuff. It's very handy sleeping on the job. Water, kettle, everything I need.'

'Loo?' Helen sounded seriously unconvinced.

'The old outside one. Don't worry,' Catriona assured her, as though remembering suddenly that other people might view her living conditions in a less positive light than she did, 'I did clean it.' Her nose wrinkled and she grinned. 'I had to.'

'But Catriona—' Helen stopped herself. How unthinkingly she had been ready to rush in with conventional protest and condemnation. Was that part of being the age she was? The point was on her mind today. 'What about baths?' she asked, and this time Catriona turned to look at her properly.

'Helen, honestly, it's OK. Don't look so horrified. You know I hate nesting and house-keeping and all that stuff.'

'But where are your things?' Helen couldn't quite abandon her concern, but knew each question was more nugatory than the last.

'I don't really *have* things,' Catriona said. 'I don't want them. My books are at Trudy's,' she added, seizing on this as though sure to reassure Helen. 'Really, nothing could suit me better for the time being, though I will look for something else, B and B, or a bedsit or whatever.' From the vagueness of her tone Helen knew she was merely trying to please.

'Oh, Catriona.' She took a last look round the dirty, dismal, crammed room, and gave up. 'Though it's coals to Newcastle if you're living here, I brought you a couple of the books we'd talked about.'

'How kind of you to remember! Oh, lovely, how good it is to see old friends again. Oddly enough, I'd just been dipping into *East Lynne*, so this will be . . .'

'Are you going to start it now?' Helen asked in amusement. Catriona, still standing, her voice trailing away, looked already lost to the world.

'Of course not.' But the little pat with which the small volume was laid aside suggested otherwise. 'Anyway, I must stop soon. What time is it? I promised Trudy I'd go up for tea, so that I could see Finn before he goes to bed. Come too, Helen, won't you? We've all missed you while you've been — so busy.' A glancing smile from under the heavy fringe hinted at a different choice of word. 'There's such a lot to catch up on, and Finbarr looks terribly grown-up by now.'

'Are you sure Trudy won't mind?' But it was purest polite form. Helen knew she was eager to slip back into life-before-Nadia, to see the baby, hear the news, be herself again.

She also thought a chat with Trudy might be timely.

Chapter Seventeen

In the event it was not Trudy Helen talked to, but Fitz. Trudy had proved to be, as might have been expected, a very laid-back and down-to-earth mother, handling Finbarr with a robust casualness which he took happily in his stride, but she was also a very absorbed one. In a drawing-room once elegantly furnished by Fitz, with cool colours, and furniture carefully chosen to be at home in the well-proportioned late Victorian house, a froth of small fluffy toys now mingled with packs of Pampers and tubs of baby-wipes, and Trudy was quite content among friends to expose a large breast and feed Finbarr as and when required.

As Trudy and Catriona were about to go through, for the second time, a thick stack of photographs of Finn from hour one, Fitz appeared in search of tea. Restricting himself to folding his immensely tall frame to bestow a beaming smile on his son, and trace a long black finger with great gentleness down the smooth, much paler cheek, he straightened to take in the scene and comment to Helen, 'I think we're in charge of catering.'

He didn't add 'again', but Helen guessed he might well have done. His practice was a large and scattered one, including many patients who could only be reached by boat, and his days were busy, and she wondered if Trudy's slapdash ways, even more in evidence since Finbarr's arrival, were not sometimes a trial to orderly Fitz. But his delight in his son was evident, and he seemed as ebullient as ever as he assembled a tray for tea with reaches of his long arms which made him look like some antique signalling device, at the same time taking the chance to welcome Helen back to the fold.

'We missed you, you know,' he said, in his deep cultured voice. 'Lapsang today, yes? Though it may provoke complaints from other quarters.'

'They just didn't fit in, did they?' Helen found herself able to say, pausing in filling a plate with stout bars of muesli stuck together with apricots and nuts, which Trudy evidently bought wholesale.

'Did you mind?' Fitz didn't bother to deny it.

Helen considered that. With Fitz, as she had found before, one did consider one's answers, with confidence in their being received with the same honesty.

'I felt it was my fault somehow, as mothers do.'

Fitz turned to acknowledge the answer with a wide flashing smile. 'He doesn't have any alternative, you know.'

Helen set down the plate, forgetting it, grateful that

with these friends so much could be overleapt. 'When Nadia's not there he's different. At least, that's not quite true. When he's not in Nadia's orbit, not in the home situation, he's different. He's successful, competent, good at his job.'

Fitz nodded, apparently content to let tea wait and to give Helen his full attention. 'He doesn't want to fight every day, or every minute, of his life. You can see that a compromise would be essential.'

Helen's set expression made her face angular and bony. 'Walter more or less wrote him off when he married Nadia, whom of course Walter couldn't abide, but I'd like to be able to like him,' she said after a moment, with a little huff of wry humour at all she had admitted.

Fitz nodded, reaching a long hand to grip her arm. 'He had to choose. He's probably not unhappy. And you don't seem an unhappy or lonely person.'

'I'm not.' Helen's face broke into a brilliant smile. Today, she was absolutely certain of that.

'Can you just let it be like that?'

She gazed into the dark eyes, full of understanding and compassion. And suddenly she knew that she could. She was free of the last niggling tug of doubt and failure. Reggie would remain as he had, after all, been for all his adult years, separate from her life, at a distance. They did not need each other's presence. Whether that was her fault or not hardly mattered. She was free of the responsibility for him as she had freed herself, more deliberately and terminally, from Walter. Free to lead her own life, while retaining the formality of contact. For she needed that too.

'Fitz.'

He turned to fill the teapot, smiling. Her considering tone told him that the subject had been rendered harmless, put away, and that this was something else, something new and more promising. 'Yes?'

'About Catriona.'

'Ah, Catriona.'

'She's sleeping on the floor at the bookshop.'

Fitz laughed, the big free booming sound making Helen laugh too. 'I told you we were glad to have you back among us.'

'I have a spare house.'

He turned to beam at her over his shoulder, but said nothing.

'Is it that obvious? Am I the last person to think of it?'

'Not at all.' Fitz put the teapot on the tray and took hold of the tray but didn't lift it. 'Most of us assumed, I think, that Little Hilltop would be let, as it had been before.'

'No, I shan't be letting it. But — with Catriona — I don't know. I dread to seem to intrude, or to impose conventional judgements. The way she lives may be right for her.'

'No,' said Fitz simply.

'She's refused to come here, hasn't she?'

'That's different. That's staying with friends. You

could offer a business arrangement. The cottage is a separate unit.'

'Do you think she's ready to settle for — for the job in the bookshop?' Helen was momentarily flustered to find it impossible to say Jake's name casually. 'She seemed to feel when she first came back that living in Luig was an easy option she shouldn't settle for.'

'I think the challenge of sorting out the chaos Percy Macleod left behind and getting the whole issue onto computer has made her feel it's a real job. And once that's done — well, I can't think of anyone better suited than Catriona to replace him, odd though that may sound.'

Will Jake not be here to look after things himself? Hadn't the idea been that because he had inherited the business he would make Luig his base from now on? Helen knew she couldn't ask these questions.

'I'd love to have her at Hilltop,' she said wistfully. But she could not be certain, on this day of seeing her son drive away, with no contact achieved in all the days they had been together, and not knowing how long it would be before she saw him again, that the idea was not attractive for selfish reasons. 'I shall think,' she said, chiefly to herself.

'Always an excellent idea,' Fitz teased her, picking up the tray. 'Now how about this tea?'

She was smiling as she followed him.

Catriona had walked nearly all the way home with her, showing her a short-cut which saved them going to the bottom of the hill and up again. Helen, her wonderful idea fizzing inside her like sherbert, had managed not to mention it yet, though she was beginning to see it would take a good deal to stop her suggesting the plan now. But she wanted to have time to herself to look at it, as far as she could, from Catriona's point of view, and Catriona's point of view was a highly individual one.

In spite of the walking she had already done today she was drawn out again into the last of the evening light, after a supper which consisted of nibbling round the edges of the food mountain left in the fridge by Nadia. How pleasant it had been to be able to have a bath without planning or waiting or going next door, to put salad and salmon mayonnaise (first making the mayonnaise and dropping the jar Nadia had bought into the bin) onto a single plate and taking it round the corner of the verandah to sit in her one hard chair, in silence, alone.

Nadia had said — laughingly, of course — that the verandah was built like a bus shelter. She had wanted Helen to pull it down and have a 'proper' conservatory added. Helen thought in view of the way the ground dropped away it might have ended up much the same shape as the present one, but had refrained from saying so.

After a supper even more prolonged than when Reggie and Nadia had been there, since she fell into *Peter Abelard*, hungry to read a dozen reclaimed old friends since unpacking her books this afternoon, she went along the lane and turned up onto the last rise of Luig Hill, the road empty now that the day's tourist traffic was stilled.

Would inviting Catriona to move in next door destroy the solitude she was so much relishing again? She hadn't thought of that aspect till now, and examined the discovery with interest. She had been so thankful to have her house to herself once more, and yet she had been eager to offer Catriona the one next door as soon as the idea had occurred to her. But might such an arrangement overload a friendship already somewhat improbable? Their lifestyles were very different, for a start. Then she remembered Catriona's smile that afternoon when she saw who had come into the shop, remembered her own relief to find her, and knew the pleasure had been real on both sides. Why question it?

She turned off the road down a winding line of turf, more a gap between stretches of heather than a path. Cars and coaches stopped on the crown of the moor because of the spectacular view, in a spot worn bare of grass and dredged with rubbish, but she had never met anyone walking here. She didn't intend to go far, tired after a day of varied emotions, but she had minded her freedom to walk being curtailed in the last few days. One of her greatest delights in living at Hilltop was being able to step more or less out of her door into this emptiness, and she had covered miles in the early mornings and the quiet evenings since she arrived. It was one of the things she had missed so much when Tigh Bhan was sold, and one of the things she had found herself oddly homesick for in the so different Shropshire countryside.

The ground fell away in one of the lips which broke

its long descent to the sound. Here Helen had found a rock perfectly adapted to her not very well padded rump, and here she sat, letting thoughts circle and drift. All day, tucked away at the back of her mind, had been the realisation that now she was alone again there might be the chance of seeing more of Jake, or even learning more about him, for she needed facts to feed on, and no amount of castigating herself for being absurd would alter that. She sat quietly, dreaming, as darkness gathered over the hills far to the west, while the long arm of the sea which intervened held on and on to its silver light.

'Are you sure you're ready for this?' Rebecca enquired, a sparkle of wicked amusement in her dark blue Urquhart eyes.

'Have I been rash?' But Helen didn't sound seriously perturbed. She had had no doubts since Catriona had finally made up her mind to move into Little Hilltop. Helen had approached the suggestion with caution, dreading being seen as bossy grown-up insisting on a 'better', that is, more conventional arrangement, anxious not to encroach upon the fragile independence it had cost Catriona so much to establish. Even so, Catriona had become very pink the moment she realised what Helen, in her efforts to be both tactful and business-like, was so clumsily saying.

'I couldn't do that,' she had said at once, with a brusqueness which showed how much the mere idea alarmed her. 'It's very kind of you, Helen, but I'm sorry, I couldn't, really not.'

They had been in Helen's kitchen, gathering together tomatoes and taramasalata and bread for a late supper for Catriona, who had just come off the hill after a trot of several miles to get the dust of the bookshop out of her lungs. Catriona had actually dropped the breadknife and gone to the door, so violent were the negative feelings, instinctive, hardly understood even by her, which instantly seized her at this proposal.

'Could we talk about why you feel that?' Helen had asked, not sure the quiet question would be enough to check that urgent flight, but knowing that if Catriona refused all discussion now it would be difficult to raise the subject again.

To her relief Catriona had paused in the doorway, standing with her head bent, her back to Helen.

'I must do things on my own,' she had said at last in a muffled voice.

'I understand that,' Helen had replied gently, and had waited, giving her time.

After a moment's silence, which gave Helen the chance to discover just how disappointed she would be if this plan came to nothing, Catriona had turned with an awkward lift of her shoulder, and said, not looking up, 'I always seem to be different from other people. I always seem to need looking after. Other people have ordinary lives with families and homes and proper jobs, and they have enough to spare to give, and help and – oh, and a million other silly things.' She had raised a hand in a gesture pleading with Helen not to say anything yet, and then rushed on. 'It's everything. Ordinary life. Like people asking you to dinner and it's all perfect, from the chairs to the wine glasses, from the smoked salmon mousse to the coffee. It's not that I want all that,' she had insisted passionately, looking up at last, 'I absolutely don't, but then I wonder why I'm different, why I seem on the outside of things, why I do the taking all the time, why I can't be the one doing the helping and giving ... ?'

Every instinct had made Helen want to rush forward and gather her up in a huge hug of comfort, but she had resisted, feeling that to do so would merely reinforce what Catriona had been saying, that she roused an impulse to console as a child did. For an uncertain second Helen had hung there helpless, almost afraid, at the glimpse of all kinds of tangled ramifications which this tortured outburst had provided.

'But you do give,' she had said, without consciously choosing this one salient fact. 'You give all the time, but you don't realise it, because you give in a different way from other people.'

It had been enough to capture Catriona's attention, and open the way to talk. Helen had managed to draw her back into the mundane business of preparing supper, deciding what she wanted to drink, going through to the sitting-room, building up the fire. And though Catriona had retreated from the searing frankness of her initial reaction they had talked into the small hours.

Helen had learned more of Catriona's grief when, as a child, she had lost her adored elder brother, her only companion in the lonely life of Glen Righ; had learned more too of Catriona's anxiety as her grandfather's instability increased and her own ignorance about how to care for him tortured her, and her fears for the future grew. She heard more details of the dark times in Dundee, realising how completely Catriona's emotional life had been put on hold, the friendships she had made superficial, the surroundings she had found herself in deeply alien.

And gradually they had talked their way round to the question of Little Hilltop.

'Think of it as digs, like any other digs,' Helen had said. 'I've no use for it, and it would be a shame to see it standing empty after we've all worked so hard on it.'

'But you could let it for holiday accommodation and make vast amounts of money,' Catriona had objected.

'I've no intention of using Little Hilltop for holiday lets. There's nothing I should hate more. And I wouldn't rent it to anyone I didn't know as it's virtually part of my own house. It has to be someone like you, or it stands empty.'

'But won't you need it when your family come again?'

'You could move out while they were here.' Helen dealt with this summarily; if it ever happened it would not be soon.

'Then I could sleep at the bookshop again.' Once the solutions became spartan and singular Catriona had brightened up immediately. 'But I must pay you properly.'

'Of course.' Helen hoped that Jake in his turn was paying Catriona properly and decided she must put out some feelers to find a balance between nothing, which was what she wanted to charge, and a rate Catriona would feel didn't damage her pride. As Catriona had seemed to think Helen's agreement on this point constituted a bargain, and abandoned the subject, there was plenty of time to arrive at some mutually acceptable amount.

Now Helen, lunching at one of the tables outside the Coach-house, having set out for a short walk and been drawn by a resplendent morning to forget all chores and walk down the headland as far as Ardlonach, was unruffled by the teasing. She had been warmed and pleased when Una and Rebecca, bringing out their own lunch once serving was over, had come without question to join her.

'We're so delighted for Catriona,' Una said at once. 'With Jake cleverly giving her a job which combines books with her new computer skills, and you providing the ideal accommodation, we're all hoping she'll forget about leaving.'

'Not that anyone's spelling it out to her,' added Rebecca.

'No, she's liable to be touchy about it,' Una agreed with her fleeting smile.

Rebecca grunted, filling up Helen's glass from the open bottle of house wine she had picked up as she came through the bar. 'One hint that we're all agreeing it's a "good thing" and she'll be off at once, convinced it's a conspiracy.'

'We mustn't let that happen,' Helen assented, her spirits going up another couple of notches with the cold wine and the hot sun and the incomparable comfort of being with people who spoke one's own language. 'I'm delighted on my own behalf, never mind Catriona's.'

'Your life will change,' Rebecca warned her. 'You realise that, don't you?'

'That might not be altogether a bad thing,' Helen answered with composure, and Rebecca laughed and raised her glass in salute.

Chapter Eighteen

Though at the last moment Helen had pangs of doubt about what she was doing, realising how short an interval of solitude she had allowed herself, she soon realised that no neighbour could be more unobtrusive, indeed elusive, than Catriona. She lived her life in a style that opened up new vistas of unprogrammed time for Helen, bringing a fresh slant of simplicity to habits long settled and unconsidered.

Although in theory Catriona had a conventional working timetable, at the bookshop from ten till four on most days, she gave no impression of being committed to a routine. She came and went at any hour, sometimes walking for miles before opening the shop, or going down before dawn to work on the cataloguing, sometimes sleeping till it was almost time to start and scrambling over the dyke and tearing away down the path at the last minute. She would work if she felt like it till the small hours, or spend the evening at Trudy and Fitz's, or at Ardlonach, where she still did the occasional stint in the bar. She also had, as Helen discovered, a whole other world of activities and acquaintances, starting with Watty and his chums, but including the fishermen who sometimes took her out with them, the townsfolk who had known her since she was a child, and ex-estate workers from Glen Righ, now often elderly, housebound or alone. Sometimes it seemed to Helen, learning about them from passing references, that they were more important to Catriona than anyone, that here she felt at her most confident and natural.

At the other end of the scale, in terms of feeling comfortable and secure, though this she talked of to no one, Catriona was still going through hoops over Connor Macleod. Whenever she ran into him by chance he was so warmly pleased to see her, carrying her off for a drink or bar lunch, or pulling up the car to talk as though he had all the time in the world, that she was always left feeling dazzled by fresh hope. Yet he never made the next move, never phoned, never 'took her out'. Invitations to Luig always came from Michaela, and Catriona had not had the courage yet to accept any except for lunch or tea, feeling that dinner, with other guests ever present, with the impossible question of clothes, was not only too daunting, but wrong for her, not her scene.

Helen quickly learned that the van parked in the lane was no indication of Catriona's presence. She might be off on foot, have lost the keys or run out of petrol. On the other hand, when the van was absent it didn't necessarily mean Catriona was too, since she and Watty had a deal going about shared use and maintenance. Once Helen, noticing Catriona's washing out in the rain (and although scanty it represented just about all her wardrobe) and deciding it would not be too officious to take it in for her, rushed into Little Hilltop with the damp bundle in her arms to find Catriona stretched out on the sofa reading *Lost Sir Massingberd*.

A house, to Catriona, was nothing more than a cupboard where she kept her belongings and incidentally slept. And those belongings, apart from the books which she brought from Trudy's and set out before doing anything else, were minimal and of little importance to her. She had accumulated none of the equipment most bedsit dwellers regard as desirable and her few clothes were mostly secondhand, revealing nothing of her personality — or everything, Helen amended.

So Catriona lugged in her heavy leather case, which stood open on the floor and was unpacked as its contents were required, and a cardboard box of provisions, extremely arbitrary in nature as Helen observed, resisting an immediate urge to supplement them.

That, she knew, she must not do. And why should she even have a view about them? Catriona was clearly in good health and, judging by her regular circuits of the moor and the higher hills inland, enjoyed a stamina most people would envy. Lesson one, Helen warned herself. This arrangement was finely balanced between success and failure — for she guessed Catriona's last-minute doubts would have been deeper than her own – and she must treat it with tact and care.

But while she was disciplining herself not to suggest adding Catriona's milk order to hers as Catriona never seemed to have any, or pressing food upon her on the pretext that she seemed to have made more than she needed, Catriona serenely embarked on life at Little Hilltop in her own fashion.

On day two Watty delivered a goat. Helen, reading for ten minutes after tea before crawling back into the dark overhangs of what had once been the herbaceous border, did her best to pin her attention on the biffing of Brigadier Ritchie Hook, and ignore first a thunderous hollow battering, then shouts, shrieks, bleats, roars, yells and laughter. Just as she was deciding it all sounded like too much fun to miss and she could be a discreet neighbour no longer, Catriona appeared round the corner of the house on the run, looking pink-cheeked and unusually animated, and guilty.

'I honestly didn't say he could,' she panted, half laughing and half apologetic. 'Only he was let down by the man he's selling to, and he'd already fetched her by then, so he thought we could put her into the walled bit by the burn, but only if you agreed, and only till tomorrow.'

'He?'

'Watty, of course.'

'Of course. And fetched *her*?'

'Yes, luckily a nanny. Easier to deal with.'

'And where is this nanny now? By which I imagine you do not mean someone who looks after children?'

Catriona, giggling, admitted, 'In the walled bit by the burn.'

'Catriona!'

'I know, I know, it isn't in the lease.' Catriona's eyes were alight with amusement in a way they rarely were. 'I really am sorry, Helen, but you see the man who wants to buy her said—'

'I don't think I can bear to hear the details, nor do I really want to know how you got involved, but I do intend to have a word with Watty,' Helen said grimly, closing *Men at Arms* and getting to her feet.

'She's called Wilhelmina,' Catriona offered meekly, trotting at Helen's heels as she headed for the walled enclosure, and giggling again when Helen raised her eyebrows, unaffected by this contribution.

All that was to be seen of Watty was a red neck and a tweed jacket with flying pockets vanishing into cover up the bank across the lane. The back doors of Catriona's van gaped open on an interior of odorous disorder.

Helen could see why Watty had been tempted to wheel and deal over Wilhelmina, a stunning beauty with a flowing apricot coat who belonged, according to Catriona, to a rare breed called Golden Guernsey. Wilhelmina did not, however, approve of her enclosure. Or at least did not think she should stay in it exclusively. During the next couple of hours she climbed out by four different routes, tumbling considerable gaps in the dyke as she did so, which

Catriona and Helen laboriously built up again. Once at large she chewed the hems off towels on the washing line, broke down raspberry canes, forced her way through the gate into the lane and had to be rounded up before she caused havoc on the road and, apparently experiencing no disagreeable sensations, ate a pizza which had caught fire under Catriona's grill and been put on the doorstep to cool. She also knocked over three pots containing the plants which Nadia, presumably not observing there was nowhere to put them in the massed borders, had left as her farewell present. Wilhelmina ate the houttuynia and the osteospermum but left the achillea. She deposited noxious droppings on Catriona's sitting-room carpet and on the way out broke the bowl in which the fruit Helen had provided to welcome Catriona was still untouched.

'How fortunate we weren't left with the billy,' Helen remarked as she and Catriona finally settled down to supper together, on the front verandah so that they could keep an eye open for Wilhelmina, though by now Catriona, having disappeared Helen knew not where to acquire it, had tethered their guest with a chain attached to a deeply driven-in stake.

How attractive Catriona looked, Helen thought with pleasure, when she laughed freely like that, her mouth, which usually had a soft vulnerable droop to it, open to show two rows of small even white teeth.

'Oh, Helen, I am sorry. I'll make sure Watty never pulls a stunt like that again.'

'Don't worry, the position will be made crystal clear

to Watty.' But in fact Helen had found the evening, if exhausting, wildly entertaining and pitting her wits and speed against the goat's, not at all sure who could be said to have won, had charged up the adrenalin most enjoyably.

She still thought it a one-off crisis, however, and when the next appeal came it was so different that she failed at first to recognise a trend. This time it was a cat. Catriona came punctiliously to ask permission for it to stay for the weekend while its owners were away.

'It will just be two days, I guarantee. I know Wilhelmina was here for five in the end, but this is nothing to do with Watty.'

'I thought cats hated strange places?'

Mere stalling, perfectly ineffectual.

'Oh, this one doesn't mind, she's so sweet, just wait till you see her.' And indeed the cat, an undeniably charming creature, spent most of its time dozing and purring on a warm window-sill. It brought its own food and its own bed and was no trouble of any kind, though Helen never grasped why Catriona wasn't simply feeding it in its own home. Unless this was a skilful move in a general softening-up process, it belatedly struck her.

'How could you suggest such a thing?' Catriona protested when accused of this, tremendously affronted. They understood each other very well by this time.

The cat was followed by a wolfhound, even gentler and less assuming than she had been, though not so keen on window-sills. Instead he laid his chin to rest on the top of bookcases or on Helen's father's tallboy, or heavily and affectionately on Catriona's shoulder from behind when he wasn't expected, which resulted in one or two spillages. He worried a lot about his tail, having learned that wagging it brought disaster and reprobation. He was so obliging that he would have kept it still all the time if he could, but so good-natured that it was permanently out of his control. Helen, seeing that this social difficulty had become a burden to him, couldn't help finding his struggles endearing, and though when he left it was nice to have tea without clutching at the cups every few seconds, or to open cupboards without having someone interestedly checking the contents of the shelves, she rather missed him.

Work on the garden, more engrossing and enjoyable as it progressed, overtook work on the house, including cleaning. Catriona never cleaned, except for running an old Ewbank she had found somewhere over the route from front door to kitchen. Otherwise she lived lightly in her cottage and Helen saw no reason not to do the same. Even in the garden she began to follow this new approach. At first it had seemed urgent to reduce the various levels of lawn to order and Watty, who had oozed back into favour, did some semi-skilled work with a scythe, and made a start on the ground elder, nettles and dockens. Then it had seemed a priority to tidy the beds under the verandah, the deep border under the western wall, the cushions of rock plants spreading unchecked across steps and paths.

But down by the burn one day, looking for the lovage

Catriona had told her grew here, Helen was beguiled by finding unexpected treasures, including a huge bog lily half buried under fallen branches. As it was a hot day it was tempting to stay in the cool green cavern, with the sound of the small waterfalls in her ears. Tempting. She paused to examine the word. When she 'ought' to be doing conventional weeding and tidying around the house, visible, on show? Who did she think was looking? How far she was from independence. She went to fetch tools and spent the rest of the day messing about by the water.

As she worked it occurred to her to wonder how Catriona, with her lack of interest in culinary matters, knew that lovage grew here, or even what lovage was. Jake must have told her. Was Jake back? Though Helen had had plenty of time to lecture herself out of foolish thoughts, the prospect of seeing him again went crackling through her with an electric effect she could do nothing about. And he was Catriona's boss; Catriona was living in Helen's spare house. Helen paused in her muddy work to consider this. Had there, deep down, been some buried idea that if Catriona came to live at Little Hilltop Jake might appear there? She examined this with an intent honesty. But no, not at any level of her consciousness had the thought arisen. She was sure of it. But she could not subdue an anticipation which left her, not breathless exactly, but strangely conscious of her breathing.

That evening Catriona reported Jake to be delighted with the progress she had made in the shop. Though at first there had been no question of her checking in at Hilltop, as it were, when she came home, a habit had sprung up of sharing the day's news, and she was as likely now to come in by Helen's door as hers.

'And is Jake here for long?' Helen tried not to ask, but the question had a will of its own.

'I don't think he's off on another job for a while,' Catriona replied, not sounding very interested, or particularly reliable as an informant.

'I don't believe I've ever heard exactly what he does.' You haven't and you are deeply curious about it, Helen told herself disgustedly.

Catriona, however, was totally incurious. 'No one knows. All a big mystery.' She strewed the contents of a sturdy leather satchel, product of Trudy's bored between-marriages period, on the kitchen worktop. 'Sorry, I left your list in the first shop so I had to guess after that, then I was down at the harbour seeing someone — oh, well, that doesn't matter—' blushing slightly and hurrying on, 'so I'm afraid the butter's not as solid as it once was.'

Someone must know what Jake did. Impossible to probe further, however. 'So what doesn't matter?'

'Oh, dear.' A curling smile defeated Catriona's efforts to look innocent.

'What livestock are about to take over my demesne this time?'

'Goodness, what made you think that? But it's only some dear Khaki Campbells, and only for a day or two, till Michie can get into the cottage he's renting from next week. Your working by the burn made me think of it. Ducks are marvellous for clearing the ground.'

'Catriona, have you ever thought of saying no?'

Helen had imagined putting up a fence to be a professional job, but Catriona assured her a suitable pen could be run up in half an hour. And so, almost, it proved. The ducks' owner, a gaunt giant of a man with flying grey hair and immense hands, produced an ancient roll of netting, Watty hacked some spindly posts from young trees he and Helen had cut down, and with sundry raids on her toolshed progress was rapid. The Khaki Campbells were indeed beautiful; but then, so had Wilhelmina been.

The only problem, apart from the steepness of the bank and the tricky question of preventing the ducks from swimming away down the burn to town, was that nobody arrived till well into the evening. By the time the fence was up, and the small unfloored wooden house Michie had brought in his pick-up set in its new spot, it was almost impossible to see. Just as Helen was beginning to worry about the newcomers scattering and being lost in the darkness, Jake arrived.

'Am I too late to be useful? Sorry, Catriona, I meant to be here earlier but got caught on the phone. I hope you don't mind my turning up like this?' he added to Helen, who was only thankful in the first place that it was too dark for anyone to see her face, and in the second that there was plenty to occupy everyone's attention.

'Not at all,' she said in a voice she thought sounded very odd. 'And you've come at the vital moment.'

But the ducks, whose main preoccupation by now was bedtime, hurried into their new home, where wheat was already waiting for them, in a tight unadventurous huddle, gabbling their unease but showing no signs of flight. The netting was secured behind them, and in the little burst of shared achievement and satisfaction Helen realised she didn't want the evening to be over.

'I think we've earned a dram, don't you?' she suggested, turning to Watty beside her as the person least likely to turn the idea down.

'Ach, well, we'd take that very kindly.'

Would she have asked them in if Jake had not been there? Helen wasn't sure and didn't care, looking round the scene in her sitting-room an hour or so later. The fire was a comfortable glow, subdued light fell from the lamps flanking the handsome old fireplace, the whisky bottle was almost empty. Michie (Christian name or surname? She never did discover) filled an armchair by the fire, vast in his flecked sweater, his glass, which he never put down, almost invisible in his big fist. Watty, round and red-faced, looked very comfortable in spite of the fact that his legs were too short for the deep sofa, and Catriona was clearly at home in this company, her face bright and happy.

While Jake . . .

Helen could never have imagined such a change in him. Though when she had first met him at Ardlonach they had talked with ease, and on her side with a startled pleasure, there had been an underlying consciousness that he had not been content in the group, contemptuous of what he was half hearing from the others even as he and Helen talked, never quite relaxing, withholding much of himself. Now he was a different person. His dark face in the lamplight looked as alive as Catriona's, his smile gleaming, his laughter easy. His sinewy legs in kilt stockings, the knees very brown, were stretched out to the fire, his boot heels on the hearth.

It appeared that Michie was, or had been, a fisherman, a white fish seine netter. Jake had gone out with him many times in the past and they had fascinating tales to tell. There was a certain amount of tub-thumping from Michie as time went by — Helen had never seen liquid flow down anyone's throat so smoothly; the man never appeared to swallow — about EC quotas, government backdowns, a way of life reduced to its death throes by ignorant politicians, but Jake skilfully steered him to less sensitive topics. Present-day gossip and news, past events in Luig and the glens, memories and history interweaving, favourite anecdotes trotted out one more time . . .

A wonderful, intoxicating — though she was drinking Chardonnay not whisky, and slowly at that — sense of timelessness spread through Helen. Not one person in this room knew or cared what time it was. They wanted to be here, doing exactly what they were doing, and no considerations of next morning, work, hangovers or anything else disturbed them. It sounded simple enough, yet Helen thought it was probably relatively rare. But it was good, and she didn't want them to go. How lucky that Reggie's parting present had been to stock up the drinks cupboard. Supply looked as though it would meet demand; unless they stayed where they were for a couple of days, which seemed not entirely improbable. She was smiling as she slipped away to the dining-room for another bottle of malt. Turning with it in her hand she started to find that Jake had quietly followed her.

'Are you sure this is all right with you?' he asked. 'It seems rather an imposition. If you want to kick us all out just say the word.'

'No, truly, I'm delighted.' Helen would not have believed she could feel so shaken by his smiling presence near her. The room with its overhead light seemed stark after the sitting-room, the summer night by contrast pressing black against the window, and she felt exposed, her feelings too plainly to be read in her face.

'Beautiful pedestal table,' Jake remarked appreciatively, looking about him. 'I love that dark grain of rosewood.' His fingers touched it lightly, and Helen saw with an almost too acute awareness the fine dark hairs on the back of his lean hand. 'Nice rugs, too. Will you let me have a proper look at them sometime, and at your books?'

'None for sale,' she warned him, trying to keep her voice light, while her heart seemed to be doing its best to climb out of its due place.

'I should hope not. And this,' Jake went on, taking the bottle from her, 'is far too good a malt to be pouring down unworthy throats.'

'Running out of choice in the whisky line, I'm afraid.' They were welcome to it, by the case if she had it, Helen thought with delicious abandon. 'I wondered, though, would they like something to eat? They probably had tea early, and they'd normally have some sort of snack later on, wouldn't they?'

'Probably, but I don't think you—'

'Just bread and cheese or something.' Hold on to this, don't let it end. 'There's plenty. I'd like to.'

'Sure? I'll give you a hand, then.'

It was the last thing she would have expected of him, but Jake was capable and deft, in the oddest way not making the kitchen feel too small for two, as Nadia had always done.

'There, that should do them. I'll carry this.' But as Jake lifted the tray he paused. 'Helen, I just want to say, I can't tell you how relieved and pleased I am that Catriona's here with you. The change in her in the time I've been away is amazing.'

'Then I'm delighted,' Helen said, smiling her pleasure. 'Though I think the job you've given her has had as much to do with it as anything.'

She did not know of the dreams of Connor which were fuelling Catriona's present contentment, but as she held open the door to the hall for Jake she was aware of a happiness spreading through her which was new to her too.

Chapter Nineteen

Catriona was shaking and clumsy with nerves as she tried to get ready in the chilly bedroom of Little Hilltop. The dress Una had lent her, taken in and taken up by Trudy, for even slight Una was not as tiny as Catriona with her immature figure, was of a soft red that suited her, and simple in style. It had a high round neck, and though there seemed to the shivering Catriona to be very little of it at the back, that comforted her, for only now had she realised how scrawny her collarbone was. That was the trouble with suddenly looking in mirrors. All kinds of deficiencies normally never noticed became glaringly apparent. Her eyebrows; she never did anything to them, didn't know what one should do to them. Her hands, very brown, the nails square and short, were, now that she examined them, hideous with scratches and old scars. Her hair. Why hadn't she thought earlier about having something done to it, having it, for once in her life, properly cut? Set, even. Set how? She couldn't imagine, staring at it in unhappy doubt. And this horrible make-up. Rebecca had selected it for her, had shown her how to put it on, had been stern on the point of using it sparingly, but now her hands were too cold and too unsteady to make a neat job of it, and unfamiliar tears of exasperation sprang to her eyes as she wiped her face clean and started again.

Never had she been more thankful to hear Helen's voice, calling from the garden door, 'How are you getting on? I just wanted to make sure you have everything.'

'Oh, Helen, it's no use, I can't go. Just look at me,' Catriona wailed, staring helplessly at the bizarre blurred face in the mirror.

'You poor girl, that mirror's in a terrible place. You can't see a thing there, I'd never realised,' exclaimed tactful Helen. 'Why not come and finish getting ready in my room where it's warmer? And I brought you this in case you needed it.' A neat black evening bag.

'Helen, how kind of you. I'd forgotten all about one. It's lovely.' Helen's presence helped as much as the kind thought. 'And my shoes are black.'

Catriona had refused, wisely, to wear high heels for the first time in her life at a party bound to last for several hours, and Una, who after long days on her feet in the kitchen went for comfort above all else, had produced some low-heeled pumps which fitted Catriona well.

'How lucky,' Helen said serenely. It had all been plotted with some care. 'Now come along, and we'll add the finishing touches. That dress is a wonderful colour for you, and Trudy's made a great job of the alteration.'

With soothing approbation and the heater pouring out even more soothing warmth, with Helen to advise on the tortured question of make-up, and add a restrained touch of spray to hold her shining hair, with a long mirror in which to view, shyly and uncertainly, the finished product, Catriona's spirits were restored.

Disaster nearly struck, however, when through the gable window they saw a car coming along the lane.

At first Catriona had planned to go to Connor's party in her van, resisting offers from Helen and Fitz to take her or, if she was determined to be independent, to book a taxi for her. She wavered only when Una said, unusually firmly for her, that she didn't want her dress coming back smelling of goat. So when Connor, somehow getting wind of all this, said breezily, 'Don't be ridiculous, I shall see to it that you are fetched and delivered,' she had needed no further persuasion. She had interpreted his intervention as meaning he would collect her himself, and she had been looking forward dreamily ever since to the moment when he would pull up at the door (albeit the kitchen door) of Little Hilltop in his gleaming Saab.

But the car which arrived was not a Saab, and the young man in a dinner jacket who got out of it was not Connor. In spite of a light application of blusher Helen was startled to see Catriona pale dramatically, and for one moment was afraid she was going to be sick.

'It looks as though Connor has sent one of the house-party,' she said, too brightly. 'Come down and meet him.'

Catriona, with a wounded look Helen hated to see, made a heroic effort. 'Of course Conn couldn't come himself. It's his birthday party after all.'

Connor Macleod, don't you dare hurt her, Helen warned fiercely as she waved them off, that tight voice belatedly telling her how matters stood. She wished quite violently for a moment that she had not let Catriona go, then realised the absurdity of this on several counts. Catriona was not her responsibility, was twenty-five years old, and could not be protected from the trials of the arena for ever.

Jake, sunk deep in the old velvet-cushioned, wooden-armed chair he'd had in his study at school, with the bothy fire and the Tilley lamp going well, sincerely believed he was deep in J.R. Harris's *An Angler's Entomology*. Whatever was going on at the big house was nothing to do with him. But presently with an oath he cast the respected classic aside and levered himself out of the chair. He'd been to Connor's parties in the past and knew what they could be like.

Not that he was exactly rigged out for attending this one. He unbuckled his kilt and flapped it violently to get rid of dust and bits of moss and grass. He dunked his face in a bowl of water, found a clean pair of stockings and spent a couple of moments pondering on where at Luig he might have left his doublet and evening shoes. A shirt would be easy; he could raid anyone's room.

And shortly he was loping across the ridges and declivities of the moor in the tenuous dark of the August night, a pace so habitual to him he would not even have called it running, his practised eye reading the ground without difficulty. Floodlit, exquisitely proportioned, unanchored against the dark trees and the dark hill, Luig House sailed above him.

He cursed again. What was he doing here?

In ten minutes, after a little quiet raiding, he unobtrusively joined the party. Unable to find his dress shoes he still wore his black brogues, uncleaned. He hadn't run his doublet to earth either, but by now half the younger men had discarded their jackets anyway after some energetic reels. Not that Jake cared, or ever had cared, what he looked like or what people thought of him, but tonight he wished for his own reasons to blend with the background.

He located Catriona in the long drawing-room, which had been cleared for dancing, and his mouth tightened. She was sitting on a small bow-fronted sofa covered in grey velvet, with his cousin Gillian, yet so obviously not with her that Jake's lips twisted again. How transparently she gave herself away. He had been startled and angered when, in casual exchanges as they worked together in the shop, her references to visits to Luig in his absence and to Connor specifically had revealed the naive infatuation to which she had succumbed. Conn had been so kind; Conn was such fun; Conn knew so much about everything. And, less explicitly, Conn had hurt her by vanishing to London when he had said he would be at Luig for the whole summer, and by not telling her he was going or when he would be back. Jake was convinced that if he had not been away himself he could have prevented this familiar cycle, through which he had seen his cousin put God knew how many credulous females, most of whom should have known better. But Catriona did not know better, Catriona knew alarmingly little about anything outside her own odd world of lame ducks, animal and human, her few trusted friends, and her impressive acquaintance with her childhood landscape. And books of course. Jake smiled this time, remembering the extraordinary things he had from time to time found her absorbed in. How well she had done that work on the inventory too; he couldn't think of anyone who would have dealt with it better. Except Helen perhaps; there was a woman of sense.

He stationed himself to one side of the folded-back double doors and dealt curtly with the greetings of a passing stream of family and friends.

'My dear Jake, you look about as tidy as when you used to rush in straight off the hill late for lunch and were sent straight out again to wash,' his cousin Mariotta commented, ostentatiously giving him a wide berth.

'Clear off, Mariotta, you're in my light,' Jake growled, and she raised her shapely eyebrows and glanced over her shoulder at the whirling couples finishing an eightsome.

'Hunting, Jake? Waiting till more civilised contact activity begins? I'm fascinated.'

He found that, most definitely, he didn't want her

to know who he was watching, or what his motives in coming here tonight had been. And he wasn't sure why that was so. But when Mariotta had moved away he looked again at Catriona. He didn't like her in those clothes; she looked unlike herself, untrue to herself. She was sitting on the edge of the sofa, answering Gillian's no doubt kind words briefly, watching, waiting.

Christ, hadn't Conn danced with her yet? Jake knew from what Catriona had said about the party that in her own mind she was Connor's partner tonight. She had enough sense, presumably, to have worked out that if it was his party then he had to be generally available, but had he remembered her at all? Jake had no faith in his cousin's ability to put the feelings of anyone in the world ahead of having a good time himself. But to be fair to him, Catriona was so remote from the type of woman he preferred that it might not even have occurred to him that he had roused any particular feelings in her.

Yes, Conn could be that stupid. His anger impelling him to move, Jake turned and went out into the hall, intending to visit the buffet, but the hum of voices in the dining-room, edging towards the rowdy small-hours level, made him turn sharply back. He should keep an eye on her. She was so inexperienced that heaven knew what she might do when the realisation finally hit her that Conn wasn't going to come and find her. Had anyone else had the grace to dance with her? Surely Michaela would have seen to it that they did?

The Campbells of Fassfern, about to leave as they

had a long drive home, caught him as he swung back. Neil and Celia were good friends, and Jake was happy to chat with them briefly. It was enough. When he looked down the drawing-room again he was in time to see the small tragedy enacted. Moments of time; gestures; body language – he was too far away for more. Connor crossing an open space of floor as sets were being made up, Catriona's face lifting to him, suddenly radiant, the turn of Gillian's head, her perceptions always hyper astute. Then a slim hand catching Connor's arm, a beautiful smiling face at his shoulder, a fall of shining golden hair tossed back. Andrea, who was supposed to be about to marry – whoever he was – some idiot. What was she doing here? But that touch on Connor's arm had been enough. With a formal smile of apology to Catriona, as though to convey that he had only intended to talk to her, he was being drawn, putty in Andrea's expert hands, into a noisy set, and to the eyes that watched him from the sofa, and the hard angry eyes that watched him from the door, it was evident that all thoughts of Catriona had vanished from his mind.

Jake acted swiftly, indifferent to how incisive his movement looked among the party throng. As he came to the sofa, Catriona now huddling back into its curves, Gillian turned her head, picking up his step in spite of the skirling music and the beat of feet.

'Jake?' He heard the perturbation in her voice, and felt the tremor in her hand as he put his over it.

'It's all right, Gillie, I'll look after this.'

She nodded, then cocked her head intently, as though listening for more than the words that were exchanged.

'Catriona.'

She raised wretched eyes to his, and again Jake felt a deep, scarcely defined dislike of the fact that she was made up, dressed and turned out so conventionally.

'Come along,' he said.

'Jake, please, I don't want to dance. Anyway, it's started already, the sets are made up, and I don't—'

'Come along,' he repeated, his voice quiet but accepting no arguments. Out of the tail of his eye he saw Gillian nod, and he put the observation away to examine later.

'But where?' Catriona asked, her voice uncertain, her chin puckering.

'With me.'

As though accepting that he was offering some sort of escape, she got clumsily to her feet. Jake scooped up the bag she had forgotten and put it into her hand. Without waiting to see if she followed he strode towards the door, and more than one observer raised an eyebrow at the thunderous rage in his dark face.

Catriona went blindly at his heels, looking at no one, as he had known she would, but when they reached the hall she summoned her resistance. 'Jake, I can't leave yet. There's still – I mean Connor will be—'

'Connor won't be.' Jake swung round on her, and the face he bent to hers was full of anger. 'He may dance with you once, but that will be that. He won't take you home, he won't kiss you goodnight.'

'Jake!' Catriona's protest was partly at the harshness of his tone, partly at the realisation of where they were, in the middle of the wide hall, with people sitting out at small tables around them. 'You don't know anything about it—'

'Yes, I do. I know too damn much about it. Come on.'

'I haven't said goodbye or thanked—'

This time he took her arm, sweeping her along a corridor which led to a side door and out, across a brightly lit paved expanse dotted with more tables, to the darkness of the gardens beyond.

'What a lucky thing I couldn't find my dancing shoes after all,' he remarked as, still holding Catriona's arm, he whirled her down a steep grass bank. 'And what a lucky thing you're so handy on your feet,' he added, ignoring her protests, 'if that's not a contradiction in terms.'

He headed rapidly across the lawn where other couples, normal couples, Catriona thought indignantly, strolled and dallied.

'Let me pick up my dress at least,' she protested. 'You nearly broke my neck on that bank.' And Jake's laughter at her return to the prosaic interrupted more than one alcoholic, sexy or promising kiss.

'Where are we going?' Catriona asked, as she wound up a bundle of skirt and took a firm grip of it.

'To the bothy.'

She opened her eyes at him in the last faint reach of

light from the terrace. 'You're taking me to your private retreat, your fiercely guarded lair?'

Jake was impressed that she was already capable of teasing him, though not quite so pleased to realise she had no other interest in his invitation, and no question in her mind about his intentions. She might as well have been rescued from Connor by Trudy or Rebecca, either of whom would have been capable of hauling her off as summarily as he had. Though he thought Rebecca might have had a word or two with Connor in the by-going. Well, that would come in its due season.

'Are you cold?' Jake enquired, as they dropped down the first slope of the moor. He himself was so inured to extremes of temperature he had to make an effort to remember other people on the whole were not. Though short of taking off his kilt all he had to wrap around her was someone else's shirt.

But Catriona, brought up in Glen Righ, was almost as used to discomfort as he was. 'I'm fine, thanks,' she said, adding as though the question had been faintly silly. 'It is summer.'

Jake grinned in the darkness. From her the lines would obviously be original.

The bothy fire was a red bank of wood ash, throwing off a sybaritic heat after their cool run through the pre-dawn chill. Catriona's shoes were soaked, her thin arms icy, but she seemed unaware of either fact, or indifferent. With an unaccustomed instinct to protect, where training and habit normally made him demand resistance to any form of weakness, Jake pulled a sweater out of the Second World War ammunition box he found useful to protect his belongings from mice, and dragged it with a matter-of-fact hand over her head.

'A dram?' he asked. 'Or something hot?'

'Oh, don't bother with anything for me,' Catriona said, neither stretching her hands to the fire nor showing any other signs of wanting to be cossetted. But Jake heard a bleak note back in her voice, now that the action was over, as though memories were returning. Coffee might help to chase them away and without further discussion he struck a match and lit the gas burner.

'What a wonderful place to live,' Catriona said, looking with admiration at the bare stone rectangle with its raftered roof and two small windows. 'No clutter.'

Jake, setting the kettle on the roaring gas, turned in amusement to look at his abode through her eyes. A few items of clothing hung from pegs driven into the unpointed walls; a couple of Portuguese woven rugs in rich colours were laid on the stone-flagged floor, and a similar counterpane was thrown over the low bed; leatherwork cushions from the Middle East padded Scottish kists; two ornate brass lamps, rescued from glen cottages and badly in need of cleaning, provided a softer light than the Tilley. He didn't think many women would think it wonderful.

'Who was the beautiful girl with the fair hair?'

He had not expected Catriona to open the subject so bravely, and his usually reserved face was gentle as he looked at her, straight, slim and fine-boned, and somehow, in the kindly light of the fire and the oil lamps, more congruous here in the soft red dress than she had looked in the splendours of the Luig drawing-room.

'She's called Andrea. She was Connor's girlfriend till quite recently, when she announced her engagement to someone else.'

'But she's come back to Conn.' It was not a question; it was steady, deliberate acceptance.

'It looks as though she has.' Jake's voice, though he was not aware of it, had never been so soft. He didn't move towards her. Instinct warned him instead to keep very still, to give her space and time to accept the implications that must be searing her.

'I think,' Catriona said at last, in a muffled voice, 'it would help to talk about something else, something I don't know about, something new.'

'Then,' said Jake, startled to find how much her courage moved him, and careful to make a small business of filling the coffee mugs, finding biscuits, pulling his ancient chair closer to the fire for her, 'I think it's time to let you into a secret.'

Chapter Twenty

The wood fire on its base of ash sent out a marvellous even warmth. The scent of mixed hardwood and softwood logs mingled with the faint homely smell of oil from the lamps, and the even more comfortable smell from Jake's sweater, of wool, heather, salt air and Jake. Catriona's feet, in a pair of looped socks the heels of which came well up her ankles, were glowing warm, and Una's shoes were drying on the hearth. Catriona had put them in the full heat; Jake, with none of his usual acerbity, had moved them to a spot less likely to kipper them.

'And truly no one else in the world knows?'

'Well, the publishers. My accountant, I suppose.'

'No, I mean real people.'

Jake smiled at her with affection. 'No one.'

'And you truly don't mind if I tell Helen? She'd enjoy it so much.'

'No, I don't mind if you tell Helen. I regard you as one unit. It's just that if it seeps into the family or the larger circle there will be no stopping it spreading, and then the whole point would be lost.' He wondered idly why his trust in Catriona was so complete, and thought the childish quality of her naivety held its own reassurance. Helen's probity, even on so short an acquaintance, he would not have thought of questioning.

'Tell me more about these weird things you do.'

'These research trips, please.' Jake leaned to nudge in a couple of half-burned logs, settled again with his back to the kist, legs stretched out in the fire-glow, big black sweater now covering the borrowed shirt. 'How about my time in the Hong Kong police?'

'Police? Wasn't that dull and respectable? I want the adventures.'

'It wasn't precisely dull,' he said, laughing at her, drowsy among the half-bald brown cushions, but still eager to listen to anything which would keep her mind off the discoveries of the evening.

For inexperienced as Catriona might be, she was intelligent enough and brave enough to know that she had made a fool of herself. Seeing Connor with Andrea, and indeed seeing him with the rest of his set, who in Catriona's eyes were all attractive, well-dressed, and supremely confident, she had accepted the truth. This was his world; his attentions to her had been the merest kindness, exactly on a par with Michaela's or Gillian's. There was a traditional friendship between the Macleods of Luig and the Finlays of Glen Righ, and she was the only surviving Finlay. She was stricken with shame as she saw how her own stupidity could have destroyed that.

She said as much to Jake, as their talk flowed without hurry or pressure from the bizarre and dangerous missions he undertook in order to – well, hardly earn his living – to supplement his income, and back to her own need to release some of her pain, which he seemed so readily to understand, while the thin, eerie light of dawn washed coldly over the fall of the moor.

Helen woke again, knowing at once that no car had come yet along the lane, and in the same instant annoyed with herself for having registered the fact. What business was it of hers what time Catriona came in, or if she ever came in? She was a grown woman. But one could use such phrases about Catriona and they would be instantly followed by the rider, 'But she's not really.'

Helen turned restlessly, feeling she had hardly slept all night. She would go down and make tea and read for a while. But no, if Catriona came back and saw the light on she would think Helen was listening for her. Well you are. And Catriona would think no such thing; her mind simply didn't work like that. And how ridiculous even to be weighing such considerations. Impatiently Helen flung herself round once more, reached for the light switch, then withdrew her hand. It really would seem like 'waiting up', an unacceptable intrusion.

She did her best to relax, limb by limb, letting herself sink down into the mattress until she could hear the tiny sounds of it giving to her weight. But by the time she had got that far her legs were tensing again. She tried harder, letting random thoughts circulate. Would Watty ever get the docks and sorrel under control? But if he did would the garden survive his preferred methods of slashing, burning and large-scale weed-killing? He was busy most days now at Luig, as Catriona had found him work there during harvest, but presumably he'd be back. And would the ducks ever leave? Helen found herself smiling. Those wretched ducks. She had given them their mash and shut them up tonight as Catriona was in her full rig. More eggs. How madly they laid, far more, she was sure, than any natural duck could be expected to do.

'Over three hundred eggs a year,' Catriona had told her, bringing in the usual five a day. How did she know these things? 'Their eggs are good for baking.'

Helen baked.

'They have a rest period in the autumn.'

Thank God for that.

But Helen could not fend off any longer the worry that had been the root cause of her restless night. Connor Macleod would eat Catriona for breakfast. Ah, breakfast – that could be the explanation. Maybe she wasn't tucked up in bed with that flamboyant and self-satisfied young man after all. It would be the sort of party where the band would play till dawn and bacon and eggs would be served before the cars rolled away . . .

I should have seen it happening. But what could I have done? What could anyone do? She has to find her own way through the labyrinths of hope and hurt. But, my God, if he's in bed with her, Helen thought, starting up, relaxation gone to the winds, he'd better be doing the responsible thinking. Catriona was just the sort of daffy bird to come home pregnant.

Don't be so *absurd*, Helen told herself furiously, flopping on her back again. That is really rushing to meet disaster. Think about something else. Think about how agreeable it has been to find the days so busy, how nice it is when Rebecca or Una snatch half an hour from their busy lives to call, or when Trudy brings Finn to see me. I must have a house-warming party. Would Jake come?

Oh, no, we're not starting on that. Grimly she heaved up on one elbow, switched on the bedside light. Ten past five. She'd never get to sleep again now. She went down to make tea just as Jake was going up the path beside the burn, headed for his sleeping bag, and Catriona, the abused red dress hung carefully on the wardrobe door in a belated access of conscience, rolled into bed and fell instantly and dreamlessly asleep.

'And when he was in Hong Kong he was attacked by a gang and knifed and—'

Catriona trailed at Helen's heels as she made her a late breakfast, chattering like a child after a thrilling time. The only difference was, as Helen did not fail to note, that she was not talking about the party.

'And guess what, he said I could tell you—'

'Go through and start on your muesli. These eggs will be done in another minute.'

'I'll eat it in here.' Catriona, not ready to be alone, started spooning it in obediently, but still managed to talk.

Helen shook her head, gently turned the scrambling (duck) eggs. 'So what are you allowed to tell me?'

She was conscious of huge relief that Jake had rescued this outrageous innocent, whom they should never have let out alone, and at the same time of a new reaction which she identified with shame and astonishment as jealousy. And much good may that do you, she thought, catching the toast as it bounced up.

'You know Brett Stark? You do know, he writes those autobiographical accounts of fighting in Bosnia and living with the Inuit and infiltrating the Triads—'

'Come along before this gets cold.'

'You must have seen them—'

'I know the name. Pull the table nearer. Coffee?'

It was nearly noon. The verandah, its door closed on a gusty but bright day, was pleasantly warm.

'Yes, but you'll never believe – oh, Helen, this looks marvellous, how kind you are,' Catriona's good manners made her interrupt herself to say.

'Well, eat it.' Helen poured coffee and settled back with her own mug, beginning to feel a promising suspicion that somewhere along the line Connor had been dispensed with.

'Guess who Brett Stark is – or half of him?'

The antennae of attraction function with uncanny

acuity, and Helen asked hurriedly, 'Are you sure that you're allowed to tell me this?'

'It's Jake! Well, he's not the writer, but he goes and does the things – is a mercenary soldier, or gets himself into revolutionary groups, hunts caribou, does research about bits of Antarctica dropping off, all that sort of thing. He's had some of the most hair-raising times you could ever imagine, while the author pretends to do them but lives in Chelsea and never leaves his study and is terrified of spiders and uses scented soap.'

'Is all this true?' Helen demanded, thinking that for someone who had come home with the dawn Catriona was in remarkably lively spirits.

'Of course it's true. Only as Jake says, it's the kind of thing that has to be kept totally secret or it doesn't work. But it's been a huge success, they've been doing it for years, making buckets of money, and no one knows. The author pretends to be one of those recluses who can't deal with publicity, and that fits the image anyway. Jake knows we won't utter a word.'

'You seem to have had an entertaining evening,' Helen observed. How far this revelation, improbable but quite credible in relation to Jake, was from her more trite fears for Catriona. But that flicker of jealous wistfulness made itself felt again, and she knew she wished Jake had talked to her by the bothy fire till the dawn came up over the hills. She supposed she was too old for such things.

*　　*　　*

Nadia phoned to ask how Helen's plans for the house were progressing, as she would have to fit their visit in with half-term, her mother's sixtieth birthday celebrations and the performance of *HMS Pinafore* the Withedine and Uppington Magna Players were putting on in the autumn.

At least she isn't planning a sixtieth birthday party for me, Helen thought, waiting for a pause in the high-pitched flow. Fortified by her growing feeling of being busy, content and more integrated in her present surroundings than she had ever felt anywhere, she was able to say with firmness, when the opportunity came, that although Nadia and Reggie, with or without the children, were welcome at any time, she had no intention of doing anything whatsoever to the house. This was not well received. But the follow-up calls, including one from Reggie under evident duress, and a long semi-literate letter from Nadia written in a childish hand and including much information about the weather and the garden, did not move her. She would see them again one day, when the dust had settled.

Meanwhile, the small events of day-to-day happily absorbed her, though it would have been hard to define exactly where their attraction lay. The Khaki Campbells departed and the backlog of eggs, which Catriona said with regret would only keep for ten days as ducks' eggshells were so much more porous than hens', were disposed of among the neighbours, with all of whom, via Catriona, Helen was by this time on friendly terms.

'The dear things did clear the ground for you,' Catriona pointed out, rolling up rusty netting.

Helen thought the trodden muddy area, covered with lavish greeny-brown squitters, hardly an improvement. She also hoped, without much faith, that the ugly bundle of netting would be removed by someone.

But nothing could disturb her serenity. Looking back to the final days at Netherdean she remembered how retirement, for which she had thought herself reasonably prepared, had come rushing up in the end like a head-on collision. There had been a sense of being abruptly devalued, and a blank fear as to how, in reality, empty acres of time would be occupied. Plans to read all the new books there had never been time for, to garden, walk, have leisure for new interests, had seemed mere whistling in the dark. Then, almost without noticing it, the fears had evaporated, submerged in everyday chores, which with Walter's exactions had increased rather than diminished.

It was hard to believe now, but in a milder form those fears had returned when she had decided to come back here and create a life for herself out of nothing. In cold fact, what did a female pensioner, living alone, with no one to look after and no family nearby, do with her days? Pad them out with small routines, go to the library, the shops, indulge in treats of coffee and cakes, watch quizzes at tea-time? Helen, scrubbing up after helping Watty excavate an ominous bright green patch in the grass at the point where her drains disappeared

ALEXANDRA RAIFE

beneath the dyke, and not impressed with what they had uncovered, or the prospect of finishing the job when Watty produced a couple of new draining tiles as he had promised, was in a hurry to get to her next job. No time for tea and quizzes.

She still wasn't sure how she had been inveigled into it, she reflected, as she sniffed to make sure her hand cream had overpowered the smell of drains.

Oh, don't give me that, a more honest and light-hearted voice mocked. You know exactly how it happened, and how delighted you were. She had been asked by Jake if she would help Catriona with the stack of mail awaiting attention at the bookshop. He had delayed replying to it until the inventory was complete and a professional valuation had been made. Uncle Percy might have had a microscopic knowledge of what the swaying piles and crowded shelves and the crammed rooms above held, but Jake did not, though he intended to learn. However, the initial work was done, and now the job of describing and offering books and answering erudite queries and requests confronted them.

Perhaps Jake would come back to dinner. Whether because they now shared the truth (or the joke as he seemed to regard it) of his alter persona, or because he felt Catriona needed his care and support, he had fallen into the habit of turning up at Hilltop more freely than he went anywhere else. He also appeared occasionally at Ardlonach, since he enjoyed the odd sparring match with Rebecca – or enjoyed provoking Dan, Helen suspected –

but since Connor and Michaela and their crowd used it as their local he tended to choose his times carefully, and would depart without ceremony if anyone who bored him came in.

But with Catriona and her network of friends from the glens, Inverbuie and Luig itself, he revealed a different self. As he did with Helen.

Was that true, or did she want to believe it, Helen queried, as she took the path down into the town at a rapid pace, full of the energy, the feeling of being fit and limber, which so satisfied her these days. But she didn't think she could be imagining it. For Jake had turned up more than once when Catriona had been busy about her mysterious affairs elsewhere, and he had been in no hurry to go. He had helped free the probing tendrils of an overgrown clematis from the roof tiles of Little Hilltop, had rebuilt a gap in the dyke which Watty had been promising to get at for days, and only yesterday evening had sat on the steps talking peacefully as the sun vanished and a sneaky wind plucked at them with an increasingly cold hand.

And I sat and hid my shivers, Helen recalled, afraid that if I suggested a move indoors the mood would be broken and he would go. I'm worse than Catriona.

Much worse, for it was obvious that Catriona never gave Jake a thought when he wasn't there, or Connor either by this time, Helen gathered. Her concerns lay elsewhere: collecting clothes for a family who had had a fire in their cottage, nursing a hamster with eczema back to health, making Watty declare his earnings and stay off the dole, or looking after Finn for a day on her own for the first time.

It was clear that all such matters were of greater moment to Catriona than a man whom she saw as an old family friend, a near-contemporary of her father's, and who was, in however informal a manner, her employer into the bargain.

Chapter Twenty-one

The first touch of autumn was suddenly threatening a summer which had seemed set to go on for ever. The peak of the grouse shooting had come and gone, at Luig only the friend or two invited to share the stalking remained, and the annual Luig ceilidh had taken place.

At first Catriona had refused to go, her wings badly burned. Connor and Michaela would be there – the ceilidh was one of the highlights of their August house-party. But it was even more of a highlight for the locals, and in the end, knowing she was being cowardly, Catriona had given way to pressure, on condition that she could wear what she liked and leave when it suited her.

It had been less of an ordeal than she had feared. Jake had come via Hilltop and he and Helen had walked her down the steep path, which in itself had lent a simplicity which Catriona found reassuring. Then several people appeared whom she hadn't seen since she came back, and she was so swiftly seized to dance that anxiety had been forgotten. It had been fun too to watch Helen's pleased surprise to be swept off by a succession of partners, from Fitz, Dan, Jake and Donald Macrae, to Postie, Michie the fisherman, Sadie's husband and a tireless Watty who danced like a red rubber ball.

When Connor arrived Catriona had found herself surrounded by friends, and twitched so promptly into a set for *Petronella* by Jake that the moment had passed before there was time for panic. But Connor had showed no sign of straying from his own party.

Growing up mostly away from Luig he, Mariotta, Michaela and Gillian had never established the links with the people of the town and glens which had been part of Jake's solitary childhood. He preferred the company of his own friends, and Catriona accepted this as natural, unaware of the anger of Jake – and Helen – to see him ignore her so carelessly.

She had been very aware of him – the tall figure in the black and yellow Dress Macleod kilt was undeniably striking and the sight of him dancing with one pretty girl after another had brought many pangs – but she had been able to enjoy herself too. And it was a step taken. She had received a bruising knock over him, and though it had brought inevitable pain and self-questioning she would get over both in time.

With that hurdle behind her she was glad to be swept along by busy days. Now that the cobwebs had gone and a few choice prints and books been arranged in the window and, it had to be said, Luig was so crawling with tourists that they would look at anything, a surprising number of customers appeared in the shop.

'I hadn't allowed for this,' Jake complained. 'I don't think Percy ever had *people* in here.'

'Me sometimes,' Catriona said.

'And were you a good customer?' His tone was immediately lighter, his face less grim.

'I was usually trying to sell something.'

'Ah.' Jake looked at her for a moment with an intent expression and saying, 'Wait there,' vanished to the upper floor, returning with three handsome leather-bound volumes in his hands. 'Look, I came across these, and thought it would be fun to return them to Finlay safe-keeping again, if you'd like that?'

Feeling more diffident than he was at all accustomed to, for Catriona's reactions could be unpredictable, he tendered the books. He had seen Catriona pick them up when they had been working together, and had observed the way she had held them close for a second, and put them back in their places with a lingering tenderness. Now he watched the slow blush rise in her cheeks and prayed she would not be offended by his offer.

'But Jake, I can't possibly—' she began.

But he had seen the way her hands received them. 'I want you to have them,' he said.

Suddenly she smiled brilliantly, tracing with a loving finger the gold tiger medallion on the top book. Sanderson's *Thirteen Years Among the Wild Beasts of India.* 'I used to adore this as a child. And these. I always called them *Edwards's*

Hists. because that was how it was abbreviated on the spine. Jake, are you sure?'

'Have them. A thank-you for all the hard work you've done – and the traps you've saved me from falling into. Who was about to send off only four vols of Walpole's *Royal and Noble Authors?* I shudder at the prospect of going off to buy armed with my paltry knowledge. The experts are going to eat me alive.'

In fact, his knowledge was already extensive, and although he insisted Percy had left everything to him because he couldn't stand anyone else in the family, Jake was his natural successor. He had another qualification for success in common with Percy – he knew a lot of people, and on a hot day when Helen and Catriona were busy in the shop and office he was away looking at the library of a friend who had inherited it in time to sell it and inject some much needed cash into his Sutherland estate.

The afternoon had dragged for whoever was standing by in the shop, for though customers wandered in and wandered round they almost invariably wandered out again, and a purchase was rare. Once Catriona and Helen had shut the door and slogged up the stone path, where the heat of the day seemed concentrated, it was tempting after a brief rest and long cold drink to go up the shady course of the burn and onto the moor, where they found themselves drawn on and on by the tawny evening light, the calm golden reaches of the sound widening below, the scents of bog-myrtle, sun-parched turf, heather now past blooming and the faint ever-present background smell of sheep wafting round them.

They talked little, the silence between them easy. Helen's thoughts drifted to Jake, as always. Every day brought contact now. People had begun to tease her.

'You're taming Jake! How do you do it?' Rebecca had demanded, and Dan had said, 'Too much home cooking. You'll have to cut it out, Helen.'

Helen was smiling as she perched on a rock, knees up to her chin, eyes slitted against the sunset light.

'I know I made a fool of myself,' Catriona said suddenly, shaking her out of her agreeable thoughts.

Catriona had this way of plunging in, as though having steeled herself to tackle some dreaded subject the only way she could begin was by taking a desperate leap to its heart. She, like Helen, gazed out over the gleaming sound, as though unable to add more.

'We all do that from time to time,' Helen said, allowing a small pause to ease the tension Catriona had so startlingly introduced into their peaceful mood.

'The thing is, I'd never felt like that before. Had those feelings before, I mean,' Catriona added, evidently feeling this made matters clearer.

'Sexual feelings?' Helen enquired, trying to strike a note somewhere between clinical heartiness and a too cautious tone which might sound as if she were discouraging further confidences.

'I suppose that's what they were.' Catriona looked away again, but the next moment Helen was surprised to hear an involuntary giggle. 'Oh, Helen, isn't it awful, not even to recognise them?'

This didn't sound as though a crisis was upon them, a possibility which had flashed across Helen's brain. If Connor had ... in thirty seconds she had made any number of far-reaching contingency plans. She decided on the positive approach. 'Was it a happy time?' she asked.

Catriona raised her head, pushing back her clumpy hair, and Helen, who as soon as she had spoken feared her question had presupposed a level of detachment Catriona might not have reached, was glad to see her expression was intent and considering.

'Yes, it was,' she said slowly after a moment. 'I suppose that's the point, isn't it? It was thrilling and marvellous and new. Thinking of Connor coloured the whole of life. Does that sound ridiculous? Does everyone feel like that? Sometimes I used to feel quite helpless, as though I only knew about love and passion and so on from books' — and she does read some very odd books, that could be a worry! — 'but then I thought about Trudy and Fitz when they got engaged, how they both went around beaming like idiots and were no use to anyone, and I remembered how Dan changed when he and Rebecca started living together. He used to be so cold and withdrawn before.'

Helen thought even now he wasn't the most outgoing person you could meet, but conceded that between him and Rebecca there was a more vibrant sense of mutual awareness than she remembered seeing in any other couple. She said nothing.

'Then I'd get afraid,' Catriona went on more rapidly.
'As though – like with houses and families and jobs
and everything – I'd be different in this too. And I
suppose I was.'

Her voice was bleak, the deep-buried fears back.

'No, what you experienced was all too normal, I'm
afraid,' Helen said, resisting the impulse to put her arms
round her and keeping her voice matter-of-fact. 'We've
all fallen for the wrong person in our time.' And married
them. 'It's part of the process. There are an awful lot of
frogs out there, and not too many princes.' And this is
not the moment to think of Jake, though images of him,
the predatory strength of the brown hands, the long back,
the hard muscles of his lean body, shook her with their
vividness.

'For me, too, though?'

'Of course for you.'

'Not too many of either so far,' Catriona said with
rueful honesty. 'I don't think I've got whatever it is
men like.'

'Catriona, that is such rubbish.' This time Helen, her
voice loving, put an arm round the thin shoulders. 'There
will be someone, I promise you.' With the deep affection
Catriona was capable of arousing in so many people,
somewhere, some day, there would be someone.

Catriona flashed her a grateful smile, which grew
amused. 'You'd really like to have a go about Connor,
wouldn't you?'

And that, Helen thought, laughing, was typical of

Catriona. You thought you were dealing with some fragile innocent who had to be protected, and then she would come out with something so bluntly down-to-earth.

'Tell me what happened at the party.'

Talking, they walked on, reaching the spine of the ridge as the sunset was squandering its full glory. Below them lay Loch Buie, the shadow cast by the promontory of Rhumore bulking black across its gilded waters.

'Taking steps,' Catriona said, pausing, speaking almost to herself. 'There's always a next one.'

Helen waited. Did this mean Catriona still believed she should leave? Had the moment come, summer ending, holiday time over? Helen found herself hoping with a violent urgency that this was not what was coming.

'Would you do something for me?' Catriona asked.

'Of course.'

Catriona's eyes had travelled beyond Loch Buie, up the narrow glen winding into the hills to the north.

'I think I must go back.'

'Back?' To Dundee, to more tests?

'To Glen Righ. I still see it in my mind as it was, with Grandfather and Braan and Watty and everyone. I haven't accepted that it's gone. I want to see it as it is, have the new picture in my brain so that I can't dodge any more. Only,' Catriona swung round to Helen with a doubtful look in her eyes, 'I wasn't sure if you – I mean, I wanted to ask you before if you'd come with me, but it would mean going past Tigh Bhan, and I thought that might be—' She was having trouble finding words for this. Someone else's marriage; divorce; adult pain.

'Catriona, I feel exactly as you do,' Helen assured her. 'Tigh Bhan has seemed to be waiting over the headland, shutting me out from this part of the landscape, as though it's something unresolved, something I haven't faced. I'm ashamed of the time I allowed to drift by there, empty, wasted time, hiding from the truth, making do. I want to go back, put it into perspective as an ordinary house where other people live.'

'I never guessed you felt like that too. How strange . . .'

'It will be much harder for you, though,' Helen said gently. 'Glen Righ was your home for all of your life. Are you sure it will be bearable to see it again?'

'I thought perhaps it would be easier to go before it finally opens as a hotel.'

Work on the revamping of Glen Righ had run into problem after problem. Even the damning valuation which had resulted in Catriona being virtually penniless had not detailed the full structural horrors which were revealed when renovation began. The grand opening planned for Easter had been postponed. A second deadline to coincide with the Twelfth had not been met. Now with the season almost over a third date was scheduled. The glen folk said, 'Aye well, we'll just wait and see.'

'We'll get the emotional bit over, then go and see Clare and the children,' Catriona said. Making the decision, and knowing Helen wouldn't mind going with her, had removed much of her dread of returning. 'You've never been to Rhumore, have you? It's a marvellous place.'

Rhumore was the only place Helen thought could be called marvellous on what she privately labelled their ghost-laying expedition.

Tigh Bhan was now a guest house and most of Lilias's beautiful garden had vanished under tarmac to provide parking space. On the slope behind, where in spring daffodils spread a glowing sheet of colour to the lip of the wild little gorge where the burn spilled down, diggers were scraping platforms of raw earth where chalets would be built. Helen and Catriona had known it was happening, but till the eye sees the mind can refuse unwelcome images.

'It's worse for you,' Helen said, as they stood on the hump-backed bridge and took in this desolate scene. 'You knew the house for so many years, and your friends the Markies loved it so much.'

'But it was your home.' Catriona's face looked small and pinched with misery, and Helen wondered if after seeing this she would want to change her mind about going on.

'No,' said Helen. 'No, never that.' She looked at the square white house and remembered slow morning silence in the big kitchen, one eye on the clock her master; remembered ironing linen pillowcases and starching tray cloths and cleaning Walter's shoes; remembered the silence of meals broken by punctilious exchanges, exasperation festering like a boil beneath the stretched, inflamed skin of habit and courtesy; she remembered loneliness. It was all behind her; gone. She thought of her narrow dark kitchen at Hilltop, simple meals scrambled together by casual helpful hands and eaten in the sun on the garden steps; she thought of cars coming and going along the lane, voices calling a greeting as the door opened; she thought of Wilhelmina and busy brown ducks that laid up a storm. She had thought she was laughing but there were sudden tears to blink away.

'You do mind.' Catriona's small bony hand, unused to the language of comfort, clutched her arm in a tight grip.

'Tears of relief,' Helen told her. 'No idea where they came from. Come on, done this.'

Glen Righ was so altered, so appallingly, resoundingly vulgar and over the top, that Catriona, after her first jaw-dropping stare, could only laugh. Indeed she laughed so hysterically that Helen thought she would choke, and as the Polo took the winding miles of track out to Rhumore fresh outbreaks still seized her.

'Those sunken baths, the jacuzzis, the fountain in the hall with those awful lights – don't they know the water supply hardly ever lasts the summer? Powder rooms, that bar called the Ghillies' Rest – if some of the ghillies I know rested there the guests wouldn't stay long. And they've put the tennis courts just where the wind screams straight off the loch. Oh, Helen, wasn't it all gloriously frightful? How glad I am we came, I can't wait to tell Clare about it.'

Helen looked forward to this visit. So far meetings with Clare, always in a crowd, had been brief and hurried, though she had heard all about her abandoning a sophisticated lifestyle in the south to come and live in a cottage on the shore of Loch Buie almost as primitive as Jake's bothy. Clare, Helen knew, had been the first friend to coax Catriona out of her solitude, but since marrying Donald she had found life on Rhumore so satisfying she could rarely be persuaded to leave it.

Now it was a pleasure to see her on her home ground in the big stone farmhouse high on its promontory, solidly built to face the hammering westerlies. Donald was on the hill, but the children were there, four-year-old Robbie and two-year-old Isla, and after lunch they all went down to a curve of white shell beach, on one of the hottest days of the summer, and revelled in the cold, clear green water.

Clare, who Helen guessed had been as anxious as she had about the impact on Catriona of her return to Glen Righ, was entertained and relieved at her reaction, and indeed Catriona's effervescent spirits had an effect on them all, adding to the mood of exhilaration whipped up by sun, wind and the shining expanses of sea and sky.

A day fairly loaded with sensations of one kind or another, Helen decided, turning into the lane with a rush of thankfulness at her good fortune to live where she did, as she did. To have done it, she thought absurdly. But she knew there was more to her happiness, to that sense of something wonderful about to happen which ran through her days, than the contrast between a dead marriage and satisfying solo living.

'Such fun,' Catriona called, coming to find Helen who was, vainly she knew, trying to arrest the march of the snowberry bushes across the fruit garden.

It was a phrase which sounded quite natural from her now, Helen thought, looking with pleasure at the slender shape in a neat cotton top and jeans. (They had returned from Rhumore with some useful loot, Clare having resigned herself to the fact that after two babies her figure would never be the same again.) 'You'll never guess who's coming.'

'I don't care who it is, so long as I can stop for tea,' Helen retorted, brushing her hair off her sticky forehead with a grubby wrist.

'I put the kettle on as I came by.'

'You're getting almost domesticated. So, who's coming? Animal, I take it.'

'Definitely human.' Catriona was clearly thrilled. 'Jake's other half.'

Helen felt actually sick in the first moment of shock. He's married. I never thought of it. Then from a long habit of self-discipline she began at once to rationalise this new fact. Of course Jake would be married, why not? In his forties, attractive, far better off than he gave any appearance of being, and he knows hundreds of people. Of course there would be someone.

'... so we'll meet him, and we'll be the only ones to know the truth. Don't you think that will be fun?'

'Him?'

Helen felt dazed, as though she had straightened up too quickly. The sun burning on her hair, the flies weaving their maddening maze in front of her eyes made her feel unsteady and confused.

'Brett Stark. Only you'll never believe what he's really called. Jake's just told me. Edwin!'

'Edwin.' Helen batted away the flies and began to laugh, jerkily, as though she was only a step away from releasing her feelings as Catriona had done over the brash horrors of Glen Righ.

'Edwin Rose. Isn't that perfect?'

'I can see this is going to be fascinating,' Helen conceded, as from the house the thin scream of the kettle summoned them, and the world swung back onto an even keel again.

Edwin, it seemed, would not contemplate staying in the bothy. Five star was his chosen level, the more opulent the better. He had wanted to stay at Glen Righ, having swallowed some highflown advance publicity, delighted that somewhere indecently comfortable would at last be available, but though he did his best to book in even he had finally to admit defeat as it wasn't open.

'Won't Ardlonach be comfortable enough?' Helen asked Jake, who had been having a prowl round her books and was now sitting with her on the verandah eating Stilton and drinking port. 'Una's food is excellent.'

'Edwin despises country house hotels, shudders at "family-run", "local produce", "house-party atmosphere". He demands as his right international glitz, full valet service, all-night restaurants, secretarial back-up, gold bath taps, access to the Internet, fax machine in the shower, round the clock contact with world money markets, and above all shelter from anything which might remind him that he's in the Highlands of Scotland.'

'Why does he want to be linked to money markets and the Internet? I thought he was a writer.'

'Barely. Have you never indulged in the doings of Brett Stark? Remind me to complete your education some time. No, it's all image. He likes power, talking money, creating waves, having people on the run.'

'Um.'

'And now you're glad you suppressed your impulse to invite him here.'

'How did you know?'

'It was written on your face when you heard he wouldn't stay at the bothy. The kind thought, the doubt about the house being comfortable enough, the conclusion that we wouldn't want you butting in anyway. And now the relief that you kept your mouth shut.'

Why was it so good to be teased? Because she could not be teased in this way without having first been understood?

'You make him sound exceedingly unattractive,' was all she said. 'I'm not sure I want to meet him.'

'Ghastly type,' Jake agreed lazily, settling his narrow haunches more comfortably into the wicker chair. 'Too late now though.'

'But why is he coming if he hates Scotland?'

'A few loose ends the publishers are querying on the last book. He could have done it by post. I told you, power, control.'

'He sounds a monster.'

Jake grinned and dug out more Stilton.

Chapter Twenty-two

The monster, Edwin alias Brett Stark, macho loner, lean mean shadowman, silent killer, ultimate survivor, cruised through Luig in his immaculate fifties Bentley, his little triangular blue eyes beaming at the prospect of seeing Jake. He was round and tiny – Rebecca was to say later that when he was driving it the Bentley rolled on at the same unchanging pace because he couldn't reach the pedals – and was dressed in a be-pocketed, belted and flapped tweed outfit that Richard Hannay would have been proud to wear when taking to the heather.

Edwin's face was plump and pink and, when he could be persuaded to take off the tweed fore-and-aft cap with the flaps tied over the crown which he pretended to believe was required wear in this barbaric region, was seen to be framed with a soft halo of fair curls. He had tiny pink hands and equally tiny feet in the most elegant of handmade shoes. He wore a half-hunter on a slim gold chain in his fob pocket. For this foray into the wilds he carried as emergency rations various expensive delicacies in a black leather picnic box, whose compartments were lined in teddy-bear-coloured velvet and fitted with tortoiseshell jars, boxes and flasks with silver tops, a tortoiseshell soap-box, a monogrammed flannel and linen face-towels in their own bags.

His chauffeur, after driving from London, had been given the evening off and Edwin, luckily encountering no locals in a hurry on the blind corners of the loch road, came swaying majestically down the drive to Ardlonach punctually at seven-thirty. He had checked in at the Balantore Castle Hotel near Fort William and was already in shock at the mockery of comfort he had found there. No bidet, no shower cap, no ice box, and when he ordered hot buttered toast it had come in a rack with shards of butter individually wrapped. He was still ruffled at the uncalled-for curtness of the waiter when asked to unwrap them, and it was soothing to be taken joyously to the hearts of those assembled to dine with him – and even more joyously by those who knew the truth of his fell alter ego.

'Dressed to kill something, I see,' Jake commented. 'No time to change for dinner.'

'Does one, here?' Edwin asked, falsetto. 'I mean, dear boy, have you?'

'Thank God you refrain from a kilt. At least in that Buchanesque rig we are spared the sight of your chubby little knees.'

Jake had come down from the bothy via Hilltop in

time to have a bath, and was, as ever, in his kilt, worn with a dark green shirt, unironed but clean. Helen thought he looked marvellous, and much enjoyed the leisurely drink and talk they had time for while waiting for Catriona. She appeared eventually, barely dry, her hair clinging to her damp neck, her shirt also unironed. Jake's appearance made no impact on her.

Jake had taken the wheel of Helen's VW – going to fetch his own car from the garages of Luig House there was always the risk of being collared by someone who expected him to be sociable – and had whipped them efficiently down the Ardlonach road. Helen had luxuriated in being driven, even for so brief a journey. One of the worst things about living alone was having to drive oneself everywhere. Then she told herself not to be fatuous. She had done the driving, on one pretext or another from Walter, for most of their married life.

Be honest, you just like being driven by Jake. Yes, I do, she had admitted, looking away down the strip of field falling to the loch, watching the bright spinnakers of a group of dinghies wheel in unison as they went about to avoid losing the wind under Ardlonach Point.

Una was too busy to leave the kitchen till almost the end of dinner, but Dan and Rebecca joined them, and Trudy and Fitz appeared in time for coffee. Dan, wary as ever with a newcomer, particularly a male intruder in the circle, viewed Edwin with the disbelief of a rottweiler confronted with a miniature chihuahua. Do they really want me to believe this is a dog? Have I got to worry all evening about not treading on it? Wouldn't it be simpler just to eat it?

But though it took him a little longer than the others to appreciate the full delight of Edwin, he got there in the end, and Helen decided as they spilled out of the Coach-house much later, reminding each other not to disturb the guests who had long ago gone to bed, that it had been one of their best evenings.

She was smiling as Jake put her into the car, remembering Dan's look of appalled incredulity as Edwin described the problems he and his mother were having getting new bobbins for their lace-making.

'Such a soothing hobby, lace,' he had remarked, twinkling innocently at Dan, whose muscles flexed in protest. 'Of course as Mummy's over eighty her eyes give her a certain amount of trouble, poor darling, but she finds working out the designs much easier now that she does it all on computer.'

'Bloody hell,' Dan had been heard to mutter as he reached for his glass, but he joined in the laughter.

The best part, for Helen, had been seeing yet another side to Jake. Edwin might relish setting himself up, but he had no hesitation in setting Jake up too.

'No, but explain to me. When you pass these manly trials like rounding the Horn on the BT Global Challenge and getting your ear pierced so that the gold earring can pay for the passage home—'

'Shut up, Edwin.'

'No, dear boy, it's not at all clear to me. Where does

the gold come from? Who makes it into an earring and at what point? When is it inserted in the lobe? And if it's meant to pay for your passage home then who gets it, and when is it torn from its fleshy coffer?'

'For God's sake, Edwin, drink your claret.'

Apart from revealing several fascinating details about Jake's past which no one had known, Edwin had also given away one or two things about his present, though this had been after dinner, when they were in the bar and conversation had become general.

'Do you wish news of the exquisite Zanna?' Edwin had enquired of Jake, nibbling a mouse-sized arc in one of Una's home-made mints, tilting his head in concentration as he checked texture and flavour, and nodding in approbation.

'No,' Jake had said shortly, glancing towards Catriona, deep in conversation with Fitz about one of his elderly housebound patients to whom she regularly read. (What, precisely, Helen often wondered.)

'She is desolate that you remain incommunicado,' Edwin had continued in his high baby voice.

'She knows where to find me.' Jake's voice had been curt, conveying a definite message that the topic was not welcome.

Only Helen, for the moment talking to no one, had been near enough to hear the exchange, and Edwin had turned to her with a theatrical sigh. 'Ah, Helen, the most beautiful anthropologist in London, possibly in the world, long-limbed, golden-haired, ready to cut the

quivering heart from her breast — her delectable breast,
I am reliably informed — for my savage partner, and he
rejects her. She has been acclimatising herself for a visit
here by a prolonged study of the nomads of Siberia —
could passion drive a fair maiden to greater lengths than
this? — and still he spurns her.'

'God, not hard to see how the books are best sellers,'
Jake had said disgustedly, but Helen had felt he was
concealing real anger.

She had also been obliged to accept, with the slight
chill that remembering her age could produce, that Edwin
would probably not, even in this mocking vein, have
referred so casually to the yearning beauties in Jake's life
if she had been twenty years younger.

That, once and for all, should put your feelings for
him into perspective, she had told herself grimly. They are
ludicrous. You must have known there would be someone
in the wings; you conceded that when Catriona's reference
to 'Jake's other half' shook you so much. Drink your wine,
as Jake had ordered Edwin to do, relax, enjoy the good
things of the evening, be a contented old woman. How
I hope I never meet Zanna.

But in spite of the chill, and the mustering-up of
good sense which it demanded, Helen learned a good
deal about Jake during Edwin's visit, and not only because
she discovered more facts about him. To her surprise
Edwin agreed to dine at Hilltop, plus Jake and Catriona
of course, and since all four knew the secret of Brett
Stark caution was no longer necessary. The truth was

both Jake and Edwin enjoyed the joke of their shared personality, and Helen had never seen Jake so relaxed. They told stories of exploits all over the world, and the books that had come out of them. The latest had centred on the armed protection forces raised by tea planters in Assam against liberationists who blew up freight trains, attacked plantations, gunned down crowds in the markets and generally terrorised anyone they didn't care for. Jake had been one of the officers hired to train the guards, and had lived and fought with them for a year.

How very improbable, Helen thought, floating on waves of Chablis and contentment as she offered Edwin a third helping of salmon (much unsolicited and delicious wild produce found its way into her kitchen these days) and hot cucumber sauce. What a splendid trencherman Edwin was, looking pinker and rounder by the moment, his smooth cheeks faintly glistening with the enjoyable effort of parrying Jake's sardonic thrusts, and at the same time eagerly stuffing himself with good things, his shining baby curls jigging under the light.

They argued about everything.

'I must congratulate you on the perfection of your cabinet, my dear Helen.' Edwin at his most fulsome. 'English of course. Oyster walnut, I—'

'Laburnum,' said Jake.

'And the inlay of box—'

'Apple.'

'Perhaps in a better light?'

'Aren't you going to pontificate about the geometric detail—?'

'Dating it as William and Mary,' Edwin darted in.

Catriona giggled. Sitting across from Helen she had been very quiet – indeed with Brett Stark in full flow there was little alternative – but it was obvious that she was enjoying herself, and Jake, playing up to Edwin, had been glad to see it. And what a good hostess Helen was, he thought with pleasure, providing with such calm ease surroundings of comfort which pleased the eye yet had the simplicity he preferred and needed.

'You could argue about the rugs now if you wish,' she was saying to Edwin. 'Are you better on rugs?'

'A barb,' he cried, desolated. 'But let me see – in this light a trifle difficult perhaps, if you will forgive me – ah, um, red ground, wool of course, hand-knotted, yes, yes, late nineteenth century, traditional garden-based design—'

'Oh, please,' said Jake. 'Elementary. And if you've quite finished troughing away at that salmon the rest of us would like to move on ...'

Entertaining as it was, the best part of the evening for Helen came when Edwin's chauffeur arrived. Edwin had been obliged to spend the previous night at Ardlonach after all as Dan, deciding it would be a tragedy if any damage came to the Bentley, had taken away the keys when Edwin started on his second bottle of port. There had been no bidet in his bathroom there either, but putting away a vast and excellent breakfast Edwin had leniently decided such niceties could hardly be expected. Tonight he was prone to linger indefinitely, but neither the chauffeur nor Jake seemed to think this a good idea.

Catriona, after a token offer to wash up which she clearly expected to be turned down, vanished to Little Hilltop, and Helen, having seen Jake bundle Edwin away with such decision, thought he would take himself off. Jake, however, didn't waste time on token anything, but set about the washing-up with his usual dexterous speed.

'If I lived in a dwelling Edwin could contemplate staying in then I'd be the one doing the entertaining,' he pointed out. 'So don't argue, just keep the stuff coming.'

It is very, very silly, Helen acknowledged, to enjoy clearing up after a dinner party so much. And it is very, very dangerous to be quite so pleased to see Jake wander back to the fire with his replenished whisky glass, looking so much at home.

'How well you looked after us, Helen,' he said gratefully, turning from toeing the ends of logs together, rewarded by a friendly blaze. 'It was very good of you – and to put up with Brett who, it has to be said, is a considerable ego-tripper.'

'But a provider.'

'Indeed. On a handsome scale.'

'And you enjoy him?'

'Over the years I've enjoyed him a lot, and also in the nastier moments hated his guts, but to be honest I'm beginning to think he's just about had his day.'

'Wouldn't you miss the colourful exploits?'

'Certain aspects I could do without.' His smile was not altogether amused. 'I suppose I'd miss the challenge, and the variety. I'm not much good at staying put.' He paused, and Helen had a sudden conviction of some disclosure, some self-revelation coming close. Then he visibly thrust it away, asking, 'Am I keeping you up, by the way? I'm afraid I helped myself to a nightcap without asking. Are you pining for your bed?'

'Not at all. It's always nice to unwind after a party.' Helen considered, in view of the delight she felt to be sharing this peaceful intimacy with him, that her tone struck a model note of friendly hospitality.

But whatever revelation had come close Jake didn't revert to it again, apparently content to talk quietly, sunk in the deep armchair, legs stretched out and ankles crossed in his familiar pose, the pleats of his kilt brushing the floor. Perhaps feeling that he had talked about himself, under whatever label, for most of two evenings, he drew Helen out to tell him more of her own life. He knew the bare bones of it. There had been many opportunities to talk by now, and though he rarely remembered Helen's age, accepting her as a contemporary, liking her adaptability and enthusiasm for new things, when he did remember it he thought she had had a lot of courage to divest herself of a husband who bored her to death. He often thought of the phrase she had once quoted from Edith Wharton, 'the green mould of the perfunctory'. It was, perhaps, what he himself most dreaded in relationships.

What he wanted to know more of, sensing accurately

that this had hurt her more deeply than the breaking up of her marriage, was how she felt about her son, and what had happened in the interval between her divorce and coming to Hilltop.

And at last, in the softly lit room where the laughter and enjoyment of the evening still lingered, with Jake looking so peacefully settled, his voice free of his usual mordant humour, she found she could probe beneath the layers of self-justification, and talk about the failure of her attempt to live with Reggie and Nadia.

'I was looking for something that wasn't there. Of course the mechanics of the household were hopeless. The arrangement would never have worked, but finding a cottage nearby would have been a practical alternative. What was wrong was my expectations, my blind clinging to nostalgia, my refusal to move forward forty years!'

'Don't be too hard on yourself.' The swingeing tone moved Jake to protest, but he was glad that she was ready to talk to him about this.

'But I was idiotic. I wanted carthorses and buttercup meadows, I wanted ditches full of kingcups and ladysmock, milk coming frozen home in pail, elm trees and haycocks, corn in stooks, a full dawn chorus.' And perhaps I wanted my father and mother, whose ghosts had been so hard to resurrect in the new gleaming house.

She kept her eyes on the sinking fire as she talked, and Jake kept his eyes on her face, liking the look of keen intelligence the years had done nothing to diminish, liking the honesty of what she was saying.

'But all those things were symbols of course. I was resisting the present. I was wanting not the past back so much as my own youth. I'd rejected Walter and my marriage, and I had nothing to put in its place. That can be quite frightening.'

'But you were able to decide what you valued, and had the courage to go for it.'

'And rejected my family as well.'

'Hadn't they had a facile image too, a cardboard cut-out Grannie to be tucked away in her annexe? Does Reggie know who you really are? Has he ever attempted to find out?'

Helen glanced up in surprise. 'Do you know I've never even thought of asking that?'

'No, you were too sure the breakdown in communication lay at your door. You won't have lost them, you know, your family. All you've done is to choose a way of living that suits you, something many people never have the guts to do. They are still there, a few hours down the road, just as they have always been. Leaving Walter didn't automatically alter your status *vis à vis* your son and his wife.'

'I felt that I should . . .'

But Helen didn't attempt to clarify the 'should'.

Jake nodded, watching her for a moment more. 'You seem very much at home here,' he suggested.

'Oh, it's been wonderful,' she assented, her tense expression lightening. 'I missed Scotland so much when I was away, having lived here most of my life, and the time in Inverbuie had made me realise how perfect this part of it is. I had to come back. And I was right. Apart from Catriona, and the friendships I've found through her – and not forgetting the crash course in animal husbandry – it does genuinely feel like home.'

And now you are part of it, or at least less likely to go away; and, when you are here, ready to sprawl contentedly at my fireside, and rouse in me feelings I can never remember feeling before.

Chapter Twenty-three

'Jake's asked me to sleep with him tonight,' Catriona said, appearing in the kitchen doorway of Hilltop with a string of mackerel in her hand. 'I'm afraid these aren't cleaned or anything yet. Do you want me to do them for you?'

Questions and protests, and the instant effort to repress them, rocked through Helen's brain. Outrage and disbelief. What was Jake thinking of? Then self-discipline took over – it's nothing to do with you; say nothing, show nothing.

'Beautiful fish,' she managed, her voice exaggeratedly enthusiastic. 'Where did you—?'

'Been out with Michie and a couple of his mates. We stopped off on Una's island and cooked some for ourselves on the way back. Mackerel always taste best in the open air somehow. Anyway, I thought I'd better stoke up. Jake will probably expect me to last out on blaeberries and strange fungal growths.'

'There's certainly plenty here if you're going to be

out for dinner,' Helen said bravely. Just talk about fish. 'Perhaps Watty would like—?'

'No, it's all right, I dropped some off for him on the way back. Perhaps you could freeze some. There, that's done. Now, I've got to nip down to Ardlonach, Dan's lending me a rucksack.'

'You're camping? You and Jake—?' There, that wasn't too difficult. And remember no one would ever imagine, least of all Catriona ... 'You're going camping?' The ordinary phrase helped to steady the whirling images.

Catriona giggled. 'I'm not sure Jake would call it that. No, just sleeping out. Absolute minimum of kit, though he's allowing me a sleeping bag, also courtesy the Ardlonach survival store.'

'And what about food?' Yes, cling to your role of anxious old dear. Ask the pointless fussing questions. Use them to blanket the pang of knowing that it is not you who is invited to sleep out on the hill with Jake in the end-of-summer night; that it will never be you; that your time for such casual adventures is over. When it was your time you slept night after night beside Walter, he wearing the same sort of striped pyjamas he wore at school, you in your Marks and Spencer nighties, the window open no more than its regulation three inches.

'Oh, you know Jake, living off the land and all that. At least where we're going he won't be making me scour out mess-tins with soapwort or horsetails, or thrash nettle stalks into fibres for lashing bunks.'

'No, but — I mean, you'll take something for breakfast?'

'Bacon and sausages?' Catriona teased. 'Come on, Helen, you know it won't be that sort of trip.'

Which is another reason why Catriona is going and you are not, Helen reminded herself grimly. Your mind is locked in the lists and ritual of sending Reggie off to scout camp, which he loathed anyway but which Walter insisted would be good for him. And here I am, thirty years later, still saying, 'What about breakfast?'

But ruthless as she was with herself, Helen's spirits lifted. Catriona was no more off to 'sleep with Jake' than Reggie had been off to sleep with his patrol leader. How irrational that flash of jealousy and envy had been. And how revealing. Someone is going to notice soon if you're not more careful, she warned herself. Rebecca's sharp eyes missed nothing, and Fitz too, in his different way, was observant and perceptive.

But perhaps, perhaps, before long it might not matter if people guessed how she felt about Jake. It was a strange, tentative thought, but lately she had begun to wonder if the unimaginable could come about. Jake was so much part of life at Hilltop these days. He came and went freely, very much at home there, openly enjoying the style of the house, of both houses, and even more openly enjoying Helen's food, so that she soon found herself buying and planning meals with greater interest and care than she ever had before. He often helped with heavy work in the garden too, having a kinder hand than Watty, whose methods were so draconian that any areas he cleared were likely to remain cleared for years to come. The only problem, as far as the work went, was that when Jake was helping there was a tendency for conversation to take over. In other respects that was Helen's greatest delight.

Nowadays he almost always came walking up the stone-walled path with Catriona, or with Catriona and her, after closing the shop, frequently staying for dinner and lingering on for those lazy evenings by the fire which he seemed to like so much, talking into the small hours, about books, his travels, the shape the world was taking, the environmental issues he cared about so much. Catriona would very often slip away on her own affairs and then, in this atmosphere of ease and frankness, Jake would gently probe Helen's thoughts, encouraging her to examine the past in a more realistic light than she had ever been capable of doing alone, enabling her to free herself of old guilts and doubts, and in his turn telling her more about his own childhood and early life.

He had been largely brought up at Luig, one of the sprawling intricate Macleod clan, but always feeling himself very much a fringe member, and even as a boy resistant to the sophisticated tastes and values of the mainstream family. His mother, the daughter of an artist, brought up in Europe's capitals and an established portrait painter in her own right, had seriously jeopardised his father's career in the Scots Guards by her exotic and well-publicised affairs, before vanishing for good when Jake was four. With his father almost totally absent Jake had grown up thinking of himself as a single unit, loosely connected to the larger family, but ultimately belonging only to himself. His commission in his father's regiment, as he freely admitted, had been an attempt to join some kind of fold, and as a consequence he had had to endure years of a conformity which went very much against the grain of his nature. That he had nevertheless made something of it, and gained from it, Helen saw as one of the strengths of his character.

It had seemed, in recent weeks, that his inveterate restlessness was driving him less urgently. He would say himself, semi-jokingly, that he owed it to Uncle Percy to do something with the shop after the compliment of being endowed with it, but had he not been ready to involve himself in the business it could have been sold without anyone giving the decision a second thought. There was no talk yet of another research foray on Brett Stark's behalf, and though Helen was strict with herself about too impossible imaginings, she did allow herself to think that Jake had found a combination he liked in the privacy and austerity of the bothy, and the empty landscape he loved where he could expend his restless energy, supplemented by the unpretentious comfort of Hilltop.

Catriona sat comfortably against Jake's side, her mind adrift from reality, swept away by the vast pure beauty before them, sailing out across the dark guts of the glens, the ridges between them etched silver by the moon, beyond the sound and the islands to the limitless shimmer of sea that without visible demarcation became the cloud-patterned sky arching back over her. She felt weightless, disembodied, yet the sensations of delight were physical, her throat tight, her breathing altered. The solidity of Jake's body close beside her kept her anchored, safe. The sense of safety was rooted, she knew, in the accord of their mood.

They had come swiftly, steadily, up the even pull of the moor in the beginning of dusk, not talking, senses open to sounds and sights, smells and feeling. As they began the climb to the first ridge darkness had thickened briefly, then the moon had swum up, warm-toned with summer, and the magic had overtaken them, the delight in every detail of their shared world.

At this height all sounds, all movement, had fallen away. No provender here for hunting owls, no distinctive brush of plovers' wings, no sound of sheep. Here there might be ptarmigan or mountain hare, but they would be mute now. The stags were not rutting yet and the heart-stopping challenges that would soon resound back and forth across the hills had not begun.

The flow of cool air against her skin, tangible as a hand, brought, in this moment of intense perception, a dozen messages. It had swept across heather and myrtle, juniper and whin, sun-baked rock and bogs parched and cracking open after the dry weather; across moss and bracken and ferns and a thousand wild flowers, across the droppings of grouse and fox, red deer and roe, across peaty pools and ice-cold burns. It was laden with the scents of home, just as inches from her nose Jake's battered hill jacket smelled of home, and the small rucksack Dan had lent her, and the boots she wore.

My world, she thought, yet I have never done this before, climbed in the gloaming to its very roof, to sleep under the moon and stars. And suddenly that tightening in her throat was too much, and with an exclamation she ducked her head against Jake's arm and pressed it there.

She felt the arm shift, her forehead dropping to Jake's chest as it did so, then the arm went round her in a firm grip.

'Too much?' His voice was full of understanding. 'How dare we, isn't that it? Not how dare we be here, but how dare we be, with our outcries and devastation, our strange conviction of our own worth.'

'Yes,' Catriona said, burrowing her head against him for a moment more, her voice muffled. Then, 'Yes,' sitting up and pushing back her hair, but not freeing herself from the circle of his arm. 'A sort of extreme reality. But also realising that this is what matters most, to me, always. I had such absurd ideas, about what was important.'

'Or you were trying to grasp other people's concept of what was important, and felt it was impertinent to know better?'

'Because I knew nothing. Yes. But everyone's reality is different.'

'And, in the general scheme of things, brief,' he reminded her.

She laughed, liking the teasing tone. 'I shall stay,' she said.

Not here on top of An Tearlach, Jake supposed, but in the life that had grown over her like a natural skin in the past weeks. 'Good,' he said, then after a pause of shared silence to say amen to that, he began to chant softly, '"With few but with how splendid stars ..." You.'

'"... the mirrors of the sea are strewn." Not accurate tonight though, there are a million stars. "Look at all the fire folk sitting in the air!"'

'"The bright boroughs, the circle citadels there."'

'Oh, Jake, what a lovely person you are, not nearly as grouchy as people say.'

'How gratifying. We're not being too original in our quotations, though, are we?'

'I don't want to be. I want the familiar, I love it. Repetition should affirm value, not debase it.'

'How right you are. Well then, "Go, and catch a falling star ..."'

'"Go and catch a falling star",' Catriona repeated dreamily. 'So beautiful, but better without the comma. The rest's a dreadful anti-climax though. "Or who clove the Devil's foot" is the feeblest effort to rhyme with mandrake root.'

Jake laughed, pulling her closer against him. I love to sit on the thin soil and wind-scoured turf of this high peak and bandy poetry with this straight-thinker, this innocent who has no undercurrents of pettiness or conceit or greed in her nature, who is swept away by beauty and not afraid to show it.

And when they were tired and ready to sleep they would lie down, here, where they were, to explore the valleys of the moon and the stately, changing patterns of the clouds till their eyes closed. He had not looked for shelter, other than to choose this small hollow lined with sparse grass rather than rock, and in the morning they would have to drop down several hundred feet to come to water and make a brew, and cook the oatmeal he had brought. He had chosen this exposed place deliberately, for its sense of limitless space and splendour, confident Catriona wouldn't notice its deficiencies.

Getting into his survival bag an hour later Jake moved to windward of Catriona, already up to her ears in her Ardlonach sleeping bag, and turned on his side to give her maximum protection.

'Ground not too hard for you?' he asked. 'Catriona?' He leaned down towards her. She was fast asleep, cold supper, cold ground, white radiance of the moon on her face notwithstanding.

Jake laughed aloud. She would never hear him.

Helen's delight at the news that Catriona had finally disabused herself of the idea that in order to have a life she should go off to disagreeable places, was so great that she paused to examine it. Was she turning Catriona into a substitute family? Dragging the thought into the light was salutary; the danger identified could be avoided. She could simply be whole-heartedly pleased about Catriona's decision.

'Only should I move out?' Catriona rattled her complacency by enquiring.

'Move out? But why? I thought you'd just decided to stay?'

'Yes, but that's why. You won't want to feel I'm tying up your other house permanently, will you? And I don't pay you nearly as much rent as I should, I know that. Shouldn't I find permanent accommodation?'

'Oh, please don't! I really couldn't bear to have anyone else living so close by. The little house would only stand empty and that would be such a waste.'

'But your family?' Catriona hesitated over the question. She knew relations between Helen and her son and daughter-in-law were not good at present, and didn't want to touch on a subject that would cause pain.

'I don't think they'll be here for a while. If they do want to use the house you could perhaps move in with me, if you didn't mind?'

'I'd love it of course, only I wouldn't want to be in the way. I could always sleep at the shop again, that worked very well. Or stay at Trudy's. Or if it's not the height of the season there's plenty of room at Ardlonach, only that's not so handy for the shop if Watty's using the van. Still, I can usually scrounge lifts.'

Helen laughed. 'I see the options are endless. You stay in the cottage, Catriona. I shall be devastated if you think of moving. And I'll tell you what we'll do — we'll have a house-warming party at last, for both of us, and to celebrate your decision to stay on at the bookshop. Una and Rebecca and Dan won't be so busy as the season winds down, and Donald and Clare should find autumn quieter, so let's get down to the planning without delay.'

'That would be fun.' Catriona knew that for her it would set a seal on her decision to stay in Luig, to accept finally that the way she was living was ideal for her. She needed known places, friends, the security of belonging. Without them she could not survive and there was no point in trying.

'All the baby-sitters will be at the party,' she observed, beginning to make a mental list.

'Then all the babies had better come too.'

Chapter Twenty-four

With a fluttery though agreeable mixture of anticipation and anxiety, Helen put the finishing touches to the buffet laid out in the dining-room. She was not usually a fluttery person and knew she was almost indulging in the unfamiliar excited nervousness, a measure of how much this party meant to her. It also struck her that the items on the table said something about her new life – grouse pâté, galantine of partridge, a deep game pie, glazed and adorned with pastry leaves, and a handsome salmon, poached in the Ardlonach fish kettle and delivered by Dan not an hour ago. A batch of Una's famous crabcakes waited in the kitchen to be fried at the last moment.

Helen had tried to stop Una contributing to the feast. 'It's supposed to be a night off for you.'

But with Una to give affection was to cook. 'It can all be done beforehand. Once the party starts I shall just be enjoying myself. Anyway, even if I lent you the fish kettle there's barely room for it on your cooker, and you've got all the rest to do. You and Catriona.'

They had laughed. It was already a joke that Catriona's contribution to the party was suggesting ever more unknown names for the guest list, and adding to every offer to help such provisos as, 'Only I don't think I'm very good at sauces,' or, 'I've not actually *made* that before, but you could show me how.'

Una had also sent, as extras of her own, a dark, rich chocolate mousse and some very professional-looking glazed fruit tarts. Posh enough to be called *tartelettes*, Helen decided, swung into euphoria again, full of gratitude and fondness. Fond in its original sense, she told herself, but this light-hearted Helen refused to be put down.

Trudy had been here all afternoon, bringing chairs, silver and glasses, raiding Little Hilltop for anything it could contribute, arranging small tables in the sitting-room and doing her best to make effective use of the nàrrow verandah.

Catriona, now chivvied off to change, had been at the shop (with orders not to bring home to supper any chance customers she happened to like) and Jake, by a piece of unlucky timing, had had to go clear across to Kincardine O'Neil for a house sale. Worry about whether he would be back in time was, Helen knew, the main cause of her tension. Without him a house-warming would be meaningless.

Was there enough food? Oh, ridiculous, there was far too much, they couldn't consume half this amount.

But how she had enjoyed preparing it. And how she was enjoying now surveying her polished, waiting house, the flowers it had been a pleasure to cut from her garden this morning, the fires nicely taking hold but low because parties got so hot and the evening was sultry anyway.

'I don't think we're going to be lucky with the weather,' Trudy had observed, coming in after collecting trails of all-too-abundant ivy for the table. 'But it gets dark so much earlier now that I don't suppose it will matter what it does.'

It was true, Helen thought, standing in the dining-room doorway to enjoy the room before going up to dress. There was more than a hint of autumn in the air, which already had that different taste, of cold and decaying vegetation, when she went out into the garden before bed. The darkness was no longer the half-dark of summer, and mornings were crisp, pale cloud streaking pale blue skies, sunlight thinner, the colours of moor and lochside subtly richer each day. Her mind swept forward to winter, and she relished the prospect, getting to know her house in a different guise, cold walks on the windswept moor and coming back to tea by big fires, robust warming food and hot toddies with the wind screaming up from the sound to howl against closed windows. She knew she was seeing Jake by the fire and downing the toddies, and laughed at herself. But nothing could shake her mood of eager happiness tonight.

And if Jake doesn't get back? The idea was too dismal to contemplate, and she pushed it aside, turning to run upstairs. Had she ever before, she wondered, got ready for a party in such a mood of expectation? Of course, long ago, when she was young. Before Walter, she amended, before a drab indistinguishable succession of duty dinner parties, duty drinks parties, Sunday lunches with the minister, a trustee, an influential parent. And their wives. One must never forget the wives.

As she began to unbutton her shirt she heard a car in the lane. Jake had made it, was coming for a bath as he sometimes did. Wonderful. She could run round to Little Hilltop, not minding if Catriona had used all the hot water. Oh, yes, Jake first. But she was too happy to be disgusted with herself. Then as she stooped to look out of the gable window she saw the car was not Jake's, the long expensive bonnet of which even she could not mistake. Yet it looked familiar. One of the others coming early to help? But it wasn't the tough little jeep Dan and Rebecca drove, or the Chrysler they teased Fitz about, more Harley Street than Harbour Brae.

It was impossible to see who was in the car before it passed out of sight. If it was unknown chums of Catriona's then she could come round and look after them, Helen decided, buttoning her shirt again and going downstairs. Whoever it was had decided against coming round to the front door. Not strangers then. She went through the lobby and opened the door to the lane. Reggie, blushing, uncertain, almost furtive with embarrassment, took a couple of steps backwards, as though disclaiming any expectation of being asked in.

'Reggie! Goodness, the last person — what on earth are you doing here?' In spite of herself Helen looked past him to the car, knowing that among the rush of questions and not altogether delighted surprise ('My party!'), the prospect that had made her heart sink was of seeing Nadia behind him, her special daughter-in-law's smile in place.

'Hello, Mother. I hope this is — I hope you don't mind. Breezing in like this, I mean, without letting you know or anything.'

Breezing in; she could hear Nadia's voice. But the car was empty. 'Reggie, of course I don't mind. But it's rather a surprise. I had no idea you were — but is everything all right?' Even as her voice sharpened with anxiety common sense reminded her that the telephone was a more efficient means of conveying news than getting into a car and driving four hundred miles. Whatever was wrong it could be nothing life-threatening.

'No, no, everything's fine. I — er — well, I just—' Reggie looked helplessly down the lane, as though assistance might appear there.

'Reggie darling, what am I thinking of? Come in, come in at once. I'm sorry, I was just so startled to see you.'

Now he rushed into explanations, disjointed and confused, as he lunged to open the door to the hall, flattening himself among the coats against the wall to let her pass, folding himself behind the door in the process and extricating himself awkwardly. Helen was conscious of well-remembered exasperation overtaking her; Reggie had been here for seventy-five seconds and already her house felt cramped and inconvenient.

'I had to come up for a meeting – a firm in Ayr – they look like being a major account. Quite a break for us. I thought I'd just pop over, as I was in the area.'

'Pop over? From Ayr?' Half as far again as his journey from Withedine, at a rough calculation.

'Well, as I was up here.' Reggie was pink and perspiring, his hands making dabbing movements as though to fend off attack. 'Up in Scotland, you know. On business.'

'Well, it was a very nice thought.' Helen, from old habit, spoke soothingly, minding his driven, hunted look. Yet part of her brain protested, But oh, Reggie, how like you to choose tonight of all nights. If you are here on a mission to make me move house or tart up the kitchen, or even if you feel some overwhelming compulsion to unburden your soul of childhood injustices, then please, my infuriating, hesitant, blundering son, why must it be tonight? But under the selfish cry of protest there was another layer still, of loving sympathy. Poor man, always the victim of his own gentleness and tolerance.

'Reggie,' she said more firmly, 'of course it's all right to come. At any time. My home is yours, you know that. Come and have a drink, relax.'

She had led him into the sitting-room and to her resigned amusement he didn't notice its odd arrangement, the sofa and big chairs pushed back against the walls and two small tables with chairs round them in the centre of the room. Instead, oblivious, he stood with his back to the fire, offering more details about the meeting in Ayr, as though believing that if he convinced Helen of its importance then she would somehow understand what he was doing here.

'Well, that all sounds excellent,' she said kindly. 'Most promising. Now, what will you have? Whisky?'

'Oh, shall I—?' Galvanised into action, the correct button pressed. Men dealt with drinks.

At least he remembers something I taught him, Helen thought, checking him with a lift of her hand, and glancing at her watch as she hurried across the hall. Less than half an hour till people started to arrive. Though Catriona should be back at any moment; no one in the world spent less time dressing. But then, what to do with Reggie? Did he urgently need to unburden himself about some crisis? That could take a minute or two. No, don't laugh at him, Helen reproved herself, lifting the whisky glass then turning back to add another large splash. Could it wait till after the party, whatever it was? She noted with objective interest that she felt no curiosity on her own part. But apart from Una, or perhaps Gillian Macleod, few of the people coming tonight were likely to leave early. Was it fair to ask Reggie to wait? But there wasn't time now. She still had to change. She must switch on the hotplate before she forgot. There was wine to open, though Dan would probably take care of that for her. A useful person to have around, Dan.

Suddenly she paused, stabbed by an unwelcome comparison. Dan, competent and cool, like most of these new friends, was so different from her bumbling, indecisive son. And the difference seemed to emphasise the gulf between her new independent life and her former trammelled one; between herself then and herself now.

There isn't time for this, she told herself fiercely, turning to go back to Reggie. But he, either incapable of facing his own company with whatever was worrying him as yet unresolved, or still thinking he should make himself useful over the drinks, had followed her. Even he could not fail to notice a table entirely covered with food.

'I say, you're not having a party, are you?' His voice was blank with disbelief. His mother, this old person living alone? Whatever for; whoever for? The disbelief was heavy with disapproval.

You guessed? No, don't say that. 'Reggie, I'm sorry this is happening on the very evening you've chosen to come, such unlucky timing. But you'll stay the night – or as long as you like, of course – so we'll have plenty of time to talk. And you'll be able to meet my friends. Some you already know – Catriona, the Urquharts—'

'Well, I certainly didn't expect anything like this.' Reggie didn't seem prepared to let her off. 'I mean, we've been worried about you, all on your own and so on. It's one of the reasons I'm here, in a way.'

Oh, is it, Helen thought grimly. Thank you for the warning. 'Well, as you see, this evening I shall be far from alone. This is my house-warming party, so in that respect how appropriate that you came tonight. You can share in wishing me well for my life at Hilltop, and wishing Catriona well, for it's her party too. I've let the smaller cottage to her, on the understanding that she moves out whenever you need it. And here is Catriona, so she can look after you while I change.'

Which dealt with quite a lot, she decided with satisfaction, having pushed an unwilling Reggie and Catriona into each other's arms and fled once more to her room. Though heaven knows what they will find to say to each other. She laughed as she ran the bath. Who cared? Only don't be too late, Jake. I think I may need your stringent good sense to get me through this, for sooner or later I am bound to be under attack.

Reggie looked miffed until well into the party, but avoiding the trenchant Rebecca, and Trudy with her bracing down-to-earth manner, he gradually gravitated towards the less abrasive female element, and Una's soothing murmurs, large quantities of delicious food and corresponding doses of alcohol administered by Dan, who decided Reggie needed to loosen up a bit, blurred his initial censoriousness and he began to enjoy himself. His lurch into the party mood was half a beat behind the music, but he never knew it.

In spite of her contentment with the scene, and the satisfying feeling of being at one with her surroundings and with these people who knew so well how to enjoy themselves, Helen, watching him, was uncomfortably conscious of other demands waiting to pull her in a different direction, to be another person.

Reggie, she saw, was surprised by the mixture of guests present, and she was annoyed to find herself wanting to argue with him about it. She could imagine him struggling to answer Nadia's questions, and wondered how he would describe the sight of Michaela Macleod, 'casually' dressed in amber velvet trousers and silk shirt, dancing a disciplined and skilful jig to uncouth mouth music provided by Catriona's friend Michie, wearing as ever his huge fisherman's sweater. And what did he make of little red-faced Watty, his intake of drams monitored by Dan, skilfully waltzing with quiet Gillian, her blind face serene above his balding head?

Connor had been invited, though Catriona had needed some persuasion from Jake and Helen to accept that that was a good idea, on the grounds that family friendships of long standing should not be lightly dispensed with.

'Particularly now that you are living here for good,' Helen had said disingenuously, and that had swayed the balance. However, fortunately or discreetly, Connor had been unable to accept, having stalking guests to look after. He was deeply entangled with Andrea once more, and her engagement had been broken off. Helen suspected that he wouldn't even notice that Catriona never appeared at Luig now, just as he had never registered her departure from his birthday dance.

How good they are to come, Helen thought, listening

to the gabble of talk. And how nice to know the babies
are tucked up next door. Fitz had just come back from
checking on them, signalling to Clare that all was well.
Trudy, deep in discussion with Sadie, hadn't noticed he'd
gone. Clare had been apologetic about Robbie who, in
roistering spirits at finding himself in such a gathering at
bedtime, especially with so much food in sight, had not
been inclined to retire, though Isla and Finn had allowed
themselves to be carried next door without protest.

'Don't worry, he'll go when he's ready,' Helen had
reassured Clare, and then had felt a guilty pang because
Reggie was there, and because when he was four she would
not have countenanced him running about for half an hour
at a grown-up party. I was such a stickler, she thought
ruefully. But that's how it was then, she instantly defended
herself, then shook her head, her face tightening, to realise
how readily such old arguments could be prompted by
Reggie's presence.

Dismissing the thought, she turned to watch the
dancing. Helen had not envisaged this when first she
planned the party. She would have thought there simply
wasn't room. But Trudy's organisation had been good and
as soon as supper was over the tables and chairs had been
whistled to the far end of the verandah, the rug rolled
up and dispatched after them. There was room for one
set for an eightsome, spectators tucking up their feet or
hanging their legs sideways over the arms of chairs. For
longways sets the neutral couple simply climbed onto the
nearest piece of furniture.

Reggie's face was a study of reluctance and dismay as Rebecca hauled him to his feet, though at Netherdean he had been put through his paces at an early age like everyone else. The dismay turned to stuffy disapproval as Jake led Helen out for a *Duke of Perth*.

For Jake had come, appearing among them just as Fitz put a square of neatly dissected salmon – refusing to let Una go near it – onto the last held-out plate. Jake, in his best green shirt, Jake bringing with him a swirl of cool air after his swift run down from the moor, Jake smiling, white teeth gleaming, Jake lively and energetic and ready to party all night.

His presence swung everything back into perspective for Helen. This was her place; here, where with such ease and speed she had been drawn into this generous group. Whatever Reggie had come to say could not change that. And if, as she suspected, he was here out of some need of his own, then she would do whatever she could to help him – when the moment was opportune.

At least Reggie had the chance to see, could not avoid seeing, the elements that were now part of her life. Though perhaps she should reassure him, she thought, spun to a standstill by Jake and supported for a moment by his arm, as hard as a piece of bog oak, till she was steady, that she didn't spend every evening like this. She laughed at the thought, and Jake glanced down at her.

'Nothing makes a party go so well,' he observed, 'as the hostess enjoying herself.'

'How could I not? Everyone's been so kind.' They

had come bearing gifts and she had been overcome by it.

She had wondered if Jake would stay long, afraid a party like this would bore him, but he was as keen a dancer as any of them, and when he set about enjoying himself no one could match him for energy and staying power.

But what was happening now? Rebecca was standing up, Dan bringing in a guitar from the hall. This was new. As everyone found places for themselves and the room became quiet Helen was glad that Jake was still beside her, sitting sideways on the arm of her chair, curving an arm along its back. And as Rebecca sang, her pure voice filling the small crowded room, Jake's nearness seemed to Helen almost unbearable, as though it was wonderful but not enough, not nearly enough. And when the applause broke out and Jake dropped his arm to give her shoulders a brief hug, she turned her face up to him with a smile which afterwards she was afraid had showed him far too much.

'Hadn't you heard Rebecca sing before?' he asked, bending to speak to her under cover of the noise.

'Never. It was beautiful.'

'Essential to any party,' he declared, adding in a different tone, 'I imagine that the evening has provided an opportunity for your son to see that your life is not without colour.' He looked across at Reggie, owlish with tiredness, driving, malt whisky and the ramblings of Sadie's husband on the subject of home rule for Scotland, and his lip curled in his familiar sardonic grin.

He's got there in one, Helen thought, not entirely

sober herself. It made her feel thrillingly on the brink of new things. Yet tonight, tonight of all nights, her son would be sleeping in the house. What an irony there was in that.

Chapter Twenty-five

Not only was Reggie there that night, but he was there the following morning, and whatever it was that he had come to say had to be addressed. He looked in bad shape. Not that he had been by any means the last to leave the party, having stumbled off apologetically to bed while people with more stamina, and more lively consciences, had insisted on putting the house to rights for Helen before they departed. Donald and Fitz had retrieved their sleeping children, Sadie had promised to deliver Watty and Michie home, and Dan had followed to make sure they gave her no problems, while Catriona, very conscious of being co-hostess, had stood with Helen to see everyone off. Jake had given them each a hug and a kiss before vanishing into the darkness of the hillside, and Helen had had to deal with some troublesome and long-dormant feelings as she took herself at last to bed, not in the least ready for sleep.

Now she was unable to feel much sympathy or

patience for her son. He had insisted that she wake him early as he had a long drive ahead of him, and she had dutifully dragged herself out at the time they had agreed, ignoring an inner protest that one of the best features of her present life was being able to sleep as long as she liked. This was one morning when it would have been bliss.

Reggie, having been vainly called and then ruthlessly shaken awake, took an interminable time to get up. He had so little with him that it was impossible to imagine what he could be doing as he tramped endlessly back and forth overhead, went up and down stairs and in and out to the car. At last he appeared in the kitchen, pale, shaky and quite unable to make up his mind what he wanted for breakfast.

Helen had decided she couldn't be bothered to make proper coffee, then had felt mean and grudging. She was pleased when her new, less-programmed self was able to take one look at the shambles that was her son and decide unrepentantly that he wouldn't know what he was drinking.

He seemed vaguely conscious that he had something to say, but his mind was dragged away by concern about the time. He kept checking the clock, his watch, and even peered earnestly for some moments at the oven timer but could make nothing of it. Eventually he asked if Helen would turn on the radio.

'I don't have one in here.' And I don't feel inclined to fetch one. Just eat.

'Mustn't be too late, Nadia will be expecting me,' he mumbled. 'Long way to go.'

'Reggie,' she said, and saw him flinch and blink at the crisp tone. 'Does Nadia know you are here?'

He gazed at her dumbly, mouth quivering, and for one appalled second she thought he was going to weep.

'Oh, Reggie.' Helen sat down opposite him and looked at him with irritated compassion. He looked as vulnerable as he used to at ten years old, when his spectacles were always crooked and seemed to be permanently held together with sticking plaster, hair standing up in all directions, brown eyes shy and anxious. 'Why did you come?' she asked gently.

He made a jerky twisting movement with his whole body, as though literally feeling the hook in his mouth. 'It isn't that Nadia would mind,' he burst out defensively. 'Of course she wouldn't, you are my mother, she knows that. But she'd — well, she'd — I mean, she likes to go into things a bit.'

What a very good way of putting it, Helen thought detachedly. Poor man. 'So you came because——?'

'Look, Mum——'

He must feel desperate to call me that.

'I just wanted, well, you know, to see if you were all right. Nadia made such a song and dance about the house, and how uncomfortable and inadequate it is, and I didn't like to think of you stuck up here all on your own. I know we didn't look after you very well when you were with us. I do know that,' he repeated, as though he was so used to being argued with that he felt he must insist on the point, 'and it wouldn't have worked out, I suppose, that sort of arrangement. But it does seem a long way for you to have come, where you know nobody, and so on.'

That was how he had seen her situation; that was how he was still seeing it.

'Did you notice anything going on here last night?' But before he could reply, Helen hurried on. That was not the tone to take. 'I've been very fortunate here, Reggie, and have been made most welcome. It's a place where people are friendly, easy to get to know, and ready to look after a newcomer, particularly someone living alone. Didn't you find my guests last night agreeable?'

'Yes, well, but — there were some pretty odd people there, weren't there? Not at all the sort of ...' His voice trailed away, and from his frowning, groping look Helen judged that his recollections of last night were not too clear. Had Dan seen to that, just as he had paced the intake of Watty and Sadie's husband? No one ever tried to interfere with Michie's drinking.

'They are my friends,' Helen said firmly. What was Sadie's husband called? 'And they are very good to me.' He still looked resistant, unconvinced. 'Reggie, I'm happy here. Don't you see that? Though it was good of you to want to make sure, and I appreciate your coming.'

He looked at her, grateful for the sincerity in her voice. 'I had to come. I had to talk to you, on my own.'

She nodded, waiting, aware that they had come to the point at last.

'I know I'm not a good correspondent, never have been,' Reggie plunged. 'And now that you're up here, well, keeping in touch is difficult, isn't it? But I don't want you to feel cut off. It's not always easy to suit everyone, with the children wanting to do their own thing, and you and Nadia—'

He paused, the words sticking in his throat, but Helen had never expected him to get so far.

'We're very different,' she said. 'I sometimes wonder if that was why you chose her?'

Reggie stared, flustered by this frankness, rushing them on so much further than he had meant to go, then some inner honesty responded to it, and Helen received a surprising glimpse of a different Reggie. Even his voice changed, becoming deeper and firmer. 'Perhaps you're right in a way. But it wasn't so much you I wanted to move away from, it was the unit, you and Father, the school – the pressures. I always felt I couldn't be what you wanted me to be, didn't have the brains or aspirations, the values even. Although I knew Father despised Nadia and laughed at her, she made me feel – well, I knew I could give her what she wanted. I suppose that's what it amounted to. But I don't want you to think that even if you and she don't—' He put his hands to his forehead, pressing the pale skin into wrinkles. 'What I mean is, I'm always there for you. That's what I came to say.'

'Oh, Reggie.' Tears stung Helen's eyes. She slipped out of her seat and went to stand beside him, drawing his bowed head against her. He didn't resist, but he didn't take his hands away from his face either, so the embrace was knobbly and inept. But it was theirs. And she had been afraid that Reggie might have come to confront her yet again with the damage she and Walter had done to him by not letting him go to a 'real' school, by letting him be an only child. 'I'm so glad you did,' she said, smoothing back the untidy hair and pressing a kiss on it before releasing him and going back to her seat.

'We're family,' he said gruffly, putting his spectacles straight.

'Yes, and that matters to me too. And Reggie, please don't feel guilty about the time I spent with you. The circumstances weren't ideal, we both agree on that, but I didn't attempt to fit in either. I didn't realise it at the time but I was resisting everything, hating change, searching for the impossible – the past. In that frame of mind nothing you offered me would have seemed right, but that doesn't mean I wasn't grateful to you and Nadia for offering me a home. Another thing was, of course, that I'd spent too much of my life in Scotland. I feel at home here, though I'm sorry my living so far north imposes such long journeys on you.'

'Yes, well, I'm not exactly sure when we'll manage to come up again.' The positive Reggie had vanished, and his eyes didn't meet hers.

'Well, since we're being frank, I'd be glad if you could convince Nadia that I shan't be doing anything to the house, and need no help on that score. The cottage will always be available to you for holidays – no, Catriona is quite clear about it, it's part of our deal – and I think we should leave it that when you want to come you come. The link is there, unbroken.'

And that was what mattered.

She cried, this time, as he drove away. She had expected him to come loaded with accusations. Instead he had brought his guilt, freeing her from hers.

The tempo of her days seemed changed after Reggie's visit, more sure and even. She could hardly have said where her time went. Squandered on trivia, she decided cheerfully, but it was enjoyable trivia, satisfying her, keeping her fit, providing her with much good company.

Jake showed no signs of going away again, and she saw a great deal of him; acknowledged to herself that her days revolved around seeing him. Sometimes they walked together, though never taking the ranging circuits he made with Catriona, and through his eyes she learned more of the moor and its endless life, minute and obscure as much of it was. He explained to her the uses of several plants which she had never guessed at, opened her eyes to details she would have walked straight past, relatively observant though she considered herself to be, but above all he shared with her his love of this landscape, empty of humans, still unspoiled. Sometimes they walked together down to Ardlonach, or down to the shore, or went out to the furthest rocky extremity of the headland. A couple of times he took her fishing for trout, but he never suggested that she went out with the fishing boats, as he and Catriona occasionally did, and Helen never had the courage to say how much she longed to go.

Slowly she got to know more names and faces, became involved, felt more securely and contentedly part of things. Inevitably she learned more about Jake, both from the long hours spent in his company, and from others in their circle.

'You've had a most humanising effect on my cousin,' Michaela commented once, when Helen was having lunch at Luig. 'Normally he keeps himself to himself and is scarcely seen. I thought he'd be even worse when he decided to live in the bothy. He was always a terrific loner as a child.'

'He wasn't happy,' Gillian put in. In general she said little, inhabiting a quiet world of her own, and when she spoke her words made an impact.

'Well, his mother was pretty unkind to him.'

'In what way?' Helen asked.

'Always making lavish promises she couldn't be bothered to keep,' Michaela replied. 'I see him in my memory as always watching the drive, waiting. She hardly ever came here, hated the place, the climate, the whole way of life. Her mother was Spanish and she was brought up mainly in Seville. Beautiful, of course, but quite ruthless.'

Hence Jake's swarthy colouring, Helen thought, the images of the lonely child catching at her.

'Perhaps that's why he always goes for beautiful women and treats them so appallingly,' Michaela went on. 'Hitting back. Now, is it warm enough for coffee outside, do you think?'

Rebecca too, had commented, 'Jake not tired yet of being domesticated? You've worked a miracle, Helen. How do you do it?' and Donald Macrae had remarked, though as a general observation, 'Jake's surely giving up his wild ways these days. What's come over the man?'

Helen thought Catriona had had as much to do with the humanising of Jake as she had, for with Catriona he showed a gentleness and protective care no one else ever saw. But Helen knew he liked her company too, and did her best to take each day as it came, determined not to read too much into his friendliness, his constant presence at Hilltop. She tried not to look ahead, but in spite of herself her mind ranged forward, turning up unsettling images. The age gap was not huge; indeed when she was with Jake she was never for one second conscious of it. There seemed a general consensus that marriage, in the ordinary sense of commitment, could never be for him, yet he seemed to like companionship, and was certainly drawn to the comforts, simple as they were, of Hilltop.

Perhaps they suited him because he hated excess of any kind. Perhaps he preferred the sort of undemanding company Helen could give him. Perhaps he liked the freedom to come and go, with a stable background of affection behind him, which a younger woman might not be prepared to give him. But over and over again she came to the inevitable question – would he not want a physical relationship? And how did she herself feel about that? Attracted, in a word. But would she be acceptable to him? Attractive was a word she didn't even consider here. Of course not; unimaginable, unthinkable. Fit she might be, but always the dread words must be added, *for her age*. The figure sixty seemed to have nothing to do with her, but she must face it. Thin as her face was its flesh had begun to sag downwards; the badger streaks in her hair were getting wider, the rest of her hair was greying; her hands were stiff on cold mornings, her thighs were no longer smooth, the flesh of her upper arms sagged.

How could Jake—? she would demand of herself in fierce anger, racked with the knowledge that all this had come too late, unbearably too late. Then he would spend an evening at Hilltop, his usual reserve in abeyance, talkative, clearly enjoying himself and reluctant to leave, and the obstinate hopes would return, against all reason.

He was growing more and more interested in Percy's legacy, which included dozens of diaries detailing much fascinating lore about his lifelong passion. These notebooks, for that was how he had used them, containing a record of so many historic and valuable documents and rare books, would be worth a fortune in themselves, but for Jake they were a key to a world he was increasingly eager to explore. He shared much of this delight with Helen, and she was often at the shop, helping with correspondence or enquiries, airing her new vocabulary of fep, aeg, teg and eps, pursuing Percy's tortuous but efficient cross-reference system, or happily browsing. She found so much pleasure in this that she had to remind herself firmly that it was an interest Jake shared equally with Catriona, whose catholic reading tastes were an endless source of amusement to him.

Catriona, in spite of her usual comings and goings, had been keeping a low profile on the livestock front, but Helen was not deceived when Catriona came to find her in the garden one afternoon, exhibiting all the signs of winding herself up to make some request. She was so hesitant, in fact, that she reminded Helen of her first appearance at Tigh Bhan, determined to welcome the new arrival out of loyalty to Lilias, but almost speechless with nerves. How gauche she had been, and how young she had seemed.

'Talk to me,' Helen commanded calmly, busy in the herb border.

'Oh, it's nothing really. But — well, there is something actually.'

Silence.

'And that is——?'

'Well, I just wanted to ask — I know it's probably not part of the deal or anything, and you must say no at once if it's out of the question, but Jake said I should ask anyway, or I'd never know——'

'And I'll never know if you don't get on with it,' Helen said, gathering up a bundle of tall fennel stalks she had left growing as long as possible for the beauty of their yellow seedheads, but which had been struck down by an unusually sharp frost. 'Um, smell this, lovely.'

Catriona took a quick unimpressed sniff, her mind elsewhere. 'It's probably not a good idea.'

'Oh, well, I should forget all about it then.'

'Helen!'

It was a wail of anguish and Helen abandoned the fennel and paid attention. 'Tell me.'

'You know that riding place along the loch?'

'Beside the caravan park?' Helen wondered what was coming. Was she to build a stable?

'Well, you know they're closing down.'

'Being closed down?' That was what Fitz had said.

'Not exactly. But they can't comply with the regulations, so they're having to give up that part of the business. The ponies are going next week, but half of them have never been boxed in their lives, so I said I'd go down and help with the loading.'

'And?'

'Well, the thing is, they've got to get rid of all the animals.'

'Catriona, I cannot bear the suspense. I don't think we've got room for a horse.'

'Oh, not one of the ponies! And not inflicted on you. I just wondered — would it be all right to have a dog in Little Hilltop? A puppy?'

'A puppy? Is that all?' Helen laughed at her. 'What took you so long? Of course it would be all right. I should enjoy it.'

'Really? Do you mean it?'

'Of course I do. I'm only thankful you've settled on

a dog. Now that you're here permanently it could have been anything.'

'It's because I know I'm staying that I thought perhaps ... I've missed Braan so much,' Catriona admitted.

'What kind of dog, though?' Helen thought to ask.

'Oh, nothing huge or awful, I promise. The sweetest little Jack Russell, well, mostly Jack Russell. They're not weaned yet. I used to have one ages ago, called Chippy. What a little brute he was. A darling though, of course.'

'Of course. So when is he coming?'

'Next week?'

'Fine. But what does Jake say? I suppose he realises it will enjoy the flavour of calf bindings and do much to improve on deckle-edges. Unless – you're not intending to leave it here during the day by any chance?'

'Oh, no, of course not. Well, only sometimes.'

Helen laughed. She thought a puppy would improve the quality of life at both Hilltops.

Jake hadn't much liked the sound of Catriona's plan to help load the garrons from the disbanded riding school ready for transportation to their new homes. The enterprise had run into trouble when the only person who knew anything about horses, the father of the caravan park owner, had died earlier in the year. Jake could imagine the ham-fisted job they would make of beating half a dozen hefty and frightened animals into ramshackle lorries, and he had resolved to go down and have a look at what was happening himself.

Just as he was leaving the shop, however, having no compunction about closing early on a rainy autumn afternoon, he was delayed by a telephone enquiry from a world-famous collector in Boston, Mass., which developed into a gratifyingly lucrative order.

He was much later than he had meant to be as he drove along the loch road, angered as he approached the stables by the increasingly squalid appearance of the adjoining caravan park. He might have a word with Fitz about that, see if anything could be done. But at least the ill-used and despondent-looking horses he had seen plodding up and down the nearer hill tracks, suffering the sack-like bumping of their riders and the sawing at their mouths by people who thought the reins were there to hold on by, would be going to new homes where hopefully they would be better off. And the finding of those new homes had been largely due to Catriona. She had not mentioned it; he had learned it from gossip in the Coach-house.

He was smiling as he turned in through the leaning gate posts to the littered yard. Catriona saw herself as so useless, yet she was a natural giver, and her care and interest were not just devoted to animals. No wonder she was so well loved in Luig and the glens.

As he parked he observed that very much the scene of noise and chaos he had expected was in progress, and he was not best pleased to see Catriona attempting to lead a big garron with rolling eyes and tossing head up the sagging ramp of a battered horse-box, backed too close to the wall of the stable. Catriona, Jake saw as he went quietly forward, had almost succeeded in coaxing the big horse in; he was all but there. Then, either in jubilation at her success, or thinking he would finish the job off for her, one of the lads closing in at the foot of the ramp leapt in the air throwing both arms above his head and giving a blood-curdling yell. The garron shied violently, slipping on the top of the ramp as it did so, the strut intended to provide footing splintering away. The frail wing, which as he ran forward Jake saw to his horror was secured to the box by nothing more than binder twine, collapsed sideways, pinning Catriona to the ground as the horse lost its balance and with flailing hoofs crashed down upon her in the confined space.

Chapter Twenty-six

It was nearly nine when Jake came back from the hospital, looking more drained than if he had done a thirty-mile run round the skyline.

'She'll be fine,' he said wearily. 'They'd have let me stay longer but she just needed to sleep.' It was all he seemed able to say for the moment, his face set, his mouth closing in a grim line, and Helen held down her own anxiety, her need for words, and pushing a dram into his hand went quickly to fetch food. Guessing that he would not want to bother about moving to the table, or even dealing with a knife and fork, for he looked more shocked than she had expected – and her heart fluttered at the thought of what that might mean – she quickly filled rolls with ham and chicken, warmed the remains of a spinach quiche, cut it into handy slices, made coffee.

Waiting and wondering, she had not been able to face having dinner, but now would eat something to keep Jake company. She had been kept in the picture – Fitz had phoned from his mobile as he started for Fort William behind the ambulance, Trudy had called to offer comfort and company, Jake had phoned from the hospital to say there was no major damage but that they would be keeping Catriona in for the night as she had received a bang on the head and was still very muzzy.

Most of this he repeated as he began abstractedly to eat, more out of a sort of impatient courtesy than because he was interested in food at the moment. Then as he began to unwind a little he ate more hungrily, and thanked Helen for taking the trouble.

'Trudy offered me supper – I stopped in on the way back, I'd promised Fitz I'd call – but I couldn't face anything. I just wanted to get back here and tell you what was happening. It really feels as though we're responsible for Catriona, doesn't it? The two of us?' He attempted a smile, but it didn't alter the distress still plain in his eyes.

'It truly does,' Helen agreed. 'And judging by the phone calls that's how everyone else sees it. Rebecca and Clare and Gillian have all been asking for news and sending messages.' She tried to speak lightly to conceal the leap of pleasure her heart had given at his words. The two of them. He felt it too. 'But how is poor Catriona feeling? What sort of state is she really in, Jake?'

His mouth twisted in amusement and some deeper emotion beyond his control. 'She's so—' His voice was husky and uneven and he cleared his throat and started again. 'She's in such an odd state. Quite funny really.'

Helen could hear in his voice that he had not found it funny at the time. 'She's doped to the eyeballs, of course, but madly concerned about the bloody horse. No one's to blame it, is it all right, where is it, who's looking after it, will it still go to its new home? You can imagine. Then she's panicking because she was supposed to collect her damned puppy today, and now she's afraid that they won't keep it for her. I'd better call in first thing in the morning on my way to the hospital to find out about that, or there'll be no meaningful conversation of any kind with Catriona.'

'But won't they be letting her home tomorrow?'

'Fitz seems pretty sure they will, but not first thing. Visiting time isn't till two but they seem pretty flexible and said I could look in earlier.'

'Oh, Jake, I couldn't come with you, could I? I just need to see her with my own eyes, even if she will be home later.'

'I shouldn't think that would be any problem.' From the hospital's point of view, he evidently meant, and Helen felt a slight chill. 'You should have heard her, Helen. Except for her concern about those wretched animals she hardly seemed to notice what's happened to her.' Jake began to laugh a little, clearly moved at the memory. 'She's lying there looking very tiny and very wan — that lovely tan of hers seems to have turned an odd yellow colour, highly unattractive.' He said this in a tone which sounded almost loving, and Helen felt a queer little lurch she could not quite identify. 'The broken wrist's in plaster, her ribs are severely bruised, in fact she's bumped and scraped from top to toe, and she barely seems to realise it.'

He passed a spread hand roughly down his face, keeping his head down, and Helen, moved but somewhat startled to see Jake, the hard man, the ruthless and heroic side of Brett Stark, so unexpectedly affected by what had happened to Catriona, filled his glass again and wondered why the silence that had fallen between them suddenly seemed so comfortless.

More than that; tense. But why?

Jake raised his replenished glass with a little gesture of acknowledgement, but looked away from her at once, gazing into the fire, his mind elsewhere.

Helen waited, aware that her heart, which she was not at all accustomed to being conscious of in this manner, was making itself felt again, bumping with a hard uncomfortable rhythm which seemed oddly slower than its normal beat, as though it was impeded and working with extra effort.

She was acutely aware of Jake's physical nearness. He was in the big armchair and she was perched forward at the end of the sofa nearest to him, a low table in the angle between them. She wanted to touch him, in comfort – or for her own comfort. His right arm lay along the chair arm, his muscular lean brown hand lightly cupping its curved end. She could reach out and that hand would take hers; the contact would release them to talk.

But Jake was talking already, turning his head with

a brusque movement to look into her face, the words impelled from him by deeply stirred emotion.

'Christ, Helen, she's so damned special – so different. When I saw that horse go down on top of her, saw those hoofs thrashing just above her head – it all seemed to happen in a flash, yet so hideously slowly. I felt as though I couldn't lift my feet from the ground, I was glued there, helpless – yet I was running, trying to get to her, and even then I was wondering how I could ever endure it if anything happened to her . . .'

Helen sat rigid, with a hideous sensation of all her blood draining away somewhere, out of her cheeks, out of her limbs, leaving her cold, stone-still, her mind floundering, pleading not to receive this message. She must respond; that is what one did when someone spoke. One spoke in return. Words slipped and slid and refused to coalesce in the recesses of her brain, fled away from her control. She gazed at Jake, incapable of hiding her shock, but he wasn't looking, looking down into the glass he now held with both hands. Then with a violent shake of his head he began to speak again, as though words for him too were beyond control, but in his case must pour out.

'There's never been anything like her in my life. She's such an incredible blend of resilience and gentleness. I've seen some tough men in my time but for sheer hardihood and complete impervious indifference to discomfort she takes some beating.' His voice warmed, amusement briefly returning. 'There's nothing of her, but her stamina is incredible. On the hill, no matter what the conditions or the terrain, she simply trots along, chatting, relaxed, as though she's strolling on the harbour wall, and at the end of the day her pace is just the same as at the beginning. And she travels light!' He was almost chuckling, a most un-Jake-like sound. 'I've never seen anyone pay less atten-tion to cold or wind, heat or rain. She rarely bothers to carry food even, regarding the whole peninsula as her back garden, but nobody could be safer, nobody could know the ground better. Yet the marvellous thing is, although she's so hardy, and so careless about how she looks, at the same time she's feminine and fine-boned, with that slim girl's body, those delicate limbs. And there's so much about her that's really beautiful, though in an exciting way you have to discover it. Like her beautifully shaped hands, in spite of the scars and scratches, the ingrained oil and paint and God knows what else. And those little even white teeth; and her eyebrows. When the wind blows back that ragged fringe you see they are so fine, so perfectly arched . . .'

Helen sat, poker-backed, numb, still on the edge of the sofa as she had sat to pour Jake's whisky. She must show nothing, say nothing till she could be certain of her voice. Then she realised that Jake did not need or want her to speak, had indeed forgotten she was there, would probably not notice how her voice sounded, and that brought such a bleak pang of rejection that tears sprang to her eyes. Clumsily, feeling stiff and uncoordinated, she put her hands down to her sides to help her move back in her seat. Without realising it she had balled her hands into fists, and they sank into the sofa cushions, making her movement awkward and effortful as she hitched herself to lean against the sofa back. Her breathing felt shallow and strange, and she did her best to draw long steady breaths.

'I never thought I'd meet anyone quite like her,' Jake was saying, more reflectively now. 'In fact, I couldn't have described such a person, or summed up that particular blend of qualities which in her satisfies me so completely. I've spent my life running after women who were her exact opposites, yet without real conviction. Going for the obvious things, yet knowing they weren't really what I wanted.'

Helen remembered Michaela's interpretation of his choices, but said nothing.

'I have been acquainted,' Jake said, pulling himself out of his absorption and turning to her with a flashing grin of self-mockery, 'with a great many extraordinarily beautiful females. Stunners, not to put too fine a point on it, and also creatures, sometimes, of intelligence and ability. But,' his face becoming sombre once more, 'although I could be hugely attracted, even carried away for a while, there was always a finite quality to the feeling, a conviction that this couldn't be all. I imagined that it was because fundamentally I didn't want there to be, that there was some lack in myself. Also, of course, I hadn't much to offer anyone. I knew I'd be incapable of settling down, staying put in one place for any length of time, living any sort of conventional life. But God,

Helen, you don't want to hear all this. What am I thinking about?'

'But you want to tell me.' She managed it composedly, humorously even, and was rewarded by a laugh of acknowledgement. It was more than she could manage to say, 'And I do want to hear,' but in some cold, rational, bleakly honest way she did. She knew that ultimately, on some distant day when this would no longer hurt, it would help to have had the impossible hopes and illusions ripped unequivocally away.

'That's been the marvellous thing,' Jake said, 'having you to talk to. Having you, as it were, almost *in loco parentis* to Catriona. I always felt that coming here, getting to know you, being made so welcome in this house, was like getting to know her family. And often, of course, it was the only way I could be close to her. I was so terrified of saying or doing anything to frighten her away. To be able to be with both of you has been so good, and I'll be grateful to you for ever.'

You wanted the truth; now you have it, Helen thought, trying to be stoical but actually feeling quite faint for a moment, as though the fabric of what she had perceived, or foolishly invented, was being torn too rapidly into shreds too small.

'It's been such a new thing for me,' Jake went on slowly, 'finding someone who fitted into my life. I mean, being with Catriona isn't like being with a different, separate person. No explaining, no justifying, no defending what I do, or the choices I've made. It all seems entirely natural to her, the bothy, the journeys, even the bookshop!'

'And will there be more journeys?' Helen knew, still, that she was not asking on Catriona's behalf.

'Edwin's been agitating for a while. Thinks Brett should move his ass.'

That told her little. 'And you?'

'It can wait.'

A silence stretched. Helen thought, I should put a log on the fire, take away the tray. She didn't move.

'She looked so battered, poor little love. But I think she'd rather have had Watty at the bedside than me – he'd have been more concerned about the pony than I was, and she would certainly have considered him more reliable on the question of the puppy.'

I don't think I can manage a light rejoinder to that, Helen decided clinically.

'She hasn't a clue how I feel of course, and I can't imagine how to begin to let her see it. She'd be appalled. I'm nearly as old as her father, and I'm sure she sees me as belonging irredeemably to his generation.'

'I'm not certain you're right about that,' Helen said, wondering why she was arguing. 'Catriona doesn't apply labels, or have preconceptions about such things. I think, to her, everyone is simply as she finds them. And everything, come to that. I don't believe she spends much time evaluating or measuring. She's too busy doing.'

'Yes, and mostly on behalf of other people,' Jake agreed, but Helen was aware of him tucking away the reassurance of her words. Once launched he had plenty to say about Catriona's activities, glad to relax in laughter about them, glad to be able to talk about her with the question of their attitudes to each other put aside for the moment.

Helen pulled herself together sufficiently to make up the fire, remove the remains of supper, make more coffee — the latter because Jake was reducing the bottle of Laphroaig at a steady pace, without apparently noticing he was doing it.

They were disturbed only by Watty, who had returned after delivering three of the garrons to a riding centre near Spean Bridge, where hospitality had been freely offered, and had heard in his pub down by the harbour what had happened. He had come up the hill hotfoot, and was almost in tears when he arrived, his nervous cap-rolling so violent that Helen thought the much-abused piece of headgear would never be fit to wear again.

When, two drams later and looking more cheerful, he had wambled off into the night, Helen thought Jake would leave too. But he seemed restless and on edge, as though dreading his own company, and she steeled herself to suggest that he slept at Hilltop, crushing down bitter thoughts of how till now such an invitation would have been impossible, and how illusory, how exclusively in her own mind, the distinction was.

'No, no,' said Jake instantly. 'Thanks all the same, Helen, but I'll go up to the bothy.' But still he made no move to leave and, afraid of certain pain but knowing there could be no evasion, Helen saw that he needed to release more of his anxieties and doubts before he would be able to sleep.

'I wonder what sort of a night Catriona is having,' he said, his thoughts far from this room.

Any route would do to where he wanted the conversation to be, Helen knew. *Better than I am,* she longed to say.

'Well, with all the pain-killers they shot into her she'll be completely out of it,' Jake went on, reassuring himself. 'And even without them she wouldn't be troubled by any concerns likely to prevent her sleeping.' He gave a little snort of laughter. 'That's the problem. She's so damned oblivious. Oh, Helen, how in the world am I ever going to make her wake up to how I feel about her or what I want?'

Don't ask this of me; don't dare, don't dare ask my advice. None of this wild protest showed in Helen's calm face. And Jake wasn't looking for an answer anyway.

'She's so completely innocent and unaware. It's not going to be easy, I can see that. Sometimes I've been very close to asking your advice, but of course there's no advice to give, is there, between two people?'

Oh, Jake, I'm so tired. So weary to the bone. I can't take any more.

'Perhaps she just needs more time.'

Helen made one huge effort; of self-immolation it felt to her, though the words in the peaceful room sounded like nothing more than sensible counsel to a friend.

'Perhaps now would be a good time to try, when she's vulnerable, and sympathy and closeness seem natural.'

Jake shot a look at her, alert with hope, with a need to accept that. 'Perhaps you're right. Believe it or not,' he went on, his tone lightening, 'but she actually let me hold her hand this evening. Though I can't be entirely sure she noticed I was doing it.'

'There you are then.' Helen wasn't sure what she meant. 'So when you see her in the morning ... Oh, and I think perhaps I won't come to the hospital with you after all, Jake, if you don't mind. I really am rather tired, and probably won't want to be up very early ...'

He was on his feet in one active movement, contrite. 'Helen, forgive me, I've been selfish. But it was so good to talk to you. By God, I needed it. That's no excuse for keeping you up half the night, however.'

Unexpectedly he put an arm round her, pulling her against him in apology and gratitude, and bent to kiss her cheek. 'I'm off. Thanks for supper – and it looks as though I'd better bring you a bottle of Laphroaig next time I'm passing. But thank you most of all for being here. It's meant so much to me.'

Somehow she went with him to the door to the lane, said, she supposed, the sort of things one said in reply to such a speech. Though in the manner of the person who has just made it, the answers were only half-heard by Jake. Then he was gone, the darkness swallowing up the dark figure.

Chapter Twenty-seven

Helen stood numb, aching, jolted out of all normal relation with her world. She roused herself to walk through the hall to the sitting-room, with some conditioned instinct that she must ... that there were things she should ... The faint impulse petered out, and though her eyes passed over the coffee things, the uncovered fire, the lamps, she did nothing about any of them, but after standing in the middle of the floor for a few seconds went dazedly out again and paused at the foot of the stairs. Then a much fiercer response stopped her; a desperate reluctance. She could not go up there, as though this was any ordinary night. She could not go alone into her room in the empty house, undress, get into bed. Where would her thoughts go, and these wild feelings that seemed to be mounting and mounting inside her, making it difficult to draw air into her lungs, making her feel breathless and unsteady and helpless? How could she lie down, alone in the darkness, putting herself at their mercy? She went through to the little lobby and, seizing the first jacket that came to hand, out into the lane. Jake would be far on his way to the bothy now. But the thought brought such instant searing pain that she knew she must keep it at a distance for the moment. Not think at all. Ah, if only that were possible.

She turned along the lane to give her eyes time to adjust to the darkness. As she went she put on the jacket. It was a soft lined corduroy one she was found of, but it was more like an overshirt and had no pockets. She needed to plunge her hands into pockets and hunch her shoulders and wrap it comfortingly around her, and being unable to do that seemed to matter inordinately. Almost she turned back to exchange it for another, but it seemed too absurd to do so, and also she found she couldn't stop walking. It was a need, a compulsion, and perhaps would be a solace, to continue moving, more rapidly as her night vision improved, out onto the road looping up the flank of the moor.

The road was a pale space of greyness; she had not intended to walk along it — what, in truth, had she intended? — but it lured her on, saving her from thought or decision or concentration, and she hurried, head down, heart beginning to pound. If any vehicle passed, which at this time was unlikely, she would see it coming for miles and could if necessary obliterate herself in the rocks and heather and broken ground of the moor. The image didn't seem in the least incongruous; it was vital not to be seen, above all not to be offered help or the distraction of human contact.

For she must think. She must face what had happened, drag out of obscurity every absurdity of hopes and dreams, and confront them with remorseless fact.

She was high on Luig Moor when tiredness brought her to a halt, her legs feeling too heavy to take another step, the stickiness of her hot face unpleasantly cooled by the sharp autumn air, heels sore because she hadn't paused to change her shoes and was wearing light loafers not designed for long walks. By now it was quite easy to see what lay at her feet, though the moon, not yet half full, was mostly hidden behind cloud. She crossed a stretch of turf and found a rock, and after a few experiments settled in a comfortable hollow on its lichened top. These physical details were unimportant however, seemed at one remove from her, and she could hardly have described the night, the slow high changing of the clouds, their movements replicated in the softly merging shadows that came and went across the rough ground below her.

First to be dealt with was shame. She closed her eyes and almost wanted to cover her ears to think how she had interpreted Jake's presence, his friendliness. She had thought he was coming to see her. She had actually thought that an attractive, superlatively fit and active young man of excellent intelligence and many interests, thirteen years younger than she was, had in some way found her equally attractive to him. Helen drew in her breath in a small hiss of pain even to think this now. She was old, a 'senior citizen', which she thought no gentler a phrase than 'old age pensioner'. She was old, greying, wrinkled, sagging. Her back ached if she gardened too long and she liked going to bed early with a book. How Jake, who loved Catriona's young, smooth-skinned, slender body, would shudder with horror to think of hers. And how could she for one second have imagined ...? With a small sob of desolation she dropped her head into her hands, shaking with humiliation.

But she must go on with this, must get it all out into the open. That blind hurrying walk up the grey road had been escape, first aid. Now the wound must be examined properly and, if that were possible, bound up. Jake had come to Hilltop because he wanted to see Catriona, or if he could not see her then to be in her orbit. He had often talked about her, and Helen hadn't even noticed, merely accepting it as a subject he and she could share. He had given Catriona a job, had developed his own interest in the bookshop because it was something they could have in common.

And Helen had imagined — yes, you did, don't duck — that he had found at Hilltop the sort of comfort that balanced his life at the bothy. She had imagined, fatuously, that by giving him good meals and hot baths and putting his shirts in her washing machine — yes, and you ironed them, you fool, that ultimate piece of inane female caring — she was giving him something his life lacked and that he appreciated. God, he was as indifferent, as deeply and truly indifferent, to such niceties as Catriona was. They were irrelevant to him. He had, very probably, been indulging her in letting her perform these housewifely rites. Poor old thing, if it makes her feel good let her get on with it. He didn't need a less stark contrast to the bothy; the bothy was his choice, conforming precisely to his taste, pared down to essentials, uncluttered, functional, satisfying.

The bothy. He had never taken her there; she had no part in that area of his life. Not area. No, that was his life. But he had taken Catriona there, as he had taken Catriona on the hill with him, ranging far back into the great hills of Morar and Lochaber, sleeping out, carrying next to nothing with them, using the resources of what seemed a barren landscape to survive. All of that was far outside Helen's scope. With her Jake would stroll down the western end of the Luig peninsula, drop in at Ardlonach for a dram, potter round the shore. Old woman's walks. And she had never noticed. That was the vital point. *Why* had she never seen this? What arrogance, what self-delusion not to see.

She was cold, too lightly clad, the brief warmth of her rapid walk draining away, her skin crawling with a disagreeable chill touch. And she was cold inside; cold, bleak and empty. She remembered Jake's voice as he had talked about Catriona, the tone she had never heard him use before, compelled by anxiety to express his feelings at last.

But he had expressed them to her.

Slowly, as though she had to dredge up the fact with actual pain, she brought it into the light and examined it.

He had, once again, sat by her fireside, and with emotions stirred by the shocks of the day beyond his normal cold control, he had talked to her, with an honesty and freedom which she now began to see was extraordinary. Why? Was there no one else he could talk to? But she would not fall into the trap of devaluing herself just as wildly as she had lately flattered herself, she decided with a first flicker of grim humour.

Jake had talked to her because he was comfortable with her, trusted her, respected her views. Jake had had no least suspicion of her reaction to him. And here she paused, for that reaction she was, even now, glossing over. He had roused in her a sexual awareness she had never previously imagined. Was that very weird at her age, somehow shameful? Wasn't she supposed to have finished with all such feelings years ago? But she knew that many women retained strong sexual needs beyond the menopause; had indeed been told once, very unexpectedly by a woman she barely knew and whom she would have thought the last person to talk so freely on the subject, that after hormone replacement therapy her libido had been startlingly enhanced.

'Orgasm at a touch,' she had said gaily, and Helen, rather taken aback, had thought her vocabulary startlingly affected too.

But I haven't had HRT. And my thoughts of Jake have not been torrid images of the sexual act. No, she thought forlornly, they had not gone so far, but there had been delicious longings for touch, for closeness. She had let herself believe, she saw now, resolutely probing, that there could be some sort of calm physical pleasure, reassurance and comfort rather than wild passion. The bed no longer empty. And then what? A peaceful amble through the years together, Jake free to pursue his own life, she there to provide background comfort and loving care. That was about what the dreams had amounted to. She had convinced herself, perhaps because she had never seen Jake with a woman, had heard such disparaging things about the relationships he had formed, none of them meaning much to him, that he didn't need love based on physical attraction or need. Jake, of all people. Had she been mad or blind or both? He might conceal his deepest feelings from casual observers, but she knew by now, beyond any doubt, that he was a man capable of the greatest feelings possible.

Only not for you. Well, she concluded, with something creditably close to a laugh, that's probably just as well. You couldn't have handled it, could you, you poor old thing? But the stir of laughter turned sour on her, threatened to turn into tears, and she moved hastily, pushing herself to her feet, brushing lichen and whatever else from her skirt, turning to go up towards the road again.

For accepting that, knowing such passion was not for her, closed the door on it. She had never known it, it had never come her way, and now it never would. Chill knowledge. Her arms wrapped round her body, her hands icy, she set off dully towards home.

But you never expected it, a small insistent voice reminded her, as she mindlessly put one foot in front of the other, her heels beginning to burn with the first fire of blisters. This time last year if someone had told you you would never feel passionate love you would have been surprised at their spelling it out.

Yes, but, I have glimpsed it, seen briefly something wonderful and special and exciting, and now I have to learn to do without it.

And I have to face Jake, perhaps Jake-and-Catriona. But instantly, reassuringly, she knew that if there was to be a Jake-and-Catriona she would be delighted. She was surprised at her conviction about this, but no examination could shake it. Her pain had only to do with her. Catriona and her happiness were quite separate.

Well, that's a relief. She plodded on.

It was hard, however, to go into the house. Tired as she was she did not see it as a refuge, and at the door she paused, puzzling over this.

Because when you go in there ordinary life begins; dreams are left behind. You go in, lock doors and put the guard over the fire, you tidy coffee cups and fill a hot-water bottle, and you embark upon your own solitary normality, for the rest of your life. She felt as though she was starting from the beginning all over again.

Catriona woke, muzzy, still half doped, a dozen confused nightmares dissipating in her head like mist rising off the hill on an autumn morning. There had been noise, crashing, light glancing off a shod hoof, the hair of a heavy fetlock tossing, the image of a huge brown rib-cage blotting out the light. She made a faint mewing sound of rejection, closed her eyes, dozed uneasily again.

When she woke a few minutes later she began to register details of where she was – pale walls, light from a big window, a strange bed. Turning her head, with a gasping wince at the pain, which made her realise that she was aching dully all over, she saw beds beyond hers, the nearest tidily made and empty, the next occupied by a small white sleeping face with a tight grey perm frilling it. The bedclothes were so flat there seemed no body to go with the head, and for a few moments, interested but unalarmed, Catriona studied this phenomenon.

'So you're still in the land of the living.' A female voice, rallying and kind, seemed almost too robust for these surroundings, and Catriona twisted her head a little further to see who was there.

A stout middle-aged woman, roped into two sections by the cord of a magenta dressing-gown tied tightly round mounds of flesh, came supported on a zimmer frame round the end of the bed and into Catriona's field of vision. It occurred to Catriona, as though it were a dim memory of a faraway time, that she could have turned her head the other way.

'Well, you're looking pretty spry, lassie, considering the dunt you had. Though you'll not be best pleased when you see yourself in a mirror. Ach, just bruising, it'll pass, never fear. Now, will I call the nurse? Is there anything you're wanting?'

The nurse. Hospital. The ambulance. Fitz. Jake. The falling, flailing body of the garron. It was like fumblingly putting one building block on top of another.

'I'm fine,' said Catriona.

'Fine, are you?' The woman sounded richly amused. 'Aye, well, if you say so.'

'Does that person have a body?'

'What's that?' Startled now, her fat face suddenly doubtful, the woman bent closer, then turned to look at the further bed, and began to laugh wheezingly. 'That's a good one, though I can see fine what you mean. That's Meg, and you couldn't ask for a quieter room mate, could you? One of these days she'll just no' be here. Now, lassie, I'm Lizzie, and it's Catriona, isn't it? I'd best tell someone you're awake and asking daft questions. It might take me a whilie though, I don't leap about these days the way I used to.'

Catriona, testing her theory, decided to turn her head to follow Lizzie's progress to the door. It obeyed, though not without some effort. Before Lizzie had got far, however, a nurse came briskly in.

'All action here, I see. And is Meg still with us? Yes, she is, wee soul. Now,' to Catriona, 'how are you this morning?'

'I'm fine.'

'Good, then you can have a wash and tidy-up because there's someone to see you. Visiting hour is two by rights, but this one's very persuasive, has come a long way, and all the rest of it. All right with you, Lizzie, if I bring someone in before you've dolled yourself up? I don't think I'll bother myself asking Meg if she minds.'

Catriona assumed her visitor couldn't be Fitz, who wouldn't have had to do any persuading in order to see her, but vaguely expected Helen or Trudy, or perhaps Una, more likely to be concerned than pragmatic Rebecca. She had not imagined it would be Jake, and missed the appreciatively raised eyebrows as Lizzie squashed herself into a chair and watched television with the sound turned so low as to be almost inaudible.

If Jake had been asked afterwards he would have said in all good faith that Catriona was in the ward on her own. His heart did something uncomfortable and peculiar at the sight of her discoloured face, her narrow shoulders in the white hospital gown, one wrist in plaster, the other arm with a dressing taped for almost the whole of its length to cover a deep abrasion from which hideous splinters had had to be extracted. Jake looked at her and his voice refused to work. His Adam's apple moved, he gathered his breath to say 'Hello'; nothing happened.

Then out of the bruises and grazes Catriona smiled at him, with the little curling smile he loved, and the smile freed him to move forward, lifting a chair with him as he went, pulling it as close to her as he could get, gingerly lifting her hand and laying it in his other palm, smiling back at her.

'My poor little love, what a squashed fragment of humanity you look. Is there anywhere that doesn't hurt?'

'Jake.' Catriona frowned slightly at the reediness of her voice; she didn't think she normally sounded so feeble. 'Jake,' she said severely, testing her powers. 'Um, that's better. I seem to be functioning somewhere in the next room. Oh, but Jake, I'm so glad you've come.' In her eagerness she half pulled herself up, then grimaced at protests from various parts of her body. 'Was the garron all right? Was he much hurt? What's happened to him? Is he still at the stables? They didn't have to put him down, did they?'

'For God's sake, not the damned horse again. No, Catriona, they did not have to put him down. He had a couple of gashes which the vet dealt with, and he is being taken this morning to his new quarters, though I haven't checked on his feelings about them or his general state of mind. Now, is that good enough for you?'

'Oh, good, I'm glad he's going to be all right. He must have had a terrible fright. But I've just remembered – the puppy! I was supposed to take him home. The mother was going away last night too, to somewhere near Dalmally. Whatever will they have done with the puppy, not sent him away with her? Not drowned him? Jake—!'

'Calm down, Watty's got him. He'll bring him up as soon as you're home. Now are you satisfied? Can we forget about these tedious animals for a while?'

Jake was determined to forget them. The mundane topic was not conducive to the tender and intimate mood he had hoped, after Helen's wise words, to encourage. How thankful he was that he had talked to her at last; he had known she would help.

'Oh, Jake, it's so good of you to come and let me know. I'd have been so worried.'

Oh, well, thought Jake, perhaps after all it hadn't been the worst of starts. 'And we've been worried about you,' he told her, very gently shaking the hand he held. 'The whole of Luig was in an uproar about you last night, phones ringing, bulletins flashing back and forth. Lots of people send their love.'

'Who?'

'Oh, Lord, surely you don't expect me to remember the entire list?' Me, for a start, you little owl. 'Helen, I suppose. Yes, I'm nearly sure she said something about it. Trudy, she's a soft-hearted lump, and Una of course, practically in tears. Not Rebecca, she's got far too much sense. Can't think why you had to come to hospital at all for a few bumps. But Dan – now he's always had a soft spot for you.'

'I know,' Catriona said simply, and Jake laughed. He knew it too, and whereas it could still strike sparks to see his old flame Rebecca so vibrantly, openly happy with Dan, he had never felt a trace of jealousy for Dan's protective affection for Catriona. No sex involved, simple as that.

And when would there ever be, for Catriona? But that seemed faraway and unimportant now. What he needed was to see that she was safe, to see her smile, to know that there were no after-effects which wouldn't mend, and to be close beside her, her hand in his.

'Thank God you weren't badly hurt,' he said, in a husky voice which was quite new, yesterday's panic briefly washing back.

'Oh, Jake, it was so horrible.' Catriona clutched his hand now, and her fingers felt very thin and small. 'The noise as much as anything, the wood splintering, the hoofs drumming, the trailer lurching. I thought it was going to topple on me too—' She shuddered and leaned suddenly towards him, and he drew her head against his shoulder and put his arms close round her, soothing her with small wordless sounds.

'I'm so glad you came,' she whispered. 'Because you were there, you saw it. I couldn't have borne trying to describe it to anyone. And you looked after me, waiting for the ambulance. That was awful, wasn't it, it seemed to take such ages.'

It had indeed been awful, and Jake didn't care to recall it. 'It's over,' he soothed her, his throat constricted, 'and you're going to be all right.'

'When will they let me come home?' Catriona asked, sitting up again, her movements cautious, and brushing the hair back from her forehead. 'Do you know? Can I come with you now?'

'They won't let you come yet.' He had already asked, but didn't say so. 'The doctor will have to have a look at you first. But if it's just general battering I'm sure they won't want you taking up a bed for long.'

'Will you fetch me? Would you mind?'

'I'll fetch you.' He couldn't say more. She wanted not Helen, not Trudy, but him.

Chapter Twenty-eight

Jake drove slowly over the high moorland road from Fort William and down the sharply descending curves to Loch Luig. Not that he thought the perfect suspension of the Mercedes, or his own driving come to that, would jolt one bone in Catriona's body, but it was such a novel pleasure to be looking after her, to have her, still looking reduced and childlike with her bandages and bruises, tucked into the seat beside him, to have this quiet, encapsulated time together with no urgency, no demands.

As they came to the caravan park Catriona turned her head to look at the deserted stables and, though she said nothing, watchful Jake saw her lips tighten, and caught the infinitesimal movement as she flattened herself against the seat, as though drawing back involuntarily from even this brief reminder.

He drove quietly on, but put out a hand to cover hers, clenched in her lap. She accepted the gesture without any movement of withdrawal. Indeed she turned to smile at him, without shyness or surprise. Jake found himself as thrilled as any teenager that a first tentative approach has not been rebuffed, and grinned sardonically as he drove, thinking of the speed of his usual technique. The careless, untender, sometimes even vengeful speed. His smile twisted into an expression of bleak distaste. It had meant nothing. This tiny acceptance of Catriona's promised so much, and, for her, how carefully he was prepared to go, how infinitely slowly. Yet, the wry thought struck him, the very naturalness and simplicity of that acceptance held its own problem – she read no more into the touch than friendly comfort. He had a steep hill to climb. But what a joy to climb it. His spirits were high as the car purred up Luig Hill.

Helen had got Little Hilltop ready – taking scrupulous care not to change its character by undue polishing or tidying or the introduction of flowers – and had prepared, as best she could, her own mind for their arrival. Now she prepared her face, pinning a welcoming smile across it as she went out to the lane.

But the moment passed without constraint. A real smile, of love and relief, overspread the aching deliberate one the moment she saw Catriona getting out of the car, Jake whipping round to stand by in case she needed help, raising a hand in a salute to Helen that was so buoyant, so jaunty even, that she could not grudge him his happiness. She had wondered what she would find to say, but the fear vanished as they went in, caught up in an effortless hubbub of questions and exclamations and the eager rehearsing of their feelings and reactions, to which no one else listened.

'Can you sit in the big chair by the fire? Will you be comfortable enough there? Or are you ready to roll into bed again? And are you hungry? Have they fed you?'

'Oh, not bed,' Catriona protested, but she looked weary enough for it as she sank into the armchair, her broken wrist in its plaster supported in a sling, her face that odd shade of skin pale under a tan. 'There's nothing wrong with me that—'

The telephone cut across Helen's worried protest and Jake's ironic laugh.

It was Clare Macrae asking after Catriona, but the rest, nearer at hand, didn't waste time with the telephone. Trudy arrived first, with a beaming Finbarr, who once he had learned to smile had done so more or less permanently, the sort of child people reached out for in delight.

Trudy wasn't handing him over to Catriona, however. 'He'd pound you to oblivion. He doesn't just sit quietly these days, you know. I'll tie him to a bush outside or something.'

'Give him to me,' said Helen, her arms out. 'Or no, perhaps you'd better keep him while I go and make coffee. I suspect you won't be our only visitors.'

'Give him to me,' said Jake, 'and you can both go and make coffee.'

'I'm not sure sending us to the kitchen is sexist if he

ends up with Finn,' Trudy said to Helen in pretended doubt. 'What do you think?'

I think I could laugh, or equally weep, to see Jake and Finbarr nose to nose and laughing, to see Catriona tucked up safely by my fire, home once more, to have my nerve ends alive, my feelings finding all kinds of depths and heights. I think I'll put the percolator on. I think, and thank God for it, someone is coming in.

'Catriona, just look at you. And I thought you were supposed to be good with animals,' was Rebecca's contribution, but she found a safe place to kiss Catriona, somewhere at the side of her right eye.

Una brought food, her unalterable expression of solace and love.

'Dan's devastated because he's had to take a group out on An Tearlach,' Rebecca went on. 'He wanted me to take them for him so that he could come and coo over you, but I wasn't having any of that.'

'Fitz said we weren't to descend on you in waves and tire you to death,' Una said, a little anxious.

'Are we a wave? I don't think so,' Rebecca decided. 'Can I have action man for a minute? Then you could leave, Jake, and we'd be still less of a wave.'

'Leave yourself,' said Jake equably, but he handed Finn over and toeing a squashed pouffe closer to Catriona's chair sat down beside her. Rebecca's eyebrows rose, and he met her eyes with a cool stare, from which he could not quite eliminate a glimmer of mingled concession and amusement.

Coffee had been made, and Una's cake cut, when Trudy, sitting by the window, announced, 'Watty smelt the food evidently.'

She waved to him to come in, and in a moment he was in the doorway, his eyes round and worried, his face red with distress and haste.

'I seen the doctor in the town and he said you'd be back about now,' he said, addressing Catriona and oblivious of everyone else in the room, a reaction they took perfectly for granted, half smiling, half moved at his concern. 'Oh, my, lassie, whatever have they done to you?'

Did he think the nurses in Fort William had kicked Catriona around and not the horse, Helen wondered with sudden light-heartedness, lifting books from a long stool and drawing it forward. 'Come and sit here, Watty. Have some cake.'

'I should never have gone off wi' that other trailer. I should have waited till they were all loaded. That bugger Ron – och, I'm sorry, but ye ken what I mean – he should never have been let to have beasts in the first place, he's no more sense than a—'

'Watty, I'm all right,' Catriona interrupted him, laughing. 'You couldn't have done anything if you had been there. It was an accident. But, much more importantly, where's the puppy? Don't say you've forgotten him?'

'Forgotten him, of course I havena'.' And with an affronted look Watty dived into his baggy pocket and produced a sleeping ball of white fur roughly the size of a croquet ball. The gesture was a huge success, and Finbarr's forehead puckered in doubt at the shout of laughter that went up. The puppy uncurled itself on Watty's grime-ingrained palm and struggled to sit up, rolling sideways a couple of times, checked by Watty's thumb, then steadying itself, blinking still milky-blue puppy eyes at this strange place.

'He's minute, I don't believe he's six weeks old.'

'That can't possibly be a dog. It's face is no bigger than a 50p piece.'

'Oh, Watty!' Catriona's voice held such a note of soft delight that the hairs went up on the back of Jake's neck. 'Let me hold him.'

'His tail's like an electric button. Helen, had you been consulted about this?' Trudy asked. 'Jack Russells have a character all their own, you know.'

'Aye, thrawn wee — wee terrors they are,' Watty amended, relaxing in relief at the success of his mission, Catriona's survival, and the sight of a large slab of Una's cake being passed towards him.

It's easy, Helen thought blankly, going out to make tea for Watty, who had tried her coffee before and wasn't up for it again. I can cope with this. Why did I think it would be such a nightmare? Everything that went on was in my own head. No one else would have had the remotest of suspicions; to them it would in any case seem utterly unthinkable. They are all still here, they haven't gone away; friendly, kind, giving people. I have descended into chasms of despair and self-reprehension and to them I am exactly the same as I always was. All I have to do is to go on as before.

So simple, but sometimes it was almost impossible to put into practice. Yet it was the only answer, the sane and in the end comforting remedy. No grand gestures were needed, no departures, no new starts. There was so much here that mattered to her, her house, her rambling, many-tiered garden which would keep her busy for years to come, the neat little town where she felt at home, accepted, and which she looked forward to knowing in its out-of-season guise. Above all there was the beauty, ever-changing, ever-arresting, of this place that had drawn her back so powerfully. A dozen times a day that beauty caught at her, a background to life which lent depth and satisfaction and its own level of emotional security.

She would stand and think, 'I can step out of my house, straight into this, whenever I like,' and still be hardly able to take it in. She had found a place to live, had stuck to her resolve, and gradually, gradually, a skin of custom and familiarity would form over every small day-to-day action.

And the raw nerve ends would lose their sensitivity, grow a new skin of acceptance too. Indeed, she realised, as the weather took an uncompromising step into autumn, with wild winds and great thundering tides breaking high over Luig harbour wall, that the pain she had flinched from, of seeing Jake and Catriona together, was not as acute as she had feared.

Honesty and rational thinking can work wonders, she mocked herself, forging over the moor on one of the walks which were growing longer now that sitting out in the garden between bouts of cutting back and tidying was impossible. She didn't feel able yet to sit peacefully indoors for long. Easier to deal with thoughts with the wind whipping at her, cold and clean-smelling against her face, stripping the golden coins of the birch leaves, buffeting the dark heather, flattening the rain-dulled bracken.

She had come to see, almost without effort, the fitness of what had happened. How simplistic, how laughable, to have thought that Jake didn't love her because she was old. It didn't happen that way. Jake would not add it up – 'Helen is fine in this respect, acceptable in that. I like such and such a quality about her. But, what a pity, she's thirteen years older than I am, so that's no good . . .'

Affection, attraction, love, whatever, did not work like that. A person is a complete entity. Jake liked and valued her, she was sure of that. Would talk to her, or so she needed to believe, about things he would not discuss with anyone else. They had found an ease together which she knew was rare for him. But whoever and whatever Helen Rathbone consisted of, Jake did not love that individual, and never would.

He loved Catriona, with her strange mixture of caring for all humanity yet blindness to the feelings this one person had for her, with her natural solitariness, her chronic incapacity to be part of conventional life; Catriona with her light supple girl's body, her gentleness and astonishing endurance.

There was an element Helen had not foreseen, though ironically it was an inevitable part of the friendship she needed to hold on to with Jake – he talked to her about Catriona as often as he could, desperate to release some of the emotions he had to guard against showing too clearly as he built up Catriona's trust.

'Sometimes I think it's time Brett Stark had another outing,' he would say in frustration to Helen, and it was she who had to persuade him, truthfully, that there was a change in Catriona's manner to him.

'She depends on your being there, Jake. You must see that. She spends most of her time with you, at the shop or the bothy or on the hill.'

'I spend most of my time with her, you mean,' he grumbled, but Helen knew he had snatched at the crumb.

'She's happy when she's with you,' Helen said steadily. And it was true. There was so much in Jake that suited Catriona's needs and temperament.

'God, if I could think so.' He rubbed his hands harshly over his face, afraid of revealing too much. 'She's so completely the person I want in my life it terrifies me sometimes. What sort of existence could I ever have offered a normal woman? Well, you know what I mean. Most women want so much more than I could ever give, in emotional and material terms, yet with Catriona I feel that what I could offer would be exactly right. But how to move things on, take us into the next stage?'

'Perhaps you're being too cautious?' Helen suggested. (Am I saying this?) 'Although in many ways she seems so young Catriona's not a child.'

Jake nodded, his face thoughtful, doubtful, longing to be persuaded.

But Helen's quiet words swayed him when the moment came. He and Catriona had been stretching their legs up at the head of Glen Righ – a quiet convalescent's stroll – on a keen autumn day that had started with a specious brightness but soon turned to squally showers. As the afternoon darkened these carried the smell of snow, and when Jake and Catriona paused above Glen Righ House to see what monstrous 'improvements' they could spy from this height, Catriona moved closer to Jake as the icy wind whirled at them. He knew it was as instinctive as moving into the lee of a rock but still it stirred him, and he put a quick arm round her, drawing her against his side.

'Are you happy?' he asked, scarcely knowing what he said.

Catriona turned to him, catching something in his voice which he had not been conscious of betraying.

'Yes, I am,' she said with her usual directness.

Still holding her, but turning her towards him and putting both hands on her shoulders, aware as he did so of the fineness of the bone structure, her lightness as she responded to his touch, Jake looked intently into her face. 'Happy with me, I mean?'

To his great surprise a slow blush rose in her face,

though she didn't evade his eyes. 'Yes,' she said again. 'I always am.'

'Catriona—' Words surged up, coalescing into a clumsy mass he couldn't disentangle, and then he realised that he was gripping her so tightly that he must be hurting her. And further realised that even if she was aware of it she would take no notice, and realised some of his feelings in a stifled gasp of laughter. 'I might have known it would be different with you.'

'What would be different?' Catriona sounded calm, but he felt an unmistakable tremor run through her.

'Catriona, have you any idea how I feel about you?'

'No.'

He laughed out loud now. 'I'm besotted about you, you idiot.'

'Jake?' Her calm was gone, her voice uncertain, her eyes wide and doubtful.

'Look, I just want you to know how I feel,' he went on hastily, that alarmed look warning him not to rush things. 'It doesn't mean anything will be different between us—'

'Won't it?' Catriona sounded so disappointed that he checked, thrown.

'Catriona?' he asked in his turn.

'It's all right. I thought for a moment that you . . . But of course you couldn't have meant that. I've got it wrong, haven't I? Just like Conn all over again?'

'Catriona.' Jake registered, astounded, that it felt like tears clogging his throat as he tried to find words. 'Do you mean that you—?' Don't frighten her, don't use words that will drive her back into silence.

'I got it wrong before, didn't I?' Catriona's voice was thin, her small face, from which the wind buffeted back the dark hair to reveal the discoloration of lingering bruises, was bleakly resigned. 'But you're – to me, you're—'

She bent her head, closing her eyes, and Jake thought she wouldn't go on, and waited to see if she would with tension coiling painfully tighter. Then he realised he was holding onto her shoulders hard again and, remembering the battering she had recently suffered, slackened his grasp with swift anger at himself.

But she did go on, though her head was still down and he had to bend close to catch the words. 'Being with you is the most perfect thing I know – right – good. Oh, *Jake*,' she cried in sudden fury at her own ineptness. 'I don't know how to say any of this. Why am I so *useless!*'

But she had said all he needed to hear. With relief surging through him as powerfully as adrenalin he raised her face to him and kissed her gentle mouth, cold in the cold wind, with a tamped-down tenderness that told her little of the feelings roaring through him, the confused resolve never to harm her, the terror of alarming her by going too far too fast.

As he held her carefully, his arms round her but not pulling her close, Catriona put her hands on his upper arms, and accepted his kiss in a trembling mixture of expectancy and uncertainty. But as his lips touched hers, as his arms drew her in, she found, without even a moment to feel astonished, that she was floating and adrift on delectable sensation. She had never imagined anything like it. It still didn't occur to her to put her arms round Jake; she wouldn't have been capable of such a definite action in that amazing moment, but her fingers closed tightly on the sleeves of his jacket and her body arched of its own accord to his. As that first kiss carried her away on unknown seas of feeling, another part of her brain was telling her that this place and time were right, that it was right the wintry wind should be driving over them, that her nostrils should be filled with the familiar mingled scents of autumn dusk, the peaty ground on which they stood, rain-streaked rock, the threat of snow. And right that in this magical new closeness, in the warm intimacy of breath and touch, there should be added the homelike whiff of old Barbour, of damp wool, of cold skin.

Helen was surprised, and detachedly impressed, at her reaction of pleasure when she saw them come in together. Jake wasn't touching Catriona, did nothing so crass or uncharacteristic as to walk in holding her hand, but he curved an arm behind her as she came forward to the fire, and moved at her shoulder, and Helen knew that all was changed between them. They were not ready to talk to her then, and she said nothing, knowing that Jake, as much as Catriona, would need time, but the new feeling was there in the room, a tangible happiness.

*　　　*　　　*

'I'm afraid you'll lose your tenant,' Jake said to Helen, days later when, in their own time and in their own way, they had let their news be known. 'Although I did suggest that when I'm away Catriona could move back in.'

'So you'll still go away?'

'Yes, that's what's so marvellous. I know I could never imagine not having time on my own, taking on new challenges, or however you wish to describe them. I'd feel stifled at the very thought. But Catriona is the one person who understands that and won't mind.' Not true, Jake, Helen protested silently. 'That's part of why I love her; she gives me the impossible luxury of freedom. And she says she wants to live at the bothy, stay there when I'm away, and I know she means it, and will accept it precisely as it is. However did I find her?'

And with that single fact all Helen's lingering sadness vanished. She could not have lived at the bothy as it was. She would have wanted to smother Jake with domestic comfort; she would have ironed his shirts.

And for herself? Suddenly she knew that she too would have been reluctant to give up a new-found freedom, a simplicity and straightforwardness she had never imagined life could hold. She had found her place, her corner, and she loved it. And how would she like now, in all honesty, the other body in the bed, the other presence across the table? When she had at such cost freed herself? It had been a passing madness, a regret perhaps for something she knew she had missed out on, but which would do nothing now but ruffle a most desirable and admirable contentment.

ALEXANDRA RAIFE
BELONGING

An encounter she never expected to face prompts Rebecca to abandon her high-powered, successful life in Edinburgh to seek refuge at Ardlonach, the family home on the West Coast of Scotland. But Rebecca does not find the haven she expects.

The sprawling old house, now run as a hotel by the cousin who owns it, is in turmoil – and full of people with more immediate problems than Rebecca's own. Never one to resist a challenge, she puts her future on hold and sets about making the venture a success. In doing so, Rebecca finds the answer to her own dilemma – and achieves at last a sense of belonging.

Praise for Alexandra Raife:

'An absorbing story with a perfectly painted background' Hilary Hale, *Financial Times*

'*Belonging* has all the emotions ... we have come to expect from Alexandra Raife's characters' *Woman's Weekly*

Alexandra Raife has worked in many countries, from Brazil to Finland, and has worked at a variety of jobs, including six years in the WRAF, but for most of her adult life has lived in Scotland.

ALEXANDRA RAIFE
SUN ON SNOW

No one really wants Kate at Allt Farr, the rambling house in Scotland that sometimes seems more of an albatross than a valuable inheritance to the Munros. But they are used to dealing with the consequences of Jeremy's fecklessness, and Kate — a cast-off girlfriend — is one of those consequences.

A fragile 'townie', Kate is unused to the rigours of a harsh Scottish winter and unfamiliar with the way of life in a house like Allt Farr. Her ignorance of country ways exasperates Max Munro, the head of the household, who has worries enough trying to run the estate. But her gentle manner, intuitive sympathy and cheerful willingness to tackle any chore quickly endear her to Max's mother and sisters. When disaster strikes, Kate finds she has earned herself a place at the heart of the family.

ALEXANDRA RAIFE
THE WEDDING GIFT

Cass falls instantly in love with Corrie Cottage, the small house perched on a grassy ledge of hillside on the borders of the Riach estate. And when Guy suggests that they take it on as a wedding present to each other, she leaps at the chance; maybe it will set the seal on their marriage as the wedding and honeymoon had failed to do.

But it is not long before Cass finds that the more time she spends in Scotland, the less she sees of Guy. And as she becomes increasingly involved with the lives of her neighbours — Gina, struggling with domestic chaos and a recalcitrant teenage daughter; socially competitive Beverley and her enigmatic husband Rick — Cass finds her loyalties shifting inexorably from London, and Guy, to Glen Maraich — and her new friends.